Reflections in Darkness

Book VII of The Quietus of Fate

By Brian C. Kershner

All of the characters in this book are fictitious, and any resemblance to actual persons, living or dead, is purely coincidental.

ISBN: 1-942082-13-4
ISBN-13: 978-1-942082-13-2

Acknowledgements

Reflections in Darkness was supposed to be a departure from everything that had come before it. It was supposed to be a blank slate and a jumping off point for new ideas and a way for me as an author to leave behind characters that I had been tinkering with for over a decade and perhaps move into some edgier material. I had played a lot with the idea of perception and the way that we as human beings view the world around us in the first six books, and I didn't know if there was any more for me to do with that topic.

I took a long hiatus from writing, and spent quite a few years crafting a new series of characters. When I felt that I was ready to dive into the process of writing once again, it felt like I was running at full speed into a brick wall. Nothing came easy, nothing flowed, and it felt like what I was trying to write was fighting me every step of the way. One of the lessons that I had learned about myself as a writer early on was that if the information wasn't flowing out of me freely and I was having to force it, than the output was usually terrible.

So the hiatus continued. The few chapters that I had written faded from my mind and languished in a folder on my computer. Finally frustrated, I sat in front of my computer once again, opened a blank document and began typing. What came out was something I never expected, and in the end it turned out that there was more of Quietus of Fate story to be told.

B.K.

Table of Contents

Epilogue

Appendicies

In the vast cold darkness of the Cosmos there was nothing,
And from the nothing emerged a throne of gold and light,
Beams of Ephemeral and Immortal Will came streaming,
Manifesting the first dawn from the unbroken night.

From the mind of the Creator came all of Creation,
the jewel of which was a world called Espre,
The facets of this solitary sphere became the foundation,
from which the radiance of the Creator's vision would glare.

Upon the face of Espre walked sacred vessels,
Filled to the brim with the Creator's love and mercy,
They struggled only how best to honor Him in their revels,
Raising their voices in praise to prove themselves worthy.

- *The Verses of The Word*
From the High Priestess of the
Church of the Creator

Prologue

A Coming Storm

Cadaria: the center of the world, the center of life, the center of the spirit and the soul. All of these descriptions were true to most of the inhabitants of the world of Espre, even if they did not bend a knee to the Cadarian Emperor. For centuries, the continent of Cadaria had been divided into the twelve kingdoms, each governing themselves in accordance with a mix of ancient traditions and policies promoting collective prosperity. For generations these kingdoms co-existed, squabbling at times about trade agreements and encroachments into sovereign territory, but these conflicts were confined and were of little import in the grand scheme. However, the tensions and old resentments and grudges would soon build to a point that they could no longer be simply resolved. Warlords and generals rose seemingly overnight and began to agitate for a unified Cadaria, each styling themselves as the only worthy choice for leadership. A great civil war erupted that led the whole of the continent to the very edge of self-destruction. One great hero emerged from the carnage and led the continent of Cadaria out of the darkness into a new era of prosperity. This hero became the first Emperor of the newly formed Cadarian Empire, Terrik Lorien. The Lorien line, like all of ruling families from the Great Kingdoms was said to be descended from great heroes who sacrificed themselves so that the world of Espre could have life. Through victory in the civil war it was theorized that the Lorien line that was touched by the

Creator Himself, and thusly the Lorien family would rule so long as the line remained unbroken. Each of the Great Kingdoms dedicated themselves to the fledgling Cadarian Empire and a new peace reigned.

The First Day of Star Fire was supposed to be a rededication to the still only decades' old peace and stability of the Kingdom of Cadaria. As the moon began its year-long journey through the corona of the distant suns, the magnificent shower of sparks and lights began. However, as soon as the streaks of black blotted out the shower of light, panic began to set in throughout the land. This day would ever be known as the Day the Heavens Fell. These streaks of dark light were dark gods that had been cast out by their ancestors, banished for their crimes of hubris against the Creator. The fall to earth cursed those that once followed these fallen gods, and turned them into foul creatures from legends and fairy tales. These creatures would soon regain their ancient names…Jeresei, Shadowwalkers, Kalbraks, and Stone. The gods themselves gained a type of mortal form, but it became evident quickly to the people of Cadaria, through the teachings of the Church of the Creator, that these monsters were nothing less than the embodiment of pure evil and were dedicated to nothing less than the total destruction of their ancestors and the humans that worshiped and honored them. Thus began the War of Darkness.

From a distance, the Cadarian Empire watched as the continent to the southeast of Cadaria fell to the dark influence of the fallen gods, their corruption spreading through the hearts of even the innocent, reducing them to mindless shells. The growing darkness consumed the continent of Mythryn, making it a desolate wasteland whose very nature shifted to the whim of the dark gods that ruled it. A haze of ash settled over the entire continent, allowing no sunlight to pierce the veil, and in the most temperate region of the world, the barren plains of Mythryn became covered with black snow and ash; a frozen wasteland.

It was clear not long after the Day the Heavens Fell, that the War of Darkness could never be truly won. A fragile peace was negotiated between the Cadarian Empire and the Dark Empire Mythryn. In exchange for the peace, a thirteenth kingdom was created in Cadaria, the Kingdom of Night, a permanent representation of the Dark Empire and its legions of death and destruction. For nearly a two thousand years this fragile peace stood.

However, the o'er-hanging fear could not be ignored. One day the bitterly won peace would fail, and the war between the faithful in Cadaria and Dark Gods of Mythryn would erupt.

* * * * * * * * * * * * *

Year Seventy-Five of the Just Emperor Ender "JustHand" Lorien XI, Creator's Calendar Year 1857.

Emperor Ender Lorien sat on the great golden Imperial Throne in his palace in the Cadarian province of Aldere looking out onto the assembled mass of courtiers and ambassadors from the thirteen major kingdoms and sighed. Ender was rapidly approaching his seventy-sixth birthday, and as the years dragged on, his tolerance for the niceties of court had begun to wear thin. The Lorien line had been touched by the Creator and had been gifted with a longer than average life, and it was days like this that Ender cursed that gift. Having ruled since the tender age of thirteen, Ender had seen many days in court, and none of them grated on him as much as this day had. The well-respected Ruby Knight of the Kingdom of Blood, Gregor Quicksilver was debating the finer points of Divine Law and Justice with the representative of the Kingdom of Night, a sharp-featured half-demon by the name of Sil.

The disagreement had begun shortly after Sil's announcement that the Onyx Knight, Tutio Illik had fallen in a freak accident while riding his horse through the lands claimed by one of the Great Dragons that called Cadaria home. Gregor simply put forward the theory that those descended from the dark gods would have to be more careful lest they meet with more Divine retribution. Sil naturally took offense to this statement, and the argument began. Many of the courtiers tried to politely end the discussion, but neither Gregor nor Sil were the type of men to let such a challenge go unmatched. Sil felt that such a remark was a blemish on his honor, and seemed intent on escalating the argument to a duel. Gregor, while never backing from a challenge loudly wondered whether everything in the Kingdom of Night had to become a life or death struggle. This further infuriated Sil, and the whole situation threatened to spin out of control.

The Emperor was about to intervene in the discussion when the doors to the audience chamber burst open, and two of Lorien's royal guard sailed through the air, landing nearly twenty feet into the audience chamber with a loud crash. The room stopped for a moment, no one sure what to do next. The members of the Royal Order of Knights, the Flashing Blade, who were in attendance immediately formed a wall between the cause of the disturbance and the Emperor. Lorien himself, though never as proficient a warrior as his defenders, reached for the Blade of the Emperor, *Allu drwo Chyfiawnder*, and stood straight to meet the coming danger.

Instead of an army of beasts or would-be assassins, a simple young woman dressed in the clothes of a commoner stepped into the room. She did not move gracefully, or even daintily. The woman moved as though she was carrying a great weight upon her that would not relent. Upon entering the chamber, the strange woman dressed in a tattered black dress stumbled slightly, and then righted herself by grasping one of the many tapestries that hung in the opulent audience chamber. However, the woman's touch drained the color from the tapestry, leaving the once brilliant scene of a victory over hordes of demons at the Plains of Steam looking like a barren wasteland of gray where the demons had triumphed. Many of the courtiers were shocked by the display and shrank back, leaving the braver warriors to face this threat. The woman stopped several feet short of the dais, just out of the reach of the line of warriors that stood before the Emperor. When the stranger finally lifter her head, Lorien could see the distant look in her eyes, as though she were somewhere far away. The woman bowed low, low enough for it to not just be a courtesy to the Emperor as a courtier or a knight would, but as someone who was truly honored to be in the presence of the Emperor of Cadaria.

"Please forgive this intrusion, my Emperor," the woman said, her head still bowed, "but the guards would not heed my words nor admit me to your presence, so I had no choice but to take matters into my own hands. If you will give me leave to say what I must say, I will gladly submit to any punishment you see fit to level upon your servant for her rash actions."

Lorien was struck by the sincerity in the woman's voice as well as the regal manner that she conducted herself with. The woman may not have looked like a courtier, but neither did she act like a commoner. The strangeness of the woman intrigued Lorien, and he motioned for his guards to stand aside.

"You have my leave to speak," the Emperor said slowly, his eyes never leaving the woman. "Rise and speak what you have fought so hard to say."

The woman straightened after a long moment and finally fixed her cold blue eyes upon Emperor Lorien. The power of the gaze was such that Lorien felt himself shudder for a moment. Finally, after a long deep breath, the woman began to speak.

"Thank you, Just Emperor Lorien. My name is Jehna Feris, of the Forer Clan, of the Kingdom of Blood, Zevarit."

Many in the room were taken aback again by the speaking of the name of the ancient Forer Clan. All of the members of that clan had been Seers, both blessed and cursed with different levels of ability to see either the past or the future. Some could only see the time of the death of those around them, while others could see with perfect clarity any action that had taken place on the spot in which they stood from any time. Most had been driven mad by the visions of the Day the Heavens Fell, and none were known to escape the fate of the corruption of the Dark Gods. Even the great Maldovrin Triplets, the last known Clan Forer members had not been spared the touch of darkness. If this woman truly was a member of Clan Forer, she could be more dangerous than some of the demons that served the fallen gods.

"Emperor Lorien," the woman continued, not deterred by the reactions of the assemblage, "I have come because my time is short, and there is much darkness coming, a darkness that will rival that of the Day the Heavens Fell. A great plague will walk across the lands of Cadaria, and old enemies will rise again to wreak havoc on the lives of those who live in the light. There is a great war on the horizon, the likes of which this world has never seen. Only those strong enough to stand against their own frailty and devotion will survive. And only those willing to set aside the blindness of this life will live to see the truth."

Sil was the first to scoff at the woman's visions.

"This woman is no Seer!" Sil announced with little time for other reaction. "She is simply a witch from the Dark Empire trying to frighten us into lowering our guard so she can strike against the Emperor. It is madness to put any validity to her words."

Jehna leveled her gaze upon Sil, and the room fell silent. Though none may have believed that the woman spoke the truth, the doubt had begun to creep into their minds, and her earlier display had caused fear to begin to fill their hearts. Her eyes closed and Jehna began to tremble and then finally opened her eyes, a knowing smile on her lips.

"It is wise for you to try to discredit me, Sil Nelerek. You more than anyone else here knows the depths that treachery can drive one to."

Jehna turned to the Emperor again and the smile faded from her face.

"Emperor Lorien, I have never laid eyes upon this man before, but I can tell you that in the tip of his sword's sheath lay a bottle of the most potent poison ever concocted in the Dark Empire, and in the pommel of his blade is a dart to be used as a delivery system. In his quarters, hidden in a text of the noble bloodlines of the Lorien family you will find several correspondence from the Dark Empire instructing him to kill not only yourself, but also the Onyx Knight. If you are interested my Emperor, I can recount for you the true circumstances of the Onyx Knight's death, and how it was staged to look like a riding accident."

Lorien did not even wait for the shocked reactions of the courtiers to fill the room before he struck. With a single blow, Sil's head was separated from his body, and the dark blood of a demon from the Dark Continent of Mythryn spread onto the floor. There were many shrieks, and some of the courtiers ran, fearing the corruption the blood contained. Emperor Lorien simply returned to his throne and laid his sword on the low table beside him, the black blood still clinging to the blade.

"Summon Alistair to deal with the blood, and when he is done, search Sil's body for the poison the Seer spoke of. I also want his quarters here and in the Kingdom of Night thoroughly searched. Gregor, you will see to the search personally as the Will of the Emperor."

"Yes, my Emperor," Gregor answered without hesitation.

"Now, Seer Feris," the Emperor Lorien said quietly, the audience chamber silent, "let us hear more about this dark time that approaches."

* * * * * * * * * * * * *

Day 224, Year Eighty-Five of the Just Emperor Ender "JustHand" Lorien XI, Creator's Calendar Year 1867:

We had another three cows die today. The only sign was just like all the others, bright green blotches on the skin and bloodshot eyes. We've had to move the rest of the herd to the south grazing fields, but the grass is so sparse that there is no telling if there will be enough grazing to be found there. A lot of the people in the village are starting to get worried, and I have to say that I am too. In just under two weeks, we've lost almost a quarter of our cattle, with no sign of the sickness before the end. Some of the more paranoid members of the council have openly stated that it is only a matter of time before this mysterious killer moves to the people of the village. I have tried to calm their fears, but I am unsure that it did any good. Hopefully, this move to the south fields will buy us some time and help to keep the paranoia and fear from spreading. As the ranking member of the council, it is my responsibility to keep the others from falling prey to their base emotions. However, I myself have at times allowed my fear to get the better of me. I gave my prayers to the Creator that he will help us find a way through, and keep us from harm.

Day 230, Year Eighty-Five of the Just Emperor Ender "JustHand" Lorien XI, Creator's Calendar Year 1867:

The south fields are no longer safe. Four more cows died today, all with the same mysterious symptoms. One of the shepherds that was tending the flock reported seeing something, but he got only a quick glimpse and couldn't be sure. He said that he saw a gaunt man, gray skin, and glowing red eyes, walking amongst the cattle. Before he could get a good look though, the man was gone. The only reason this was reported was because the shepherd thought he saw this man touch one of the cows that eventually died. I must admit that I officially did not put much stock in this report, but I have known the shepherd most of my life, and if he says that he saw such a man, then I have no choice but to believe. Nothing in the ancient scripture can account for this, and none of the wise men that have traveled through the area over the past few days had anything that could be called a valid explanation. Many more people have expressed their fear of the situation, and I understand their concerns. The situations that you do not understand are the ones that you most fear. Two families have already expressed their intentions to move on. In fact, just as I walked back to my home to pen this entry, I saw that one of the families had already begun the process of gathering their belongings into a wagon. I pray that they find happiness wherever their journey leads them. If things do not go better in the coming days, I fear that more of us will follow this same road.

Day 233, Year Eight-Five of the Just Emperor Ender "JustHand" Lorien XI, Creator's Calendar Year 1867:

Disaster has struck, and I pray that the Creator will have mercy on those of us who remain. The family that set out two days ago was discovered dead in their wagons less than a mile from the edge of the grazing fields. Only the family was killed, stricken by the same mysterious affliction, as the oxen wandered around on their own, finally making it back to the viable grazing lands. The bodies were burned immediately, where they sat in the wagon. None of us dared to get close for fear that the affliction would jump to us. It is clear that we cannot leave and only a fool would think that this plague would not eventually visit all of us. Fear has begun to grip the hearts of all of the inhabitants here, and they are not alone. I too am fearful of what is coming, and I only pray that I will have the strength to see my flock through this time of trial. What I do now, I pray that the Creator will guide me and see me through, for I do not know if I have the strength to make it through alone.

Day 235, Year Eighty-Five of the Just Emperor Ender "JustHand" Lorien XI, Creator's Calendar Year 1867:

Death has come to our quiet little village, and I am afraid that before long it will claim all of us. The gray man walked through the village openly at dawn, and everything he touched died within a matter of hours. He called himself Pestilence, the vanguard of a great darkness that would consume our entire world. Over half of the population has already been stricken with this plague, and there is no telling how many more of us will be left by the morning. This may be the last entry in my journal, and I pray that whoever finds it is not trapped within this same nightmare. The Creator have mercy upon us for our failings. May the light shine upon us on the Other Side.

Day 235, Year Eighty-Five of the Just Emperor Ender "JustHand" Lorien XI, Creator's Calendar Year 1867:

I am the last. The Crawling Plague has wiped out the entire village. Even now as I write, I can see the skin of my arm turning gray, and the green spots beginning to appear. It won't be long now, and the Creator will welcome me to the Other Side. My words may not be clear, as my sight has begun to fail. Please, if anyone ever reads this account, beware the gray man Pestilence; in his path lay only devastation, and in his hands lay only death.

* * * * * * * * * * * * *

Year Eighty-Five of the Just Emperor Ender "JustHand" Lorien XI, Creator's Calendar Year 1867:

The word of the deaths in the village of Kalid in the southern reaches of Cadaria had spread through the countryside like wild fire, and the diary of the Village Elder sat on Emperor Lorien's table open to the final horrifying entries. In the months that had followed the demise of the village, thousands of others had fallen victim to the Crawling Plague, and no one, not even the wisest of the Kingdom of Knowledge, or the Academy of Arcane Arts had any answer to the cause or the cure for the plague. The Crawling Plague had even spread to the Imperial Lands of Aldere, and some of the Emperor's royal guards had already fallen victim.

The plague had gotten its name because in its final stages, the victim's body was wracked with such pain that they could only crawl and did not have enough strength left to fully lift their own body weight. Gray splotches covered the skin until all color was gone, and the victim wasted away to nothing. As Lorien looked over the last entries again, his eyes fell to the small gray blotch on the back of his right hand, the hand that always held his sword. He knew it was just a matter of time before the rest of his body would show the signs of the plague, but for now he would have to remain strong.

A knock suddenly came at the door, and Emperor Lorien hurriedly closed the diary and covered his hands with the long flowing fabric of his regal robes.

"Enter."

The doors remained closed for a moment, and then opened. A wise-looking older man with a long black beard and slightly soiled robes entered the Emperor's private chambers. The normally wide smile that always hung on the face of Alistair Ravenheart was not present and the Imperial Sorcerer was obviously not the bearer of good tidings. However, as Emperor Lorien looked on the face of his old friend, he found it hard to believe that there could be any good tidings with the darkness that had begun to descend upon Cadaria.

"My Emperor, I am pleased to see you remain in good health," Alistair said quickly.

"I take it you have bad news for me, old friend."

Alistair's lips curled into a frown and he nodded his head slowly. Good news had been in increasingly short supply over the past few months.

"The Dark Seer Jehna Feris has disappeared from her quarters at the Academy of Arcane Arts in Jelan. The grounds have been searched several times, but she is nowhere to be found. The guards who stayed at her door reported nothing out of the ordinary, and there was no trace of magic or any other means for her escape or possible abduction. It is as though one minute she was there, and the next she was gone."

Lorien nodded his head for a moment and then sighed. There was still so much about the strange woman that they didn't understand, and now it looked like they never would.

"However," Alistair said slowly, "in her effects there was a letter addressed to you with today's date upon it. I brought it as swiftly as I could."

Lorien started to reach with his right hand, and stopped short, placing it on his desk and then taking the letter with his left hand.

"Thank you Alistair, you performed your duties well as always."

The old sorcerer held his ground, his jaw tight and a look of great burden in his eyes.

"Was there something more, old friend?" Ender asked slowly.

"I am sorry, my Emperor, but your daughter, the wife to your son Kaitain, has been stricken by the Crawling Plague. It is said she did not suffer too much, and fell into a deep slumber before the end. It seems she was spared the worst."

Ender fell silent and unconsciously looked at the back of his right hand, a strange itch seeming to fill the spot.

"Kaitain? Marlae?"

"Both are fine," Alistair replied, "they appear to have escaped any infection at this point."

Ender sighed deeply.

"Thank you old friend. I need some time alone."

Alistair bowed deeply and then turned to leave the room. Ender reflected for a moment before cracking the seal on the scroll that sat in his lap. When Lorien read the words, his heart fell. The day he had dreaded was finally upon them, and the prophecy that the Dark Seer had spun all those years ago was now about to come to pass.

Emperor Ender "JustHand" Lorien

It has begun………

Jehna Feris, the Dark Seer

Chapter XLV

Bargains

Year Eighty-Five of the Just Emperor Ender "Just Hand" Lorien XI, Creator's Calendar Year 1867

The death of a father is never an easy thing to bear, and as Kaitain Lorien watched, his proud and strong father faded from the stalwart and just man that he had been to a mere shell of life that hung on out of nothing more than stubbornness and habit. The great and powerful Emperor of Cadaria was reduced in his final days to a bed-ridden mumbling old man. A force that Kaitain could not understand, a force that threatened the entire continent, had stolen away the life from the seemingly invincible soul of the Cadarian Empire, and not even the wisest of the members of the Academy of Arcane Arts in Jelan had any answers. Kaitain had just recently passed his thirty-fifth birthday and had served as his father's ambassador to the thirteen Great Kingdoms on many occasions, and he knew in his heart that the time was right for him to take up arms against whatever force was causing the plague. Regardless of the wild and unsubstantiated theories that were whispered in the halls of power, in Kaitain's mind there could be only one source. For years there had been rumblings about the Dark Empire of Mythryn wanting to break the millennia long truce and begin a war against the rightful powers of Cadaria. The Dark Gods of Mythryn had to be the cause of the Crawling Plague, and as soon as the power was in Kaitain's hands, they would be made to pay for what they had done.

When the knock came at the doors to the heir's chambers, Kaitain knew immediately what had come to pass. He had felt it the moment that his father died and the power of the ancient Lorien bloodline passed to him. The light streaks of gray that had begun to grace his temples had vanished from the mirror, and the old scars from bandit attacks began to fade. The ancient powers said to be granted by the Creator Himself had entered him, and Kaitain's life force had been suffused with the same power that had once shaped the heavens. The door opened to reveal Kaitain's father's old friend, Alistair Ravenheart, and in his hands lay the Imperial Sword. Its name came from an ancient tongue and its name meant Power through Justice. *Allu drwo Chyfiawnder* had served the Lorien family for generations, and its origins had long passed into the mists of antiquity, remembered only by scholars and historians. The bright golden blade gleamed in the light, and it had been through the judicious use of this sword that Ender Lorien had earned the name JustHand. Without a word, Alistair knelt and lifted the sword to the rightful ruler of the Empire of Cadaria. Kaitain took the sword, accepting his position as Emperor.

"Let me be the first to swear my loyalty to the rightful Emperor of Cadaria, Kaitain Lorien, the Just Emperor Lorien the Twelfth."

Alistair kept his head down as he spoke the words. It took no recognition of the passing of the title, it was decreed by the ancient accords that had ended the Unification Wars that the successor would assume the title when they were called by the power in their blood. The calling had struck Kaitain hard, and yet he felt ready, as though he were always carrying the responsibility of the empire on his shoulders.

"Thank you, Alistair. My father trusted you, and I always felt that the trust was well placed. For that reason, I will request that you continue to serve as the Imperial Sorcerer and liaison from the Imperial Palace of Aldere to the Academy of Arcane Arts in Jelan."

Alistair rose to his feet and smiled.

"I thank you for your kindness in this great hour of sorrow, my Emperor. If there is anything I can do to repay this great honor you have bestowed upon me, I will do it without hesitation."

"There is, Alistair," Kaitain said after a moment, "find the cause of this Crawling Plague, and eradicate it."

Alistair fell silent for a moment and shook his head.

"Emperor Lorien," Alistair began, the title tasting like ash on his tongue, "we at the Academy of Arcane Arts have searched every corner of our texts, scoured the countryside, and have yet to come up with any clue as to the origins of the Crawling Plague or the identity of this man referred to as Pestilence. This gray man seems to have disappeared after the plague started. None of our magic has been able to cure or even impede the spread of the disease. We have even gone so far as to petition the clerics and healers from the Temple of the Creator in Albitonin for aid. Some seem to be totally immune to its effects while others are ravaged within hours. There are very few avenues of exploration left open to us at this point."

Kaitain fumed for a moment, and then squeezed the hilt of the Imperial Sword…his sword.

"And what about the Dark Empire of Mythryn? Has there been any thought that the Dark Gods there could have created this plague and loosed it on us to start a war?"

Alistair stood silent for a moment and then responded slowly.

"That was one of the first avenues that we explored, Emperor Lorien, and while we have not been able to rule out the possibility, we also have not been able to confirm the Dark Empire as the source."

"Is there anyone else that we are aware of that could create this Crawling Plague? Is there any other force that could bring this gray man to our Empire to kill our people?"

Alistair fell silent. He knew where this conversation was going, and where it would eventually lead the empire. Kaitain seemed intent on a war with Mythryn, and had felt thusly for years. There was going to be little that Alistair could say to keep a war from breaking out, but there was perhaps one more option. Even as the thoughts entered his mind, his stomach twisted into a knot and his heart felt like a chunk of ice in the center of his chest.

"There is, my Emperor, one more avenue that we could explore. As you know, the Ancient Dragons that call Espre home are older than even the Dark Gods that fell from the Heavens. They perhaps could give us answers."

Kaitain fell silent this time, his head bowed and his eyes closed. Many nights, Kaitain and his father had sat discussing the Dragons of Espre. They were aloof and powerful creatures that seemed neither to answer to others of their kind or even the ancient gods. Some were good, some were evil, and some were everywhere in between. Working with the Dragons was always a possibility if a war were to break out with the Dark Empire. Approaching them was always a danger because it could be seen as a sign of weakness if the wrong member of their race was approached. There had been a tenuous peace between the Empire of Cadaria and the Dragon Realms for many years, and upsetting that peace could cause a war to be fought on two fronts, something Cadaria could not afford.

"Very well, Alistair, you may approach one of the dragons, one that you feel will not take offense to the request, and one that you do not feel will return to attack us. If there are any repercussions for this course of action, I am afraid to think of what perils might befall you, old friend."

Alistair saw the look in Kaitain's eyes, and for the first time was scared of the young man he had watch grow from a baby. The death of a father changes people, and it would either make the young man stronger, or it would destroy him from the inside out.

"By your word, my Emperor."

* * * * * * * * * * * * *

Year One of the Just Emperor Kaitain Lorien XII, Creator's Calendar Year 1868

On the outskirts of the Kingdom of Night, Alistair Ravenheart found himself both afraid for his life, and afraid for the lives of everyone he had ever known. A massive dragon, thousands of times larger than the largest man lay stretched across the barren cave floor underneath a great swamp.

CHAPTER 45

It had taken several months to track down the dragon, and now at the moment of truth, Alistair was concerned if he would survive to return to Aldere. With a low loud snort, the dragon slowly raised its head and flashed its gleaming white teeth.

"So," it said in a rumbling voice, "you are the human that had been trying to find a dragon. Are you some deluded hunter? Do you wish to make a feast of me? Leave now little man, you are not even enough to be considered a snack."

Alistair shivered as the foul voice passed over him like a hurricane. The force of the beast's voice was incredible, and it took all of the magic within Alistair to remain standing.

"My Lord Dragon," Alistair began, falling to a knee, "I have come to seek out your guidance and wisdom in a matter of grave importance. I am willing to offer you my life in exchange for any information that I could share with my Emperor about the great plague that had befallen my people."

The dragon stayed silent for a long moment before lifting its head higher and fixing its gaze on the tiny human.

"And what is the life of a tiny human wizard worth to me? I could simply destroy your home, destroy your Academy of Arcane Arts; I could even destroy your Empire if I saw fit. So, why is one life important to me?"

Alistair's heart sank.

"However, in your own pathetic human way, it took bravery to come here and make your offer. For that I will do you a courtesy. I will make you a deal, human."

At that, the dragon pulled itself up to its full height, towering over Alistair and the exertion made the ground rumble and shake as though an earthquake had struck the area.

"I will give you the information that you seek, if you find something for me. There is an artifact called the Dragon's Tear. I want it. I will tell you who created your little plague and how to cure it, if you find it for me."

Alistair sat silent for a moment, having been knocked to the ground by the rumbling beneath his feet.

"My lord, I do not know how long it will take me to find this item of which you speak, and all that time my people will be dying. I must know now who has caused this terrible affliction, and how it can be stopped."

The dragon roared, and its rage could be felt as the temperature in the cave rose sharply in a matter of moments. Alistair knew is life was at an end, and so too were the hopes of all of Cadaria.

"You dare to make demands of the great Demon Dragon Shadowweaver? You dare to believe that your life and the lives of your pathetic species means anything to me? I have killed millions of you insects in my lifetime, and I will live to kill millions more. You are filth, vermin, and you should have been exterminated long ago. Tonight, your people shall suffer greatly wizard, and it will all be because of you. I will tell you how to stop this little plague of yours wizard, but for your impudence, your cities will burn and your children will grow without parents. The suffering and pain I will cause will make this plague seem like a simple fever, and it is all on your head wizard. You and your impudence will always be to blame. Think on that tonight as your cities die. Now listen, before the destruction begins. Heed well the information you have paid for with so much blood."

* * * * * * * * * * * * * *

Kaitain Lorien sat on the throne in his audience chamber and stared in horror at the news. The Kingdom of Night had been attacked by a flight of dragons. Alistair's plan had failed and it had cost the lives of thousands of people. If the wizard had survived, there would be more than just the blood of innocents on Alistair's hands. His execution would be slow to be sure; slow and painful. There was no price that Alistair could pay to make up for this failure, and his death would serve no real purpose other than alienate the Academy of Arcane Arts at the time when they would be most needed. How could Kaitain denounce the most powerful wizard in the world and still save face with the Academy?

Just as Kaitain slumped in the throne, there was a gentle breeze that filled the room. The audience chamber was never known to be drafty, except when the correct series of doors were opened. As Kaitain straightened, he became aware that he was no longer alone. Reaching slowly for the Imperial Sword, Kaitain scanned the room. Assassins were not uncommon in the Imperial City of Aldere, and several attempts had been made on his father's life over the years. Just as Kaitain's hand found the hilt of his sword, a sweet and gently voice lifted onto the air of the chamber.

"My Emperor, I apologize for this intrusion, but I needed to speak with you."

Kaitain found the source of the voice a moment later, coming from a servant's entrance on the far side of the audience chamber. Kaitain had seen the young woman many times in the years that he had lived in the palace, and knew instantly who she was. The young woman's name was Irene Drage, an apprentice to Alistair Ravenheart, and one of the most accomplished students at the Academy of Arcane Arts. She had not yet gained the rank of Sorceress, but if she was studying with Alistair, it was only a matter of time. Many would consider Irene beautiful, and the woman had always fascinated Kaitain. She had long brunette hair that washed down her back like a cascading waterfall, and her eyes sparkled like stars in a clear night sky. The dress that she wore would barely qualify as clothing in more corners of the world. It was made of a thin, nearly transparent white material that clung to her body as though it were wet, showing off every curve and feature. Her lithe body seemed almost to tremble in the presence of the Emperor.

"Irene Drage, I trust you have a good reason for disturbing me."

Irene wavered for a moment, and then straightened as though the fear had been expelled from her body. She now moved more confidently, striding gracefully to the front of the dais where she bowed slightly and then straightened.

"I am flattered my Emperor that you remember my name. It has been many months since you have spoken a word to me, and so I am grateful that I made an impression upon you."

Kaitain was captivated by the woman's voice. There was something intoxicating about her, and Kaitain could feel himself relaxing back onto the throne, his enthrallment with the woman deepening.

"I was saddened to hear about the passing of your young wife," Irene continued softly. "She was a beautiful woman and too strong to have been claimed by the terrible plague. I was however relieved to hear that your daughter survived. To lose three members of your family to the same plague would have been too much to bear I'm afraid."

Kaitain nodded, the pangs of loss swelling up inside him.

"Marlae will be a strong heir to the throne, and if she is paired with a good man, the Lorien line will live forever," Kaitain answered softly. "But you did not come here to discuss my family Irene, I am sure that this has something to do with your mentor."

Irene flashed a quick and enticing smile.

"You are as perceptive as you are wise, my Emperor. This visit does indeed have to do with my teacher. Alistair is a proud man and would do anything to serve the Empire…"

Kaitain cut her off quickly and sat straight on the throne.

"If you are here to beg for his life, save your pleas. What he has done has brought shame upon his family and himself. There is nothing that can stave off his execution."

Irene smiled again and shook her head.

"On the contrary, my Emperor. I am not here to beg for the life of my teacher, I am here to give you another way to exact your vengeance and still save face with the Academy of Arcane Arts."

Kaitain smiled for a quick moment and then let his features go cold.

"I'm listening."

Irene seductively straightened her dress and then locked her perfect hazel eyes on the Emperor.

"As you know, any action taken against Alistair Ravenheart would strain your relations with the Academy of Arcane Arts where he is viewed as a father and mentor by many of the most powerful wizards and sorceresses in the world. In the war that is coming, you cannot afford to be without their support, especially now that it seems you will be fighting on two fronts. The best way to dispose of Alistair would be to first publicly forgive him for his mistake and reward him for the attempt he made."

Kaitain rubbed his chin and frowned.

"If he survived," Kaitain responded flatly.

"Ravenheart still lives," Irene answered quickly. "And with him he carries the means to end the Crawling Plague and cure those who are still infected. Also with him he carries the name of an ancient artifact that has great powers. It was his refusal to return this artifact to the dragons that caused the attacks. Alistair was right to refuse this request because the destruction in the Kingdom of Night would be dwarfed by what the dragons could do with this artifact in their possession."

Kaitain sat forward, nearly hanging on the woman's every word.

"What is this artifact, and what does it do?"

"It is called the Dragon's Tear, my Emperor," Irene answered, "and it will do anything that its possessor wishes. It can remake reality in whatever way they demand. The dragons would surely use it to eradicate every last human from the face of Espre. No matter the cost, it can never be allowed to fall into their clutches."

Kaitain nodded absently, but his thoughts were elsewhere. With the power of the Dragon's Tear in his hands, he could reverse the damage done by the Crawling Plague. He could bring back his wife and his father. He could bring back all those killed in the Kingdom of Night. He could even slay the Dark Gods and the monsters of the Dark Empire of Mythryn. The possibilities were endless.

"How do you know of this artifact and the fate of Alistair Ravenheart?"

Irene smiled again.

"I am a sorceress, my Emperor, it is my responsibility to know everything that could benefit or harm the Empire."

Kaitain could feel something in her words, another track of thought that was left unspoken. It had always been the gift of the Lorien line to be able to feel when people were telling the truth or when they were holding back information. There was something more to Irene's purpose than just being a good servant of the Empire.

"And what do you want, Irene?"

Irene frowned.

"Emperor Lorien, as a dedicated vassal of the throne, I am bound to bring any information that I have to you as quickly as possible without thought of reward for myself. My actions are their own reward."

Kaitain smiled. Irene was telling the truth, but she was also plainly omitting what she wanted. It was perfectly played.

"Then perhaps if something were to happen to poor Alistair, you would accept the appointment to become the Court Sorceress?"

Irene smiled and then blushed slightly.

"If that is my Emperor's will."

"Very well," Kaitain said flatly. "Then let us discuss the honor that we will bestow upon our good friend Alistair."

A maniacal laughter rang through the audience hall as Irene simply smiled and plotted her next move.

****

In the streets of the capitol of the Kingdom of Night, Galateria, people were dying. The flight of dragons that had descended upon the city were merciless. The ancient sword of the Onyx Knight stood on the memorial to the fallen hero, Tutio Illik, and without a new champion to take up the sword, the Kingdom of Night would never stand against the dragons. Upon a hill, overlooking the destruction sat a young man. His gleaming red eyes soaked up the death around him, and he felt pity for the people that had once been his friends. It was his nature, the joke of his birth that made him an outcast and prevented him from saving the people that had once been kind to him. His father had been a dragon, his father had cursed him with a twisted form, and it was this curse that had caused him to be cast from his home. Now the people below suffered, and it hurt to watch.

Devlin turned away from the destruction, but the visions would not leave his mind. The people below may not have wanted him, but he would not turn his back on them.

What are you doing?

"Go away, I don't need you."

If you're thinking about going down there and attacking your own kind, then you certainly do need me.

"They are not my kind. They are dragons, they are filth, vermin. Every last one of them needs to be destroyed."

Even you?

The voice taunted Devlin in the back of his mind, just as it had during every day of his life. As long as Devlin could remember, the voice had been there, urging him on, protecting him, and keeping him sane in a world that seemed to want to rip itself apart in insanity.

"I'm going to help them."

If you are intent upon doing so, would you at least listen to me first? I can make you famous if you'll just listen to me for once.

"I'm going to die today. Will that make me famous?"

You'll only die if you don't listen.

* * * * * * * * * * * * *

The battle for the Kingdom of Night was over and Galateria was saved. Standing in the middle of the town square was Devlin Rannoch surrounded by the pieces of the statue of the Onyx Knight and the bodies of fallen dragons. The ancient sword of the Onyx Knight, Discipline, raised above his head, the townspeople cheered and lauded praise upon their savior. The battle had not been an easy one, but Devlin had survived. And just as the voice had said, he would now be famous throughout the world, the great savior of the Kingdom of Night.

All you have to do is trust me……

The Price of Excellence

Year Seventeen of the Just Emperor Terrik Lorien I, the Creator's Calendar Year 67

Arturious Demascious labored at is forge, the heat nearly searing his skin. For nearly five years, hour after laborious hour, Arturious had been working on his masterpiece, the first obsidian weapon in the Empire, a true masterpiece. As the heat in the room began to build, Arturious could feel the anticipation build within him. Then suddenly, the glowing black stone before him cracked. Before he could even utter a cry of shock, the stone blade exploded, sending shards of obsidian flying in all directions, many of them piercing Arturious' skin. Blood flowed freely from his wounds, but the flow of red did not compare to the tears streaming from his eyes.

For twenty years, Arturious had been the only master weapon smith in the entire Cadarian Empire, and probably had been before the Cadarian Empire was even formed. However, metal held no more challenge for Arturious, there was no life in the metal to expand upon. It was as if the metal had no soul. When Arturious turned his attention to stone however, he found a wealth of untapped energy within every stone. First he started with granite, then slate, then even moved to gemstones like emerald and jade. Each and every crystal that he experimented with was fascinating in its own right. However, when Arturious stumbled upon a piece of obsidian, he knew he had found something special, something that could change the face of weaponry.

There was a life and a spirit within every piece of obsidian. It was like the stone housed a soul; a soul of fire and purity. When heated, the stone moved of its own volition at times, taking strange and wondrous shapes. At the same time though, Arturious found through love and guidance that he could mold the stone into a form that he desired. However, all of his attempts to form a perfect blade had met with utter failure.

Arturious soon discovered the cause of his failure. Obsidian was created in the hottest portions of active volcanoes, and as the stone cooled, it collected impurities. These impurities made the stone far too unstable for fine smithing and it sometimes had explosive results. Because of this Arturious had but one choice left open to him. He would have to collect obsidian from the heart of the last active volcano on the face of Espre. The very site where the dark gods impacted on the Day the Heavens Fell. The place known only as the Endless Crater.

* * * * * * * * * * * * *

Year Twenty of the Just Emperor Terrik "Godslayer" Lorien I, Creator's Calendar Year 70

The first War of Darkness between Cadaria and the Dark Gods of Mythryn had seriously impeded Arturious' quest, but finally he had reached his destination. Arturious cared little for the war or the plight of those who suffered both directly and indirectly from the conflict. He had done his part for the Cadarian Empire long before there was such a thing, and his debt of blood had been paid more times than he cared to count. Life, death, emperors and gods mattered little. Only the work mattered, and the war was an impediment that needed to be overcome if he was going to succeed in his task. The Endless Crater stretched low before him, a gaping hole in the world where the mightiest of the Dark Gods crashed down from their heavenly fall. Arturious had heard rumors during his journey that Emperor Lorien had slain one of the mightiest of the Dark Gods in personal combat and it had ended the War of Darkness with a truce. Arturious had never cared much for the politics of war, though it was the industry of war that made it possible for his work to continue. Arturious was particularly proud of the sword that he had crafted for the Emperor, though it was only one of the many powerful blades that had been crafted. A greater weapon still lay hidden, the greatest of Arturious' creations with metal. But hopefully the time for its emergence would never come.

Slowly and deftly the old man made his way down the face of the Endless Crater, sampling the obsidian he found along the way. The rocks at the top were too impure, too much of the Dark Gods' corruption lay upon them. While most would never dare to get this close to the crater and risk corruption, Arturious had no fear of such things. No one could be made evil that did not truly wish to be, or was not already corrupted within their soul. His pure purpose would keep him safe form whatever lay below.

****

Day 142 Year Twenty of the Just Emperor Terrik "Godslayer" Lorien I, Creator's Calendar Year 70

I have stopped for the moment to sample a few more rocks here. I'm nearly one hundred feet below the surface, and so far the corruption in the obsidian remains. There must be more pure stone down below. I would assume that the closer I get to the core of the world, the more pure stone I will find. As I continue my descent, I will make more notes about that which I find…

It's been several more hours now, and there is much more heat here. The descent has been harder than I expected, and the obsidian here, while much more pure, is not suitable for my work and makes my descent far more difficult. It coats the walls of the chasm everywhere, and my hands are showing the effect, even with my thick gloves. It seems that I was right about the cutting quality of this stone. If lightly putting my hand upon an outcropping can draw blood, can you imagine what effect a blade would have? But I must find pure stone to make it work, and then find a way to strengthen the stone without dulling it. There must be pure stone here…

All sense of time seems to have left me down here in the darkness, and my torch will not stay lit. It is only because of the eyesight of my ancestors that I am able to function at all, let alone keep this journal of my activities. I have built a small fire, and it is helping. But I have made a miraculous discovery here. There is virtually no corruption in these stones at all. It is almost like the touch of the Dark Gods does not extend this far into the world. If that is true, than what made the rest of this chasm? I shall continue to descend, and perhaps I will find the answer when I find my pure obsidian…

Success! I have reached the bottom. There is a light down here, it is an eerie green light that seems to permeate everything. But I have found what I was searching for. The stone here is free from corruption, and with the heat, there is a vein of pure obsidian that I can draw enough material from to create my master blade. However, the unexpected discovery has been a path that leads away from the bottom of the Crater. It seems to lead away from the chasm deeper into the core of the world, almost as if it were built here before the fall. I will continue my search, and upon my return I shall forge the most powerful weapon the world has ever seen…

The world is over…the world is over…Dorovar…I must return…can't sleep. Can't ever sleep. Must work, must keep working. War is coming, much war, big war, war to end everything. Have to keep working…must not stop, must not rest, he will come…Dorovar…he will come to take me…to make me do it….to make me end it all. He will come to take us all. Pestilence…Famine…Death…War…must not stop…must not rest. Dorovar. Dorovar. The dragons will come, the dragons will kill, the dragons will suffer. The Dark Gods must not know, the Dark Gods must never know what they have. They could destroy us all, they could make it all go away. They could kill Dorovar…no…no one can kill Dorovar…no one can stop the Conquest….no one can kill us…nothing can kill us. No one can stop us. We must not stop, we must not rest, no…we must make, we must take, we must live. We will live forever, we must live forever. The Creator cannot touch us, the Creator cannot stop us. The Creator fears us. We must not stop, we must not rest, we cannot sleep. Sleep is death, and death cannot touch us. It cannot stop us…..He cannot stop us….Dorovar…

* * * * * * * * * * * * * *

Year Sixty-Five of the Just Emperor Terrik "Godslayer" Lorien I, Creator's Calendar Year 115

Emperor Lorien walked into the former residence of his friend Arturious and sighed deeply. For the last few years, the often enigmatic and irrational weapon smith had kept mostly to himself and shut off all contact with the outside world. When most of the world had stopped caring about the man often referred to as a lunatic, Emperor Lorien's love would not allow him to forsake the man who had done so much to help establish the Lorien family as the rightful rulers of the Empire of Cadaria. When no one had spoken to or seen Arturious for several months, Terrik became concerned and went to visit his friend. All that was to be found in Arturious' house was a cold forge, a stack of half-finished weapons, stacks and stacks of journals with nearly incomprehensible writings, and thirteen special weapons. The note attached to the weapons told of the thirteen Great Kingdoms of Cadaria and how these weapons would be gifts to the champions of those kingdoms. These knights would become known as the Knights of the Flashing Blade, and would serve to protect the Emperor in times of dire need.

There was a sound behind Terrik and he spun to see a beautiful woman standing in the doorway. The Emperor's grasp on the hilt of the Imperial Sword loosened and he smiled at his wife.

"It seems our friend is gone," Terrik said slowly.

"So it seems," the woman replied.

Terrik scowled. His wife had always kept her council to herself. She was older than Terrik, but still retained the same beauty as the day they had met. There was talk that she was a Seer, a gift from the Creator to guide the Lorien line to rulership. Most simply scoffed at the suggestion because the Empress had never shown any talent other than infuriating her husband.

"I bring a request from my clan, husband."

Terrik sighed. The Clan Forer had been much trouble since its inclusion into the Imperial line. They seemed to think of themselves as experts on everything, and professed to have knowledge about things that predated the existence of Espre, as if they had been touched by the Creator Himself. Though that was not out of the question, it was unlikely. The Creator had gifted some of the bloodlines with amazing abilities, the most profound of which was the long life granted to the members of the Lorien family. However, it was only the chosen, the pure bloods that truly benefited from the gift. It was also said that only one member of each of the Blessed Families carried the gift, the Touch of the Ancestors. Only time would tell if that were true or not.

"And what is this boon that your clan requests of me?"

The Empress strode past her husband and bent to pick up one book out of hundreds that lay strewn across the floor. She regarded it for a moment, but did not open it.

"We request that this book be stored in the archives and protected from all. It is never to be opened or the knowledge within it used. The rest of the books and weapons should be destroyed with the exception of the thirteen in the corner. Those should be moved to the Imperial storehouse."

Terrik scratched his chin.

"If the knowledge is not to be used, and the book never to be opened, let us just destroy it with the rest."

The Empress held the book to her breast quickly and shook her head.

"This book cannot be destroyed, my husband."

The look on the face of the Empress was one of sorrow and regret. It was almost as if the book held some great evil, and if she were to relinquish it, it would spill out upon the ground like the corrupted blood of the Dark Gods. And for the first time in their marriage, Terrik saw true fear in the eyes of his wife.

"Why?"

The Empress looked down at the book for the moment, and then sighed.

"Even the destruction of this book cannot prevent what will come to pass, and if the book is destroyed, the dark future that it predicts may come quicker."

Terrik shook his head.

"Very well then, Liette. I shall do as you and your clan requests. The guardianship of this book will fall to your clan for the rest of time, and if there are no more of your clan to protect it, than it will fall to those whom you do not wish to possess it. Do you understand?"

"My clan will persevere, my husband," Liette answered.

The Emperor nodded and watched as his wife left. Soon agents would be dispatched to destroy all that remained of the great man known as Arturious. As Terrik looked down at the note again telling of the great knights that would rally to protect him, only one thought kept running through his mind.

There are twelve kingdoms in Cadaria…

* * * * * * * * * * * * *

Year Eighty-Three of the Just Emperor Ender "JustHand" Lorien XI, Creator's Calendar Year 1864

There are places in the world where fear is a palpable thing; it has mass, form, and a face. Every child knows the face of the creature that wears the name fear, it haunts them as completely as any ghost. However, all children are given a gift once they reach the age of maturity. Perhaps it should not be called a gift. All children forget the face of their greatest fear, that thing which haunts all their dreams yet their parents are unable or unwilling to see. Deep within the deepest darkness this creature sleeps, waiting for the time when its pact with the primal forces of nature will no longer bind it; when it will be able to reclaim the hearts and minds lost to it through the ages. Of all the primal emotions, fear is one of the most powerful. It can drive a person to do almost anything.

At the bottom of a chasm, a single form deftly made its way down the long and treacherous mountain face. The form hung there, suspended by only the strength within his hands and arms, still thousands of feet from the solid floor of rock below. His hands were stained with his own blood, the treacherous rocks of the solid wall of razor sharp obsidian had taken their toll on the sensitive flesh. The descent had taken nearly three days, and though he did not require sleep, he was still tired. It would take another two hours to reach the bottom, and after that, there was no telling how long before he would reach his destination. The Vault of Terrors was considered to be a legend at best. There was no proof that such a place ever existed except for a few scribbled notes in the margin of the diary of the world's most notorious madman. While he was a genius of engineering and metallurgy, the genius did not translate to everyday life. This man, Arturious Demascious, was paranoid in the worst sense of the word. He believed that there were monsters around every corner, and that if he slept they would come to get him. So, through strange magic and rituals Arturious never slept, not for the last forty-five years of his life. Then finally, one day, he just disappeared. All that was left behind was a set of thirteen blades that he had been working on before his disappearance, and the madman's diary. Most of the historians of the time could not make any sense of the words in the diary. The book had been quickly snatched up by the equally legendary Clan Forer, the mystical seers whose portents foretold a coming darkness unlike anything the world had ever seen. This darkness was said to rival even the Day the Heavens Fell. The book was stored in the basement of a church under heavy guard for hundreds of years. Eventually the madman's dairy passed into obscurity for almost a millennia.

It had taken many bribes and many years of searching to uncover the location of the church, but a daring thief was able to recover the book at the cost of the lives of the guards and everyone else in the church. The man laughed to himself as he batted the large leather-bound book that was hidden inside the pouch hanging on his side. It was not a perfect crime, but sometimes the prize is worth the risk.

Finally, the lone form reached the bottom of the rock face. Looking up, the man could see the last glimmer of light from the surface, light that barely made it down the several mile drop to the depths of the planet. It took only a moment to light a torch and look around the makeshift chamber. There was evidence that someone or something had been here before. There were ashen remains of what must have been a fire pit, and a few bones strewn around that may have been from unlucky animals that found themselves cooked as food. There was only one way, other than the rock face, out of the chamber, and that was a long narrow passageway that snaked its way out of sight, heading off to the west. After a deep breath of the moderately stagnate air, the man began the long walk that he knew was ahead of him.

Without the light of the sun, it was impossible to know how long he had been down there, wandering through the twisting and turning labyrinth of passageways that seemed to go everywhere and nowhere all at once. Every single passage had the exact same markings, and the dim light of the torch went a long way toward making the passageways look even more similar.

CHAPTER 45

I wonder how long I've been down here, the man thought to himself as he turned yet another familiar looking corner. And then suddenly, the passageway opened up into a huge room, and what's more, there was light.

As soon as he had entered the new chamber, the man whistled softly and then pulled the large book out of his bad and flipped through the pages until he came to the scribbled words that he knew by heart.

'The Vault of Terrors lies within the heart of darkness, illumed by the light of creation, bathed in the fire of perdition, and contained within is the end of all that was, is, and will be.'

"Fool," the man said, his voice breaking a silence that had stood for a thousand years.

The man looked for the first time closely at the massive ornate door that stood before him. It had to be thirty feet tall and easily that far across. The edges of the door were wreathed in fire, a fire that burned like ignited oil upon water. It slipped and slid over the surface of the door, flowing like water over every carefully carved feature. Then, he heard it.

"*Dorovar……*"

The sound was like a thousand voices whispering the name in unison.

"*Dorovar……*"

"Who's there?" the man spoke, the whispering voices filling his head to the point of overflowing.

"*Dorovar……*"

"Who is Dorovar?"

"*I am Dorovar……*"

Suddenly the door moved. It slid back about half a foot before stopping, however the ring of fire that had been surrounding the door remained just as it was, and though there was no longer a surface for the flames to flow over, they still moved as though the door was in its original place.

"I have come to open the Vault of Terrors."

"*And why have you disturbed Dorovar……*"

"I have come to open the Vault of Terrors. Is Dorovar the guardian?"

"*I am Dorovar……*"

Again the door moved.

"*I am the nightmare of all creatures, I am the destroyer of worlds, I am that which comes in the last moments of life to bear the souls to the Other Side. If you desire the opening of the Vault of Terrors you must first complete the Trials of Dorovar.*"

The lone form dropped the old book to the floor and removed the long flowing cloak that had helped shear the wind during his descent.

"I have not come for a test, I have come for the power contained here. This world will fall under my boot, and nothing will stand in my way!"

The door moved again, this time accompanied by a blast of hot air. The air moved so quickly that the man fought to hold his ground. The voice came again, this time no longer a whisper but a loud roar.

"*NO ONE DEMANDS ANYTHING IN THE FACE OF DOROVAR!*"

The wreath of fire exploded that moment, enveloping the man in flames. The lone figure closed his eyes instinctively, waiting for the hot searing pain through his skin. The pain never came. When he opened his eyes again, he found himself surrounded by the flowing, water-like flames. The voice once more spoke, this time it had returned to a whisper.

"*I am Dorovar……You are unworthy of the gifts that Dorovar has to offer you. But perhaps you can be useful. Choose. You may serve Dorovar, or you may die.*"

Fear struck the next moment. This was not what he had intended at all. Never did he expect to find any kind of intelligence within the Vault, now he was faced with the only option that would allow him to keep his life.

"I will serve, Lord Dorovar."

Finally, the pain that he had been expecting came. The fires that danced across the surface of his skin now began to burn, and burn fast. The flicking fires burned away all traces of the clothing that the man had worn, stripping him down to his bronzed skin. But the fire was not content with merely burning the fabric of his clothes, and it began to lick at his flesh, but instead of burning, the flesh began to rot and congeal, much like after death. The bronze color faded away, and the remaining flesh was gray, pitted and pocked. His tongue shriveled in his mouth and then his gums began to dry and bleed. The fires flicked at the tender lenses of his eyes, and at that moment, he could feel the dry and burning pain. Suddenly, like an explosion in the back of his mind, the lone figure's eyes erupted, the tender membrane ruptured and flowed down his face like tears, mixing with the congealing flesh of his face forming a truly horrific amalgamation. If death had a form, that is what he had become.

"*You belong to me now. You are now my first. You are Pestilence. You are no longer a man, you are a tool. You will spread the plague and disease that I have created upon the land and the dead shall join my choir. When enough voices have been added, they shall sing me into the realm of the immortals, and then I shall finally have my revenge and my peace. Go now, Pestilence. Go.*"

Pestilence vaguely remembered that he had a life. Vaguely remembered that he had a name. But all that was gone. There was only his work. He would kill, and keep killing until no living being remained on the face of the world. That was all that remained. All there was, all there would ever be. Dorovar.

Boundless Love

Year One of the Just Emperor Kaitain Lorien XII, Creator's Calendar Year 1868

Faith and love take shape in many different ways. High Priestess Hannah Ironheart, the Celestine Knight of the Kingdom of Stone sat in private meditation in the Temple of the Creator known as the Heart of Stone. From the tender age of five, perhaps even before the moment of her birth, Hannah's life had been dedicated to serving the interests of the Creator in every way possible, and it was only because of the Dark Gods and their perverse affront to the natural order that Hannah supplemented her role in the church with the unavoidable calling of the military. Her martial skill and utter dedication to the cause eventually rocketed her through the ranks of the military until she was the most trusted and valued holy warrior in the kingdom. When Ender "JustHand" Lorien invited Hannah to the Imperial Palace in Aldere, Hannah was overjoyed. It was not the promotion to the ranks of the Knights of the Flashing Blade that filled her heart with joy, it was the fact that her new position would give her greater opportunity to spread the word of the Creator to the world, and to strike down the Dark Gods of Mythryn whose very existence were blasphemy. The order of the Flashing Blade was a great honor, but her allegiance to the Emperor was far second to her allegiance to the Creator.

CHAPTER 45

As Hannah knelt in prayer, the doors to the Heart of Stone opened to admit a man that Hannah knew well. She did not have to open her eyes or turn around to know who had entered. No one but Erik Relcan was bold or presumptive enough to disturb her meditation. Halfway into the Heart, Erik went to one knee and waited to be addressed. Hannah smiled to herself. She could make him wait as long as she wanted, and he would say nothing. There was a bit of a thrill in that power. However, Hannah remembered her vows of honor and humility. She would have to reflect on her moment of failing later. It was her piety and her devotion that had granted her not only her station in life, but the Creator's blessing which had slowed the process of her aging. Were it not for these boons, Hannah would have been well into her dotage, but devotion had its rewards. Quietly she finished a prayer to the Creator for strength and patience before bowing slightly and turning to face her visitor.

"I trust you have important news?" Hannah asked quietly, her voice barely above a whisper.

"Yes, my Lady," Erik replied.

Hannah noted that Erik had used her Imperial title of Lady rather than the title granted her by the Church. The news was from the Imperial Court, and she steeled herself for the terrible tidings that she had felt coming.

"I carry to you a summons from the Just Emperor Kaitain Lorien, Emperor Lorien the Twelfth."

Hannah felt her heart fall. The Emperor was the embodiment of the Creator upon the world of Espre, the chosen champion of righteousness. The touch of the divine was not something to be taken lightly, and while the world would mourn the passing of a great leader, Hannah was secure in the knowledge that his soul would rejoin his sainted ancestors in the Heavens.

"Read the summons."

Hannah's tone was flat, with little trace of emotion. Erik could not tell if Hannah was happy or sad at the news of the Emperor's passing. However, as he regarded her for a moment, he could feel the pangs of love growing in his chest. Since the moment they had met, Erik had been madly and deeply in love with the woman that the rest of the Kingdom of Stone Albitonin both revered and feared. Hannah was a just woman, a lovely woman, but her dedication to the Creator made her seem aloof to matters of the world, and it always seemed as though her mind was in the Heavens with the only one she would ever call master, and the only one she would truly ever love.

Erik cleared his throat and began to read.

"Lady Hannah Ironheart, Celestine Knight of the Kingdom of Stone Albitonin. As a member of the Knights of the Flashing Blade, your duty and responsibility to guard the Emperor from all harm now transfers to the newly recognized Emperor of Cadaria, Kaitain Lorien. At the earliest possible time, you must return to Aldere to bend a knee to your new lord and master."

Hannah felt a dagger of hatred and anger pierce her normally placid heart. The Knights of the Flashing Blade had more important duties than a ceremonial welcome to their new ruler. It was insulting, degrading, and a waste of valuable time. Though Hannah tried to keep the thoughts from showing on her face, when Erik stopped speaking, she knew that her control over her emotions had slipped. She would have to meditate upon that fact later.

"Continue," Hannah said flatly.

"This is also a notice of the unfortunate set of circumstances that have befallen the Empire, and to inform you of your new assignment for the Throne. The dragons of Cadaria have broken the truce, and have launched an attack upon the Kingdom of Night. As the closest major kingdom, you are to rally support efforts immediately to assist the new Onyx Knight in rebuilding the capitol of Galateria."

New Onyx Knight? Hannah thought to herself. *Our comrade has been replaced already without a full explanation of his death? The new Emperor seems to be in a hurry to make his mark upon the Empire. Or is he worried perhaps that the Knights of the Flashing Blade will not bend to his will so easily? I know that some of my brothers in the order are close to their retirement. I wonder how many more changes there will be to the order before all is said and done. At least I can count on Gregor if something should go wrong.*

"This new member of the order," Erik continued, "is named Devlin Rannoch. His unique nature and talents made him a perfect choice for the title of Onyx Knight, and his recent heroism during the dragon attacks could not be ignored. You are to give him whatever assistance he requires for as long as it is required. The notice is signed by the Just Emperor Kaitain Lorien."

Both Erik and Hannah remained silent for several moments. Finally Hannah stood and took her heavy war mace named Spirit from its cradle beside the shrine to the Creator and hefted it over her shoulder. The weight felt good in her hands, and she could feel its power coursing through her body. While there was never a proven connection between the creator of the sacred weapons of the Flashing Blade and the Creator, Hannah could always feel her maker's touch more strongly upon her when Spirit was in her hands.

"Rally a quarter of the standing troops and have them gather whatever supplies they can carry. We will march for Galateria in the morning. Also, the remainder of the force shall mobilize under commander Adlone and prepare for possible dragon attacks. There is a band of eccentric dragon hunters that often works in this area, find someone to make contact with them and request their aid."

"As you wish, Lady Ironheart."

Erik stayed bowed, his head held low. Hannah waited for a moment, and realized that he was not going to leave. There was something else, something that Erik was hesitant to mention.

"Was there something else, Erik?"

The words burned in his mind like wildfire. There was so much he wanted to say, and it had nothing to do with the message that had been entrusted to him. War broke out within his heart and mind, pushing him even farther to say what he truly wanted…no, needed to say.

"My Lady," Erik said finally, the rational part of his mind winning out, "there has been a courier from your sister."

Hannah felt her breath catch in her throat. The Ironheart family was a family divided. One had followed the path of the Creator while the other had bent their knee to the Dark Gods of Mythryn. There had been little to no communication between the two sisters over the years and even less since Hannah had become a member of the Flashing Blade.

"Shall I read it, my Lady?"

Hannah debated for a moment. She trusted Erik with all of her heart and soul, but this matter was not for anyone's eyes, save hers. There could only be one message, and it was a tiding of evil.

"No, Erik. Leave it there, and I shall read it shortly. I would like however for you to ride for Oradrim immediately and request that Lady Leonora Wastri, the Jade Knight, meet me at Galateria. I shall draft a letter for her before you depart. Return to me when you are ready to travel."

"Yes, my Lady."

Again Erik lingered. The war within him was becoming stronger by the minute. He had waited for so many years in the shadows, watching her, loving her, waiting for the chance to say and do all the things he had dreamed about. She would have to love him. She would have to know how he felt. They had spent so many years together, close to one another, and it was everything he could do to control himself in her presence. However, there was no more control left within him. He had to tell her how he felt.

"Dismissed."

The word was like a slap to his face. And though he tried to resist, Erik rose, bowed deeply and then left the room. His blood boiled both with love and anger. Hannah would love him…she had to.

* * * * * * * * * * * * *

CHAPTER 45

Candlelight filled the room where Hannah sat and quietly prayed. It had been several hours since Erik had delivered the message from her sister, and still the parchment sat unopened on her desk. For most of the day, Hannah kept herself busy with the preparations for the trip to Galateria, and it had kept her mind off the letter. But now, in the privacy of her chambers, there was nothing to keep her mind from it. There was a temptation to simply burn the letter, ignore its very existence. Sadrina had turned her back on the family the moment she had joined with the Dark Gods on Mythryn. She had once said it was a holy quest, a chance to touch the divine and become closer to the will of the Creator. The argument had been a fierce one, debating the nature of good and evil. When the argument was over, they were no longer sisters; they were simply strangers who shared the same name. Sadrina had changed all that when she took the name of the god she called husband.

Finally, Hannah seized the letter and pulled apart the seal that held it. Her heart fluttered for a moment, and she closed her eyes to steel herself against the dread that began to fill her. There was an evil omen that accompanied this letter, and Hannah knew that the price for reading it could be high. As her eyes scanned the words, horror filled her heart and silently she began to say a prayer to the Creator.

Hannah,

It has been too long since we have looked upon each other sister, and many years since we have spoken. I do not know if you have even read the many letters I have sent you over the years, just as I do not know if you will read this one. I pray however that you heed the words I am about to write. There are changes happening in this world, and I am sure you have felt them too. The Dark Gods are divided of mind and of intent, and I fear that before long some terrible tragedy will befall us all should we remain divided.

There is an evil force rising in Cadaria, and I can feel it going stronger by the day. If it has not yet taken hold of the young Emperor, it soon will. Forces have conspired to place young Kaitain on the throne, and before long, their machinations will bring about a terrible tragedy. But that is not the only force I fear.

I have seen her my sister. With my very eyes. A dragon calling itself Abysm Nightwalker demanded an audience with the Dark Gods. Though the Council has no business with the dragons, the audience was allowed, and when the dragon arrived, she was with him. It took every bit of control within them to not cast her out, but I spoke to the Council and we all agreed to hear her words.

She spoke of terrible things my sister, nightmares that make the Day the Heavens Fell look like a rainbow. She said there are dark times upon us, death will walk upon the face of Espre, great plagues will befall mankind, hunger and starvation will shroud even the richest and well-fed lands, and great wars will tear apart not only Cadaria, but Mythryn as well.

There may be little love left between us sister, and there may be no love between Mythryn and Cadaria, but this new threat is more important than borders or blood. If there is nothing done, there may be no Cadaria or Mythryn left because of our stubbornness. If you will agree, I will send my daughter to negotiate peace between Cadaria and Mythryn. However, I will entrust her welfare to you to ensure that the new Emperor does not harm her.

The Dark Seer also spoke of Kaitain, my sister. She said that the plague upon the land might pale in comparison to the hell that he could unleash. He bares careful watching, and if all of this comes to pass as the Dark Seer has prophesied, there may be nothing, not even the Dark Gods, that can stop it.

Please my sister, I beg of you. Heed my warning, and heed the warnings of the Dark Seer. I shall await your reply, and if I do not hear from you by the dawn of the first Day of Star Fire, I shall have to take other steps. War may be inevitable at this point my dear sister, but we must try.

All my Love,

Sadrina Annis

Dark Queen of Mythryn

Hannah shuddered upon reading the words, and let the scroll fall to the floor. If the Dark Seer had truly returned and had given more of her dark prophecy, then perhaps there was nothing left but to hope that the Creator would see them through the dark times ahead. If there was truly more danger coming, if the gray man Pestilence had only been the beginning…

After a moment more of thought, Hannah shook herself back to the reality of the moment. She would draft a letter to her sister and request that her niece be sent to act as an envoy of peace. If Kaitain Lorien truly had the best interests of Cadaria in his heart, he would listen. If not, then Hannah would know for certain that the words the Dark Seer had spoken were true.

At that moment, there was a knock at the door. That would be Erik. He had made all the preparations necessary for his journey to Oradrim, and the letter for Leonora sat sealed on the desk. Hannah had been right in the request for Leonora's council.

"Come in, Erik."

Slowly the door opened. Erik stepped into his Lady's presence with head bowed. It took only a moment for the letter to be placed in his hand and for him to be quickly dismissed. He was to give orders that Hannah was not to be disturbed before the march to Galateria in the morning. Erik would faithfully carry out his orders, but the burning within his heart and mind would not abate. It would be a long and lonely ride to Oradrim.

* * * * * * * * * * * * *

In the stables, Erik saddled his horse and took a deep breath before placing the sealed letter for the Jade Knight into his pack. It would take several days to make it to Oradrim, and by then the Army of Albitonin would already be in Galateria. As Erik was about to mount his faithful steed, there was a rustling in the shadows. His hand on his blade, Erik stepped back from his horse and waited. After a moment, a tall man in a dark robe emerged from the shadows.

"Erik Relcan," the man said slowly in a pleasant sounding voice. "I have been looking for you."

There was something striking about the man. While he was not handsome, his features were intriguing. In his eyes was a wild energy, like a hurricane barely contained. While Erik should have remained on guard for anything, there was something about the man's presence that put Erik at ease. After a moment, Erik's sword had returned to its sheath.

"What do you want?" Erik said finally.

"You certainly get right to the point, don't you, Erik?" the man said, taking several steps forward. "But you aren't always like that, are you? You sometimes have problems saying what you really mean, don't you?"

Erik took a half step back before he realized it. The gentle calm that the man's demeanor had brought only a few moments before had been shattered by the directness of the questions. The stranger's eyes now burrowed into the very depths of Erik's soul, ferreting out every secret that Erik held dear.

"I know how you feel about her, Erik," the man continued taking a step forward. "I know you love her more deeply than anything in this world. I know that you desire her, not for her body, not for her mind, but for her heart and soul."

Erik turned his back and tried hard to suppress the tears that inexplicably began to form in his eyes.

"You don't know what you're talking about. I serve my Lady faithfully because that is my duty. It is merely my desire to serve her to the best of my ability."

The man took another step forward.

"And do you serve her with all your heart?"

"Of course," Erik answered.

"And your soul?"

"Without question."

"And does this unquestioned devotion of the heart and soul include your love?"

Erik thought for a moment. It was an honest question.

"Yes, I love my Lady for that is what she deserves."

"Would you do anything for her?" the man asked.

"Yes."

"Would you give your life for her?"

Erik answered without hesitation.

"Yes."

The man finally rounded on Erik and locked eyes with him.

"Does she love those that serve her?"

Erik exhaled and gave the practiced answer.

"My Lady loves all of those who serve her. She is an extension of the Creator's love and will upon the face of Espre. She loves all as the Creator loves them."

The stranger did not laugh, smile, or react at all.

"And would all the others give their life, soul, and heart to her as you have?"

Erik faltered. He could not answer the question. He knew the answer that his temple training wanted him to give; he knew the answer that he should give. However, that was not the answer he wanted to give.

"No."

Erik was shocked to hear his own voice speak the word. His heart and mind were on fire with emotion.

"Then why do they deserve her love? Why do those selfish cattle deserve the love of the woman that you would die for?"

"They don't."

Anger and hatred for all those pretenders began to well up in Erik. He had never thought of it that way before. This stranger understood better than anyone. The other sheep that claimed to serve Hannah would never willingly give themselves to save her, nor would they lay down their lives simply if she asked them to. Only Erik had that type of love and devotion in his heart. Only he deserved Hannah's love.

"How much do you love her, Erik?"

"Without bounds."

The man finally smiled.

"And because only you deserve her love, you of pure heart who would lay down his life to protect her, don't you feel that she is wasting her love upon those other pretenders?"

Erik thought for a moment. How much time did Hannah waste praying for those who did not care about her, who did not love her?

"She is going on a mission to a kingdom who was once at war with Albitonin, isn't she? Didn't those people once wish her dead and curse her very name?"

The anger flared deeper within Erik.

"And now she will lavish her love, the love that only you deserve, upon the people that hate her."

All restraint in Erik nearly snapped. He could not allow Hannah to waste herself upon these undeserving wretches. They were beneath her, they were scum and she was a goddess. But there was nothing he could do. He had been sent away. His love had been cast aside so she could give her love to people who hated her. He began to hate Hannah…No…How could he hate the woman he loved so completely?

"It's not her fault," the man said softly, his voice soothing the anger that was welling up in Erik's soul. "It is the Emperor that is sending her on this mission. She does not want to go. She does not want to give her love to anyone but you, Erik, you must know that."

Of course…it all makes sense now. The Emperor is taking my love away from me. If not for the Emperor, if not for her place in the Flashing Blade, she would be all mine, and she would not have to waste herself upon all those miserable curs.

"I have a way to save her from the machinations of the Emperor and of the usurpers that would steal her love from you. I have a way for you to be together in peace forever, and all I ask in return is that you perform a small task for me."

Erik regarded the man for a moment. The truth that had come from his lips had been more profound than the teachings of the Creator that he had studied seemingly from birth. For the first time in his life, Erik had clarity, and the vision before him was one of absolute harmony. No matter the cost, Erik would pay it to save the woman he loved from this danger.

"I'm listening," Erik said smiling.

* * * * * * * * * * * * *

Erik Relcan rode out from the Heart of Stone, leaving a cloud of dust in his wake. Upon his leaving, the young stable-hand emerged from his place in the bales of hay. He was going to ask Erik if he needed any help with his horse, but then the man had begun to talk to himself. There was no one around, but it appeared as if Erik was having a very animated conversation with thin air. The stable-hand shook his head, and went back to work, trying to clear the thoughts of the strangeness of the morning.

Silent Night

Year One of the Just Emperor Kaitain Lorien XII, Creator's Calendar Year 1868

Emperor Kaitain Lorien sat silently in his chambers, the sweat still covering his body. Under the covers of his spacious bed lay the naked form of Irene Drage. Their pact had been sealed with passion, and now that the veil of lust had lifted from his mind, Kaitain began to weigh the consequences of what he had just committed to. He would have his revenge, there was no doubt, and if Irene's plan worked as flawlessly as she predicted, there would be no blame cast in either of their directions. Alistair had recently returned to the palace and was met with a welcome befitting a conquering hero. The cure for the Crawling Plague had already begun to circulate through the kingdom, and it was only a matter of time before the cursed plague was eradicated forever. The cost of the cure had never been mentioned, and it would never be spoken by anyone; agents of the Shadow Guild would see to that.

In the darkness of the chamber, something moved. There were very few in the palace that knew all of the secret passages, but those who did were loyal to the Emperor. There were things that the Emperor needed done, acts that would have turned the stomach of most in the Empire, but they were necessary. Assassinations, the destruction of insurgents, and other delicate operations needed to take place outside the view of the public, and for that, the Shadow Guild was employed. The Shadow Guild itself was made up of seventy-five people, never more, never less. There were five masters that trained the agents, and no agent knew the names of the others. The Emperor would make contact with one of the masters, and they would assign the mission to one of their subordinates. Even the masters themselves did not know the identity of all the agents, even the other masters. It was this anonymity that made the Shadow Guild the most effective. Kaitain was given the names of the five masters in the effects of his late father, as well as a list of the operations that were currently being undertaken by the Guild. Kaitain was shocked to learn that one of the members of the Knights of the Flashing Blade was a master in the Shadow Guild. However, the Flashing Blade could not know this task, even in part. The master who had always acted with the most discretion had been assigned this task, and his name was Geoffry Aramour.

Geoffry was the court poet, bard, and herald. What most people saw was a simple man who was a master of verse, music, and rhyme. The great stories that Geoffry told created such a picture in the mind that all who would listen to his words felt as though they had lived through the epic tales. The songs composed and performed by Geoffry were equally soul-stirring. Melody could ensnare the heart and soul, wrenching out smiles, tears, or even the darkest pain of the soul. In all, Geoffry was a master. However, it was his gift for murder that was even more astounding.

Like his prowess with the lute or harp, Geoffry was equally well trained with poison, blades, and other implements of death. However, Geoffry's true calling was to make any assassination look like a simple accident. When it was learned that the former Onyx Knight, Tutio Illik had been involved in a plot to assassinate Kaitain's father, Geoffry had been dispatched to deal with the issue. Tutio's death marked the first and only time a member of the Knights of the Flashing Blade had been marked for termination. The master-stroke was the implication of the ambassador from Galateria, Sil, in the Onyx Knight's death. However, Kaitain began to feel that it would not be the last time that the Shadow Guild was used against the Flashing Blade. Some of the words that Irene had spoken festered in Kaitain's mind. The Knights would eventually betray him. They were too powerful to be fully controlled, and those he could not trust he would remove from power one way or another.

Already someone Kaitain felt that he could control had replaced the Onyx Knight. This Devlin Rannoch was the type of man who would always be viewed as an outsider and would never curry the type of favor that the former Onyx Knight had. He could never be a revolutionary, and owed his new life to the Emperor. He would be easily controlled. However, there were others that could cause a problem.

"You summoned me, my Emperor?"

Geoffry's voice took Kaitain away from his thoughts.

"Is it done?"

Geoffry smiled in the darkness. He liked this new Emperor. Kaitain always got right to the point, and Geoffry was sure there would be more work for himself in the future.

"Yes, my Emperor."

Kaitain smiled.

"Good. Arrange for a servant to find him in the morning."

"Yes, my Emperor."

Geoffry began to leave.

"I have another job for you."

Geoffry stopped and could not contain the smile. This Emperor would be very fun to work for. Already he had carried out three assassinations in the name of Kaitain Lorien, and it seemed that there would be no end to the new run of business.

"The Shadow Guild cannot be trusted for the plans that I have in mind. I need a group of assassins that I can trust with my life, which will protect and obey me to the end. I want you to find and train such a group for me Geoffry. They must have no other allegiance, no other agenda but mine. And they must not hesitate to eliminate anyone regardless of the situation."

"I understand, my Emperor."

"Even if you were the target, Geoffry," Kaitain added.

Geoffry smiled.

"I understand, my Emperor."

Kaitain smiled as Geoffry silently exited the room. Yes, this new group of assassins would certainly have their work ahead of them. But no hired hand would be loyal enough to be trusted. Irene had made that point clear enough during their conversations that led deep into the evening. Only blood could be trusted and fully controlled. And so a great plan had been hatched. A plan that would change the face of Cadaria.

Kaitain's thoughts drifted back to the Knights of the Flashing Blade, the very men and women that would lay down their lives to protect the Emperor. Kaitain scoffed at the thought, a wave of disgust passing through him. How had he not seen it before? If the Onyx Knight could plot against the throne, what prevented the others from doing the same?

Bernhardt Yeoman, the Moonstone Knight of Pellatori. He was a proud member of the Iron Legion, which made him bold, headstrong, and stalwart. However, Bernhardt was not stupid. He was loyal, almost to a fault. He carried out his orders, and was a valuable soldier. He would never be the start of a rebellion, but if he were to put his might behind those who did begin an uprising, that army would be difficult to defeat. Bernhardt would bear close watching, and great efforts would have to be made to keep him away from the other members of the Flashing Blade who could cause problems. Perhaps Bernhardt could lead the counterattack against the dragons. That would keep him in the thick of battle and away from the politics of court. Kaitain would have to remember to send a dispatch in the morning.

Lady Chelsea Zarova, the Garnet Knight of Saldarine and Seraph Kore, the Emerald Knight of Thorigald; the odd couple of the Knights of the Flashing Blade. Their kingdoms had been at war until their marriage, but now were uneasy allies. Together they were a powerful combination, possibly enough to defeat all the other members of the Knights of the Flashing Blade. Chelsea was the more levelheaded of the pair, she thought about the larger picture, and if there were going to be a leader of a revolt, she was a prime candidate. Seraph on the other hand was driven by duty. Their marriage had been arranged to cement an alliance, not out of love or devotion. It was rumored that Seraph loved another and secretly had made his love in to a mistress. Kaitain would have to have his spies check into the identity of this woman that could be useful leverage against the Emerald Knight. However, as long as the two knights were still man and wife, they could be a danger to the throne. Perhaps there was yet a way to set the two kingdoms at each other's throats and still keep the loyalty of the people. That would be a job for Geoffry for certain. A few careful assassinations and planted evidence would start a war surely. Naturally, the Emperor would have to condemn such a civil war while supporting each side. That would be an avenue worth exploring.

Sir Gregor Quicksilver, the Ruby Knight of Zevarit. He was the longest serving member of the Knights of the Flashing Blade, but nowhere near retirement. The man was said to be nearly a hundred years old, but did not look a day over thirty. Like some other members of the Flashing Blade, Gregor was a devout servant of the Creator, and Kaitain wondered if his devotion to his faith was stronger than his devotion to his Emperor. Gregor would merit careful watching. But there was another danger. It was said that the Sacred Sword Valor, which Gregor wielded, was the strongest of the blades, and had the power to control the others. Perhaps it was true, or perhaps it was fiction. The first Emperor of Cadaria took that secret to the grave. Gregor was a learned man who tempered his judgments with both what he knew and what he felt. Many said that it should have been Gregor not Kaitain who took the throne after the death of Ender Lorien. Though no one was foolish enough to speak those thoughts in open court, Kaitain had heard the whispers. Traitors would not be suffered lightly, but to dispose of a man like Gregor would take great care. He would have to die fighting, fighting a foe of such power that it would need his talents. The dragons would not be enough. However, when Kaitain started his war with Mythryn, a Dark God would be the perfect enemy to loose Gregor on. If Gregor died, it would get the meddlesome knight out of the way, and if he were victorious, a god would be dead. Either way, Kaitain would win.

Like Gregor, Hannah Ironheart was a delicate problem. She was too dedicated to the Creator, and if there was one more devout than Gregor, it was Hannah. This woman flaunted her love of the Creator above all things, even above her position as the Celestine Knight. But Kaitain had already come up with a way to dispose of Hannah. Like Gregor, Hannah could not simply disappear, that could create problems, especially since the woman was the High Priestess of the Church of the Creator. In time Kaitain would be able to groom his own replacement for that post, if he didn't simply abolish the archaic practice altogether. No, there were better ways to eliminate a habitual meddler like Hannah. A pious woman like that could not resist a request to help those who were suffering. So, Hannah would find herself in Galateria just before a flight of dragons attacked. The informant who had let Kaitain know of the impending attack disappeared quietly, Geoffry had seen to that well enough, and not a single word of the attack had gone past the Emperor's private audience chamber. Only Irene knew of the impending destruction. The pious one would surely fall, and if she didn't the newly anointed Onyx Knight would be there to finish her off. Kaitain smiled to himself. Hannah Ironheart was a liability because of her standing with the religious community and because she was truly a woman that could not be corrupted. There was no vice or sin of her past that could be manipulated. The death would be quick, and Kaitain would be sure that Hannah would be happier in the Heavens with her precious Creator.

Jaccob Aldora, the Topaz Knight of Hedorah. Once a beloved student of the Academy of Arcane Arts, Jaccob had left the teaching of Alistair Ravenheart because of a difference of opinion about the use of magic. Jaccob had felt that magic should be used more offensively to crush the enemies of the Empire, while Alistair felt that magic was not to be used as a weapon, only for defensive measures. It was only through his prowess and devotion to the Empire that Jaccob merited any notice at all. When the Topaz Knight, Jeriv Tonash retired shortly after the ascension of Kaitain to the Throne, Jaccob had been elevated to the position of Topaz Knight. Though Kaitain had never met Jaccob, it was this thirst for power and the need to crush the enemies of the Empire that made Jaccob the perfect choice for the position. Naturally, Alistair loudly voiced his opposition to the appointment, but the Emperor's will was not swayed by the argument of a traitor. As long as Kaitain kept the young man focused on the enemy, his mastery of magic could never be a threat. If he ever became a threat though, Jaccob had plenty of vices and failings that could be exploited. At the best of times, Jaccob was a drunk and a lecherous man, no stranger to the beds of prostitutes and common women alike. It was even said that since his appointment as the Topaz Knight, his habits had not changed. The blemish upon the position would be enough to guarantee control.

Controlling Leonora Wastri, the Jade Knight of Oradrim, however would prove much more difficult. Her studies into the limitless energy of the soul had made her one of the most formidable women in the world. It was said that not even time could touch her. There were many stories of her feats of great strength and speed, or her defeating armies with her bare hands. It was said that she had once met and destroyed a dragon on her own and had emerged with only a scratch. Though she had never publicly acknowledged the story, neither had she denied it. Her studies of the mystic arts had granted her a form of invulnerability such that disease, poison, magic, or time could not affect her abnormally. It was also said that she had conditioned her body in such a way that age would never touch her features. The most intriguing of her strange powers was that she no longer needed to eat or sleep, and her vigilance was revered through all of Oradrim. It was said that the brilliant emerald light of Wisdom burned so brightly in the Jade Knight that not even the blackest night could keep it from shining. Kaitain fretted about the woman on many nights. She was beautiful in an ethereal way, almost as though she had been touched by the gods themselves in such a way that she had transcended the ugliness of the mortal world. People were easy to deal with when they could simply be killed and forgotten. However, legends were another story. Legends had a way of continuing long after the death of the mortal form. The only way to truly destroy a legend was to destroy that which made the legend. Kaitain would have to discredit the woman before he could destroy her. It was clear in Kaitain's mind that she would never willingly bend her knee to the new Emperor. Leonora would be the troublesome one. The legend, the myth, the enlightened warrior. However, Kaitain had learned that Leonora had received a strange dispatch from Hannah Ironheart telling of a plot to assassinate the Emperor. The Jade Knight was on her way to Aldere. Soon enough, Kaitain would know whether or not the woman could be trusted, and if she could not, there would be ways enough to make her pay for her arrogance.

Of all the Knights of the Flashing Blade, it was Natalia Pressen, the Sunstone Knight of Bellnoc that Kaitain most feared. It was not a fear, as one would have of a dragon or one of the Dark Gods, it was a fear as one would have of one they fully respected. Natalia was a master of the Shadow Guild, the most perfectly trained assassin of the guild, trained both in the arts of martial combat and arcane lore. She was the head of her class at the Academy of Arcane Arts, and it was said that she and Jaccob Aldora had a bit of a competition growing up. When Natalia left the Academy to join the Shadow Guild, she swore her allegiance totally to the Empire. It was not the Emperor that she served, but the Empire. That in itself was dangerous. If the Emperor was a danger to the Empire, Natalia would be honor-bound to kill him. However, the Shadow Guild had methods to deal with rogue members of their ranks, even Masters who chose to defy the will of the Emperor. Should Natalia rise against him, Kaitain was assured that the Grand Master of the Shadow Guild would make sure her rebellion was a short-lived one. However, there was still use left for Natalia. Kaitain soon would make a demand of his most accomplished assassin, and she would either carry out the assignment, or she would be destroyed. Unlike some of the other Knights of the Flashing Blade, Natalia could never be a serious threat.

Sir Orren Eldrath, the Sapphire Knight of the Kingdom of Rashaleb, was as mysterious as he was fickle. Orren was born under the sign of the Great Fates on the anniversary of the Day the Heavens Fell. From that point forward, it seemed that the improbable happened with regular frequency around Orren. When he was old enough, Orren was admitted to the Academy of Arcane Arts where he excelled in the manipulation of fate and probability, as well as time itself. However, soon it appeared that his thirsts for knowledge were too dangerous to be contained in the Academy and he was expelled for continuing to practice dangerous magic. In addition to his dangerous tastes in magic, it seemed that Orren was a specialist in the sword, able to use it from a young age as a blade master would. His level of skill was frightening to many, and it bred a great deal of mistrust and fear. Kaitain smiled at the thoughts of Orren Eldrath. He was a man who thirsted for power and knowledge, and men like that could be controlled easily. Greed could be fed with knowledge, and the opportunity to study the Dark Gods would be a large enough carrot to dangle before the tempestuous youth. Kaitain easily counted Orren among those he could control and use. However, there could come a time when Orren's luck would run out.

It was only a matter of time before Kaitain was able to force the ninety-year-old amethyst Knight into retirement. He had long since served his purpose, and would no longer embarrass the other members of the Flashing Blade with his incompetence. Kaitain spent many weeks reviewing the candidates for the position before finally settling on Tolon Moor. Tolon was raised as the son of a slave girl in the service of the lord of Celidar. When he was old enough, Tolon was sold to the gladiatorial arena of the southern provinces where he was taught every weapon imaginable. With an uncanny ability to master any weapon that was put in his hand, Tolon defeated all who crossed his path, and after one hundred victories in the arena, Tolon won his freedom. Instead of retiring to luxury as was the norm for champions of the arena, Tolon traded the garb of a gladiator for the uniform of a soldier and gladly joined the Army of Steel. This devotion and thirst for blood and war made Tolon a perfect choice for the position of Amethyst Knight. He wanted no power, he wanted no wealth; he merely wanted to fight. Because of his humble birth, he would never question authority, and would be the perfect enforcer of the Emperor's will. If need be, Tolon could even become the Emperor's Executioner. If there was to be division in the ranks of the Knights of the Flashing Blade, Kaitain was sure that Tolon would be able to end it quickly.

The touch of divinity was said to have strange effects on people, but to Kaitain, the cost that the Tiger's Eye Knight, Xaran Firesoul, paid was too high. Blind since birth, Xaran's parents contemplated ending the child's life before they began to see the true gifts that their child had. Before his third birthday, Xaran was given to a monastery where the wisest of monks in the land of Menoris trained him. In time, Xaran's mind and body became weapons all their own. His ability in unarmed combat were second to none, and his mastery of the teachings of the greatest minds in Cadaria made him wise far beyond his years. However, Xaran was touched in a way that robbed his eyesight and plagued his dreams. It was said that like seers, Xaran could see the future, or the past with eerie accuracy. There were those who felt that while Xaran's eyes could not perceive the world around him, he could see the world that could not be seen by mortals. Many times the monks of the temple found Xaran holding conversations with people who were not there, and it was surmised that Xaran could communicate with the spirits of the ancestors, or even the gods of the Heavens. Like so many other members of the Flashing Blade, it did not seem that there was anything that Kaitain could tempt Xaran with in other to ensure his obedience, but unlike the other members of the Flashing Blade that had been marked as problematic, Xaran's gift could not be discarded so easily. The ability to talk with the ancestors was rare, even more so now that the Clan Forer was nearly extinct. However, a man able to see the unseen might be able to see the plots revolving around him, and so Kaitain would have to find a way to utilize the talents of the blind man without allowing him to see the true nature of the requests. If Xaran were too wise, he would have to meet his fate and join the ancestors that he spoke to.

The last of the Knights of the Flashing Blade was perhaps the strangest and least seen of the group. Sir Vallic Ultiv, Serpentine Knight of the Kingdom of Iltorp, did things his own way, and held to his own religion of sorts. He did not believe in the gods, the Creator, or the Dark Gods. He instead prescribed to a strange religion of balance, and he preached it wherever he went. All things must have balance, and there must be good and evil if the world is to survive. This belief often kept him at odds with both Gregor and Hannah, and perhaps he would be a derisive enough influence to keep the others in line. It was possible that Vallic could not be of any pure use to the Emperor, but it was his distracting personality that would be enough to keep the others on edge. Perhaps it was time that the Serpentine Knight took a more active role in the business of the Flashing Blade. That in itself would keep the others off-balance.

Just then Irene stirred in the bed behind Kaitain. She sat up slowly, the soft satin sheet falling from her naked frame, her luscious body encased in the moonlight streaming in from the window.

"Trouble sleeping, my Emperor?"

Her voice was like that of a gentle nightingale, filling the room with a sweet song that was intoxicating to the mind a soul.

"Simply thinking about the future."

Irene stayed silent for a moment.

"The future is a dangerous thing, my Emperor," she said finally. "It is always in motion and the wisest man can find himself consumed with it. It is like vapor, like a gentle whisper in a noisy room. If you hold onto it too tightly it will slip through your fingers like water. You must let it happen, you must let it come to you. Fate does not bend to any master."

Kaitain turned to face Irene, soaking in her beauty and reveling in the lust in his heart. The words she had spoken flowing through him, stoking the fires of ambition in his heart.

"It will bend to my will. I am the Emperor of Cadaria, and there is nothing outside my domain, not even fate."

Irene smiled and weighed her words carefully.

"Only the gods can control fate, my Emperor."

She let a quiet laugh slip past before speaking again.

"Let us talk of more…pleasurable things, my Emperor."

With that, Irene opened her arms, beckoning Kaitain back to bed. Slowly Kaitain moved back up the bed and embraced his lover once more. The passion ignited between them again as the minutes passed into hours. Though while his body was very much wrapped in the embrace of the beautiful woman beneath him, his thoughts were elsewhere, her words ringing in his mind.

Only the gods can control fate…

Absolute Power

Year One of the Just Emperor Kaitain Lorien XII, Creator's Calendar Year 1868

Stepping into the large corridor, Irene could feel the tension in the palace. From a young age she had been able to feel the emotions of the people around her, and the stronger the emotion, the more overwhelming to her senses. At times she could swear that she was the one feeling the emotions of the people around her, and it had caused uncomfortable and at times debilitating outbursts as a child. When she was old enough, her parents who were wealthy members of the Imperial Court, sent her to learn at the Academy of Arcane Arts in Jelan where she quickly became one of its most gifted students. Alistair Ravenheart, the Headmaster of the Academy, quickly recognized that Irene was not a common student and before too long, he began to teach her nearly exclusively. Even in those early days, the lessons came easily to Irene, and she was able to grasp the concepts of even the most complex and abstract arcane lore. However a problem quickly began to present itself. It was small at first, but the more she learned, the more prominent the problem became and it prevented her from realizing the full extent of her abilities.

Like every problem, there is eventually a solution. Alistair could teach Irene everything about magic, but Irene had difficulty making the correlation between the theory and the application of the lessons. She had power to spare, but it was the subtle thread that held the power to the form that was eluding her. Then, one morning, as if someone lit a torch in a dark room, the connection was made. Finally she could see the subtle flows of magic all around her that Alistair had talked about on so many occasions. In a matter of months, Irene had mastered everything that Alistair had taught her, and it seemed as if the student was teaching the teacher a few lessons along the way. Irene found ways to refine some of the lessons, making them easier to understand, opening Alistair's eyes to avenues he had never dreamed of. When the appointment to the Imperial Court came for Alistair to become the Imperial Sorcerer, Alistair left his position as the Headmaster and accepted the great, if political, honor. As a reward for being such a good student, Irene was allowed to accompany Alistair as his apprentice.

For most of the early years, Irene was not alone in her lessons with Alistair. Though many of the teachers at the Academy of Arcane Arts frowned upon having families, Alistair embraced it. His beautiful wife was also a teacher at the Academy, and she was as skilled in magic as she was breathtakingly beautiful. However, the more Irene was around Estelle Ravenheart, the more she realized why Estelle was so loved. It was not because she was beautiful on the outside, it was more than that. Every part of Estelle was beautiful. Her eyes, her hair, her smell, her touch, everything about her features, but more than anything else, her heart. And it was Estelle's heart that would betray Irene, and betray Alistair as well.

Irene began to feel the love that Estelle felt for her husband, and it filled and suffused her so fully that Irene fell in love with her teacher as well. When the jealousy began, it was magnified by Irene's emotional mimicry. Then, one fateful day, Estelle was found in her bed, having passed away in the night. There were no signs of anything out of the ordinary, but many felt that it was impossible for a perfectly healthy twenty-five year old woman to simply die in her sleep. There was a full investigation, but nothing ever came of the search. With Estelle's death, the feelings for Alistair faded, and there was nothing more than the respect for her teacher and a hole in her heart.

The loss of a wife changed Alistair, and while he sometimes was more reserved and distant, he was also more loving. He showered affection upon both Irene and his daughter Quyhn. It wasn't too long before Alistair began to tell everyone that he had two daughters, and both were equally loved. Having been separated from her family for so long, Irene clung to this love like a dying man clings to a piece of wood in the middle of an ocean. She began to think of Alistair as her father and Quyhn as her sister.

The two young women were inseparable for a time, learning their lessons together, growing in the powers of magic, pulling pranks, and doing everything that they could to keep their father on his toes. However, when the new powers began to well up within Irene, the relationship between the two women became strained. Irene felt as though Quyhn was holding her back, keeping Irene from fulfilling her full potential. As the years passed, the two woman remained civil, but the sisterly relationship was dead and gone. Irene cared only for magic, and all the wondrous gifts that she had been given by birth.

The Crawling Plague changed everything. Naturally that was a common statement around all of Cadaria. No one was untouched by the Plague, even if it touched no members of a person's family. Everyone knew someone that had been infected, everyone knew someone that had died from it. The Crawling Plague changed families, businesses, lines of ascension, everything. Even the vaunted Emperor of Cadaria was not immune to the effects of the Crawling Plague. Irene watched daily as her master, the great sorcerer Alistair Ravenheart tried everything he knew to cure the Plague, but all his efforts seemed to be in vein. Irene tried to give him clues, tried to help him find the solution, but his mind simply would not grasp what was so obvious to Irene. The cure was so simple, and in front of him all the time. Irene could have cured the Plague, ended the suffering, but something held her back. She did not want the Plague to end. She needed it to continue for some reason. So, she kept quiet. Alistair would find the cure eventually. However, the mystery of her silence plagued her until the death of Emperor Ender Lorien.

Again, connections were made in Irene's mind when she saw the new Emperor, Kaitain Lorien ascend the throne. Here was a man who would thirst for power, here was a man that could help her become what she deserved to be, the Imperial Sorceress. From there, the rest of Cadaria would only be a step away.

Where are these thoughts coming from? She thought to herself at the time. She never had any desire for power. *The mundanes have done nothing but destroy this Empire. You had the power to cure the Crawling Plague, they didn't. You have the power to destroy the Dark Gods, and all they do is bargain and bide their time. Not even the dragons are powerful enough to stand in your way. You must control Cadaria, and the way to do it is through this pompous Emperor.*

At his official coronation, Irene had been introduced to Kaitain for the first time. They had seen one another many times before, but never had they spoken. As the two smiled at one another upon introduction, the train of thought within Irene sparked again.

Look at the fool smile. He wants you. He doesn't know why, but he has to have you. That is all it will take. Just a few subtle spells whispered in the middle of the night and the use of your body for a few hours and he will be yours. The Crawling Plague has damaged him, and it will take only a gentle push and he will jump at shadows. He will do whatever you wish him to do. Once you give him a gentle push, he will be so consumed with his petty desires that he will not want you anymore, but you will still have the power. One night of pain is worth the lifetime of power. Look into the fool's eyes. You can see how powerless he is. He is a child where you are a goddess. Like all the mundanes, he will be crushed beneath the weight of his own stupidity. He will give us what we want, and then we will destroy him.

Irene smiled to herself at the memory as she continued walking down the corridors in the palace. Today was to be a special day in her life, and the fear and tension in the palace increased around her. She knew what had happened, and the practiced response would not seem forced or even contrived. It would be genuine enough. The young page that came her way had a look of fear in his eyes, and Irene felt the smile leave her face and the cold expression return.

"Apprentice Irene Drage," the page said as calmly as he could manage, "Emperor Lorien summons you to appear at once."

And so it begins…

* * * * * * * * * * * * *

Many in the Imperial Audience Chamber had tears in their eyes, and when Irene saw Quyhn standing near the dais, tears streaming down her face, Irene went quickly to comfort her. There were no words spoken between the two women, as Quyhn could do nothing but sob on her old friend's shoulder. When Emperor Kaitain entered the room, his face was a mask of pain and anguish, but Irene could feel the true emotion under the rugged façade. He was overjoyed.

"Children of the Empire, it pains me today to bring you this news. Our friend, our hero, and our mentor, the great Alistair Ravenheart is gone from us."

There was a ripple of sadness and shock through the room, and Irene focused her strength to prevent the emotions of the palace from overwhelming her. She carefully allowed several tears to fall from her eyes, something that Quyhn noticed immediately. Quyhn held Irene's hand and the two woman stood close together. Irene could hear the joyous laughter in the back of her mind.

"Sometime in the night," Kaitain continued, "Alistair was working on refining the cure for the Crawling Plague. He believed, according to his notes, that there was a more effective way of distributing it. However, there was a terrible accident. Apparently, from what we have gathered from Alistair's notes, the cure contained a bit of the Crawling Plague itself, and Alistair's experiments somehow triggered acceleration in the Plague. He died in a matter of moments and had no chance to call for help. The page who discovered him also died horribly from the Plague. In order to prevent further contamination, both bodies have been burned, and their ashes have been given a burial in the already corrupted lands outside the palace. It is an unfortunate end to such a great man, and it deeply pains me that he cannot be given the hero's burial that Alistair so much deserves. So, in memory of the great man that brought us the end of the Crawling Plague, I henceforth declare this day, forever and always, the Day of the Ravenheart."

Through the sobs and tears there were smiles and cheers. Irene restrained her own smile. Kaitain was proving to be more adept at winning the hearts and minds of his people than she had initially suspected. He could be a very impressive pawn in the game ahead. Out of the corner of her eye, Irene saw the Headmistress of the Academy of Arcane Arts, Fiona Ebonsight step forward. She was the perfect choice to run the Academy when Alistair had stepped down. Beside Fiona stood her daughter Aris, a talented sorceress in her own right.

"Emperor Kaitain, may I be allowed to speak?"

Fiona had never been one for the niceties of court and had a far more practical mind. When she saw things that needed to be done, Fiona did her best to make sure they were done for the benefit of everyone, not just herself. Because of that, the subtle manipulations of the Imperial Court were often lost on her. Any decision that could only benefit one person was never the right decision.

"The Throne recognizes Sorceress Fiona Ebonsight, Headmistress of the Academy of Arcane Arts in Jelan," Kaitain said slowly.

Fiona bowed low and then took a step forward.

"Emperor Lorien, though it pains me to hear of the circumstances of the loss of our great mentor, I know that the business of the Empire must go on. Since the beginning of the Lorien reign over the Empire of Cadaria, a strong sorcerer or sorceress has stood beside the throne helping to guide the growth of the Empire. My Emperor, you have proved to be a just and capable ruler, and it would be a shame if you would have to continue on alone for anything length of time. The burden upon you might be too great for even you to handle."

Kaitain frowned.

"Does the Academy of Arcane Arts feel that it is in a better position to handle the weight of the rule of Cadaria than I am?"

There was a stifled gasp throughout the audience chamber. Tension was building, and Irene could feel it close to a breaking point. Fiona had made a critical misstep, just as Irene knew she would. Fiona was not a manipulator or a diplomat like Alistair was, she did not know how to handle the temper of a man like Kaitain.

"On the contrary, my Emperor," Fiona replied without missing a beat. "The Academy of Arcane Arts simply wishes to stand beside the Emperor to assist him in the days ahead, to provide wisdom and guidance."

After a moment, Kaitain rose from his throne, forcing everyone in the room to one knee. It was obvious to everyone in the room that the Emperor was angry, and as he took hold of the Imperial Sword and took a step down the dais, fear entered Fiona's heart.

"The Lorien line had stood strong for twelve generations, nearly two thousand years of uninterrupted rule. There is wisdom in my blood, and the only guidance I require is that of the ancestors that watch over me. They will not allow me to falter. Is the Academy of Arcane Arts as wise as the ancestors? Are you as wise as the men who have guided and shaped this empire for two millennia? Can you offer advice that is more important than the words of the emperors long past? I think not. You presume much in your words Sorceress."

From her knees, Fiona shuddered.

"No disrespected was meant, my Emperor. Whatever punishment my ill-chosen words have merited, I will bear without question. I submit to your will."

Kaitain smiled. Fear resounded through the room. Irene was impressed with the visage of the Emperor. Though unstable, the power within him was undeniable.

"There is a wisdom to your words, Headmistress Ebonsight. You are a credit to the Academy, and I would want nothing more than for you to return to Jelan and take up your position and teach the new generations of the magically inclined."

Fiona bowed her head.

"But there will be a new Imperial Sorceress. She is the apprentice of Alistair Ravenheart, and he had confided in me several times her skill and worth. He had said on many occasions that she deserves to be recognized as the equal of the greatest sorcerers in Cadaria, and I trust his word. Therefore, from this day forward, Irene Drage shall be the Imperial Sorceress until her death."

The proclamation brought mixed reactions from the assembled members of the court. The delegation from the Academy of Arcane Arts reacted with a mix of shock and horror, while others whispered gossip of a relationship between the Emperor and the new Sorceress.

"Emperor," Aris Ebonsight said after a moment, "if you will permit me?"

Kaitain nodded slowly.

"Irene Drage is a very skilled woman, and an accomplished Adept, but she had yet to pass the trials and does not hold the rank of Sorceress."

Kaitain frowned again.

"Are all members of the Ebonsight family so insolent? Do you question the word of the hero Alistair Ravenheart? Do you question the word of the Emperor?"

Irene could feel Kaitain's rage growing. Everything was progressing as planned. This decision would alienate the Emperor from the Academy and ensure that only Irene's word about magical matters would find their way to Kaitain's ear.

"The audience chamber is to be cleared at once. I shall hear no more of this. I will hear no more petitions from the Academy of Arcane Arts for the period of one year because of this insult. Any who dare oppose this decree will be executed."

The guards were in the room in a moment, clearing everyone out of the audience chamber. There was screaming, chaos, and incredible fear in the room. Only Irene and Quyhn remained when the dust had settled. When Kaitain returned to his throne and locked his eyes upon the two woman, his features changed from anger to concern.

"I'm sorry you had to witness that, Quyhn, especially today," Kaitain said slowly. "It will take time before many will accept my rule and learn that while I am my father's son, I am not my father. I have a vision for the future of Cadaria, and though it will be born from tragedy, the Empire will be stronger for it."

Quyhn nodded. There was still too much shock and pain within her to properly process all of the information.

"I understand that you have no other family Quyhn, and I do not feel that you would be safe in the Academy of Arcane Arts after what has happened today. So, if you wish, I would make you a member of the Imperial Family, a member of my family. You would be a sister to my daughter, and would be allowed to call me father. I can never be a replacement for the great Alistair Ravenheart, a man that I looked upon as an uncle for most of my life, but I would be there for you in your time of need."

Quyhn stood speechless for a moment, and then found the strength within her to speak.

"That is a very gracious offer, my Emperor, and I would be a fool not to accept such generosity."

Kaitain smiled and strode down the dais and took the young woman in his arms.

"You are forever more Quyhn Ravenheart Lorien, a member of the Imperial Family and second in line to the throne of Cadaria. You are now my heir as much as my own daughter, and I hope that the two of you will grow to become great friends. I have recently summoned her back from her studies in Menoris to fulfill her new duties. I am sure in time you will begin to look upon one another as sister, and our family will be stronger for it."

Quyhn closed her eyes for a moment, and in that instant, for the first time since she learned of her father's death, she felt safe.

* * * * * * * * * * * * *

The hour was late when all of the business of the court was finished and Kaitain could retire to his private chambers. As expected, both Irene and Geoffry were there waiting for him. The day had gone nearly perfectly, and there were only a few loose ends to tie up.

"You did well, Geoffry. I compliment you on a job well done."

Geoffry took a bow and returned to idly strumming his lute.

"Quyhn may prove to be a problem, my Emperor," Irene said slowly. "There is doubt within her already as to the nature of her father's death, and the longer she is in the palace, the more those doubts will fester within her. Perhaps in time she will need to be fostered to another family of the Imperial Court, one that can be trusted to keep her away from the matters of court, one that can be trusted to keep up appearances."

Kaitain nodded.

"Why don't we simply eliminate her?" Geoffry said coldly.

Kaitain could not help but let the smile creep onto his face. Assassins were predicable; their answer to every situation was the same. If someone was causing a problem, make them disappear and the problem disappears.

"Right now, the little Ravenheart is too valuable to eliminate, in fact, my own daughter is more of a threat than Quyhn will ever be. Perhaps she will have a calming effect on Marlae. Besides, if she were to die too soon after her father, it would look too suspicious."

After a moment of silence, there was a knock at the door. Without a word, Geoffry melted into the shadows and escaped the room through a hidden passage. Irene stood in the far corner of the room opposite the Emperor, to help keep up appearances.

"Enter."

The door opened to reveal the last person the Emperor would have expected. Leonora Wastri was a stunningly beautiful woman, perfect in form, perfect in features. Her long flowing hair hung down to her shoulders and her bright green eyes shown clearly in the dim light of the room. She was dressed informally, in the loose fitting robes of a monk. To her back was strapped the sacred weapon of Oradrim, a weapon known as Wisdom. Wisdom was a type of polearm known as a naginata, basically a short spear with a long curved blade attached to the end. It was an elegant if not unruly weapon, one that required a great deal of training to wield properly. As soon as the door opened, Leonora fell to one knee and bowed her head.

CHAPTER 45

"Lady Leonora Wastri, Jade Knight of the Kingdom of Soul, Oradrim, at your service, my Emperor."

Kaitain felt his breath catch in his throat for a moment. It was said that Leonora could read the hearts and souls of men simply by looking in their eyes.

"Rise, Lady Wastri. Your presence here is a surprise. To what do I owe a late night visit from a member of the Flashing Blade?"

Leonora stood and closed the door behind her. Her eyes scanned the room for a moment before they fell upon the Emperor.

"First, my Emperor, let me swear my allegiance to you as I did to your great father. His loss has wounded us all, and it is unfortunate that a great man such as your father could fall to anything as petty as a disease."

Kaitain nodded.

"My father was a great man, and he is sorely missed."

"When I arrived, I had heard of the death of Alistair Ravenheart and I feared that I was too late. Another member of the Knights of the Flashing Blade, Hannah Ironheart, alerted me to a possible plot against your life, my Emperor, and I felt it was my duty to bring this news to you, and if it was your will to discover the source of this plot and destroy it."

For a moment Kaitain stood speechless. It was Irene that broke the silence.

"And you feel that this plot is somehow connected to the death of Alistair Ravenheart?"

Leonora looked at Irene for a moment.

"Yes, great Sorceress, I do. A man such as Alistair would not be as foolish as it seems he was in experimenting with the cure. I have known Alistair for many years, and he would have been content with finding the cure. I feel that he was murdered, and that it was made to look like an accident. I fear the same fate may be in store for you, my Emperor."

Kaitain nodded.

"Perhaps you are right," Kaitain wondered out loud, "perhaps we were naïve to believe that Alistair's end could be anything other than murder. I simply did not want to believe that something so terrible could have happened."

"It is most difficult to believe that murder can happen to those that we love and value, my Emperor," Leonora commented. "If not for the warning from Hannah, I may have believed in the accident as well."

Irene took several steps forward.

"And what is the nature of this warning?"

Leonora paused for a moment and then spoke.

"According to Hannah, a dark sorcerer has infiltrated the ranks of the Academy of Arcane Arts, and has begun to influence the minds of the most influential members of the Academy. If this sorcerer succeeds in his manipulations, the entire Academy could be turned against you, my Emperor."

Kaitain froze for a moment. This had not been part of his plan, but it seemed that the fates were conspiring to assist him.

"Then I take it you heard of the problems in court today?" Kaitain asked.

Leonora nodded.

"Very well then," Kaitain continued. "Lady Leonora Wastri, I task you with uncovering the source of this plot and destroying all involved, no matter how deep the plot goes. You act with the full sanction of the Imperial Court and the Throne."

Leonora bowed deeply.

"By your word, my Emperor."

As Leonora turned to leave, she stopped and turned back to face Kaitain.

"Was there something else, Lady Wastri?"

Leonora nodded.

"Then by all means, speak."

"There was one more passage in the message from Hannah, my Emperor, one that concerns me more than the plot against your life. It said that the dragons have learned of a great weapon, a weapon called the Dragon's Tear, a weapon that could unmake the world. Hannah said that she had heard rumors of it in Galateria, and that she would investigate them while she was following your orders. If such a weapon does exist, it must not be allowed to fall to the dragons."

Kaitain frowned. The Dragon's Tear was for him alone. No one was to possess it other than him.

"I shall send troops to investigate this weapon, Lady Wastri, and I appreciate your candor. It seems that a war with the dragons is inevitable."

Leonora nodded and quickly left the room. Kaitain felt the smile creep onto his lips, and behind him Irene could feel the pride well within her.

All according to my plan. Soon the Emperor himself will be nothing more than an inconvenience that I can cast aside as I did that old fool Alistair.

Chapter XLVI

Hunger

Year Two of the Just Emperor Kaitain Lorien XII, Creator's Calendar Year 1869

New Year's Day was usually the cause for a celebration that would resound throughout the world, and this New Year's was supposed to be special. This New Year's marked the beginning of the first full year under the reign of Emperor Kaitain Lorien, the twelfth member of the Lorien family to hold the title in just under two millennia of uninterrupted rule. In addition, it was supposed to be a celebration of the faithful of the Creator triumphing over the scourge known as the Crawling Plague. The hero Alistair Ravenheart had given his life to bring back the cure from the evil dragons, and now for the first time in years, there would be no deaths from that horrible disease. However, the celebrations this year would have to wait. There could be no rejoicing in the face of war. Emperor Kaitain "Dragonsbane" Lorien had declared the first ever war against the race of dragons, and all available troops were being called forth to help in the defense of Cadaria from this new enemy. The dragons had struck the first blow in their attack of Galateria, and now the forces of Cadaria were ready to strike back. It was rumored that the Emperor had put the famous Knight of the Flashing Blade, Sir Bernhardt Yeoman, the Moonstone Knight in charge of leading the counterattack against the armies of the dragons. It would promise to be a bloody war, one whose outcome was still uncertain. But if the Just Emperor decreed that the battle could be won, then it would be so.

All of the warriors in the small town of Yelsin in the Kingdom of Iron, Pellatori, had been called up to join the Moonstone Knight's army. It was a great honor, but to the families left behind there would be endless nights of worry and fear. Would their loved ones return? Would the battle be won? The more horrible question was whether or not the dragons would retaliate against Pellatori the way they had against Galateria. In the darkness of one of the homes in the middle of the night, the wife of one warrior contemplated the end that would befall them all.

Isabel Relin was a bright young woman who had been married to an aspiring young warrior. It was considered a good match for all involved, and the two would eventually come to love one another very deeply. However, the call to war had a chance to end their young life together. As Isabel sat in the kitchen of their small house, she could only listen to the sobs of the other women and children in the village. They wished their husbands and fathers good luck in the coming campaign. Isabel had no such kind words for her husband.

"Isabel," her husband had said, "I have to go. It is my duty to the Moonstone Knight to take the fight to these dragons. They are the true enemy and they may have been the cause of the Crawling Plague. I must do my duty."

"And what about your duty to me?" Isabel had countered. "You are my husband. We are to have a life together. How can you throw it all away like this? The dragons don't care about our little village, and the great Bernhardt Yeoman doesn't care about you. He wouldn't know if you were there or not."

"But I would," he had said finally. "I'm not going to argue with you about this. You knew this is what I was when we were matched, and you knew that this day would come and that I would have to go."

The words that Isabel had spoken then had been ones of hatred, anger, and bitterness. She never realized how much she loved her husband until that moment, and the chance that they would have the happy life that they had always spoken about in the stillness of the night had been destroyed. There in the darkness, all she had was the New Year's dinner that she had prepared for the village. Enough to feed seventy people. She had worked for days to make sure it was all ready, and now the great and powerful Emperor Kaitain Lorien, sitting upon his throne had ruined it all. How could a man such as that who had never known hardship issue the orders to send common men and women to their deaths? How could his whim be the only thing responsible for the destruction of families? As Isabel sat at the table, the food for the feast before her, she began to eat. Each bite seemed to fuel the hatred of the Emperor even more.

Pompous ass, sitting on his throne…

Chew.

What does he know about family?

Bite.

How could he do this to us?

Swallow.

"Dorovar…"

I hate him.

Bite.

I hate him.

Chew.

I HATE HIM!

Swallow.

"Dorovar…"

Suddenly Isabel became aware of the voice that filled her head. As she looked up from the table where over half of the food was already gone, she could see a man's form moving though the house toward her. He was gray, his skin, his hair, his nails, everything except his eyes. His eyes burned with this fire, this obscene fire. And as Isabel looked upon him, she was not afraid. She had heard the stories of the gray man named Pestilence that had brought the Crawling Plague to Cadaria, and though the plague had been cured, the gray man had never been found. As she looked upon the horror, she could not stop eating. The hunger within her grew and no matter how much she ate, it only grew stronger.

"Do you feel the hatred?"

The gray man's voice was like a dagger in her mind. It bore deep into her and made her shiver with every word. Her flesh crawled and her eyes watered, but the hunger seemed to grow more with every bite.

"Do you know who has caused you this pain?"

Isabel's mouth was full but she grunted the Emperor's name. Even now the gray man grew closer and the fear gripped her heart. But she could not stop eating. The food was nearly gone, and the hunger ravaged her body even more.

"I can release you from your pain."

Yes. She wanted release. She wanted the pain to stop. She wanted the hunger to stop. She wanted it all to stop.

"I can give you the power to make those who did this to you suffer."

Yes! They would all suffer. They would all starve. They would gorge themselves until they could breathe no more. They would hunger and starve and choke on their own blood and bile. They would know the suffering that she had; they would know the depths of sadness and pain. They would know hunger.

"You must give yourself to him."

The food gone, the hunger mounting, Isabel found her voice again.

"Who?"

A green light filled the room. The light seemed to be alive, full of substance, and full of joy. It held the room like a ghost.

CHAPTER 46

"Dorovar…"

The voice came from the light and it shook Isabel to her very core. She had head the voice in her dreams. It held her at night when she cried. The voice had comforted her. She trusted the voice.

"Dorovar…"

The gray man went to one knee, the green light enveloping him. The light suffused his being making him nearly transparent. In that pale light, Isabel could see the gray man for what he truly was, and he was beautiful to behold. The Crawling Plague had not been a curse upon the land, it had been a gift, the love of Dorovar given to those deserving enough to be his servants in this life and beyond.

"You must bring me more souls. My tomb confines me to this place, and I must have more souls to fuel my chorus."

The voice of the light became stronger, and the light pulsed with the words.

"I must have my vengeance upon those who imprisoned me here. We must make then all suffer. I have started a war with the help of my first servant Pestilence, and now we shall unleash a new plague upon the land. One that will drive all hope away from our instrument of destruction. One that will make them fight even harder. One that we can blame upon our true enemy. You will be that plague my child if you will dedicate yourself to my will. Will you give your soul to me? Will you serve the will of Dorovar?"

There was no answer needed, and the green light moved from the gray man to Isabel, and she felt the light penetrate her. It surrounded her and held her, and the hunger grew. As the moments passed, she could feel the change flow through her body. Her already lithe form was sucked dry, leaving her with a nearly skeletal visage. Her face retained a subtle beauty however. Her cheeks were sunken in, and the bones of her jaw and her cheekbones were clearly visible, as were her well-pronounced eye sockets. Her hair straightened and grew down the length of her back; dry, split, and frayed. It hung like a cloud behind her. The clothing that she wore hung loosely and then fell away from her body, leaving her naked and hideously beautiful. A moment later the green light pulsed and Isabel was surrounded with a haze that obscured her features, and she looked like a ghost, a beautiful ghost. All the beauty that she had possessed when she had been mortal had been magnified by the power of Dorovar even with her newly gaunt frame. Standing naked in the center of the room, the woman who had once been Isabel looked down at herself. The name that was tied to her old life no longer held her. She was no longer a wife, she was no longer the member of any community. She was now Famine, the second child of Dorovar, and she would make all of the enemies of her lord and master pay. Death would follow in her wake starting with the village that she had called home all her life.

"Now Famine, my child, take your new powers and bring suffering to all those who stand in your path. Bring them the touch of Dorovar and add their souls to my growing chorus. When enough have died and enough souls have added their voices, I shall be free of this prison and the chorus of souls will sing me to the Heavens where I belong. Then and only then will I be able to exact my revenge upon the demons that put me here. Then and only then will every last dragon that breaths everywhere on this world be made to suffer as I have. Let them feel my pain. And once they have all felt my wrath for what they have done to me, I shall make the Creator pay for his part in my suffering. In the end they will all burn in the fires of their own making. From the ashes I shall rise, alone in my Heavens, alone in my world, alone in my creation. I shall remake all as I see fit. Such is the might of Dorovar!"

Laughter resounded throughout the village, and as the dying began, Famine found that she was laughing the loudest.

* * * * * * * * * * * * *

Deep in the forests of Iltorp, Vallic Ultiv sat in careful meditation upon the recent events. The new Emperor, a child whom he had met only a hand-full of times and whom had always had a sour disposition, had declared war upon all of the dragons on the face of Espre. It was a bold if not foolish moved, but the will of the Emperor was not to be questioned by anyone, not even a member of the vaunted Knights of the Flashing Blade. And now, in a time when all the members of the Flashing Blade were most needed to defend the Empire as their charter demanded, it seemed as if

Emperor Lorien were taking great pains in ensuring that no two members of the Flashing Blade were ever in the same place at the same time, and if they were, one of his appointees to the Order would be there. But as Vallic sat and thought, the Knights of the Flashing Blade were not the organization that he had been recruited to all those years ago by the grandfather of this new pup of an Emperor.

Once the Flashing Blade was a group of honorable men and women, those who had a deep-seated respect for the Empire and what it would become. As members came and went, some prescribed to the values that the Cadarian Empire had been founded upon while others were simply zealots that fit the ruling Emperor's agenda. Though Vallic had never understood why they were appointed, he did his best to work with the new members and to keep the peace. However, once this pup Kaitain took the throne, it seemed that the respect for the loyal order of knights was lost. Two of the knights that he had appointed barely deserved to be called knights at all, and it seemed that before long the Knights of the Flashing Blade could become extinct.

Hannah was off on some humanitarian mission. Natalia, Leonora, and Gregor were on secret missions for the throne. Bernhardt was leading the fight against the dragons. Chelsea and Seraph were trying to keep their kingdoms from a full scale war. The new ones Jaccob and Devlin were also on missions for the throne, but there was nothing secret about them. They were winning support for the new Emperor in their respective kingdoms and trying to build names for themselves. The other new knight, Tolon, was also knee deep in trouble for the new Emperor, on a fool's errand to seek wisdom from the Maldovrin Triplets. If he survived the attempt, he could be the only new member who warranted any respect at all. As far as Vallic knew, there had been no summons for Orren or Xaran, which made perfect sense. Neither man was predictable to say the least, and often both were too steeped in their own studies to be much use to anyone other than themselves. However, when their duty called, Vallic knew they could be trusted to do what had to be done when it had to be done.

Letting his mind touch the cosmos, Vallic could feel the ripples of power flowing everywhere in the world. There was something dangerous on the horizon, something that threatened to tip the balance between good and evil, light and dark. There was a great shadow hanging on the edge of thought. It was there, like smoke, impossible to grasp but there nonetheless. Reaching out with his senses, he tried to touch the mind of the young emperor. Many times Vallic had touched the mind of Ender Lorien, and the two had shared many moments that helped to shape the Cadarian Empire into a prosperous place. However, Kaitain's mind somehow was hidden from Vallic's view. It was as if the man did not exist in the pattern of the cosmos. His energy had been suppressed. Perhaps it was due to the Crawling Plague's touch on the lands of Aldere, or perhaps it was a manner of protection put into place by the new Court Sorceress. Whatever the reason, it unnerved Vallic.

Suddenly a great pain pierced through Vallic's body and it shook him from his meditation. The sounds of hundreds of screams resounded through his soul, the sounds of death. A similar feeling had struck Vallic the day the Crawling Plague had struck the land, and now Vallic feared that a new, more terrible horror had been unleashed upon the Empire. Focusing as best he could through the pain, Vallic reached out to find the source of the pain. Finally he found it, a remote village in the south of Pellatori. Concentrating, Vallic focused his energies and in the next moment, only the gentle winds disturbed the grass where Vallic once sat.

* * * * * * * * * * * * *

Horror comes in many forms. It is the hideous visage of the undead, the shriek of a dying child, a nightmare that forbids sleep. None of them compared to the vision that awaited Vallic in what had once been the village of Yelsin. Men and women lay in the streets motionless, food lying about them half eaten, marks on their bodies that could only have been caused by human teeth. As Vallic looked around it seemed that the inhabitants had tried to consume everything. Flesh was ripped and torn. Crops were eaten from the fields before they were ripe. Pieces of the very houses that they people lived in had been ripped from their moorings and eaten. One man laid face up, a stone stuffed in his mouth. It was obvious that the man had suffocated. But as Vallic made the rounds through the unimaginable horror, the bodies of the men and women were the most perplexing. It looked as though none of them had eaten a meal in several days. They had wasted away to nearly nothing. Merely skin and bones, nothing but a shadow of their former selves. The devastation in this village made the Crawling Plague look like a simple fever. Whatever was causing these horrible afflictions would not let the killing stop with the cure of the Crawling Plague.

Vallic knelt by the body of a fallen woman. Reaching into her mind, he saw the last moments of her life. He saw the phantom of a woman who walked through the town, and he felt the hunger that entered the dying woman's soul. It was not a hunger that any food could cure. The more the woman ate, the hungrier she became. She ate bread, corn, meat, and when none of it would sate her hunger, she turned on her husband. The knife in her hand ended his life and his hunger, but even as his flesh crossed her lips, and his blood smeared across her face, it was not enough. She ate and ate, but the hunger grew until finally she could contain it no more and she simply stopped. She wasted away to nothing in a matter of minutes, and just as with the Crawling Plague it was a horrible death, perhaps more so. Where the plague killed only the body, this new afflictions, this Wasting Disease, seemed to destroy the soul as well. Without another moment of thought, Vallic concentrated. The danger would have to be fought, and quickly.

* * * * * * * * * * * * *

"How could this happen!"

Emperor Kaitain stalked around his audience chamber. All of the courtiers had already been dismissed, and the rumors were beginning to spread through the Imperial Palace like wildfire. Sir Vallic Ultiv had brought the bad news, the kind of news that no Empire could survive once let alone twice. On the heels of the Crawling Plague came this new horror.

"My Emperor," Irene said calmly. "There is only one possible cause for this new affliction. The dragons could not be responsible so quickly for such a disease, it is not their way to attack in this manner once an open war has been declared. This is no doubt the work of the Dark Gods of Mythryn."

With the Imperial Sword clutched in his hand, Kaitain paced the audience chamber.

"The bastards launch this kind of attack just when we are starting our war against the dragons. If we focus our attention on them now, then we will be forced to fight a war on two fronts, and we would most likely lose. The brilliant devious bastards. We must do something to stop them Irene, we must crush them."

Vallic Ultiv stayed silent for most of the Emperor's fuming, but chose this moment to speak.

"My Emperor," Vallic started slowly, "while I would never openly disagree with your decrees, I must speak. When I felt the touch of this Wasting Disease, I felt a darkness like I have never felt before. It was deeper and more foreboding than even that presented by the Dark Gods. While I cannot dispute the fact that the source of this affliction could be Mythryn, I am not however convinced that the Dark Gods are the cause. For nearly two millennia the Dark Gods have abided by the truce hard won by the first Emperor of Cadaria, and they would have no cause to break it now."

Kaitain locked his eyes on the mysterious member of the Flashing Blade. It was said that Vallic was incapable of lying.

"You can feel these abominations, Vallic?"

Vallic nodded slowly.

"Then hunt them down!" the Emperor raged, bringing his fist down upon the arm of the throne. "Use whatever means you have to, do whatever you must, but I want this gray man Pestilence, and this woman calling herself Famine destroyed. Find out what you can from them, but I want this horror they are causing stopped. Kill them!"

Vallic bowed and left the audience chamber quickly. The dismissal was implied. Irene kept quiet until Vallic left the room. She had been waiting for this moment, but it had come sooner than she expected.

"I have done some research into the backgrounds of the Knights of the Flashing Blade as you requested my Emperor, and I have discovered a very disturbing piece of information. It seems that Hannah Ironheart is the sister of the Dark Queen Sadrina Annis of Mythryn."

CHAPTER 46

The Imperial Sword clattered to the ground. Betrayed. How could the wool be pulled so completely over the eyes of the Throne? The Celestine Knight was a traitor. She had been providing information to her sister this whole time. They were in collusion, there could be no doubt. This could not be tolerated. An example would have to be made.

"Execute her."

The edict was quick and powerful.

"My Emperor, you are most wise in all things," Irene began, "but perhaps there is another way that this situation could be handled. I have learned through my sources that the daughter of the Dark Queen has been sent to Lady Ironheart to sue for peace between Cadaria and Mythryn. This is a situation that could be turned to our advantage."

Kaitain fumed.

"They talk of peace and attack us like this? They are all cowards. But you are right Irene, we will capture the Dark Princess and use her as a bargaining chip against her mother and the other Dark Gods. We will make them pay for what they have done."

Irene smiled.

"You are very wise, my Emperor."

Kaitain picked up the Imperial Sword and an evil smile graced his face.

"But that does not relieve the burden from the shoulders of Lady Ironheart. An example must still be made of her. I want you to send Geoffry to meet the Dark Princess when she arrives, and to bring her directly here. As for Hannah, I want you to personally issue the termination order to our new Onyx Knight. Consider it his proof of loyalty to the Empire."

Irene bowed deeply and left the room, wondering if she could really control the fires of madness that she had stoked within Kaitain. She could hear his maniacal laughter resounding from deep in the palace as she began to draft her own instructions for both Devlin Rannoch and Geoffry

Aramour. Yes, Kaitain was beginning to fall farther and faster than she anticipated. She would have to find a way to add another layer of control, another part of him to distract. Smiling to herself, she reached for another piece of parchment and began to draft a letter to Thorigald.

Revelations in Darkness

Year Two of the Just Emperor Kaitain "Dragonsbane" Lorien, Creator's Calendar Year 1869

For most of his life, Gregor knew that he was different. As the son of the Ruby Knight Ivan Quicksilver under the rule of Emperor Kaldawyn Lorien, the tenth Lorien Emperor, Gregor was destined for great things. He would join the Army of Blood as soon as he was old enough, bringing great pride to his father as a member of the Regiment of Blood, the most senior military organization in the Kingdom of Blood, Zevarit. From there Gregor would train with his father and be ready to take up the position of the Ruby Knight when his father retired. However, the best-laid plans are the first to be thrown away when the uncertain future rears its head.

With the death of Emperor Kaldawyn Lorien by what was widely believed to be the blade of a Mythryn assassin, everything in Gregor's life changed. The new Emperor, Ender Lorien, despite his personal misgivings and in an effort to stave off growing unrest within the royal families, declared a renewal of the Shadow War. As was his duty, Gregor's father went off to war, a war that he would never return from. Emperor Ender Lorien brought Gregor to the Imperial Palace in Aldere where Gregor learned the news of his father's demise fighting the Dark Gods of Mythryn on their own soil. It was a senseless and pointless mission, one that was never going to succeed, but Gregor's father had gone anyway. The only remainder of his father's existence was his weapon. It was the sacred sword known as Valor, the sword crafted by the legendary Arturious Demascious generations past. Another member of the Flashing Blade had retrieved the sword from the Dark Empire, and his name was Vallic Ultiv, the Serpentine Knight. For many years, Gregor hated Vallic for only bringing home the sword and not the body of his father, but eventually Gregor learned to forgive the man, knowing he was fulfilling his duty the best he could. Valor was placed in Gregor's hands that day, and he had become the Ruby Knight. At the time, the sword was larger than Gregor, nearly six feet in length from the hilt to the tip of the blade. However, once Valor was placed in Gregor's hands, everything within him changed.

The touch of the divine is a strange thing. It comes in many forms and does different things to different people. For Gregor, it steeled the emotions of his heart and dedicated him fully to the path that laid ahead of him. From that moment in time on, there could never be duplicity in the head of the Ruby Knight. He was clear of focus, could see through the lies and manipulations of others, could feel the aura of evil around him as though it were smoke, and fear never touched his heart again. Not even death would be considered a hurdle for Gregor. It was as though death would be a welcomed release from the world. Gregor had seen something through the power of Valor, and though he had never spoken of it to anyone but his wife, it was rumored that the Creator himself had spoken to Gregor and told him what lay ahead.

For a time after his ascension to the rank of Ruby Knight, Gregor traveled to every corner of Cadaria, meeting the other members of the Knights of the Flashing Blade, and also meeting the royal families of each of the kingdoms. Gregor firmly believed that while Cadaria was divided, the Knights of the Flashing Blade had the responsibility to help cure the ails of the Empire, regardless of what kingdom they lay in. After a time, Gregor became the most loved of all of the members of the Knights of the Flashing Blade, and it was even whispered in some corners of Cadaria that Gregor was more popular than the Emperor himself. It was this rumor that led Gregor finally back to Aldere after nearly ten years to speak to the man who had given him the great honor of becoming the Ruby Knight.

CHAPTER 46

When Gregor returned to Aldere, there were many who thought that he would challenge Ender Lorien for the throne; that the prophecies about the fall of the Lorien line were going to come true at the hands of the Empire's greatest servant. However, on that day, the assembled courtiers witnessed what some would call the greatest moment in the history of the Empire. The speech that Gregor gave on that day was inscribed into legends and taught to every aspiring child across the Empire.

****

Year Forty of the Just Emperor Ender "JustHand" Lorien XI, Creator's Calendar Year 1822

Gregor Quicksilver strode into the throne room, his famous sword Valor in his hand. The courtiers in the audience chamber shuffled out of his path, both fearful and curious about what was going to happen in the next few moments. As he approached the dais, the royal guard impeded Gregor's path. If he had wanted to, Gregor could have cut the men down without a thought, but he stopped several steps short of them and looked past them to the man who stood before the throne.

"My Emperor," Gregor said proudly, "may your humble servant approach?"

Ender Lorien thought for a moment and then nodded his head. Without a word, the royal guard parted, but did not depart the throne room. There was a palpable tension in the room, and as the two powerful men stood mere feet from one another, the tension grew. Ender looked over to the low table where the Imperial Sword lay, and then looked back at Gregor.

"Do I have reason to draw my blade as you have, Gregor?"

At that moment, Gregor fell to one knee, and placed the sword Valor at the feet of the Emperor. There were gasps of shock around the room, but before any action could be taken, Gregor began to speak in a proud, clear voice.

"Emperor Lorien, I have wronged you. As I have traveled your Empire, I have seen and heard many things. I have healed many wounds, both physical and mental, and I have defeated many enemies of the Empire. I have ended uprisings, and quelled unrest. All of this I have done in the name of the Empire and in the name of the Just Emperor Ender Lorien, the man who gave me the position once held by my father. However, my Emperor, I fear that while in doing the will of the Throne, I have been elevated in the eyes of the people to that of your equal. I am but a humble servant, my Emperor, and though the whispers persist even now, I have no designs upon the throne of Cadaria."

Gregor took a deep breath, then continued.

"All I have done, my Emperor, I have done for you. All I have done, is to honor the memory of my father who loved this Empire more than he loved himself. However, my Emperor, you are the foundation of this Empire, and if you were to fall by my hand, the Empire would suffer, even if I felt that I would be more just or more powerful than you. I have no thirst for power, my Emperor, and I have no desire to be seen as your equal. For these wrongs, I would surrender my sword and my place as the Ruby Knight of the Flashing Blade. My task was to save the Empire at any cost, even if I must save it from itself. In order to do my duty, my Emperor, I must ask that you allow me to retire."

The silence that followed Gregor's impassioned speech held for several long minutes before Emperor Lorien took a step forward and retrieved Valor from where it lay on the first step of the dais. When he began to speak, he spoke not to Gregor, but to the assemblage of courtiers in the audience chamber.

"It is always said that the proudest day of a father's life is the day that his son surpasses him. I learned many lessons from my father when I was a child, and I hope in the short time that I had with him, that I was able to teach my father as well. However, I never had the chance to surpass the greatness that my father held. As I am the Emperor of Cadaria, all who dwell within its borders are my children. I love all of you as I love my own children. And so, I have never been more proud of my children as I am today. This great man, this great champion Gregor Quicksilver has done what I wish I could have done. He has surpassed his father's greatness, and he has surpassed the greatness of his surrogate father."

Gregor looked up at the Emperor, tears welling in his eyes. Ender looked down at Gregor and smiled.

"From this day forward, let no man question the ideals or the drives of the Ruby Knight. He had proven himself to be a true defender of the Empire, and has shown all of us the way to build Cadaria into a place my father always dreamed of. From this day forward, the Ruby Knight shall be my personal champion and personal defender in all things. I trust Gregor Quicksilver with my life, and I would also trust him with the lives of my children. Were it not for his position with the Knights of the Flashing Blade, I would make Gregor a part of the Lorien family. However, because I cannot, I will do the next best thing. I shall find a woman whose beauty of spirit matches Gregor's and I shall bind them with the Emperor's blessing."

* * * * * * * * * * * * *

Year Two of the Just Emperor Kaitain "Dragonsbane" Lorien XII, Creator's Calendar Year 1869

Gregor sat cross-legged on the deck of the great ship *Nemious*, looking out over the rolling waves toward the black haze that covered the Dark Empire of Mythryn. There was something discomforting about the mission that he had been given. The Dark Gods may not have had a hand in the Crawling Plague, or in the new Wasting Disease that Gregor had heard about during his journey, but the new Emperor, Kaitain Lorien, seemed to be convinced that they did. A war with Mythryn was not the wisest course of action at the present time, especially with most of the armies of Cadaria involved in skirmishes with the dragons. Gregor felt that he needed to be with the rest of the Knights of the Flashing Blade eliminating the threat of both the Wasting Disease and the dragons. Gregor's thoughts turned to his wife. She was somewhere in Galateria trying to put right the damage that was done by the dragon attacks there, and he had not even had an opportunity to say goodbye to her before he left for Mythryn. Of course, this was nothing new. Many times for the Throne, the Knights of the Flashing Blade were sent on urgent secret missions, so secret that even other members of the Flashing Blade could not know of them. Still, Hannah deserved to know that her husband might not return from his latest mission.

Another set of thoughts entered Gregor's mind. Why was this mission so necessary? Wouldn't Gregor's talents be better use trying to find a cure for the Wasting Disease? Wouldn't it be more beneficial to take the fight to the more dangerous of the dragons? Wouldn't resources be better spent identifying all of the dragon nests throughout Cadaria and eliminating them? Emperor Kaitain must have had more information about the actions of the Dark Gods than he had given Gregor. However, that was the right of the Emperor to say and do whatever he felt he needed to do in the best interests of the Empire. As Gregor's father had said on many occasions, the Dark Empire of Mythryn would have to be dealt with eventually. It was too big of a threat to remain ignored, and the truce that created the Kingdom of Night would not last forever. As the years passed, Galateria was becoming less an extension of Mythryn and more a true Kingdom of Cadaria.

Within hours, Gregor would feel the shores of Mythryn for the first time. The same place where his father had met his end. In his heart and in his mind, the chorus of pain and anguish began, despite how hard Gregor tried to ignore it. The circumstances of his father's death had always plagued his mind, and his now comrade in arms Vallic Ultiv had never been willing to provide any answers, even after Gregor became a member in good standing of the Knights of the Flashing Blade. There had been a thirst for vengeance; this need to see those who were responsible for his father's death brought to justice. But it was not justice that Gregor wanted. It was revenge. Those thoughts always brought Gregor pause. He was a man who had dedicated his life to the Creator, a man who wanted nothing more than to serve the Empire with every fiber of his being. It was not within him to desire revenge. If the Creator willed that justice would befall those who were responsible for the death of his father, then so be it.

* * * * * * * * * * * * *

Hours had passed since Gregor had begun his long trek through the countryside of Mythryn. The captain of the fishing vessel who had given him passage told Gregor that the Dark Citadel of the Fallen was only a few miles from the shoreline. However, it had been several hours, and Gregor was beginning to doubt the word of the simple fisherman. Just as doubt began to well up within him, Gregor heard the sound of men in armor moving from the other side of the next hill. As he deftly and silently climbed the ridge, Gregor could see the vast plain below, filled with men in black armor. Upon their heads were helms that made them look like demons, and after a quick count, Gregor would doubt that there were less than ten thousand troops below. That was too many to handle even for a Knight of the Flashing Blade. There was only one course of action left to him. Slowly, Gregor stood and drew Valor from the sheath strapped to his back. The eerie inner light of the blade was magnified at Gregor's will, and within an instant the cries went up from the men below.

"My name is Gregor Quicksilver," he called proudly to the men below. "I am the Ruby Knight of the Flashing Blade, emissary from the Kingdom of Cadaria, serving in the name of Emperor Kaitain Lorien. I have come in good faith to speak to your leaders. If you will, take me to your lord and master. If you do not wish to do so, you can try to take me by force. However, I control the high ground, and my power is unlike any you have ever matched yourselves against. I do not want to have to shed any of your blood, but I will if I must. So, what is your decision?"

The battle cry from below was the only answer that Gregor needed.

* * * * * * * * * * * * *

Gregor Quicksilver looked up at the sky, the light blocked by the magical haze that covered Mythryn. Small cuts covered his arms and legs, and as he fell to one knee, he felt the soaked ground below him give slightly. All around him, the broken bodies of the fallen dark knights littered the hillside. Many had fallen back down to the plain below. Blood soaked the ground, a great pool of it splashing around Gregor. His clothes had already been soaked in the blood of his enemies, and he was sure his skin had been stained red as well. At the crest of the hill, another wave of soldiers stood, still marveling at the skill of their enemy. Gregor would need just a few more moments to gather his strength again. They had come at him in waves, moving to the top of the hill the best they could to attack him. The wiser ones however had circled around and come up from behind him. They could come in more force that way. While the armor of the dark warriors would have been enough to repel most blades, they were no match for Valor. The pieces fell away like cut paper, the bodies beneath splitting just as easily. Gregor took no joy in the killing, but his opponents had given him no choice in the matter. Either they would fall, or he would. To die this close to his destination was unthinkable. No member of the Flashing Blade would be kept from achieving his or her goal. So far the cost to the Dark Empire had been high. Over a thousand troops had met their end at Gregor's hand, and many more would fall before it was over. They were beginning to mass again, ready to surge forward. A wicked smile flashed across Gregor's lips as he stood again and held Valor aloft.

"I thought you were warriors of the Dark Empire?"

The taunt passed through the ranks of his enemies but was not answered. Gregor smiled to himself again. They were well trained, and though they were beginning to fear their opponent now, it was the fear of their masters and their growing ranks that bolstered their resolve.

"Alright then, let's continue."

They were on him again in the next moment.

* * * * * * * * * * * * *

Pain. The red haze of battle began to clear from Gregor's vision, and all that was left was pain. Gregor's arms ached from swinging Valor time and time again. The cuts on his legs and body made it difficult to stand. Blood was flowing freely from the jagged wounds on his arms, legs, and chest. Halfway into the second wave, Gregor's breastplate had been shattered by the massive war hammer of one of the dark warriors. The blow had nearly ended the battle for Gregor then and there. However, he had staggered back into another of the warriors who had not been prepared to deal the lethal blow. It took Gregor only a second to recover his wits and kill not only the man with the hammer, but his unwilling assistant as well.

Agony coursed through Gregor's veins again as he fought to straighten up. The flowing blood had turned the hill into a swamp, thick mud coating everything and making it hard to move. In some ways that benefited Gregor. It meant that his enemies could not swarm him as quickly. However, it also meant that Gregor could not rely on his superior speed to fight enemies both in front and behind. Several thousand were dead now. Either they were killed by Gregor's hand or the falling bodies of their comrades. If Gregor had enough blood left in him, he could survive another assault, however, there would not be enough of him left if any more came. By now the alarms in the Dark Citadel of the Fallen had been sounded, and the more elite troops of the Dark Empire were being rallied to deal with the incursion. Finally, Gregor said a silent prayer to the Creator and steeled himself for the next charge.

"To think, I had heard that the warriors of the Dark Empire were powerful enough to kill any member of the Flashing Blade in single combat. I see that the stories of your prowess have been greatly exaggerated. Well, come on again. How many thousand of you do I have to kill before you finally get to me?"

The charge that Gregor had prepared for never came. Dark warriors stood, watching, and for a moment Gregor thought they were all going to swarm him at once, overwhelming him in a single strike. In his weakened state, it would have been a sound strategy, and quite possibly would have worked. Finally, the ranks of the warriors parted and a striking woman in a pale violet dress stepped into the clearing created by the fallen bodies. She literally walked over the land and bodies, the mud and blood repelled with every step. The woman's black hair was nearly shoulder length, and in her eyes Gregor could see power. It was as if her body was merely a vessel for a greater power that dwelled within her. There was a frown upon her face, a look of disdain that was focused on the bloody and battered Ruby Knight.

"You are as brave as you are stupid, Gregor Quicksilver," she said after a moment. "A smart man would have surrendered by now and let his miserable life end with some dignity."

Gregor sneered.

"This battlefield is not a place for a child. So unless you would like to fall upon my sword, I would suggest you let your toy soldiers continue their attack."

The woman laughed.

"You shame yourself with your pride, uncle. I have the power of a god at my disposal while you simply claim to serve one. I shall lead you to the Queen of these lands, and she will determine what will be done with you."

With that the young woman turned her back on the Ruby Knight and began to walk toward the Dark Citadel of the Fallen. Silently the dark warriors watched for Gregor's next move. As Gregor took several steps forward, following the young woman, confusion began to set in.

Did she call me uncle?

* * * * * * * * * * * * *

Deep in the Dark Citadel of the Fallen, Gregor stood before two empty thrones in an empty audience chambers. He had not been offered any healing, nor had he been shown any courtesy whatsoever. However, Gregor could not blame his hosts. Was he a guest, or was he a prisoner? Either way, this was giving him time to recover his strength. If they wanted a fight, he would be ready for one. Already some of the smaller wounds on his body had mended, and as he focused more of his divine power, the larger wounds would begin to heal. That however would take several hours of concentration and peace.

After several more minutes of silence, the doors to the audience chamber opened admitting three women and one man. One of the women was the young woman in the pale dress who had called him uncle on the battlefield. The second of the women wore a long blue gown, a crystal crown upon her head, her bright blue eyes shining like stars. The third woman wore a simple brown robe with a hood pulled up over her head, but enough of her face was revealed for Gregor to know that she was a woman. In her hands she held a gnarled staff, the kind that Gregor had seen on many occasions during his visits to the Academy of Arcane Arts. The man, rather than sitting on the other throne as Gregor expected, moved to Gregor's right and stood with this hand on the hilt of the blade that hung from his hip. Apparently this man was the personal guard for the woman on the throne, and must have been very good if they thought he was the only protection the three women needed from Gregor.

"Gregor Quicksilver," the woman on the throne said slowly. "I should have known that you would have been the one that the coward Kaitain sent after us. You are by far one of the most powerful and accomplished of the Flashing Blade, and now I see what my dear sister sees in you."

Gregor's mind whirled for a moment. There could be only one answer.

"And you don't appear to be as thick as I expected," she taunted. "My name is Sadrina Annis, the Dark Queen of the Empire of Mythryn, heir to the Heavens, and sister to the Celestine Knight Hannah Ironheart."

Gregor stayed silent for a moment, not allowing the shock of the moment to pass through him. He had to control his emotions if he were going to survive.

"You have already met my eldest daughter, Darrien. As you may have already surmised, while I am a mortal, she is the daughter of the leader of the Dark Gods. The woman on my right, you know quite well."

At that moment, the third woman pulled back her hood, and Gregor's memory flashed back several years to the day the Dark Seer Jehna Feris descended upon the Imperial Palace with her prophecy.

"It had been many years, Sir Gregor," Jehna said softly. "I never got the chance to thank you for your kindness in supporting the validity of my visions."

Gregor nodded, too stunned for words.

"The man standing beside you is Alderin, the personal protector of the Imperial Family. He too is a child of the Dark Gods."

Alderin nodded his head slowly, but in true warrior fashion did not lose focus on his target.

"I suppose you are wondering why your life was spared…"

Gregor stiffened.

"You didn't want to lose any more soldiers."

Gregor's taunt passed through the room with no response, until a roar of laughter rushed into the room from one of the open doorways.

"I did not think that arrogance was a trait of an enlightened man."

That voice….it was familiar.

"But it is good to see you have such confidence in your abilities. Though, I think you need to work on your left side parry. That isn't the way I taught you."

When the man stepped into the room, all strength fled from Gregor's body, and his sword fell to the floor. The face, eyes, hair, beard, posture…it was all the same. And he hadn't aged a day.

"Father?"

Even In Death

Year Two of the Just Emperor Kaitain "Dragonsbane" Lorien, Creator's Calendar Year 1869

While citizens who lived in Galateria all of their lives had been able to learn to tell time in the magically created constant state of night, Hannah Ironheart was still having difficulty. For months now, Hannah had been engaged in the relief efforts to assist the Kingdom of Night to recover not only from the Crawling Plague, but also the attacks by the dragons. Just when it looked as though the efforts were beginning to pay off, the new hideous Wasting Disease struck. The mages and mystics tried all that they could to try and make the suffering easier for those stricken, but no matter what was tried, there seemed to be no relief in sight for those suffering. The Crawling Plague had been painful, and seemed to stretch on for a long period of time before it became fatal. The Wasting Disease on the other hand was brutal and efficient. The only way to prolong the victim's life was to deny them food, which seemed to work. However, before long, the true hunger would set in, and the victim would die just the same. They could either eat themselves to death, or their families could listen to them howl and beg for food as they slowly starved to death. Neither end seemed to be a less cruel one.

Hannah slumped down onto the simple cot that served as her bed. She had yet to be able to get comfortable in the simple house that served as both hospital and residence. The smells of death filled the house, and while Hannah tried to comfort herself by thinking how those poor wretches had rejoined the Creator, as the days passed, her composure was beginning to slip. On top of her stress and concern for the citizens of Galateria were the worries for her husband. There were not many times that Hannah allowed herself to think about Gregor, but in the quiet of her residence, she allowed herself a private and silent moment of reflection.

In the beginning, when the Emperor had matched them, the church viewed the match as the ultimate blessing of the Creator, but Hannah had her doubts. She had always found Gregor arrogant and the worst kind of the Creator's followers. Anyone who felt that they could kill in the name of the Creator did not deserve to be seen as the instrument of the Creator. But, as Hannah began to know the man who would become her husband, she began to admire his zeal and true love for both the Empire and the Creator. To him, the Emperor was the right hand of the Creator, the chosen vessel of the Creator's love, and the people of the Empire were the people of the Creator. All who dwelled in Cadaria were blessed, and that was something worth defending. While Hannah never felt that killing was necessary, she began to see the choice. There were forces in the world that would always oppose the Creator, whether they were the Dark Gods of Mythryn or their followers. For some reason, Hannah always saw the followers as a greater threat.

Those who are born to a path have no choice but to walk it. Hannah often thought that about the Dark Gods of Mythryn. In her mind they were tragic figures, to be pitied and wept for. They had no choice in the path they had to walk because they had been cast out from their home for some yet unrevealed reason. Or perhaps the reason had been revealed. The Dark Gods surely made it known, but because they were the enemy their words could never be trusted. However, those that flocked to the banner of the Dark Gods worried Hannah the most. They joined a crusade that they perhaps didn't fully understand, and yet they were willing to give their lives. They had clarity in their choice; they saw the truth and the right in what they were doing. In Hannah's mind, she was no different. Did she truly understand the Creator's plan, or was she simply clinging to a life that was easy and clear? It was a life where she did not have to make decisions of her own. She had a life where she went where she was told, married who she was told to marry, and followed every path that was laid before her. There was no responsibility that was truly her own. Perhaps that was the way she always wanted it. Or perhaps, she simply was waiting for her opportunity to rise past the expectations and become something greater.

The church-taught humility hammered her mind the next moment. She was a servant of the Creator, nothing more. Only the Creator's Will could elevate her past her present station, and to desire more was hubris. Could a mere candle be greater than the sun simply because it wishes to be? It was folly to desire more than what the Creator had predestined. All mortals were tools, toys, children in the wilderness of the Creator's Will, and to defy that will was to meet with pain, anguish, and a horrific death.

There had been many in the Church's community that had heard whispers from the more extreme members of the church hierarchy. They said that these awful plagues were the result of the wicked ways of the human race. They were a punishment from the Creator that would help them to find the path back to righteousness. The voices constantly said that only the most pious amongst the race would survive the purge, and it would mark the beginning of a new world, the rededication of the human race to the will of the Creator. While most laughed at the thought in public, in private, the words were very much in the back of their minds. What if the Crawling Plague and the Wasting Disease were plagues created by the Creator? What if trying to heal those infected was an affront to the Creator's Will? Here Hannah found herself beginning to weep. She had been ordered to help those that could not be helped, and now it was possible that the very act was an affront to the being that she valued so much above herself. Had her devotion to the Creator damned her soul? Had her devotion caused needless suffering? There in the darkness of her quarters, Hannah wept, as the solace she had once found in her faith was outside her reach.

* * * * * * * * * * * * *

Sitting alone on the shoulder of the statue to the former Onyx Knight, Devlin Rannoch stretched his wings and let the cold air buffet against the wings for a moment. The air swirled around him, wanting to lift him onto the breeze, but Devlin easily resisted the urge to try to fly over the Kingdom that now called him a hero.

"You, a hero? You can't be serious. All you are is an opportunist. Everything you have ever been is because of me, and don't you forget it."

"Shut up, old man."

Devlin's voice broke the silence. Luckily there was no one around. Many of the citizens of Galateria already were fearful of Devlin, to add the appearance of mental instability would only deepen that fear.

"That's right Devlin, just keep talking to yourself; that will really inspire confidence. I really worry about you sometimes."

"I don't need your concern or your help."

This time Devlin's voice did not carry. The words echoed in his mind only. It was not a practice that Devlin liked to carry out, but in this situation it seemed the most prudent course of action.

"You need me more than you like to think. I know what goes on in that pea brain of yours.... I know what you want and what you need. But in order to get it you have to play the good little solider for a while. Once you have the trust and confidence of the Emperor you can do whatever you want. But for right now, you follow orders. Be a good boy for once in your life and try to stay out of trouble."

Devlin snorted. He never liked following orders, he never liked doing anything he didn't want to do. Perhaps that was what made him a good fighter. He did what he had to do to survive. But now survival had a totally different set of rules.

'That's right, you're starting to get it. If you don't do what the Emperor commands, you become a threat to him, and he will kill you. Now, are you ready to make the deal? Are you ready to do what has to be done?"

Devlin sighed.

"I don't understand why this is happening," Devlin said to himself. "This order from the Emperor makes no sense. Why would he order the death of one of his own Knights of the Flashing Blade? Isn't that a foolish decision considering the situation? You have a war on two fronts and you're going to destroy one of your most effective weapons?"

The parchment from the Emperor had been simple and direct in its message. Hannah Ironheart had become a liability and was to meet with an untimely demise. However, the deathblow could not be struck by Devlin himself, it would have to come from an outside source.

"Do you, a simple half-breed, proclaim to know the mind of an Emperor? Do you think you know what it takes to rule this entire empire? Just do what you are supposed to do and then there will be no question about your loyalty. This is a test, nothing more. The perk for the Emperor is that he gets a thorn out of his side at the same time. Now, do you know what you have to do?"

Devlin sighed again.

"It's already been arranged. They should be attacking any time now. Of course, there will be several that attack the town as well to keep me occupied. That way I can show up just after the killing blow has been struck on the good little Lady Ironheart. There will be no suspicion, and the loss of life will be minimal. Not only that, it will further the Emperor's agenda against the Dark Empire."

Laughter swelled in the back of Devlin's mind.

"Sometimes you are very devious my boy. I think the Emperor will be quite pleased with this. Who knows, you may be the highest-ranking member of the Flashing Blade in no time at all. Then we can make our move."

"This is no time for ambition. We have a job to do."

The laughter continued.

"True. Time to be a good little soldier Devlin. Do what must be done."

* * * * * * * * * * * * *

Erik Relcan sat on his saddle looking down at the city of Galateria, knowing the horror that was about to descend upon it. The poor inhabitants of Galateria had already suffered horribly, but truly it was only the beginning. Soon the hatred and the distrust would begin, and it would make the beginning of a civil war the likes of which Cadaria had never seen. It was a small price to pay for the heart of the woman that Erik loved. He would destroy the whole of Cadaria if it meant that Hannah Ironheart would love him. For years Erik had dreamed of the moment when he could take Hannah into his arms and hear her confess her love for him. So many nights the dreams had kept him awake, but there never seemed to be any way for those dreams to become reality. That all changed when Erik had learned of the plot to assassinate the woman that he loved.

The man who brought him the news had his own agenda, that much was clear, but none of that mattered as long as Hannah was in danger. Erik had to protect her, no matter what, and he would help this mysterious man destroy the Empire if need be. Nothing would stop Erik from saving his love, not even death.

In the distance, Erik could hear the cries and screams of terror. The battle was beginning. The hideous creatures from the Dark Empire were descending upon Galateria with the intent to kill Lady Hannah Ironheart and plunge the Kingdom of Night deeper into the darkness that already held it. Erik spurred his horse into a light gallop. He had time to get where he needed to go, but there was no sense in putting himself at risk too early. There would be time enough for that.

* * * * * * * * * * * * *

Horror. That was the first emotion that rocketed through Lady Hannah Ironheart as she took up her War Mace known as Spirit and watched as the advancing horde of red-skinned beasts flooded toward her. The already critically undermanned Army of Galateria had mobilized as quickly as possible, but it was clear they were greatly outnumbered. Summoning all of her strength, Hannah charged the ranks of Jeresei, unafraid of the fate that may await her.

Several of the agile beasts lunged at her all at once, their long razor-sharp claws barely missing her flesh. With one swing of her mighty mace, Hannah sent a group of the demons flying through the air. With the Creator as her guide, she was a goddess on the battlefield and the demons stood no chance. There was a rallying cry from deeper in the city, and many of the members of the Army of Galateria were called away to assist the Onyx Knight in defending the center of town. It seemed the Jeresei had coordinated their attack to cause the most amount of casualties possible. However, as much as Hannah wanted to lend her aid to her comrade, there were many sick and injured people in the houses around her, and she could not allow them to be executed by those beasts. So, Hannah stood her ground alone as another group of Jeresei bore down upon her position.

When they were within striking distance. Hannah let her voice hit the turbulent air.

"Know beasts that you stand against the Celestine Knight, Lady Hannah Ironheart of the Knights of the Flashing Blade. I am the defender of this place, and the sworn protector of the Empire of Cadaria. What you do to the least of us you do to me, and as the Creator is my witness I shall give my last breath to keep you from inflicting any harm upon those I am sworn to protect. If you do not flee now, I shall call down the Creator's vengeance upon you and I shall make you pay for every soul you harm a thousand times over. Flee now before me you beasts, or I shall make you pay with more than your lives."

For a moment the beasts hesitated. After a handful of heartbeats, one of the braver of the beasts charged. Bracing herself, Hannah called upon the strength of the Creator and extended her hand, catching the beast by the throat and crushing it without a second thought. Several of the other creatures took a step back, unsure what to do at that moment. What Hannah did next nearly broke their resolve. With one quick motion, Hannah pulled at the throat of the beast and separated its spirit from its dying body. The ethereal spirit writhed in pain in her hand.

"In the name of the Creator, I consecrate the spirit of this beast and allow its soul to find peace in the realm of the blessed spirits. "

The spirit cried out in pain and then vanished.

"Whatever gods you worship," Hannah said fixing her gaze upon the Jeresei, "they will bring you no aid against me. I shall smite you here on the plane of mortals and also in whatever afterlife you believe comes to you. When you reach the gates of hell I shall be standing there waiting for you."

Not giving the creatures any time to react, Hannah charged, her mace Spirit shrouded with a strange ghostly yellow glow. The Jeresei to their credit held their ground and struck back as best they could, but they were no match for the immortal metal of Spirit. One by one they fell screaming to the ground, their bodies crushed by the sheer force of Hannah's blows. Before long dozens of the beasts lay dead, and Hannah felt the thick blood of her enemies crawling over her skin. From behind her, there was the sound of applause. Hannah turned and saw another group of the foul demons had circled around behind her and were preparing for an attack. Sitting atop the house that she had been staying in for several days was a woman Hannah had never seen before.

She sat on the very edge of the roof, a short blood-red dress clinging to her body, her long pale legs hanging, crossed at the ankles. Her long red hair flowed behind her, caught on the breeze. The woman's skin was too pale, the color that Hannah would expect to see on a corpse. Nails painted black as death, the woman's hands sat on her lap, daintily crossed as would be expected of a lady of high status. After a moment, a cruel smile graced the woman's placid features.

"Very good, Hannah, I am impressed."

The woman's voice was melodic, and she didn't so much speak the words as she did sing them. A wave of intoxication passed over Hannah, and she felt drunk. It was as if the woman's voice was making her head swim. Mumbling a silent prayer, Hannah steeled herself against the effects of the voice.

"To think that someone as frail as you would be able to destroy so many of these lovely creatures is amazing. I would hate to see what would happen if you were to truly get angry. Oh, but I forget myself, don't I? A pious woman like you would never allow anger to rule her like that, nor would passion ever rule you. What a pity for your husband."

Hannah let the taunt pass over her. The woman's heavily accented voice made her origin difficult to place. Some of her words sounded stilted, as though she was nobly born, but others were a smattering of common and vulgar dialects.

"You know my name, will you grace me with yours?"

The woman laughed and seemingly floated down from her position atop the roof and stood at the vanguard of the Jeresei force.

"Syren. Syren Belloch. The Empire will know my name before too long noble-born. Those in the halls of power shall tremble at the very mention of my name, and my progeny will tear out the throats of anyone who stands in the way of the righteous. The time of your Empire is over, and the rule of the Dark Gods will not be impeded any further."

Hannah felt the words like a blow to her stomach.

"Your Emperor was a fool to start a war with us by sending his Ruby Knight to the Dark Empire, but now that the war has begun, there will be no truce this time. No amount of begging and pleading by your weak Emperor will prevent the Dark Gods from assuming control of Cadaria. You Knights of the Flashing Blade will be the first to bend your knees to the new leadership, unless you are lucky enough to die first. I almost envy you Hannah. You will be with your precious Creator and he can comfort you as you watch the world you helped to build burn down around your comrades. How delicious."

The words were intended to destroy whatever will Hannah had left. However, they had just the opposite effect. Scathing though they may have been, the words did nothing more than steel Hannah's heart. She knew as long as she still held breath that Syren's vision of the future would never come to pass, and it would take much more than simple Jeresei to stop her. After a moment, Hannah held her mace aloft.

"Try to take my life if you can, witch."

Time slowed as the Jeresei charged. They swarmed around Hannah, ripping and tearing at her flesh with their long black claws. However, as they got close enough to attack, they were close enough for Hannah to strike. One by one they fell, Spirit causing mortal wounds to anything it struck. But their strikes were taking their toll on Hannah. Strength was beginning to drain from her arms, and as the blood continued to flow from the jagged wounds all over her body, Hannah could feel her spirit beginning to give out. Calling upon the last of her power, Hannah struck down the last of the Jeresei and then fell to her knees, surrounded by blood and bodies. Again the mocking applause came from the tall pale woman.

"Excellent, Hannah, it seems you are more powerful than even my masters envisioned. It is too bad that you will not consent to be our ally as your husband has."

Hannah's eyes went wide. Surely Syren was lying. It was just an attempt to break her spirit.

"You lie," Hannah said weekly, her voice cracking.

"Why should I lie when the truth is so much more fun?" Syren countered wickedly. "Deny it if you wish, it makes no difference to me. You'll be dead in moments anyway."

The mists and darkness coalesced the next moment in Syren's hand, creating a rapier that appeared to be made of nothing more than darkness. It glowed with an inner energy, and while the outline of the blade was clear, the rest was blurred and undefined. Syren strode slowly over to Hannah, relishing every moment of the kill that was coming. Hannah tried to raise her weapon, but all strength fled from her, and the only sound that reached her ears was that of Spirit falling to the blood-soaked ground. Syren raised her blade and was about to strike. The last thing Hannah saw before passing out was a man's form leaping in front of the blade.

* * * * * * * * * * * * *

It was several hours later when Hannah awoke. She was surprised to find that she was still alive. Hannah lay in her bed, a simple white sheet pulled up over her body. The healers had been at work on her, and she lay naked under the sheet with the exception of the mass amounts of bandages that helped to keep her wounds closed. It would only be a matter of time before her granted powers would help to speed her recovery. As Hannah began to sit up, she saw motion out of the corner of her eye. The wings were her first clue as to the identity of her visitor.

"You need your rest, Lady Ironheart," Devlin Rannoch said softly. "The healers tell me that you are lucky to be alive."

Hannah thought for a moment but stayed silent.

"It seems that you were saved by a man named Erik Relcan. Do you know him?"

Hannah nodded.

"He is an acolyte at my temple."

Hannah's voice sounded weak to her, almost as if it were someone else's voice.

"His body was found lying next to yours, dead. There was no apparent wound, and the healers could find nothing that would have caused his death. All they could say is that it seemed as though his life had been drained from him. You are very lucky to be alive."

Hannah stayed silent for another moment before finally speaking.

"Erik saved my life, and he deserves a hero's burial. I would like his body returned to the temple in Albitonin where he can be laid to rest with honor."

Devlin nodded.

"I'll see to it personally."

****

Cold. When Erik Relcan awoke, that was the first sensation. It was cold. For a few moments, his eyes would not open, and then finally, he forced them open. Darkness. There was nothing but darkness. Then suddenly the sound of stone grinding against stone, and a faint light flooded in. Even the dim light blinded Erik, but he did not need to see to know the voice that rang out through the silence.

"You once said that even death could not keep you from your love, Erik," the voice said. "And I am here to make sure you keep your word."

Sight Without Sight

Year Two of the Just Emperor Kaitain "Dragonsbane" Lorien, Creator's Calendar Year 1869

There are few places that inspire awe and peace at the same time. Those that do are coveted simply because they are so rare. One such place existed in the whole of Cadaria; it was known as the Peaks of Patience, the tallest point in all of Cadaria, casting its shadow over nearly the entire Kingdom of Knowledge, Menoris. As the protector of Menoris, the Tiger's Eye Knight, Xaran Firesoul found himself at the highest point of the Peaks of Patience many times in his life, for he found himself the most at peace there. From an early age, Xaran was fascinated with the Peaks of Patience, and the monks that raised him had always been very support of the curiosity. However, upon his eighteenth birthday when Xaran set out to climb the Peaks, many tried to stop him, fearful that Xaran would never return from such an endeavor. At that age, all monks made the attempt, and even those who were thought to be unable were never prevented from the attempt. The concern for Xaran was that he was blind.

From birth, Xaran Firesoul had been blind, but he never let his handicap prevent him from following the same path as the others raised in the monastery. Xaran did the chores that were assigned to him, and though he could not do many of the lessons, or read the materials required of him, Xaran found other ways. From an early age, Xaran befriended a young girl by the name of Sidena Doran. The two would sit in Xaran's simple room, and Sidena would read passages to Xaran late into the night, so that Xaran could keep up on his studies. For several years this practice continued, until the day that Sidena was dispatched on the mission for the monastery that she never returned from. It was said that she was lost when the boat that she was traveling on capsized, but her body was never found. For the first time, Xaran became aware of the fact that he could not weep, could not express his sorrow for the loss of someone he valued and loved. Sidena was important to him in so many ways, and though he had never seen her face, in his mind he knew what she looked like. In an effort to honor her memory, Xaran rededicated himself to excellence and took every possible avenue open to him to continue to learn and excel. From that point, there was nothing that stood in Xaran's way.

This rededication more than anything led to Xaran's desire to climb to the top of the Peaks of Patience and make his mark there as all the other brothers of the order had before him. Though the concerns were valid, Xaran would not be denied his right, and set out alone in the middle of the night with seven days' worth of provisions. When Xaran did not return after eight days, there was concern for his welfare, and when the eight days became two weeks, many feared that Xaran was dead, killed by his own foolishness. Finally after the third week passed, search parties were sent to recover Xaran's body. When one of the search parties finally reached the top of the Peaks of Patience, they found Xaran there, sitting at the highest point, in deep mediation. Only two days' worth of his rations had been eaten, and it seemed that Xaran had been there for quite some time. When Xaran was questioned about his experiences upon his return several days later, he would only say that he was communing with the spirits that made their home in the Peaks of Patience and had lost all track of time. From that point forward, Xaran spent much of his time at the top of the Peaks, speaking with the spirits of the ancestors and with those that could only be described as akin to gods.

However, these weren't the only beings that Xaran found at the top of the Peaks of Patience. Many called these mountains home, from the lowliest of vermin to the majestic eagles and hawks. There was a more profound hunter that made its home in the clouds above the Peaks, and its name was Khalas Skydancer. Most humans had never seen a dragon, and if they had they probably would have run in fear or attacked out of ignorance. The latter was the possibility that concerned Xaran the most. The evidence of which was the war between Cadaria and the dragons. It was started through ignorance and arrogance, and while Xaran did not have any right to make his opinion known, as a member of the Knights of the Flashing Blade, Xaran felt as though his ability to protect the Empire was being wholly dictated by a man who possibly was not intelligent enough to rule an Empire. But that was not for someone such as Xaran to decide. The Lorien line had been touched by the Creator and destined to lead the Cadarian Empire before there was a Cadaria, and Kaitain Lorien was a descendant of that line.

Xaran's thoughts turned back to Khalas Skydancer. Their first meeting had been a truly memorable one. As Xaran sat on the highest peak, he listened to all around him and heard something moving on the wind. It was something so large that it could change the very pattern of the wind without disturbing the clouds. It radiated awe and fear at the same time, so much so that the other animals around the peak cowered in terror. Yet Xaran sat silently and still, unaffected by fear or curiosity. It was as if he were a single reed standing proud in a hurricane. Later Xaran had learned that it was this placid tendency that had intrigued Khalas, and had perhaps spared Xaran's life. As Xaran remember the first meeting, he felt the swirling of the winds around him again, the same motion that always alerted him to the presence of his friend.

"Greetings my great friend, you seem to be disturbed today."

Xaran's voice was calm and soothing as always. Emotion was an ally so long as emotion was controlled. It was when emotion was let loose that it began to cause problems. Those who were ruled by their emotions were erratic, difficult to control or predict, and often more of a danger to themselves than they were to their enemies. One who could control their emotions and make them a tool were the most dangerous in the world because they could focus all of their emotions when it was most needed and become a truly frightening weapon.

"And you seem as pliable as always, Xaran," the great beast's voice answered.

The swirling of the wind stopped and Xaran knew that the Great Cloud Dragon had come to a rest on a nearby outcropping or rock. Despite its size, Khalas was nimble, quick, and very light on his massive feet.

"Water too seems pliable my large friend, but water has a way of making its own path when it needs to."

A great laugh hit the air and washed over Xaran like a wave.

"It is so rare to find wisdom in one of your people Xaran. And it is a shame that it is not someone like you who will take the human race into its golden age. With the rule of your Kaitain Lorien, I doubt there will be a golden age for humans on this world. What has he taken to calling himself now? Dragonsbane is it? The arrogance."

"All of us must do what we are destined to do," Xaran responded after a moment. "To know the path chosen for you and to choose not to walk it would bring discord to the harmony of the universe. Isn't it you who once told me that everything gravitates toward balance between the furies of the world? Order, Chaos, Good, Evil; they must all be in balance otherwise the universe will take steps to rectify the imbalance, sometimes with disastrous results."

Xaran could hear the dragon reach up with one of its clawed hands and scratch its long beard. During their many visits, Xaran had created a picture of Khalas in his mind, and he could see the wizened old dragon now in his mind, scratching his chin and smiling looking down at the much smaller human. To think that he would find such a friend in this time was nearly impossible.

"You might have made a good dragon, Xaran, if the Creator had been kind to you and blessed you with a noble birth. But I suppose that everyone has their purpose, and yours apparently is to remind me that not all humans are worthless prey."

Xaran let the jibe pass over him without reaction. The two often played with gentle insults, the kind that were usually leveled in court where an open insult could mean death.

"I trust that the Creator has a plan for me, and if he does not, the universal balance certainly does. My comrade Vallic has often told me that balance has a mind of its own, and at times balance and the Creator do not agree and balance must go its own way."

Xaran could feel Khalas smile.

"Your friend is very wise, Xaran. If there is time, I should like to meet him."

Xaran nodded.

"I am sure that he would like that."

Silence stood between the two friends for a moment. It was obvious to Xaran that Khalas was avoiding something, and that there was a thought in his mind that was grating on him.

"In answer to your unspoken question," Xaran started slowly, "the Emperor has given standing orders to all members of the Flashing Blade that they are to destroy any dragon on sight."

Khalas growled.

"And is that to be the end of our relationship then? A fight?"

Xaran smiled and stood gently from his position, his hands outstretched.

"Since I have yet to see a dragon, I cannot very well carry out my orders."

The laughter that hit the air was a mixture of relief and delight. Many times Xaran and Khalas had sat speaking about a great deal of topics ranging from the divine to the mundane, and Xaran had heard his friend laugh many times, but never like this. Perhaps there had been doubt in Khalas' mind as to whether or not he would have to make an enemy out of his good friend.

"I see that you are adhering to the letter of the decree and not the spirit."

Xaran frowned.

"You seem almost disappointed my friend. Isn't it you who once told me not to believe the spirits for they always have their own agenda. That every lie has mostly truth, and those who speak in riddles are the wisest of us all? To ignore the greatest of my teachers would be an insult to not only myself, but also to you."

Khalas pondered the thought for a moment, and then produced an item from a large pack that hung beneath its wing. Many dragons had taken to utilizing such satchels to carry valuable items, as it was easier to protect them with their impressive abilities. Xaran could feel the item as soon as it was produced. It radiated a great power, a power unlike anything he had ever felt before. The item was magical that much was for certain, but when compared to the magic that enchanted Xaran's staff known as Faith, the item was a river where as Faith was a droplet of water.

"I bring you a gift my good friend from the assembled Council of Dragons. I am a member of the group known as the Nine and Nine, this fact I reveal to you here where only the air can hear us. In the beginning of all things, there was the Creator and the Dragons. We are the sons and daughters of the Creator's love, his first children and in our opinion the pinnacle of his powers. When the Creator laid out the worlds that would carry his works, his progeny, and all other manner of thing, it was the dragons that named everything. Plants got their names from us, as did all manner of beasts. It was one of our race that coined the term human. Because of this, the dragon race has always seen itself as the right hand of the Creator; an extension of his power and an extension of his love."

Xaran sat back down upon the stone, letting the knowledge flow into him. It was obvious there was much more to the story, but for Khalas' part, it was quite possible that there was only so much that Xaran would understand.

"In the beginning there were ninety-nine breeds of dragons, and the greatest of each of the breeds formed what was then known as the Council of the Winds. In order to ensure that all facets of the universe; Order, Chaos, Good, Evil, Balance, were represented, each member of the Nine and Nine became a champion of a facet or a combination thereof. Eleven of us for each combination. That way there could never be a stalemate among any group, and there could never be a stalemate in the whole of the dragon race. We would always have direction. In the centuries and millennia that would follow, this ruling council would continue, even as more breeds of dragon were born. Now, as the war between the humans and the dragons begins again, we are faced with a choice that we should never have to make."

Xaran let the information sweep through him and tried hard not to come to any conclusions. However, there was one statement that would not leave Xaran's mind. It gnawed at him as the moments of silence passed.

"You said the war was beginning again?"

Khalas sighed. It was obvious from the labored breath that this was not a happy subject for Khalas and it appeared to Xaran that the ancient dragon was trying to pick his words carefully.

"Not many of your race are very perceptive my friend," Khalas said after a moment. "And because of that, much of the truth of the origin of the universe had to be hidden from you. However, you do not see like other mortals, and you are not so closed into your perception of reality that you cannot grasp the truth. For that reason, I will be able to make you understand one of the most basic and most important facts that you will ever know in your life."

It was Xaran this time that took a deep breath. For much of his life Xaran realized that there was more to his existence than that he had come to know as reality. A great haze stood between him and the truth he sought, but the more Xaran learned from the dragon Khalas, the more the veil of haze seemed to lift. Answers were there, just beyond his reach, and before long, they would be within his grasp.

"There are other worlds, other realities that the Creator oversees, and his agents make sure that the balance is maintained across the entire span of the universe. On many of these worlds, humans are the dominant species as they are here. However, on most of the worlds, humans have not yet crawled from the primordial ooze. On one of these worlds several thousand years ago, the dragons and the humans tried to co-exist. However, like what is beginning here, dragons were mistrusted and feared because of their tendencies and their power. That fear eventually became hate as it seemingly always does. Then the war started. The pathetic humans of that world tried to bring us down with their primitive weapons, and tried to kill us with their sheer numbers. At first, we simply defended ourselves, as they were unable to truly harm us. As the war stretched on, you humans began to learn quickly how to harm us, and before long, one of our number was killed by a man who fashioned himself an expert dragon hunter. This victory was heralded through the land and more of these dragon hunters arose. It was then that the war escalated and the dragons began to fight harder. We began to attack the human cities, we began to exact revenge for the horrible crime of the death of one of our own."

Xaran nodded.

"And how many did you kill to exact this revenge?"

Khalas snorted.

"We warned the humans early on that the death of any dragon would result in the death of one hundred thousand of their own."

For a long moment Xaran could not speak. One hundred thousand humans was nearly the entire population of the Kingdom of Menoris. Granted that was the smallest of Cadaria's kingdoms, but the loss was no less staggering.

"You think us cruel?"

Xaran shook his head without hesitation.

"The dragons are old and powerful beings with limited number. In comparison, humans are not even infants and must seem like annoying ants to you. Would we hesitate to kill a colony of thousands of ants if they took our food? I think you reacted as we would."

This time Khalas fell silent. Xaran could feel something from the dragon, a strong emotion that he had never felt from his friend before. It felt almost like regret.

"As I said Xaran," Khalas said after a moment, "you are much wiser than most of your race. You humans are very much like we were in our beginning. We were brash, undisciplined, and our power threatened to destroy us until we learned that the power we had was not ours to wield. It was a gift to us from the Creator and should only be used with the full understanding of the consequences of such an action. When the humans attacked us, we thought we were invulnerable. We thought our age and our power protected us from those so much weaker than us. It was this arrogance that did not allow us to see your resourcefulness, and did not allow us to accept the simple fact that if we let the conflict escalate we would feel some of the loss. The outrage caused by the loss of one of our own sent the Council into a murderous frenzy. Dragons began to slay humans by the hundreds without need for revenge any more. Most of my race felt the humans had to be exterminated. And so we killed. And killed. And killed. Finally, the only creatures left standing on the cinder of a planet were the dragons."

Khalas fell silent again, the sorrow deepening in his voice, and his breathing becoming labored.

"And what did the Creator do?"

Khalas stopped breathing for a long moment and then laughed.

"None of my brethren would believe that a human could perceive the fact that we are accountable to the Creator for anything, even the destruction of a planet full of humans."

Xaran smiled.

"You said it best yourself my friend. The dragons are an extension of the Creator's power. If the Creator allowed that power to be used for such destruction, the cosmic balance that he works so hard to protect would be easily shattered. So, in order to rebalance the universe, the Creator would have had to take action against his children."

Khalas laughed again.

"And so he did. The Creator, in the first of his sweeping changes to the universe, decreed that the dragons would have to atone for their great sin. The Creator cast us to the mercy of the universe, and we were not allowed to find rest on any world without the express permission of the humans of that world."

Xaran was stunned.

"So the Creator consigned you to a fate that was controlled by the whims of the humans?"

"The Creator is not without a sense of poetic irony and poetic justice my friend. We drifted for many centuries and were turned away from many worlds before one of our number made a deal with a group of humans from a planet very far from here several millennia ago. The chief of their group was a man by the name of Dorovar. He was a religious figure not unlike your Hannah Ironheart, a truly pious man that believed in the good of all of the Creator's creatures. So we executed the deal that allowed the dragons to make a home on that world."

Xaran felt the next part of the story in the back of his mind, like a dagger in his mind's eye.

"And the cycle started again."

Xaran could hear Khalas nod.

"It took several years, but the fear and mistrust spread again, followed by the inevitable hatred. However, unlike the first humans that we had encountered, these humans were far more adept at causing harm. Somehow they had learned to control the elements in a manner that you refer to as magic. This time the war was far bloodier, and we suffered many losses. However, the result of the battle was far more devastating. The magic employed by the humans and the powers used by we dragons made the core of the planet unstable. If we had stayed there, the dragon race would have ceased to exist. So, in order to finish our deal, we tricked the man named Dorovar and gave him the gift of immortality in order to escape our bond to the world. We fled the planet and left the mortals there to burn in their ignorance and hatred."

It was at that moment that Xaran's stomach turned. The thought of such a bargain being executed and such a fate befalling two worlds full of people was impossible to imagine. And yet, had happened.

"And did you have to make a deal to come to rest here?"

Khalas took a moment before answering.

"This is actually the fifth world that we have inhabited after the destruction of our first home. Luckily for us, the humans on the other worlds were still in their early years of development and understanding, and we used our powers to help guide and control them. Once the humans began to show signs of the fear and resentment, we concluded our deals and found another home. The same was true on this world. We came here when you were just beginning to realize the extent of your consciousness, and so our representative executed a deal. However, we were betrayed. The deal we executed with the humans became null and void on the Day the Heavens Fell. The Creator changed the rules for us, and therefore, our deal with the mortals cannot be concluded. This is our world now, no matter what happens, so that is why I have approached you my friend. We must find a way to stop this war from concluding in the same was that it did on Dorovar's world. My gift to you from the Council is our attempt to secure your aid in our endeavors. We have much information to share with you my friend, and I hope that you will trust me long enough to hear what the Council has to say. If you do not believe us, or do not trust us, I will guarantee your safe passage to and from the Council, and after the meeting if you choose to go to your Emperor and assist him in our extermination, I will understand."

Xaran stood and brushed the dust off his clothes and took up his staff.

"My friend, I will hear what your Council has to tell me, and then if I decide to assist you I will accept your gift, otherwise I am sure it will be destined for someone more worthy than myself. A great sage once taught me that to accept a gift without knowing the cost was akin to embracing a dagger by the blade."

Khalas bent low and allowed Xaran to reach for his long mane and ease slowly onto the dragon's massive back.

"This sage must have been very wise."

Xaran smiled.

"I only know his words, not his face or his name. He came to me once in a dream and taught me lessons the likes of which I could never forget should I live to be a thousand years old."

Khalas laughed as they began to glide through the air.

"I know this man of which you speak, and if you are lucky, you may live long enough to meet him."

Seeing in Darkness

Year Two of the Just Emperor Kaitain "Dragonsbane" Lorien, Creator's Calendar Year 1869

Deep in the darkest reaches of the Kingdom of Night, Galateria, there lay a small twisting valley near the center of a group of mountains in the northern reaches of the kingdom. The entrance to the valley had been long forgotten, and could only be reached from high above, from a small path in the rock face several miles up. At the northern tip of the valley lay the entrance to a cave, the inhabitants of which were perhaps the most sought individuals on the face of Espre.

In the whole of the world there were very few pure-blooded members of Clan Forer left, and so the talent for being able to see the future was a dying ability. Other than the Dark Seer, the only known seers were the enigmatic women known as the Maldovrin Triplets. A great many would-be heroes had tried to find the way to meet with the Triplets, but few who found them ever returned from the journey. The mountain passes in the Kingdom of Galateria were always treacherous, the home of some of the most undesirable criminals and beasts. However, the man that sought the wisdom of the Triplets was no ordinary man. Tolon Morr was the sworn servant of the Emperor of Cadaria, a Knight of the Flashing Blade, and more than that, he was a soldier. The Emperor of Cadaria gave him the mission to find the Triplets and ask a question of them, and that he would do. This was to be the test of his loyalty to his new master, and the position of Amethyst Knight did not come without a price. However, the promise of power and status could not be ignored, and the greatest honor that could be bestowed upon a citizen of the Kingdom of Steel, Celidar had fallen finally at the feet of Tolon.

It had taken three weeks to find the entrance to the twisted valley, and by that time, Tolon had been forced to kill several dozen criminals and beasts. From the criminals Tolon removed a finger as proof; proof that he would use to buy the loyalty of the local magistrates of Galateria. It was always good to have friends, but it was better to have friends that you were positive could not betray you. The climb down into the valley was a difficult one, and a lesser man would have fallen to his death. When Tolon reached the floor of the valley, there were many skeletons marking the fate of others who tried to find the blessing of the Triplets.

Tolon had heard stories of the Triplets over the years, most of which he discounted as myths. The Triplets were supposed to be touched by the Creator, blessed with incredibly long life and the ability to see the future with pure and unerring clarity. On top of that, the blessing of the Creator was supposed to make each of the women incredibly beautiful and utterly desirable to both men and women. It was said that no man or woman could refuse a request of the Triplets, and it was supposed that was why so many had not returned from seeking their guidance. It all seemed foolish to Tolon. There was no woman that walked Cadaria that he could not refuse if he chose to, and no manner of witchcraft could slay his mind.

When Tolon found the entrance to the cave, the first bit of fear began to creep into his mind. What if the stories had been true, and this mission that the Emperor had sent him on was a fool's errand? Would the Just Emperor send him on a mission that he could not survive? Tolon shook the thoughts away. The Emperor would not send him on an easy mission. This was to be a test of his abilities, and it could not be a true test if anyone could accomplish the deed. The reward was worth the risk. So, holding his breath, Tolon stepped into the cave and followed the dim light that led toward the back of the cavern.

For several minutes, Tolon followed the faint light ahead of him, and finally reached a portion of the cavern that widened into something akin to a great hall. It nearly rivaled the size of the Emperor's audience chamber.

The entire floor of the cavern was covered with a thick red and gold embroidered rug, and fabulously crafted golden lanterns hung from the walls adding a great deal of light to the chamber. Three chairs sat at the far end of the chamber, and appeared from a distance to be made of gold with satin cushions. There were many tapestries hanging from the cave walls depicting scenes from Cadaria's history, the largest of which was the Day the Heavens Fell. Taking a deep breath, Tolon strode further into the chamber.

"That is far enough, Sir Tolon Morr," a beautiful female voice rang out from seemingly everywhere in the chamber, "you have disturbed us."

Tolon stopped in his tracks and quickly dropped to one knee. The Emperor had reminded Tolon to treat the Triplets as though they were the equal of the Emperor in every way.

"I apologize for the intrusion great seers. I have brought a request from the Just Emperor of Cadaria, Kaitain Lorien. He asks only for your indulgence and your assistance in a matter of some urgency."

A moment later three women dressed in black appeared before the chairs at the back of the cavern. Each of them was strikingly beautiful with delicate ivory skin and flawless features. They were not quite identical, but were similar of build and posture. Each stood tall and straight, graceful like a statue. The sister to the far left had very short hair, no longer than the bottoms of her ears, and her pale blue eyes shone out brightly despite the light in the chamber. Her dress clung to her body as though it were not really there, an extension of her skin only. The gown that stretched all the way to her ankles accentuated every feature. The middle sister stood slightly taller than the other two, her shoulder length hair glistening and in the light seemed to move as though blown by a breeze though no air moved in the chamber. Her dark green eyes were not as bright as her sisters' but seemed deeper and full of life and power. On the end stood the shortest of the three, nearly head and shoulders shorter than the middle sister. She had a childlike innocence in her eyes that seemed to be tempered by a great wisdom. Tolon could almost see the burden that she bore on her soul, as though it were a great anchor that kept her soul from ascending to the heavens.

"You have sought out the Maldovrin Triplets for your Emperor," the middle sister said. "It has been long since we have received such a request."

"Jania," the shortest sister said softly looking up at the tallest, "I do not think this one knows the true nature of his visit, and the information we could give him would be dangerous."

"Jerrica is right, Jania," the first sister added softly, "I do not think we can trust this one with the information the Emperor wishes."

"That is enough, Jordyne," Jania chided. "It is impolite to have such conversations in front of our guest. Let us hear what the young knight has to say, and perhaps we will learn to trust him as the Emperor has."

The three sisters nodded in unison and then sat. With a single motion from Jania, Tolon approached slowly, confusion beginning to cloud his mind. The way the three women spoke, it was almost as though they knew what the Emperor had written in the letter than he carried. Inwardly Tolon wondered if they knew of the orders that the Emperor had given him, and the duty that he was to carry out upon receiving the information. When Jerrica looked Tolon in the eye and her polite smile changed into a frown, Tolon thought that it was all over for him. The extent of the powers of the Triplets had been rumored at, but no one had brought back any tales to corroborate or dispute the rumors.

"I do not like this one," Jerrica said after Tolon's approach was halted by Jania's outstretched hand, "he schemes and plots and uses women for the basest of purposes. His mind is up to no good where it concerns us as well my sisters. You should see the perverse pictures in his head."

Jordyne laughed.

"The thoughts he had about what he would do with you are most amusing dear sister," Jordyne teased. "How long has it been since such requests were made of us?"

Tolon could see Jerrica shiver.

"Do not even joke about such things, sister. I do believe though that he is much fonder of you and Jania than he is of me however. In fact right now he has some interesting thoughts about what the two of you could do together."

Both Jordyne and Jerrica laughed, but Jania remained silent. Tolon was mortified. He closed his eyes for a moment and tried to purge all of his thoughts and think of nothing more than the letter that lay in his satchel from the Emperor. That was the purpose of this mission, nothing more. He would have to control himself, even the thoughts that he did not know he had. When his eyes reopened, there was a knowing grin on Jania's face.

"It seems that this one may serve his purpose well. There is no duplicity within him. He wishes only to fulfill his mission and nothing more. Very well, Sir Tolon Morr, we shall hear the requests from the Cadarian Emperor."

Tolon breathed a quick sigh of relief and then retrieved the scroll from his satchel and unrolled it. With a quick clearing of his throat, Tolon began to read the words so delicately scribed upon the parchment.

"Great Seers, it is my honor to be allowed to request your wisdom and advice at this time. Because I know that your time is precious, I shall not take up more of it with meaningless platitudes and shall come to the point. A certain artifact has come to my attention, one that could aid Cadaria in its war against the dragons and the Dark Empire of Mythryn. In order to save my people, I must know where this artifact is stored and how to retrieve it. If it is within your power, great seers, I must request that you tell me the location of the Dragon's Tear."

Tolon put away the scroll and looked across the faces of the Triplets. They exchanged some simple glances between them, neither seeming alarmed nor surprised. It was as if they knew the request had been coming. Tolon continued to wait for several moments before Jania spoke.

"The Cadarian Emperor asks much of those who do not claim to be part of his Empire. And what boon does the Emperor propose to offer us in exchange for this vital information to the safety of the Empire?"

Tolon had been waiting for that question. He quickly recovered a different scroll from his satchel, cracked open the seal, and held it out toward the Seer.

"Written on this parchment is a list of goods, services, and land that the Emperor is willing to offer in exchange for this information."

Jania took the scroll, looked over it briefly and then let it fall to the ground. Jerrica laughed softly.

"These offerings have no significance to us," Jordyne said slowly. "Your Emperor forgets that we are not simple women who have no sense of the world. We know about the wars that rage outside this valley, we know the price of the information better than anyone. No amount of land or goods will be enough to pay for this. We require something more. We require something that will impress upon the Emperor the gravity of his situation and of the information that he requests."

Tolon took a deep breath and then spoke.

"We request," Jerrica said quickly, "that the woman known as the Ethereal Sorceress, Irene Drage be put to death by the hand of the Emperor himself. Once that price has been paid, we will deliver the information, and not until."

Tolon took a step back as if struck. The Triplets had just demanded the execution of the Imperial Sorceress. Such an insult would not be tolerated. Tolon reached to his belt and withdrew the ancient battle-axe named Strength that marked his position as the Amethyst Knight.

"I was sent by the Emperor to retrieve information, not relay demands. I have been authorized by Imperial Decree to execute you as enemies of the Empire if you do not relinquish the information."

Jania looked at Tolon for a moment and then laughed.

"And who is going to carry out this execution order, my dear Amethyst Knight? Is it going to be you and that axe of yours? Do you even know the true nature of the weapon that you so wickedly wield? Do you know how much blood was shed so that weapon could come to be? If you think you are strong enough little man, then try. Try to strike us all down right here and now, we will not resist you."

Tolon stood transfixed for a moment, not believing the challenge that had been laid before him. Then making the decision to carry out the orders of the Emperor, Tolon took a step forward…or at least he tried to. The muscles in his legs would not respond. It was as though all the will had been sapped from his body. Panic began to set in. What sort of magic had the women used against him to make his body rebel like this? He had been bewitched from the moment he stepped into the cave, and now he was at the mercy of the Triplets.

"He thinks it's us," Jerrica said flatly.

"Not a very bright one, is he?" Jordyne answered.

Jania stood the next moment and approached the frozen form of Sir Tolon Morr. Fear began to enter Tolon's heart, and he felt his life draining from his body.

"It is not we who have prevented you from carrying out your grizzly orders my dear knight. That is why we had no fear of you though we knew all along your ultimate motivations. The weapon that you wield is known as Strength. The will inscribed within the blade of the axe has but one lesson to teach. With great strength comes great responsibility, and those who cannot use the strength granted to them by this weapon will not use any strength at all. It is your own weapon that forbids your strike Tolon. Strength has a greater purpose before it, one that will not allow it to spill our blood and be subject to the consequences. Now, you will turn around and take your failure back to your Emperor. Tell him our terms, and if he is willing to carry them out, when you bring us back the head of the sorceress Irene Drage, we will give the information to you. However, the Emperor will not fulfill our demands because he is a pompous pig bent on the conquest of something he cannot hope to understand. From this day forward, we will hear no more requests from this Cadarian Emperor, and any who approach with such requests will be destroyed long before they see this valley. Thus is the decree of the Maldovrin Triplets."

The control over his body suddenly returned, Tolon lowered his weapon and locked his eyes on Jania's. There was a sadness there that Tolon could not understand, but with a single nod, Tolon turned and began the long trek home. When Tolon was well out of earshot, Jania turned to her sisters and shook her head.

"It is unfortunate that his fate will be what it is destined to be. His heart deserves so much more."

Jerrica and Jordyne nodded in agreement.

"However, if we interfere and prevent the tragedy that is going to come from his next actions, are we any better than the Emperor Lorien?" Jerrica asked.

Jania frowned.

"We have no choice."

"There is always choice, sister," Jordyne countered. "Choice is the only fate for beings like us. We must find a way to undo what will be done and still preserve the future that is destined for all of Cadaria."

"And how many thousands must die, sister?" Jerrica asked.

"Humans die," Jania answered flatly. "We must put our faith now in the agents of the Creator. He will do what he must to protect us."

* * * * * * * * * * * * *

Lightning flashed as the storm began to roll in over the vast and normally quiet countryside. It had been a long time since the sounds of warfare had echoed over this plot of land. The last great war had reached its climax here, a battle of such epic proportions that the gods themselves came down from their high perches and marveled at the brutality and ferocity of their creations. The ground ran red with the blood of hundreds of thousands, and for hundreds of years to come; the field would be called the Plain of Blood. It was said that nothing would grow on the torn and desecrated ground, and the more superstitious people swore that the souls of the men buried there would never rest because of the horror and utter mercilessness of their ends. Nearly two thousand years had passed since that fateful day when forces battled for ultimate supremacy in the world each fought to control. History would ultimately recognize the forces of Terrik Lorien as the victors of the war, but in the centuries of peace that followed no one would forget the sacrifices that it took to create that peace. There were no evil dictators or monsters that roamed the countryside, just quiet life. Years faded into decades, and decades to centuries. So many years had passed since the final blow of the Founding Wars had been struck, and now the lands quaked with the power of the storms that raged above. Something stirred on the barren, dormant Plain of Blood.

From a dark, twisted tree a hawk perched, surveying its territory. No predators roamed this land, for there was no game to be found. But as the hawk craned its neck, it spied something. A form, a silent dark form, stood amidst the wind, looking at the approaching storm. The hawk waited a heartbeat. It knew there would be little time before the storm would hit, maybe enough time for a single pass over the stoic figure, then it would have to wing toward the higher peaks of the Mountains of Pain to find shelter and outlast the coming heavenly assault. Gingerly, the hawk removed its talon-laden feet from the blackened bark of the old tree and let the strengthening wind flow under its unfolded wings. A steady current lifted it into the air, and effortlessly the hawk guided itself through the flows of wind toward the form. The hawk had seen many humans in its short existence, but there was something different about this form. While it may have been human in shape, with a very human looking cloak wrapped 'round, the smell that radiated from it was much different. The hawk lifted itself higher into the streams of wind and felt the first traces of water in the breeze. The storm was coming quicker than it had anticipated. After a moment, the hawk dove down and passed in front of the form at a very safe distance. For some reason, the hawk was leery of the form, much as it would be of a larger falcon or eagle. It was a respect, primal and deep.

* * * * * * * * * * * * *

Looking up into the sky, ancient eyes watched the hawk twirl in the wind and then retreat back toward the hard gray peeks of the mountains to the west. It was no doubt looking for shelter from the coming storm, but the man wondered if the creature knew that the storm was not one of natural origin. Lightning pulsed with the flow of blood through the man's veins, and as he looked up again at the advancing storm, a bolt of lightning erupted from the angry black mass and struck the magnificent creature, and it fell toward the ground, spinning out of control. The man sighed hard and raised his hand toward the heavens. The hawk righted itself after a moment and continued on its path toward the peeks as though nothing had occurred. A feeling surged through the form, he could feel the anger of the storm as he had deprived it of the kill it rightly deserved. But the anger was quelled quickly as it found solace in the fact that thousands of deaths would soon be caused by its mere presence. The cycle would begin anew, and the world would be bathed in the blood of the innocent.

The man felt a sick turn in the pit of his stomach, feeling the thoughts of the advancing storm. The carnage that would ensue would rival that of the Founding Wars, and could very well bring an end to all life if the storm had its way. Moments later, the first droplets of rain began to fall to the ground, but this was no ordinary rain. Where the drops should have been thin blue, there was thick, viscous red. A drop hit the man on the forehead, and after dabbing at it with his fingers and pressing them to his tongue, his fears were confirmed. The blood of the dead; the tears of the dying, were being cast to the ground as in the ancient prophecies, long forgotten even by the gods. It took only a thought for the man to shield himself from the falling blood-rain, but he stood transfixed, watching the scene that would play itself out in front of him.

Drops of blood ran together as they hit the ground, forming small pools and then soaking deep into the soil. Sudden vivid flashes hit the man's mind. He saw the thousands of dead and dying strewn over the plain screaming and crying in agony as hundreds more were struck down. Every flash of recognition was met with a twisted, contorted face, crying in pain, cursing the gods that made them to suffer at the hands of their own kind for no real purpose. On the battlefield there was neither good nor evil, just banners that flew, showing the colors and symbols of long-forgotten kingdoms. But as the man shook himself from thoughts of the distant past, he was mortified at the sight of the split earth and the deformed form that pulled itself from the ground.

Luckily no flesh still clung to the body that had lain in the earth for a thousand years, but the torn and tattered uniform looked as though it had survived its long sleep well. The red fabric hung loose from the skeletal remains as they moved, and the remaining pieces of armor clattered as the infernal thing emerged from its grave. The bone, yellow and dull from its long slumber moved as though it was still laden with flesh and muscle, and the man watched the thing stretch like a man crawling out of his bed from a nap. When it turned toward the ancient form, a light shown from under the damaged breastplate. A piece of steel shaft, apparently from the spear that had killed the former soldier was still piercing through, and a bright ruby light pulsed through the cracks. However, this dead soldier was not alone for long, as more skeletal troops rose from their interrupted eternal sleep. Some of the monstrosities still bore the devices of their old kingdoms, and as more of them rose, former enemies fell in ranks together. Pleasure seemed to flow from to storm as the skeletal legion formed up and began its long march through the plain. As the march continued, the form of the creatures changed. No longer were they the fallen soldiers of an age long passed. They were no living breathing men in appearance, wearing the device of the Kingdom of Water, Thorigald. The ancient form did not have to guess where this army was headed. The capital city of the Kingdom of Fire, the Ivory Towers of Saldarine, was only a few days march away, and the hundreds of thousands there would be a fitting sacrifice for the growing storm.

The form turned away from the departing army and pulled the hood of his cloak back. His hair had grayed at the temples over the thousands of years that had passed since his birth. His eyes did not shine with the same fire as they had when he watched the first of the many wars that would occur in his life finally ended thanks to his help. But that had caused the end of his home, the end of the life that he knew, and the end of peace in his heart and mind. It had also caused the death of his wife. But the purpose of his life had been sealed with the bargain that gave him the powers of a god. No matter how many worlds he had to watch die, no matter how many lives were destroyed because of his intervention, or were saved by the same, the purpose would not change. Evil could not be allowed to triumph, no matter the cost. Sighing to himself, the ancient man reached into his pocket, and pulled out a dark blue stone and shook his head as his frail hands pulled it apart slowly. As the portal formed, the ancient man silently prayed that the Will of the Creator would prevail this time, and that the cost would not be too high.

Chapter XLVII

Betrayal

*Year Two of the Just Emperor Kaitain "Dragonsbane" Lorien,
Creator's Calendar Year 1869*

Monsters surrounded her. They were beginning to close in as the seconds passed. The strength in her body had begun to fail, and there was no chance to defend against the next attack. Her armor shattered and her defenses down, it was only a matter of moments before her life would be ended…

…Hannah Ironheart woke with a start, drenched in blood and sweat. The thrashing during her dream had reopened one of the many wounds on her body, and blood began to drench the simple white sheet that covered her bandaged body. A healer would be at her side the next moment, working on the wound and trying to keep her calm. His voice fell on deaf ears. Hannah's mind was filled with a horror that shattered her normally placid heart. Quickly she began to recite a practiced prayer to the Creator in an effort to calm the fears that raged through her.

After several minutes of work, the wound had been closed again, and the healer had gone off to tend to other patients. Hannah found the quiet peacefulness again in her mind, but just as she started to close her eyes again, a voice intruded upon her self-imposed peace.

"Bad dreams?"

Hannah did not have to look to know the origin of the voice. Devlin Rannoch, the newest member of the Knight of the Flashing Blade had begun to make quite a reputation for himself in the Kingdom of Night Galateria. He had nearly single-handedly saved the capital city from destruction not once, but twice, and in that time had personally slain nearly a dozen dragons. On the battlefield, Devlin was possessed of great power, but also with great intelligence. His strikes were precise, and unlike some other soldiers and great warriors that Hannah had seen, there was no arrogance in his movements. No matter the level of danger the opponent presented, Devlin treated every battle as though his life was on the line and would not be the first to make a mistake in combat. Hannah wondered if the ability to underestimate was even in the half-breed's makeup.

Hannah nodded in response to the question after a moment, keeping her eyes closed and trying to maintain the fragile serenity of her spirit.

"I suppose even the most spiritually inclined of us can feel fear from time to time, eh?"

Hannah was not sure if the comment was meant as an insult or critical commentary on the state of the empire.

"And I suppose that the Hero of Galateria would not know the touch of fear?"

It was a tender jab at the rough exterior of her comrade, but Hannah would remember to pray for forgiveness for her rudeness and intolerance later. When Hannah opened her eyes finally and focused them on Devlin, he seemed amused at her comment.

"Lady Ironheart, if there is a day in my life that I have lived without fear of some kind or another, I would not remember it. When your body is twisted and your blood is tainted with that of the enemy of the empire that you wish to serve, there are those that would just as soon see you dead as follow you into combat. When I was just starting out in the army, before I left to find my own path, I often wondered if it would be the claws of a dragon that sealed my fate, or the blade of one of my supposed allies."

Hannah reflected for a moment and then shut her eyes again. To be sure, this young man had strange battles to fight both within and without. Perhaps Hannah had judged him too harshly, and had not taken the time to find the reasons for his appointment to the Flashing Blade. In time, Devlin could be a wonderful addition, if his motivations remained as pure as they were currently. His next words however would shock Hannah to the core and change the way she looked at everything.

"I guess you and I have a lot in common then, Lady Ironheart. You now know the same fear as I, considering the Emperor ordered me to make sure you didn't leave Galateria alive."

* * * * * * * * * * * * *

"*Just what the hell to you think you are doing?*"

More often than not, the voice was an annoyance, today however, the level of distraction was elevated and prescient in a way it had never been before. Unlike most conversations, the conversation between the voice and Devlin could take place in a fraction of the time. As quick as a thought, the battle of words would raise, and Hannah Ironheart sat only a few feet away pondering her response to the revelation.

"I'm doing what I need to do. The order was wrong and you know it. I was playing the good little soldier boy, and then I saw her fight, and I saw that man give up his life for her. If she would have run, if she would have let those Jeresei cut down the sick and innocent, then maybe I could have justified the Emperor's orders. But now, I would much rather have her as an ally than an enemy."

"*And at the same time you are making an enemy of the Emperor of Cadaria. Very very bright decision.*"

"Yes, well," Devlin thought for a moment, "I don't seem to be alone in that category."

The voice stayed silent for a long few moments before finally speaking again. It had always shared Devlin's mind, and there was no thought that Devlin could hide from it. Devlin never knew the source of the voice, and it had taken a few years when he was young to realize that not every person had a voice in their head that talked to them. Most people simply thought he was an eccentric child with a vivid imagination. Others thought it was a madness brought on by his unusual heritage. While Devlin had never ruled out the fact that it was due to his heritage, the fact that it might have been a madness was a certainty.

"Now that is the most insane thought you have ever had. You can't be seriously thinking about making a move against the Emperor of Cadaria."

"I'm not thinking anything…"

"Remember," the voice cautioned, *"you can't lie to me. I know every thought before it even enters that puny brain of yours. What you are considering is pure suicide. Even if she believes you, and even if she decides that you are no longer a threat to her life, the chances on her actually assisting you in overthrowing the Emperor is laughable. There is a better chance that she will run you through at the first opportunity for treason and take your fool head back to the Emperor to buy her way back into his good graces. You've just failed your test and outlived your usefulness my dear boy."*

"We shall see…"

* * * * * * * * * * * * *

Shock filled Hannah's body and mind. Even if what the brash young man had said was true, what was his motivation for telling her? Surely he knew that his life would end one way or another at the uttering of those words. If he had truly been sent to kill Hannah, then the Emperor would destroy him for his failure, or Hannah would murder him at the first opportunity. If he was telling the truth, as soon as the Emperor learned of his treachery, the decree for his immediate termination would soon follow. There was no endgame here that would benefit Devlin Rannoch, and so, Hannah decided, it must have been the truth.

Through sheer force of will, Hannah pulled herself to a sitting position, much to the dismay of the healers that were still tending to patients in other portions of the makeshift hospital. Devlin's voice had been low enough to that point that no one else could have heard his words, but now, there was need for more privacy, privacy that could not be found among the sick and dying.

CHAPTER 47

"Lady Ironheart, please," the healer said rushing to her side, "you must lay still, otherwise you risk losing more blood and perhaps dying."

Hannah ignored the healer's pleas and gently swung her legs to the side of the bed and let her feet touch the cool wooden floor. Pain was rocketing through her body, and she knew it was only a matter of time before she would feel the rush of hot blood against her skin again.

"My weapon."

There was a look of shock on the healer's face, unsure how to respond. Devlin while surprised at the woman's strength did not discount her fortitude as quickly as the healer had. He retrieved the war mace from the side of the bed and offered it to Hannah. The moment Hannah felt Spirit return to her hand, a warm rush of power and vitality filled her. It was as though a light had been sparked inside her. All around her she could see the wispy trails of the spirits of the dead that still clung to the dying in the room. Some refused to relinquish their hold on the mortal world, while others lingered, waiting for their loved ones to join them on their trek to the heavens. They all suddenly looked to Hannah and Spirit, feeling her power and love radiating through them. In that same instant, Hannah could feel their gratitude and freedom pass through her, steeling her. The effect was akin to that of the salve being spread across a wound. The pain in Hannah's body eased, and the power Spirit wielded slowly began to knit some of the smaller wounds on her body. After a moment, Hannah pulled herself to her feet, much to the shock of the healers in the room. It was inspirational for not only the living in the room, but the spirits of the dead as well. Hannah held the sheet wrapped tightly around her, but her thought was not to her own modesty, but more of respect to her position as the High Priestess.

"We have much to speak about, Devlin," Hannah said softly, but with power returning to her voice, "but we must do so someplace more private."

Devlin nodded and began to lead the way to the home of the Onyx Knight, the home that Devlin had recently come into possession of.

"Looks like the new tenant will have a similar fate to that of the previous one," the voice said softly in the back of Devlin's mind.

* * * * * * * * * * * * *

The estate of the Onyx Knight was little more than a small house on the northern end of the city of Galateria. The previous champion had not been one for finery or for the opulence that his position could have afforded him; he instead preferred to live as those that he protected did. Perhaps that is what set the members of the Flashing Blade apart from all others in the empire. These thirteen warriors were supposed to be the greatest in the Empire, more formidable than any fighting force that could be assembled, and they carried with them the sanction of the Emperor in all actions that they took, provided it was within the laws set down by the Empire. They could act as judge, jury, and executioner in all matters of law, and answered to only one law and one justice, that of the Emperor. There was no position within any of the individual kingdoms, not lord, not general, that could give them an order. And yet, none of their number took advantage of this position in the way that most could. None had huge palaces, or shrines in their honor. None demanded huge wages, or bounties for their deeds. They each drew a modest salary from the Imperial Treasury, and were granted what land they needed in the kingdom they called home. The only real reward for their service came upon their retirement, when they were awarded a parcel of land and drew a pension for the rest of their lives. In the nearly two thousand years since the formation of the Knights of the Flashing Blade, only five had ever made it to retirement, and three of those died shortly afterward of advanced old age. It was understood that an appointment to the Knights of the Flashing Blade could have only one true ending, death in the service of the Empire. The position was its own reward. To be recognized as one of the thirteen most powerful warriors in the Empire of Cadaria was an honor. One that seemed to be perverted by the new emperor.

Devlin had heard of the appointments made to the Flashing Blade by Kaitain Lorien, and he had been sickened by them. Devlin had manipulated himself into the position. Jaccob Aldora and Tolon Morr had been appointed because they would be easy for the Emperor to control. Now the Emperor was obviously trying to rid himself of those he thought could be a threat. It was certainly a transparent effort. Now, there was a possibility it could backfire, if and only if Hannah would hear Devlin's proposal.

CHAPTER 47

Hannah sat on the only chair in the receiving room in the Onyx Knight's estate, while Devlin stood leaning against one of the four onyx pillars that stood in the center of the room. Lanterns hung along the walls and at the top of each of the pillars casting enough light in the room that the two knights could clearly see each other's expressions. Devlin could also see blood beginning to seep from several of the bandaged wounds on Hannah's legs and sides. As if in answer to Devlin's silent concern, Hannah smiled, and waved her hand dismissively.

"Spirit has begun to heal my wounds. My friend will not let me suffer so long as the Creator shines His love upon me."

Devlin nodded wordlessly.

"So, Devlin Rannoch, you should enlighten me as to the substance of this order from our beloved Emperor."

Even seeing the look on the Celestine Knight's face, Devlin could not tell if there was a note of sarcasm in her words or not.

"Shortly after you arrived, I received orders from the Emperor through one of his agents. The orders were simple. You had been named as a traitor to the empire, and as such I was to make sure you were executed. However, because to name you openly as a traitor could have negative repercussions in the Kingdom of Stone, and with other worshipers of the Creator within the Empire, your death was supposed to be in battle. As such, I was instructed to use my connections to those who openly followed the Dark Gods of Mythryn to prepare a trap for you. If those creatures failed, it was to be my blade that would end your life and service to the Empire."

Hannah drank in the words slowly, and then commented.

"Emperor Lorien was not concerned about the response of the Kingdom of Stone. He was worried about the response of my husband."

Devlin looked at her puzzled for a moment.

"Gregor Quicksilver," Hannah answered the silent question.

A smile crept to Devlin's face. It all now began to make sense. Gregor was sent off on a not-so-secret mission to the Dark Continent of Mythryn to eliminate any response to the death of Hannah Ironheart if it were discovered that she had been assassinated at the command of the Emperor.

"And now Gregor is on the other side of the world fighting the Dark Gods so that he would not take revenge against me or the Emperor for your death," Devlin responded quickly.

Hannah nodded wordlessly.

"Now, Lady Ironheart. Why would the Emperor consider you a traitor to the Empire and order your death? I would think that Kaitain Lorien would view you as one of his most powerful allies, and keeping you in the fold would also ensure the loyalty of your husband…"

"You are putting far too much faith in the relationship between Gregor and I, Devlin. If Gregor had to make a choice between his loyalty to me and his loyalty to the Empire, there would be no choice. Gregor serves the Empire first, at the cost of all else."

Devlin shook his head.

"So he will defend Kaitain to the death…wonderful."

Hannah smiled.

"You listened my young friend, but you did not hear. I said that Gregor would serve the Empire first, not the Emperor. Gregor believes that despite the fact that the Lorien line was touched by the Creator and destined to lead the Cadarian Empire, the emperor is not larger than the Empire itself. There are others in the Flashing Blade that feel the same way. We will defend the Emperor as that is our mandate, but we will not do so at the expense of the Empire. When the Emperor himself becomes a threat to the empire, then he must be removed."

Devlin smiled.

"You know, Lady Ironheart, you are coming dangerously close to treason with that line of thought. No wonder the emperor wants you dead."

After a moment, Hannah shook her head.

"That is not why Kaitain wants me dead, I am sure. If my hunch is correct, Kaitain has discovered my familial connection to the Dark Kingdom of Mythryn. The current Queen of Mythryn is my sister, Sadrina Annis, formerly Sadrina Ironheart of Albitonin."

"I knew it," the voice said in the back of Devlin's mind. *"It was obvious there was something else. Now do you see why she has to die? She is a traitor. She is obviously in collusion with the Dark Kingdom, and the Emperor wants her dead for it."*

"She is no more in collusion with the Dark Kingdom than I am, old man," Devlin responded in his mind. "The fact that her sister has fallen into shadow doesn't implicate her at all."

Devlin loosed the belt that held his scabbard to his side and let it fall to the ground. There was no need to remain armed, and to show a gesture of faith to his guest, Devlin stood unarmed. If Hannah wanted, she could have easily struck him down before he could act. Hannah, seeing the gesture, let Spirit rest on the ground beside her, far enough out of reach that she could not easily retrieve it, but still close enough that she could benefit from its restorative effects.

"So tell me, Devlin Rannoch, how is it you were able to rally forces to commit this murder, and who is this Syren Belloch that attacked me?"

Devlin eased back against the column and looked at one of the hanging lanterns, collecting his thoughts.

"When I was young, the people here in Galateria had no problem accepting me, but as I grew older and my dragon features became more prominent, it was more difficult. So, I left when I was old enough to protect myself. I wandered for a while, and was approached many times by agents of the Dark Empire to join their cause. I even met one of the Dark Gods once. Nice woman by the way."

Hannah didn't react to the comment, but made mental note to ask about that experience later.

"So, I was able to keep in touch with some of the agents from time to time, and would assist them against the dragons when they began to encroach on the borders of Mythryn or Galateria. It paid well, and it was an opportunity to strike back at those that cursed me with this twisted body. So, when it came time, I called in a favor. I was expecting something a little more traditional, one of the Dark Guard perhaps. I had never seen this Syren before until she arrived and attacked you. I have heard rumors about her through. It is said that she lives on the essence of others. She is a kind of an energy vampire, draining the soul, the essence of her victims, and then leaving them a mindless husk. It is said that she and her progeny are some of the more dangerous and unpredictable of the servants of the Dark Gods, and that more often than not they follow their own agenda. If it can be believed that they serve the Dark Gods at all."

Hannah frowned.

"Almost as though they knew who to send against me. Perhaps my polar opposite. My goal being to save souls and send them to the Creator, while her goal is to destroy them to extend her life. Perhaps we have all underestimated the cunning of our enemy."

"I think that may be the problem," Devlin responded at once, "seeing them as our enemy. I have had many dealings with the Dark Kingdom over the years, and they have always behaved more like they are shown in the old stories. Wanting to live out their time in prison here and make their way the best they can. I do not believe that they would take the fight to Cadaria if Cadaria did not bring the fight to them."

Hannah smiled.

"Now it seems you are the one dangerously close to treason my young comrade. The Emperor would surely have you cast out and murdered as a sympathizer if you were to ever voice those opinions openly."

"Had I not met them," Devlin said, "perhaps I never would have formed my opinions."

Allowing herself to relax, Hannah remembered a lesson Xaran Firesoul once taught her after a meeting of the Flashing Blade that had ended in an argument over the state of affairs with the dragons of Cadaria.

"You should not judge those you have never met, for seeing the actions without knowing the motivations can cause irrevocable mistakes in judgment."

"Strange words coming from a servant of the Cadarian Empire," Devlin responded.

"I thought so too at the time," Hannah replied, "but perhaps we are the short-sighted ones. Sometimes it takes the blind to truly see."

"What the hell is she talking about?"

For a moment, Devlin wondered if that was the old man's voice, or his own.

"So tell me, young Onyx Knight, of this meeting with the Dark God."

* * * * * * * * * * * * *

It was a hot summer day, deep in the forbidden forests of the Kingdom of Night Galateria. Devlin had been tracking the adult Shadow Dragon for some time, but the darkness and the brush had made the tracks difficult to follow. It was wounded for sure, hundreds of arrows and the huge ballista bolt had pierced its abnormally thick hide, and the blood had spattered everywhere. Even with all of that, the dragon still had been too much for the detachment of Dark Guard that had been sent to deal with the incursion. For Devlin's part, he had helped all that he could, but all the tactics in the world could not have prepared them for the viciousness of the wounded beast. Only a handful of the one hundred and fifty soldiers still lived, and most of those that did would not for long. Attacking in mass as they had left them open to the dragon's devastating counter attack. The billowing cloud of gray death that had been vomited forth by the dragon had caused many to shrivel and die immediately. Some of the stronger warriors held on, hopelessly weakened. They would surely die soon enough, their vitality drained. Devlin had managed to escape the attack and rounded on the beast, striking it deeply in the neck, the blow that had caused the great beast to flee. Devlin had seen the tactic many times. The dragon would hit hard, fall back, and while the forces trailing it bunched up again, the dragon would spring the trap, loosing its breath upon them again, or swooping in with a well-placed sweep of its massive tail. After spending many years hunting dragons, Devlin had been able to learn most of their tactics and devise counters. However, this prey had proved to be more of a handful than expected.

Suddenly the trail went cold, and before Devlin could regain his senses, the great beast swooped in again. It was too fast, too accurate, and Devlin was about to feel the great teeth and jaws of the beast snap him in half. However, at the last moment a bolt of blue energy struck the massive beast in the chest, sending it spiraling sideways through a grove of trees. Many of the thick trunks were snapped by the weight of the dragon, but in the end, it was the dragon that lay broken against the trunk of a nearby tree. It would cause no more problem for the Kingdom of Galateria.

Devlin looked for the source of the attack, wanting to thank his savior, and then he saw her. The woman moved gracefully though the forest, the grass and the underbrush seeming to move out of her way by their own volition. Her pale blue eyes glowed in the soft light that penetrated the haze that constantly shrouded Galateria in darkness. But Devlin could see an additional glow there, something within the blue. There was an almost golden hue around the edges of her corneas, one that spoke of a hidden power. The woman approached slowly, then finally spoke.

"Are you injured?"

Devlin looked down at his arms, and aside from the standard cuts and bruises that went along with dragon hunting, there seemed to be no additional problems.

"I'm sure I'll be fine. I've had much worse."

The woman nodded.

"I'm sure you have, Devlin Rannoch. Thank you for your service to the Kingdom of Mythryn and to that of Galateria. I'm sure the Cadarian Emperor will gladly thank you and reward you for your quick work. Provided of course that you ensure that you do not mention our involvement. Working for the Dark Gods of Mythryn could shorted your life considerably."

Devlin stood silent for a moment. Was she saying what he thought she was saying?

"Yes Devlin. I am a Dark Goddess of Mythryn. You may call me Serrina. That name will serve as well as any other. My brothers and sisters will be very thankful for your work here, and if at any time you decide to make our relationship a more permanent one, we will be happy to receive you. But in the meantime, soldiers from Galateria will be here in a few minutes, it seems they have witnessed my little display. Take your credit Devlin Rannoch, and I hope that we will meet again."

Then, just as quickly as she appeared, the Dark Goddess was gone.

****

"Very interesting," Hannah said after a moment. "I never understood why my sister spoke so highly of the Dark Gods, and I never thought that they could show compassion or act out of anything other than their own self-interests. She could have just as easily let you be destroyed by the dragon or by the soldiers from Galateria. It is very interesting that she responded in the manner that she did."

Devlin nodded slowly, and then looked into Hannah's eyes. There was still much to do, still much to accomplish. But this was a delicate moment of transition. How would the Lady of Stone choose to act now?

"We have much to speak about Devlin, but for now I am tired. I fear that the agents of the Dark Kingdom are very adept at their vocation, and have done quite a bit of damage to my body. Within a day or two I should be fit to travel. And once I am, it will be time to act. We will need to see our allies if we are to take the necessary steps. First though, I have something that you must do, as I will not be able to do it myself."

Devlin frowned.

"Why do I get the feeling that I am not going to like this job?"

Hannah shook her head.

"If it were not for my condition, I would go myself. But if the Emperor has indeed learned of my connection to the Dark Queen Sadrina Annis, then he has surely learned of the fact that the Dark Princess is on her way here to sue for peace on behalf of Mythryn. There is no telling what will happen if an agent of the Emperor gets to her first. It could be the final blow that starts a full scale war with Mythryn, and if that happens, I fear that Cadaria may soon cease to exist. You must now decide Devlin, if you serve the Emperor or the Empire, because in this case, they are mutually exclusive."

"Where and when will she arrive?"

Hannah smiled and began to lay out the details to her new ally.

* * * * * * * * * * * * *

The road to the ports of Thorigald was not the most well-tended road, but then again, in a state of war, there would be no well-tended roads. Besides, with the number of dragon territories that lay between Galateria and Thorigald, the road was the least of Devlin's worries.

"You couldn't leave it alone could you? You couldn't just kill Hannah and become the champion of the Emperor. No, you have to get all righteous and follow your heart and all that garbage. For once I wish you would just listen to me and be the devious, conniving creature that we all know you to be. You are half dragon. When will you get that through your head? It doesn't matter how many you kill, doesn't matter how many good deeds you do, and it doesn't matter how much of a hero the commoners think you are. How long you remain alive will only be dictated by how useful you are to the Emperor. And right now, I would say that your use is up."

"To this one perhaps," Devlin answered, "but there is always the next one."

Loss

Year Two of the Just Emperor Kaitain "Dragonsbane" Lorien, Creator's Calendar Year 1869

Pain comes in many forms. The most common is physical pain, that feeling of fire and lightning shooting through the nerves that invigorates and torments in the same breath. Physical pain is fleeting, and as days and weeks pass, it begins to fade. Some physical pain can last for years, or for a lifetime, but tolerance for it grows as time passes. The other type of pain is the more troubling of the two. Emotional pain rockets through your mind and body just like the worst physical pain. It can be as crippling as the loss of a leg or an arm, and can be as deadly as a blow to the heart. Like physical pain, emotional pain has a source. However, the source of emotional pain could be nearly anything; a scornful word from a lover, the death of a pet, losing a job or a large sum of money. The worst emotional pain, as anyone would attest to, is the loss of a loved one. Such a pain could stay in one's heart for many years, but unlike physical pain, no tolerance could ever develop to combat pains of the mind and heart.

Deep in the forests of the Dorsen Islands south of the continent of Cadaria, an ancient man strolled through the trees and underbrush, looking at the untouched beauty of nature all around him. Even the pristine landscapes around him would not abate the agony in his heart. It was like his heart was bleeding in his chest with every step, and no matter where his mind turned, the pain was always with him. Part of him would always be broken by the events of the past, and to him, there was nothing more than a shadow of the great man that he once was. The Creator had given him many tasks to keep him busy after the death of his wife, but no matter what he did, or where he went, she was never far from his thoughts. Her death had no meaning, and that was what stuck in his mind the most. She was not on an assignment for the Creator, nor was she following any request. She had simply been in the wrong place at the wrong time, and now she was gone. As the ancient man continued to walk through the forest, he could feel the tears welling up in his eyes.

"Still haven't been able to let her go?"

The ancient man stopped. The voice had come from somewhere behind him, and though the voice had been gentle, it was powerful enough to rustle the leaves on the trees for a great distance. Those who traveled in the forests of the Dorsen Islands did so with the full knowledge that the Dragons of Espre ruled nearly all of the islands, and there was nothing that would save a mortal from their wrath upon intrusion. The ancient man had nothing to fear from the dragons. For many years he had been an ally of the dragons, and as an emissary of the Creator, he had been afforded an amount of respect from the dragons. However, as the years went on, more respect was earned through deeds that benefited the dragon race.

"Is this when you give me the old speech about finding a new path and taking solace in the good work that I'm doing?"

The ancient man's voice was thick with anger and bitterness. It had been a long time since he had spoken of his wife with anyone, and the last thing he wanted to be told was that his feelings were wrong. Everyone grieves in their own way, and to be told that he was wrong for what he was doing made him angry.

"Work for the Creator is neither good nor bad, you know that old friend," the dragon said from somewhere in the forest. "If you should take solace in anything, it should be the amount of time you and your wife had together before the end. Most mortals would give everything to spend several hundred years with the person that they loved. I would think you would count yourself lucky."

The ancient man stood silently for moment. The initial urge was to be angry. However, the ancient man had learned to suppress his anger when it came to his wife.

"Show yourself, dragon."

After a moment, an old man dressed in white with a long white beard emerged from deeper in the forest. Unlike a normal man, this old man had the eyes of a serpent, cold blue eyes that glowed with an unnatural energy.

"Come now, Evan, is that any way to talk to your oldest friend?"

Evan Sinn stood silently, looking at the old man as he approached, and despite himself could not prevent the laugh from escaping his lips.

"Most people who consider themselves my old friends don't tend to live very long, Tarot. Do you have a death wish?"

Tarot stepped forward and put his hand on Evan's shoulder and smiled.

"We dragons do not make friends with you mortals lightly, Evan, and those that we truly see as friends could never be a threat to us. Besides, you are far more interesting than the rest of your race. I find it curious that you chose to be a servant of the Creator rather than becoming a god."

Evan pulled away from Tarot and took a half step back before completely turning his back on the dragon.

"We are all servants of the Creator, Tarot; gods, mortals, and dragons alike. Those who believed they were above the will of the divine were those who were punished, and in history as you well know, it has cost the lives of many innocents. My world was not immune to the destruction, and it was the arrogance of the 'gods' that doomed my world to ash."

Tarot nodded.

"You are a very interesting mortal, my friend. But, I trust since you are here, you have something that you need to say to the Council?"

Evan shook his head.

"I have a warning from the Creator, and it is leveled at you and only you, Tarot."

The old man's face changed at that moment. The look on his face was one of both anger and shock.

"The Creator would not send a warning to the dragons through a messenger such as yourself, Evan. I know better than that. If the Creator wanted to tell the dragons anything, he would have done it personally."

Evan could feel anger well up within him, and he reached deep down into himself and took hold of the nearly limitless power that was stored within him. It was never an easy thing to grasp the power of the Creator, and more often than not, Evan simply relied on his god-like powers gifted to him so many centuries ago. However, in times of great need, the Creator allowed Evan to draw upon the power once used to shape the cosmos. Such challenges to the Creator's authority were considered to be 'great need'. Evan's body was suffused with white light.

"Though you may be the Elder Dragon and the leader of the Council of the Winds, that does not give you the right to question the decree of the Creator. If you are not willing to uphold your position as the speaker for your race, than I will replace you with someone who will. That is my right as the Voice of the Creator."

The old man closed his eyes for a moment and then nodded his head. Friendship was one thing, but when the Voice of the Creator made a decree, it was to be obeyed without question. Evan was once a very kind and honorable man, and while that had changed little over the centuries of service, after the death of his wife, Evan had changed. He was darker, more impatient, and seemed to have bouts of both uncontrollable anger and depression. Time was once Evan's greatest ally, but now had become his greatest enemy. It is said that time heals all wounds, however, in Evan's case, time had made the wounds cut deeper into his heart and soul. It was as though pain was one of the only languages that Evan remembered how to speak, and he internalized his pain instead of letting it out and dealing with it. However, unlike most members of his race, Evan was isolated and had only his pain to depend upon. His life was one of loneliness and pain now that his wife was gone, and he was cut off from the race that gave birth to him. He could not form relationships with his own kind, as he would outlive not only them but also their children and grandchildren. He could not form a relationship with the gods because while he was technically their equal, they would never accept him because he was once human. He could not seek shelter with those that were known as the Dark Gods because their very existence was an affront to Evan's role as Voice of the Creator. The only race he could turn to was the dragons. They understood who and what he was, and the nature of his powers. However, he was an outcast, driven by mortal emotions that the dragons could never understand. So, he was left with nothing but his own pain and anguish to keep him company through the long and difficult years in service to the Creator.

"As the Creator wills, so shall we obey."

Tarot was quick to give the answer that would cause Evan to back down from his provoked state. Tarot was powerful; probably the most powerful of all of the dragons, but even all of that power might not have been a match for the Voice of the Creator.

"I knew you would see things my way, old friend," Evan said after a moment, his form still bathed in the white light of the Creator's power. "Heed my words well. The Creator has seen the course that lay ahead for this world and the fate that may come to pass if the current course of events continues. In order to prevent a great tragedy from befalling this world, the Creator has sent me to make this request of the Council of the Winds, the ruling body of the dragon race. It is the will of the Creator that this petty war with the people of Cadaria shall end now. If this war continues, the Creator shall be forced to lend his aid to the humans in an effort to avert disaster."

Tarot was shocked by the words, but kept silent. That decree would certainly not be well received by the council.

"Secondly," Evan continued, "all efforts to recover the artifact known as the Dragon's Tear shall cease immediately. That item is too dangerous to be possessed by anyone, even the dragons. If any member of the dragon race continues to pursue the item, the retribution from the Creator will be without measure."

Tarot nodded his head silently. For the Creator to make such demands of his oldest children meant that the threat posed by the Dragon's Tear was grave, even to the Creator himself. However, there was more to this. Tarot had heard whispers about the magnificent powers of the Dragon's Tear throughout the members of the Council of the Winds, and even heard it spoken of by some of the younger dragon races. Though Tarot would officially discourage the pursuit of the artifact, his curiosity had been peaked.

"Thirdly," Evan said finally, "events have come to pass that have placed the entire breed of dragon in grave danger. Preparations are to be made for all dragons to leave this world upon the orders of the Creator."

Tarot's blood ran cold. If the Creator was honestly suggesting that the dragons abandon their home…

"And is the Creator aware of the situation that keeps us on this rock?"

Tarot's question was full of venom. The mere suggestion that the dragons leave their home was both aggravating and frustrating. It had been the Creator's decree that forced the breed of dragons to make their fateful deals with the pathetic humans, and now it was another decree from the Creator that was seemingly absolving them from that order. Dragons followed a set regimented code of conduct, and any violation of that conduct had dire ramifications for the entire breed. A race without rules was a lost race. That is why the humans suffered as much as they did. Their rules of order and civilization seemed to change at a moment's notice. They had no consistency, no pride, and no sense of honor.

"The Creator understands the dilemma that faces the dragons, and while he cannot reverse his decree and save face with his oldest children," Evan replied carefully, "the Creator is willing to give you the means to resolve the issue, if the dragons are willing to hear it."

Tarot stood silent for a moment.

"I'm listening."

CHAPTER 47

* * * * * * * * * * * * *

Gregor Quicksilver stood in the darkened audience chamber, his faith and resolve shaken to the core. For most of his life, his beliefs and his code of conduct had been based on the assumption that his father was dead, and that his father had given his life in the defense of the Empire of Cadaria. If his father was still alive and had been living in Mythryn all this time, what did that mean? Had his father turned his back on the oaths that he had sworn to defend the Empire? Was his father a traitor?

Ivan Quicksilver had always been a proud and forthright man. Duty was his faith, and the violation of duty was the worst sin imaginable. For him to turn his back on everything he had stood for must have taken an incredible revelation. As Gregor's eyes returned to the face of the Dark Seer, he remember his first meeting with the young woman and how her words had shaken the very foundation of the Empire. If she had been the cause of Ivan's fall from grace, Gregor could understand it. But if she had been alive and a seer at that point, just how old was this woman?

"Your mother's eyes always told her emotions," Ivan said after a moment, "and I see that you are very much the same. You are confused, and with good reason. There is so much to tell you Gregor, and I fear that while you deserve to hear the truth, you are not ready."

Gregor's blood boiled. In the volatile mix of anger and confusion that filled his heart and mind, the anger was beginning to win out. The betrayal stung him deeply, and it would not be too much longer before his restraint snapped and he attempted to draw Valor and end the Dark Empire once and for all.

"Now I know that look," Ivan said after a moment, rounding on his son, "that is the look of the weight of duty. You were sent here to kill as many of the Dark Gods of Mythryn as you could before they killed you, isn't that right?"

Gregor nodded silently, his muscles tense, waiting for the right time to strike.

"Would it surprise you at all to learn that was the mission I was sent on as well? However, just like you I was never intended to succeed in my task."

Gregor smiled.

"Then maybe I'm a better soldier than you are father. My Emperor would never send me on a mission he did not feel I could complete."

Laughter came from Darrien Annis, the young half-god princess of the Dark Empire.

"He is much like you were when you came to us, Ivan. So sure of his own abilities that it blinds him to the truth."

Her eyes quickly fell back to Gregor, and the fires of hatred that came from her gaze felt as though they could burn through Gregor's skin.

"I welcome you to try to strike me down, Ruby Knight of Cadaria."

Ivan took a step back, as did the man identified as Alderin. Gregor reached for the hilt of Valor and drew it effortlessly from the long sheath strapped to his back. Part of Gregor's mind told him that this would not be a fair fight and that he could strike the woman down in a heartbeat. The other half of Gregor's mind cautioned him from being overconfident. He had faced wizards and sorcerers before, and while they had occasionally caused him problems, his abilities had always been enough to carry him through the confrontation. Easing into a practiced defensive stance, Gregor waited as the woman in the pale violet dress took two steps forward, smoothed the wrinkles out of her gown and locked her eyes back on the Ruby Knight. After a moment, Gregor lunged forward, the blade of Valor sweeping down in a long arc, the point of which was intended to split the young woman's beautiful face. However, mere inches from her scalp, Valor stopped, seized mid-swing by some unknown force. Gregor brought all the force that he could manage to bear, trying to will Valor to strike his opponent. For several long moments, his muscles flexed and burned with exertion, finally beginning to give out due to the strain. Suddenly the mysterious force flared and began to push back. Gregor did what he could to hold his ground, but finally both he and Valor were thrown across the chamber where he struck the wall with such force that the stone cracked.

Blood trickled from Gregor's mouth, and as he slowly began to push himself up to his hands and knees, Valor floated from the floor beside him and the blade pressed itself against his throat. The look on the young woman's face was unchanged.

"That's enough Darrien," the Dark Queen said softly, "I believe you've made your point."

Valor clattered to the ground the next moment, and Gregor found himself being helped up by Alderin. The man's hair was brown and wavy, seemingly moved by a breeze that only surrounded him. His skin was cool to the touch and pale, as though the blood of his body carried no heat. The look in the man's eyes was similar to those of the Dark Princess; cold, unfeeling, and distant.

"So you see, my son," Ivan said stepping toward his fallen offspring, "the errand you have been sent on is a suicide mission. Darrien only possesses a fraction of the power that her father holds, and while he is the greatest of the Dark Gods, the others are not far from his level of power. If they wanted to, the Dark Gods could have wiped Cadaria from the face of Espre with only a thought. However, they are merely trying to make the best of their imprisonment here. It is the Cadarian Empire that has pursued war with the Dark Gods, not the other way around. The Lorien family has been waging a private war with assassins and the sorcerers of the Academy of Arcane Arts in Jelan for generations."

Gregor finally found his way back to his feet and locked his eyes on the Dark Seer. The words that his father had spoken made sense. However, he was not ready to believe it yet.

"Dark Seer," Gregor said finally, "once you thanked me for helping your words come to light in the presence of the Emperor of Cadaria, and now I ask that you repay that kindness by answering a question for me. From you and only you will I trust the answer."

Jehna Feris took a step forward and nodded.

"I shall See for you great Ruby Knight, as it is the least I can do to repay the kindness you showed me those many years ago."

Leaving his sword Valor laying on the ground behind him, Gregor walked forward and met the Dark Seer in the center of the chamber and whispered his question into the woman's ear. For a long moment, the Dark Seer fell silent. A pained expression crossed her face, and suddenly her eyes opened wide, and a single tear fell from her right eye. The tear was of blood. The Dark Seer whispered her answer to the Ruby Knight, the blood still on her cheek. When Gregor stepped back, the look on his face was one of pain and sadness.

"The Dark Seer has given me the answer that I feared, and now I know that all you have told me is truth."

The Dark Seer returned to her position beside the Dark Queen and gently wiped the blood from her face. Sadrina Annis rose from her throne and approached Gregor, whatever fear of the larger man having been erased by his impassioned words.

"I am very sorry that truth must find you thus, Gregor," Sadrina said softly. "Your father had an equally difficult time accepting the truth. Unfortunately before he was able to see the light, a great deal of my private guard met their end. They were good men, but the price I paid was well worth the ally that I have gained. Ivan has been of great help to the Dark Gods in ferreting out the schemes of the Cadarian Emperors, and I hope that you will be equally useful."

Gregor pulled away from the Dark Queen as though he had been struck.

"I have not agreed to betray my people," Gregor said strongly.

"And I am not asking you to betray anyone," Sadrina countered. "I am merely asking you to uphold the agreements that the first Cadarian Emperor made with the dark gods after the death of our leader by his hand."

Gregor could feel a rush of contempt pass through him.

"If your Dark Gods are so great," Gregor spat with venom, "then how is it that Lorien the First was able to slay your great leader?"

Sadrina shook her head and returned to her throne. The woman slumped onto the throne and fixed her eyes back on the Ruby Knight.

"Is it not clear to you, Gregor?" Darrien said shortly. "When the Dark Gods came to this world on the Day the Heavens Fell, they caused much chaos and destruction. Humans often fear what they don't understand and the men and women of Cadaria could not tolerate such an affront to the Creator existing on this world with them. So, it was the Cadarians and not the creatures of Mythryn that started the War of Darkness. The only way to keep the entire population of Cadaria from being destroyed was to create some measure of peace and understanding between the two kingdoms. Our leader knew the only way to prevent such a terrible tragedy was to force peace talks. The only way he could accomplish that was by a tender act of sacrifice and mercy,"

* * * * * * * * * * * * *

Year Nineteen of the Just Emperor Terrik Lorien I, Creator's Calendar Year 69

The fighting through the Imperial Palace was fierce, and as Emperor Lorien stood before his throne surrounded by his elite guard, the Imperial Sword clutched in his hand, fear began to enter his heart. The forces of the Dark Gods of Mythryn were bestial and cruel, but they were effective. That paired with the incredible powers of their leader had reduced the armies of the twelve Great Kingdoms to shells of their former selves. Terrik could hear the fighting raging outside the doors of the throne room, and it would only be a matter of moments before it spilled into the audience chamber as well. Suddenly, some incredible force shattered the great doors of the throne room, and a wave of the red-skinned beasts known as Jeresei flooded into the room.

Though Emperor Lorien did his best to defend himself, the forces of the Dark Empire were too much. Within a matter of moments, the entirety of the elite guard had been wiped out, but to Terrik's great surprise, the beasts did not advance. They stopped short of the dais and then held their ground as if they were waiting for something. After a few moments, Terrik could feel an incredible power approaching the audience chamber. It was unlike anything he had ever felt before, and it almost seemed to shake the entire palace. Finally, Terrik saw the source of the power and his palms began to sweat and he had to redouble his grip on the Imperial Sword.

The man who entered the throne room stood slightly taller than Terrik, with long dark hair, a firm, stocky build and a firm jaw. The black armor he wore seemed to drink in all the light around him, and no light reflected from its surface. From the man's back sprouted angelic wings that seemed to radiate a pale light that surrounded the man like an aura of smoke. His blue eyes housed the rage of a typhoon. The red-skinned beasts parted the way for the winged man to approach the dais. A clear crystalline sword was clutched in the stranger's hand, the blood of many smearing its flawless features.

"You are Emperor Terrik Lorien?"

Terrik nodded and clutched the hilt of the Imperial Sword firmly.

"I am the leader of those whom you call the Dark Gods."

Fear welled up in the heart of the Cadarian Emperor. How could he stand in combat against a god?

"This war was not of our making, but if we are forced to, we will finish it," the Dark God said angrily. "Your people brought the fight to us, and we defended ourselves, but we will not sit idly by while you send assassins and mages to disrupt the life we are trying to build on Mythryn. I could kill you, Emperor Lorien, but that would solve nothing. Another would come to take your place, and the war would continue and you would be a martyr. And yet, I cannot let the cycle of violence to continue. There must be peace."

Terrik frowned.

"How could there ever be peace when creatures like you with such power exist? If you simply walk away and take your armies, my people will know that one day you might return."

The Dark God smiled.

"You are wiser than I expected, Terrik. The Cadarian Emperor must be shown to be the equal of the Dark Gods in power, and for peace to be accepted, you must be given a victory. The story will go forth that a duel of honor took place between the leader of the Dark Gods and the Emperor of Cadaria. After a climactic battle, the Dark God fell under the Imperial Sword's might. This will give Cadaria a victory, and it will ensure that your people will believe the truce that you will forge with my second."

Terrik's eyes went wide.

"And how will anyone believe this tale?"

The Dark God dropped his sword and motioned for the Jeresei to leave the chamber.

"Strike quickly and strike true, Terrik. Make my death a monument to the touted mercy and enlightenment of the human race."

As the Imperial Sword fell, taking the Dark God's life, Gwydeon Sandar could only smile and wonder at the irony of his final words.

Hunting Dragons

Year Two of the Just Emperor Kaitain "Dragonsbane" Lorien, Creator's Calendar Year 1869

The dark and fog-filled cavern stank of death, and as the mud gave gently under the light footsteps of the self-titled Lady of Cadaria, Jillian Corven, the rank musty air filled her nose and seemed to hang upon her like a cloak. For three long months Jillian and her team of trained dragon hunters had tracked the foul beast from haunt to haunt until they finally located its hatchery. The adult female grey dragon had recently laid a clutch of eggs, and had been hunting to replenish her lost strength by raiding the local villages and cities. The mayor of one of the smaller villages whose taxes were quickly coming due had the most to lose from potential cattle loss, so Jillian and her team had been hired to rid the region of the menace. It was several days into the hunt that Jillian had learned of the eggs, and it satisfied her all the more that she would be able to rid the world of a new generation of the abominations.

For years, Jillian had dedicated her life to the extermination of the foul lizards that lorded over the landscape of Espre like gods. Ever since the large black dragon known as Shadowweaver destroyed her home, Jillian had invested every part of herself to learning all she could so that she could more effectively dispatch the bane of her existence. For many years Jillian had wandered the lands, learning from those she could. Monks had been a good source of information, so had the Great Library of Menoris. But her true education came through the process of hunting her prey, learning the habits of each of the breeds, learning their sources of food, preferred nesting grounds, everything about their lives. Along the way, Jillian had crossed paths with others of like mind, those with the compunction to do what must be done at any time, and at any cost. So far, Jillian and her team had identified and hunted at least a dozen breeds of dragon, and had leads on perhaps a dozen more. Each hunt brought new dangers and new opportunities for revenge.

The crunch of a fracturing skull under her feet shook Jillian back to the moment, and forced her to refocus on the situation at hand. This foul beast that called itself Feartooth had been a crafty opponent. She had taken great pains in trying to disguise the path back to her lair, and had on three separate occasions doubled back upon her route to make sure that she wasn't followed. However, for as crafty as the creature thought she was, she was no match for Kiara Aren, the tracker of Jillian's group. Through night and swamp, and mountain climbs, Kiara had successfully followed Feartooth's path, never losing faith or scent for a moment. When the trail had finally descended into the dank pit beneath a swamp in the far reaches of Pellatori, Jillian felt a bit of anger and trepidation. The Moonstone Knight was not one who suffered the interference of those he did not consider his equal, and since the decree of the Just Emperor Kaitain Lorien assigned the war against the dragons to Bernhardt Yeoman, there were few that would dare to hunt in his domain. However, Jillian was never one to let something as petty as the law come between her and her prey.

The temperature in the cavern had slowly been rising the deeper Jillian moved into the cavern. While Jillian did not relish the thought of attacking an adult dragon on her own, this had been the method that had worked well in the past. Any time there was an underground incursion; Jillian would attack the beast in close-quarters due to her speed and agility and if necessary would attempt to flush the beast out in the open where the rest of her team waited with magic and ballistae to attempt to fell the beast. If the team moved quick enough, the dragon would not have a chance to react from the time it emerged from the mouth of the cavern to the time it was struck by one of the implements of death that awaited it. Rarely had the situation worked to plan, but at least they were ready if it ever did.

The heat that filled the cavern had begun to cause the mist to thin on the cavern floor. Now Jillian could see broken and battered bodies of the would-be dragon slayers that had attempted to make prey of Feartooth in the past. Most had been burned to a crisp, while still others showed signs of being either ripped apart by sharp claws, or bitten in half by even sharper teeth. Their weapons and armor had proven to be of little use to them against the might of the dragon, as was typically the case when mortal weapons tried to match the immortal strength of a dragon. Jillian herself chose to wear no armor, and bore no shield. Such things would prove of little use against her foe. Her only need was the specially-made sword which hung at her hip. It took Jillian nearly half her life to save the money required to purchase the materials, expertise, and spells to forge her blade, but in the end it had been well worth it. Scaleripper was crafted from the finest and lightest metal in all of Cadaria. During its forging, instead of being cooled in water, it was cooled in the nearly congealed blood of dragons, while spells were cast to assist the metal in drinking in the foul liquid. The blade of the sword would begin to crave the blood of dragons to fuel its enchantments. The more blood it tasted in its life, the stronger the blade would become. Scaleripper would impart increased speed and nearly superhuman strength to the user in the face of its prey, and would make the wielder a match for all but the oldest and strongest of the creatures. While theoretically anyone could wield Scaleripper, it was specially made and weighted for Jillian's lithe frame.

A wave of tension passed through Jillian as she descended deeper into the cavern. She was getting close, and she could feel the anticipation pass through Scaleripper. Because it had tasted the essence of the foul beasts, it thirsted for more of their blood, and could feel when they were close. Jillian felt her blood run cold as the desire for death passed from her weapon into her heart. It sang to her, sang to her of death and revenge, and hate. The need to kill enveloped Jillian, and as Scaleripper was freed from the confines of its scabbard, the end of the hunt was upon them both. The end of the cavern's enclosed descent was in sight, and at the very edge of the limited light, the widening cave was apparent. There, just beyond the precipice, the quarry lay, quiet and waiting. While Jillian could take the stealthy approach, sneaking into the hatchery, the chances on it being successful was limited. The younger dragons had much keener senses to alert them of enemies. A single misstep could alert the parent to the incursion. However, a quick decisive strike could be enough to end the battle quickly. Jillian took a slow deep breath, careful to remain silent, and then held Scaleripper aloft as she charged through the opening.

Jillian ran quickly, her sword high. Deeper into the cavern, before a clutch of eggs stood the foul Feartooth, its eyes locked on the approaching attacker. To Jillian, the next few moments played out in slow motion. Feartooth dropped down to stand on its four feet, let its jaws fly wide and sent a billowing haze of hot air rushing from its mouth. The hot, dry heat passed over Jillian, threatening to sap her strength and her resolve, but Scaleripper would not let her relent. The burning fires would be upon her the next moment, but a quick roll to the left would save Jillian from a molten fate. Jillian came up to a knee after a moment and then pushed off, propelling herself toward the dragon. While Feartooth was slow to recover from the fiery assault, it was still in good enough position to dodge Jillian's high-arcing slash. Falling back onto three feet, Feartooth slashed with its clawed front foot, missing Jillian by a fraction of an inch. Taking advantage of the larger creature's plodding yet powerful assault, Jillian brought the blade of Scaleripper quickly slashing down on the back of the dragon's outstretched hand, drawing a plum of blood on contact. A roar ripped from Feartooth's massive jaws, and in an unexpected turn, the dragon flapped its massive wings sending a gust of wind through the room knocking Jillian down, and lifting the creature onto the foul winds of the cavern.

"Fool woman," the dragon spat, "hundreds have tried to end my reign over this area, and many were stronger than you. I give you credit for wounding me, but that is all you will accomplish with this reckless assault. Pray to whatever gods you believe in, woman, and prepare yourself to meet them."

Another burst of hot breath accompanied the taunt, but Jillian was ahead of the dragon's tactics. She had seen it many times before, but now Jillian had the advantage. Making a run for the clutch of eggs, Jillian dodged the barrage of fire and flame that bellowed from Feartooth's open mouth, and when she reached the clutch, she smiled and turned to face the hovering beast.

"Now let us see you send that barrage of fire again, Feartooth. I don't think you will risk the health of your brood just to deal with one lone dragon hunter."

Confidence poured through Jillian again, and she felt the weight of Scaleripper in her hands. It would only be a matter of time before Feartooth would have to come in for the kill, and then Jillian would have another measure of vengeance. But instead of the roar of agitation that Jillian expected, the response from Feartooth was one of amusement.

"I think you underestimate the fortitude of my hatchlings, dragon hunter. Perhaps your grand plan was not as grand as you thought."

It was then that pain flashed through Jillian's body. A small yet razor-sharp set of teeth had sunk into the flesh of her left arm, sending a river of blood flowing down to her fingertips. Strength began to flee her body, but the power and thirst of Scaleripper would not let her falter. In a single deft move, Jillian ripped her arm free from the hatchling's grip, pulling a large chunk of her own flesh free, and then spun around, a long slash separating the hatchling's head from its body. Pain flooded trough Jillian's body again, and the contest between desire and death began anew. As blood poured out of the open wound, her muscles began to fight her will, and demanded rest. Sleep pulled at the corners of her mind, and the need to collapse nearly overwhelmed her. Feartooth's roar drew her attention again. Now Jillian found herself trapped between a dozen hatchlings and the aggravated mother. The next few moments would determine the outcome of the confrontation. Feartooth dove the next moment, jaws wide, and talons bared. At the last instant Jillian rolled under the massive creature, the grasping talons missing their mark by a hair's-breadth. Popping back to a knee again, a hard, nearly aimless slash found a target in the drooping tail of the passing dragon. As cold steel met unprotected flesh, the flesh and sinew gave way sending the last foot of the creature's massive tail crashing to the ground. Another roar of pain hit the air, and Feartooth could no longer control itself as it sailed through the air and careened head-first into the back wall of the cavern. Feartooth slumped to the ground, blood flowing freely from the severed tail. The dragon's breath was shallow and ragged, but she was still breathing. The hatchlings, little more than blind could do nothing more than stumble around, the thick smell of blood in the air making it difficult to find prey.

Jillian took her time moving toward Feartooth, careful not to let the wounded beast surprise her. After a moment, Feartooth stopped thrashing about, the pain from the gaping wound overtaking her considerable strength. With one hard downward slash, Feartooth's reign of terror had been ended. Its massive head separated from the rest of its body, blood pouring out, soaking the floor in thick red and black. After catching a breath, Jillian made quick work of the remaining hatchlings, dispatching them all with surprisingly merciful blows. The eggs would be handled later, incinerated with the rest of the beast's lair. Settling back against one of the many rock ledges in the cavern, Jillian ripped a portion of her sleeve and quickly tied off the bleeding wound on her arm. It would take some doing before that arm was back to normal, but it was a small price to pay for the dispatching of her enemies. Slowly walking back toward the entrance, Jillian began to reflect back on the battle, checking her tactics. She should have cleared the egg clutch before advancing on the dragon. Perhaps stealth would have been the better course of action after all. Well, regardless of the flaw in the plan, she was alive and Feartooth was dead. That was the only result that really mattered.

When Jillian finally emerged from the cavern, she sighed deeply upon seeing the relieved faces of her companions. There was no real need for words. The fact that Jillian had returned meant that the battle was over, and they had struck another blow against the vile dragons. Now the real work would begin. Killing the dragon was just the first part of the act. The rest would take as much time as the tracking, but would be much more lucrative in the long run. Kiara Aren, the second longest reigning member of the team of dragon slayers quickly made her way over to Jillian and began tending to the wound on her arm.

Kiara had been a promising acolyte in the Temple of the Creator once upon a time, until her gift for the arcane overrode her gift for the divine. While it had been a difficult choice for her to make at the time, in the end, it turned out to be no choice at all. The more her powers began to manifest, the lesser her control over them became. The outbursts of arcane power would soon interfere with her studies in the Temple, and it would only be a matter of time before she would be expelled from the Order of the Creator anyway. So, as a preemptive measure, her teacher, Erik Relcan, had sent her application to the Academy of Arcane Arts in Jelan along with the recommendation of himself and the Celestine Knight, Hannah Ironheart. Those two recommendations had been enough to easily guarantee her admission to the academy. However, her tenure there would not nearly be as successful as her admission. Within a few weeks, Kiara had found all but the studies of alchemy tiring and in conflict with her beliefs and lessons from the Temple of the Creator. To her it seemed nearly impossible for the world of the arcane and the world of the divine to coexist. Either the Creator was responsible for all things on the face of Espre, as the temple taught, or He was not, as the academy taught. It could not be both. Kiara could not live with a foot in both worlds. So, after she was confident she had enough control over her abilities to not be a threat to herself or anyone else, Kiara left the academy. However, when Kiara returned to the Temple of the Creator, she found that it would not be as warm a homecoming as she expected. Though no one would say it openly, Kiara was viewed as an outsider, corrupted by the teachings of the heathens in the academy. What's more, her continued studies of the properties of alchemy were forbidden by the Temple, and would eventually lead to her complete expulsion from the Order of the Creator. She was excommunicated, and would never be allowed to return under pain of imprisonment and death. To that end, she was also forbidden from even taking part in any organized rituals or worshipping of the Creator at any temple. And so, cast to the wind, Kiara wandered until she met the woman that would become her salvation, Jillian Corven.

When Kiara had first met Jillian, Jillian had already begun to make a name for herself as a dragon hunter. By that time she was considered one of the foremost experts on the creatures, even though her findings were never included in any teachings or studies because of the fact that she was low-born, and also because she was a woman. Kiara had been working as an apothecary in a small village when Jillian and her rag-tag hunting group passed through after a hunt. Several of them had needed their wounds treated, and Kiara had volunteered her services in exchange for some of the blood and organs taken from their latest kill. Kiara had always heard of the amazing alchemical properties of dragon organs, and so a deal was quickly struck. Kiara found Jillian's group circling back to her small village many times to continue the deal, healing for supplies. In time, Kiara's research would bear fruit, and she would learn to concoct many alchemical potions that would fortify the strength and speed of those who used them, as well as some that would impart a measure of the dragons' amazing abilities. These continued encounters had proven Kiara's value to Jillian, and their alliance was formalized soon after. Once a full member of the group, Kiara again proved invaluable, using her alchemical talents to track the dragons by the very scent and potency of their blood. And of course, as the fighting of dragons was dangerous work, having a healer along was a benefit of its own.

"Seems like this one was tougher than you expected," Kiara said softly as she applied a poultice to the gaping wound.

Jillian shook her head.

"I got careless. I should have known the hatchlings would have taken a swipe at me if I got too close. I tried to use them as leverage, and they made me pay the price. But, I won't make the same mistake again."

"You say that every time," Kiara laughed.

Jillian smiled and then looked toward the other two women standing nearby. Angelina Lynn Sador and Jacqueline Escandi were the other two core members of the Dragon Hunters. Jacqueline was a former member of the Iron Legion, the most elite defense force of the Kingdom of Iron, Pellatori. However, her frustration over her lack of advancement due to her gender forced her to look elsewhere, and making a name for herself as a dragon hunter seemed to be the right course of action. Angelina Lynn Sador however came to the Dragon Hunters through a similar path as Jillian, and was the most recent member of the group, but had quickly shown her usefulness. When the Cadarian war with the dragons began, Angelina's village had been one of the first destroyed, just on the southern border of the Kingdom of Night, Galateria. Her hatred was palpable for the overgrown lizards, and she had taken great pleasure in her test for admittance to the group as she slew a young dragon. When she emerged from the den, she had been nearly covered from head to toe with the dragon's blood, and the white dress that she wore would be permanently stained from it.

"There should be quite a bit to recover this time," Jillian said to her companions. "Take the normal measure. Organs, blood, eyes, teeth, what scales you can recover. It should easily compensate us for the supplies this trip. Make sure to take the horns for Kiara, and the rest of the head for the mayor. Burn the hatchlings, they shouldn't be worth much to us this time."

Jacqueline frowned.

"Were there any unhatched eggs?"

Jillian thought for a moment. Jacqueline always seemed to frown after a hunt where she was not involved in the kill. But, Jillian could not expect less from a trained soldier. While Jacqueline would have been useful in the cavern, she was more useful manning the ballista. Jacqueline's military training had given her access to all types of siege weapons, and those seemed to be the most effective defense against dragons on open ground or in the air.

"I don't know off-hand, but if there are, we should try to recover them. The last one we recovered, we got a good price for from that exotic animal dealer in Hedorah. In fact, I think we made more money off the egg that time than we did off the rest of the dragon and the reward combined."

"I didn't trust him," Angelina said finally. "He seemed too eager to take it off our hands. How do we know what he was going to use it for? He could be breeding an army of dragons for himself to make a move against the emperor."

"Or he could be making the world's biggest omelet," Kiara countered. "Who cares? If the money is right, I would to sell to the Dark Gods. As long as the adults die, we have plenty of years before we have to worry about the eggs, and it ensures we will always have business."

Jillian smiled, and then shook her head.

"If you were in this to get rich Kiara, you got into it for the wrong reasons."

"Oh, I got into it for the right reasons, Jillian," Kiara countered, "getting rich is just a pleasant side effect."

The four women laughed at the retort and then quickly went to work. Safely harvesting the organs of the dragon would take several hours, and it was painstaking and bloody work. The complication was the need to salvage as much of the dragon's blood as possible while harvesting the organs. Unlike any other type of prey a hunter might bleed, dragons of considerable size could not be hung from a tree and left for their blood to drain. It was a long and arduous process, but very rewarding in the long run. Dragon's blood was a sought after material for alchemists, wizards, and weapon smiths of all types. By the gallon it fetched the most gold of any of the creature's parts. However, those of intelligence and experience would also purchase other portions of the dragon for alchemical potions or spell components. After several hours of work, the four women emerged with their spoils, as well as five unhatched dragon eggs.

****

Several days' worth of travel later, Jillian and her dragon hunters had returned to the beginning of their trek through the mountains and valleys of Pellatori, to the little town of Archreach. The mayor had been pleased with them upon their return, and had immediately mounted the head of the dragon Feartooth above the doors to the town hall. It would serve as a trophy and an inspiration to the rest of the inhabitants of the region. However, Jillian saw it as something different. If any dragon in the region learned of the dragon head adorning one of the buildings in this town, it would soon be obliterated as a measure of retribution, and the rest of the region would soon suffer a similar fate. However, Jillian kept her own council on the subject, as she was not getting paid to prevent threats from unknown dragons, only to combat the threat from existing ones. Besides, proactively hunting dragons was never as lucrative a proposal as hunting one that had caused damage. Revenge was a fine motive, but full-time vengeance led to poverty very quickly.

After finishing their business with the mayor, the team was ready to make their way to Pellatori for supplies and then to Hedorah to sell the dragon eggs, however, their plans were interrupted by the presence of an imperial page in the inn where they had been given rooms before their hunt began.

"Are you Jillian Corven?" the fresh-faced page said quickly upon the women's entry into the inn.

Jillian frowned.

"I am Lady Jillian Corven. What do you want?"

The page looked puzzled for a moment and then reached into his pouch and recovered a sealed scroll.

"The Just Emperor Kaitain 'Dragonsbane' Lorien commands the presence of the dragon hunter Jillian Corven on a matter of some urgency. You are to report as commanded within ten days of receiving this summons."

Without taking the scroll, Jillian spoke.

"And if I choose not to report?"

The page took a step back as if struck.

"If you fail to report to the Imperial Palace in Aldere within ten days, you will be considered an enemy of the Empire and jailed accordingly. If after a trial you are found to have willfully refused a summons of the Emperor, you will be put to death as a traitor."

Jillian thought for a moment, and then took the summons from the page.

"Then I suppose I have no choice. Tell your Emperor that I will be there in ten days. No more, no less."

The page nodded, a look of revulsion on his face and then left the inn. The innkeeper who had been watching the exchange chose that moment to speak up.

"You're skirting the edges acting like that girl. This new emperor could string you up for talking like that."

"He's not my Emperor," Jillian said finally. "I bow to no man. If he wants me to grace his palace with my presence within ten days, then he can wait until the twenty-fourth hour on the tenth day before I report. In the end, it will be on my terms."

The innkeeper laughed.

"You won't live long with an attitude like that girl."

Jacqueline drew her dagger and let it fly. The tip buried itself in the wood of the support beam just inches from the head of the innkeeper.

"Watch your words, old man," Angelica said coldly. "You are addressing the Lady of Cadaria, and you would much sooner answer charges from the vaunted emperor than incur her wrath."

Jillian laughed for a moment and then turned to her companions.

"I shall go to answer this summons from the Emperor. You three resupply in Pellatori as planed and then meet with Blade in Hedorah. I shall meet you there. I expect no less than five thousand a piece for the eggs, or at the very least four thousand and a pick of one of his finest trackers."

The three women nodded at the commands and went to gather their belongings for the trip. Jillian stood alone in the inn common room for another few moments looking at the still-sealed summons from the Emperor. Her fame had brought her to the attention of the Emperor at last, but she knew it was only because of the war. If he wanted her expertise, it would be at a very high price. A price he would never be willing to pay.

Royalty

Year Two of the Just Emperor Kaitain "Dragonsbane" Lorien, Creator's Calendar Year 1869

The Celestial Princess Marlae Lorien sat in the Great Library of Menoris flipping through one of the many volumes of history of the Lorien family, vaguely taking note of names, dates, and important other facts. For nearly two years now she had been a student of the monks who maintained the Great Library, and for two years she had been nearly bored to tears by their stringent and unending devotion to the tedium of history. It had been weeks since her father had been elevated to the position of Emperor, and Marlae tired of the tedium of her daily routine. Her attention to her studies waned, but was brought back as her instructor rapped his writing tool against the edge of the table.

"Princess Marlae," he said in his droning monotone voice, "pay attention to your studies. A proper lady of the Empire must be able to speak intelligently on all manner of subject if she is to be seen as a woman to be respected."

Inwardly Marlae groaned. Her father had always taught her that respect was earned through the level of her position. Now that she was the next in line for the throne of the Empire of Cadaria she would be respected by all of the subjects that bent their knee to her father. But that wasn't enough for Marlae. Respect was not enough. Marlae wanted to be feared. For the next hour, she tolerated the lessons of her instructor, and then once the merciless tedium was at its end, Marlae returned to her room.

During her walk back to her rather sparse and entirely too small quarters, Marlae felt the presence of her constant shadow several steps behind her. Gabriel Shadowfall, the member of the Imperial Guard appointed as her personal bodyguard, had been with her for the last ten years. At first, Marlae had been annoyed by his constant presence, but over time she learned to tolerate him. It had gotten to the point that she hardly noticed him any longer.

"You needn't walk so far away Gabriel. What would happen if some assassin were to leap from the shadows in front of me? How would you ever get to him fast enough?"

Gabriel didn't respond to Marlae's favorite taunt. If he had been one step closer than the practiced five paces behind her, he would have been chided for being too close, one step farther, it would have been no different. There was no pleasing the young woman, and no matter what was done, she would find some fault. It was always the same with Marlae. Her meals were either too hot or too cold, her drink too old and stale, her bathwater the wrong temperature, her clothes not quite the right color. When they finally reached her quarters, Gabriel deftly moved past his charge and entered her room. After a cursory look around and the standard glare from Marlae, he returned to the door.

"Is there anything else I can do for you, Princess?"

Gabriel had become accustomed to using only her title when addressing Marlae. Anything else would have been responded to with a chide of some type. The severity of which always depended upon the Princess's mood.

"Fetch my lunch, Gabriel. It should have been here by now."

"As you wish, Princess."

Gabriel bowed slowly, another practiced and necessary routine, and then closed the door behind him. Drawing guard duty for the Princess of Cadaria was supposed to be a grand position for a member of the Imperial

Guard, but it had become more of a joke and curse as Marlae got older. Marlae's honor guard usually consisted of no less than a dozen of the finest members of the Imperial Guard, and while once the whole of the Guard jockeyed for position to be named to the detail, now it seemed more a punishment than an honor. Few appointees lasted more than a month on the detail. Marlae would always find something wrong with them....too tall, too fat, too smelly, too hairy...she could not have her guards be too attractive, and yet not too repulsive either. They were to be nameless, faceless, pushed into the background. Heroes of famous battles were not even considered for the detail. Nothing could detract from the radiance of the Celestial Princess.

As Gabriel returned from the kitchen with the Princess's lunch, he heard a shriek come from her quarters. Drawing his blade, he bolted down the narrow hallway and threw his shoulder into the partially open door nearly shattering it. Marlae stood against the back wall of her quarters while a terribly frightened page stood near the doorway, white as a ghost.

"Are you alright, Princess?" Gabriel said slight, his weapon still bared.

"Gabriel, where were you? This man came into my room unannounced. He could have killed me, or worse. I should report you for dereliction of duty."

Gabriel looked over the page for a moment.

"Explain yourself."

The page took a deep breath and then held out the sealed scroll in his shaking hand.

"I bring a message from the Emperor of Cadaria to the Celestial Princess. The guards at the end of the hall cleared me for this delivery. I knocked but there was no answer. I simply intended to leave the scroll for the Princess for when she returned. I did not expect anyone to be here."

Marlae bristled at the words.

"My father would never send someone as incompetent as you to deliver what must be an important message. Gabriel, I want you to execute this man."

Gabriel stood transfixed for a moment. He could not believe what he was hearing. All of the color drained out of the page's face. The young man's mouth moved but no sound would come out. Fear had taken his voice.

"Princess, this man is an Imperial page fulfilling his duty. I agree he was hasty in entering the quarters of a member of the Imperial Family without invitation…."

Marlae's hands immediately went to her hips and her lip curled in displeasure.

"He was reckless and careless, Gabriel, and I will not have such incompetence in the service of the Just Emperor. Now, unless you want to share his fate, I suggest you follow my orders this moment."

Gabriel took hold of the page's collar and started to drag him out of the room. The look of fear on the page's face deepened.

"Where are you going?" Marlae said, placing her hands on her hips and glaring at Gabriel. "I told you to execute him. And I mean now!"

Gabriel balked for a moment, but the Princess did not relent in her stance and stared at Gabriel. Finally, the restraint in Gabriel relented, and his blade flew free, and he ran the young page through. There was a gasp of shock and pain from the young man, and as he slid from the tip of Gabriel's blade and slumped to the floor, the look of betrayal and horror was still painted on the young page's face. Gabriel too was horrified with the action, and though he had no choice in the deed, the knowing brought no comfort. After a moment, Gabriel cleaned his blade and turned to leave the room.

"Have the servants come this instant to clean up the mess, Gabriel. And have this failure's body put on display in the city center to prevent further treachery."

"As you wish Princess."

Gabriel turned away again.

"Gabriel?"

Gabriel turned back, and there was a sudden flutter in the pit of his stomach. Was she actually going to apologize for demanding the execution? Was she going to express gratitude for his quick and decisive action?

"Where is my lunch?"

* * * * * * * * * * * * *

Marlae Lorien sat alone in her quarters, the blood stain still on the floor where the page had been executed by her loyal personal guard and protector. The two guards that had let the page into the hallway unescorted had already been dismissed from their posts and were probably well on their way to their new assignment as chamber pot scrubbers in the Imperial City. The letter from her father had been a typical one, notifying her of his ascendance to the position of Emperor and a brief statement on the changes to the structure of the ruling council. The death of Alistair Ravenheart and the adoption of Quyhn Ravenheart into the Imperial Family grated on Marlae. However, the most disturbing news was the appointment of the harlot Irene Drage to the position of Imperial Sorceress. It was clear to Marlae how she got her position, much the same way as Marlae's mother had. Had not her sainted mother gotten pregnant after the drunken night of debauchery, she never would have found her way into the royal family, but the need for an heir was strong, and the wedding had been blessed by the Temple of the Creator. All the same, a woman who had to resort to sexual favors to get her position did not gain any respect or curry any favor with the Celestial Princess. The last few lines of the letter contained some contrite platitudes from her father and a request for her to return from Menoris to take up her post as the heir to the Empire.

The chosen heir was supposed to act as the Voice of the Emperor. Marlae was now expected to become the emissary from the Just Emperor to the Thirteen Kingdoms and to ensure that all was going according to the desires of the Emperor. However, rather than seeing this as a chore, Marlae began to see it as an opportunity. Through visiting the different kingdoms of Cadaria, Marlae could begin to form alliances and solidify her power-base in case anything…unfortunate…was to befall her beloved father.

To further this, Marlae had requested that the Tiger's Eye Knight, Xaran Firesoul meet with her before her departure for the Imperial City of Aldere. When there came a knock at the door, Marlae waited for several moments before responding. As expected, the knock came again. Marlae smiled to herself, knowing that she could extend this indefinitely, but relented after the fourth knock.

"Come in Gabriel."

The door opened slowly revealing Gabriel Shadowfall.

"Princess, the Tiger's Eye Knight Xaran Firesoul requests an audience."

Marlae smiled to herself. She was going to like having the vaunted Knights of the Flashing Blade at her beck and call. She had always found the Emperor's personal defense force to be full of pompous and self-important zealots, too well known for their supposed prowess. Perhaps Marlae would have to invest in a private force of her own, one that would assume the positions of the Flashing Blade when she became Empress.

"You may show the honored knight into my quarters, Gabriel."

Gabriel nodded and then opened the door widely. Xaran Firesoul entered the room a moment later. Marlae regarded the new arrival for a moment. Perhaps in his way, Xaran would be considered handsome by common women, but for a lady of refinement like Marlae, he was simply not good enough for her to notice. His shoulder-length hair was wind-blown and unkempt, and his clothing was little more than the common robes and garb of a monk. The sacred staff Faith was clutched in his hand, being used as a walking stick. A single piece of white fabric covered his blind eyes, making the Tiger's Eye Knight seem wiser. Upon entering the room, Xaran oriented himself for a moment and then bowed in Marlae's direction. Though blind since birth, Xaran often moved and acted as though he had sight. Some of the rumors said that Xaran could see through the magic of the staff Faith. Marlae discounted these rumors and simply chose to believe that his keen hearing allowed him to know where people were.

"Xaran Firesoul reporting as requested Princess Lorien. How may I be of service?"

Marlae smiled for a moment and then looked to Gabriel.

"Leave us."

Gabriel nodded and left the room, closing the door behind him.

Marlae sat on the edge of the bed, away from Xaran and looked back at the man before her. As the representative of the Kingdom of Knowledge Menoris, Xaran was an invaluable source of information not only about the pulse of his kingdom, but also the current goings on in the ranks of the Knights of the Flashing Blade. While Marlae was sure she would receive a briefing upon her return to Aldere, she was not content to wait for the partial information she would receive from the agents of her father, the Just Emperor. She wanted the unvarnished truth, as much as she could get.

"So, Sir Firesoul, as you know, my father is now the Just Emperor of Cadaria, and as his only child, that makes me the Voice of the Emperor. As such, I would like for you to tell me the status of the Kingdom of Menoris, as well as the status of the Knights of the Flashing Blade."

Without eyes to read, Marlae could not get a feel for the blind man at the door of the room. There was no change in his features, and there was no way to determine whether or not he was surprised by the request made of him.

"The Kingdom of Menoris is currently engaged in research into the threat from the Dark Gods of Mythryn as well as that from the dragons of Espre. As per the command of the Just Emperor Kaitain Lorien, the scholars of Menoris are compiling all legends and facts related to the dragons and their habits, as well as any information that has been gathered about their habitats in order to facilitate the counterattack. The Army of Menoris has yet to be mobilized into action as there are no known dragons near enough to be a viable target. As for myself, Princess, I have yet to see any direct orders from the Just Emperor, and will be leaving in the morning to follow up on rumors of a bandit assault on the edge of Menoris."

Marlae was puzzled by the last statement.

"Why would a simple bandit attack warrant the attention of a Knight of the Flashing Blade? Why not simply dispatch a small force from the Army of Menoris? Why can't the local magistrate handle the issue?"

Xaran inclined his head slightly.

"The local magistrate was injured in the bandit attack and is not expected to live. As a member of the Knights of the Flashing Blade, I have the duty and authority to act as a magistrate. Additionally, all armies of all kingdoms not currently involved in hostilities have been ordered by decree of the Emperor to remain at battle readiness in case a threat becomes confirmed in their area. To send a detachment to deal with these bandits would be in violation of those orders. Therefore, as the ranking magistrate, as well as the only free military asset in the area, I am duty bound to deal with the issue."

Marlae felt her teeth grind at the answer. There was more to this than the man was letting on. It had always been a trait of the Lorien bloodline to detect when someone was not being utterly truthful. However, it was only when the mantle of the chosen passed to her before Marlae would know for sure. However, all her life, she had felt a flutter in the pit of her stomach any time that someone was lying. Xaran may have been telling the truth, but it certainly wasn't the whole truth.

"Very well. What is the operational status of the other members of the Knights of the Flashing Blade?"

Xaran's placid exterior did not change, and he stoically responded to the question.

"Bernhardt Yeoman is currently leading the Iron Legion against a known dragon lair in the north reaches of Pellatori. Chelsea Zarova and Seraph Kore are attending to another series of peace talks between their kingdoms. Apparently Saldarine is accusing Thorigald of attempting to assassinate their Chancellor and threatening an all-out invasion over it.

Hannah Ironheart and Devlin Rannoch are assisting with recovery operations in Galateria after the recent rash of attacks from the local dragons. Gregor Quicksilver is leading the counterattack against the Dark Continent of Mythryn over the Wasting Disease. Jaccob Aldora, Leonora Wastri, Natalia Pressen, Orren Eldrath, and Tolon Morr are all currently on assignment from the Emperor, whose details I am not privy to. Vallic Ultiv, per the usual, is researching whatever he chooses to."

The last statement struck Marlae. How could a member of the Knights of the Flashing Blade be free to do whatever he wanted as a matter of course? It seemed very strange.

"What do you mean 'per the usual'?"

Xaran smiled.

"Vallic is the oldest member of the Knights of the Flashing Blade, Princess, and he is very set in his ways. His beliefs often clash with other members of the Flashing Blade, and he doesn't often work well with others unless there is no choice. We consider him the last resort. But, Vallic is usually the first to know if there is a threat to the Empire, or even a potential threat. He was the first to discover the Wasting Disease, and is most likely investigating some other possible threat to the life of the Emperor."

"And if the Emperor were to order him to undertake a task for the Throne?"

Xaran's smile widened.

"I'm sure Vallic would consider it and accomplish the task when it suited him."

Marlae felt her blood boil. Such an attitude should not be tolerated, especially from a member of the Flashing Blade. She would have to see to this Vallic Ultiv and make sure that he was brought in line. If his will could not be subjugated, then he would have to be eliminated.

"Is there anything else you require, Princess?"

Marlae thought for a moment. She was sure there was more information that she could extract from Xaran, but she debated on whether or not it was worth the time. Finally, she decided against prolonging the conversation.

"No, Sir Firesoul. You are dismissed."

Xaran bowed slightly, but not slight enough to be insulting, and turned to leave. As soon as the door opened, and Xaran left, Gabriel returned.

"Is there anything else that you require Princess?"

Marlae smiled.

"Fetch the servants and have them draw my bath. Make sure the water is the proper temperature this time. Then you may pack my things, we are returning to Aldere."

Gabriel nodded.

"I will return to pack your belongings after you have had your bath, Princess."

As Gabriel turned to leave, Marlae stood and crossed her arms.

"You need to learn to listen better, Gabriel. I said that you are to pack my things as soon as my bath is properly drawn. I'm sure your modesty will prevent you from peeking."

Gabriel swallowed reflexively and tried to prevent the crimson from filling his cheeks.

"As you wish, Princess."

Gabriel bowed, and then left the room closing the door behind him. Marlae let her smile grow wider. There was nothing quite as pleasurable as teasing Gabriel at every opportunity. She would have to make sure to drop things several times during her bath so that he could fetch them for her.

* * * * * * * * * * * * *

Xaran Firesoul lifted the pack onto his back, and slowly began his walk through the palace toward the southern gate. While part of him regretted lying to the Princess, he felt it had been necessary. No one needed to know yet about the clandestine meeting that had been planned between himself and the dragon known as Khalas Skydancer, nor the offer that had been made to him. Xaran might eventually involve some of his friends within the Flashing Blade, but the Princess was not one that he trusted even remotely enough to put his fate in her hands. The first he would trust when he was ready was Vallic, and even his normally stoic and passive nature would be tested by the revelation of the friendship with the massive dragon, the so-called enemy of the empire. Xaran's thoughts drifted through a great many subjects as the walk through the palace became a walk through the countryside. To those uneducated, Xaran looked like a simple wandering monk, keeping to himself and drawing as little attention as possible. Those who knew who he was would greet him from time to time, but most would simply leave him to his work, assuming that he bore the weight of the Emperor's decree upon his shoulders. However, on this occasion, the only weight upon Xaran was the weight he created for himself. The result of this next task could mean a civil war between the members of the Knights of the Flashing Blade, or at the very least could make him a traitor to the Throne. It was not a position he relished.

After several hours of walking, Xaran could feel the change in the air. Night had begun to descend on the countryside of Menoris. Deviating from the well-worn path, Xaran moved deeper into the forest in the bowl valley of the surrounding mountain range. There in the center of the forest was a crystal clear lake known as the Mirror of Souls. This lake was known by Xaran through his relationship with Khalas to be the home of one of the dragons of Cadaria, and as such was left undisturbed by all of the animals in the area. This was the meeting place that Khalas had determined, and it should have been a private enough place to have a conversation.

Just as Xaran took a seat on one of the large rocks that surrounded the lake, he heard a rustle in the trees behind him. The sound was not from a dragon, or even from simple wildlife, but from humans. Three of them to be precise. Listening closely, Xaran could hear the sounds of clattering armor. The sound would not be audible to most men, but Xaran was far from the typical man.

CHAPTER 47

"There is no point in trying to stealthily approach," Xaran said clearly into the evening air, "I know you are there."

The sounds of movement became more pronounced, and after a few moments, Xaran could make out four distinct sets of footfalls behind him.

"Sir Firesoul," one of the men said gruffly, "we were sent by the Celestial Princess to assist you in adjudicating an issue with bandits."

Xaran sighed. He knew much better than that. The Princess had not believed him, and had sent members of her royal guard to spy on his activities. That moment, Xaran began to feel the familiar swirl of wind around him.

"How very unfortunate for you," Xaran said softly. "My associate does not appreciate unwelcome guests."

Xaran could feel the wave of confusion pass through the four soldiers.

"And which associate do you refer to, Sir Firesoul?" the lead soldier said drawing his sword.

Xaran shook his head.

"The one right above you."

It would be over in a moment. No sooner did the soldiers look skyward than Khalas struck. It was quick, brutal, and efficient. Khalas swooped from above the soldiers, crashing down to the ground, crushing two of the men under the weight of his great forefeet, while snatching a third in its massive jaws. The fourth was quickly battered with Khalas' great tail, sent sailing through the air and crashing hard into one of the nearby rock faces, shattering a myriad of bones and ending his life painfully. Khalas roared and the whole valley seemed to shake.

"I trust all intruders meet a similar fate my friend," Xaran said calmly, still unmoved from his place on the rock.

Khalas reached up and pulled the remains of the soldier from his razor-sharp teeth.

"Only when they deserve it Xaran, and I am afraid on this occasion, I had no choice."

Xaran rose slowly and turned to face the massive creature.

"We will have to dispose of the bodies so that they do not arouse suspicion. However, when they do not arrive in the village to the south I fear that we may be discovered regardless of how careful we have been to this point."

Khalas laughed.

"Oh, they will arrive at the village to the south, Xaran. They will prevent a dragon attack with their lives. My friend Sheyruushk will see to it."

Xaran shook his head.

"If there is a dragon attack this close to Menoris, the army will be mobilized to hunt down the lair of attacker."

Khalas laughed again.

"Let them come. If they can breathe water, and fight on the bottoms of the lakes and oceans, then my friends will deal with them. Otherwise we have nothing to worry about. Now, we have much more important things to discuss. Come my friend, we have a long journey ahead of us."

Temper and Temperance

Year Two of the Just Emperor Kaitain "Dragonsbane" Lorien, Creator's Calendar Year 1869

The Kingdom of Hedorah was known for a great many things, including the marvelous high reaching towers that formed the Flying Kingdom's famed skyline. As the sun set behind the great white buildings, they were fired with all of the late evening colors, reflecting reds, oranges, and purples. Unlike most kingdoms of the Cadarian Empire, the trading and work in Hedorah continued late into the night. As the center of trade for the whole of the Cadarian Empire the inhabitants were forced to live a completely different schedule, and the twelve hour day quickly became either eighteen or twenty in Hedorah. Unlike all of the other Great Kingdoms, Hedorah was a single city that took up the whole of the island kingdom. Most of the business after dark took place in the so-called Tavern District where many of the local businessmen gathered to discuss the happenings of the day.

Deep in the Tavern District was an upscale tavern known as the Hawk's Head Tavern. For many years it had been known as perhaps the best tavern in the whole kingdom, and perhaps in the whole of Cadaria. It had been visited on many occasions by emperors, ambassadors, and heroes of the empire. This night was no exception. At the bar of the Hawk's Head sat one of the most powerful warriors in the whole of the empire, one of the thirteen chosen to serve as the personal guard of the emperor, a member of the Knights of the Flashing Blade. Sitting in his customary seat, Jaccob Aldora took another long drink from is mug of ale, and casually wiped his mouth with the sleeve of his overcoat. For the last three hours Jaccob had been in the same spot, drinking, carousing with the barmaids, and listening to the gossip around him.

As he took another long gulp and emptied his mug, Jaccob couldn't help but think that his life should have turned out differently. Not so long ago Jaccob had entered into his studies at the Academy of Arcane Arts in Jelan, and he was in heaven. Listening to all of the instructors, doing research, spending time with the other students, it was the perfect place. Jaccob could have easily seen himself spending the rest of his life in the academy, studying to perfect his craft, becoming an instructor and passing his knowledge on to the next generation of students. But that could not come to pass now. All it had taken was a few hasty words exchanged in anger, and Jaccob found himself expelled from the academy, cast to the winds of fate, and left to his own devices.

Jaccob looked down to the short staff that stood against the bar beside him. While it wouldn't have looked like much more than a simple wooden short staff to most, it actually was one of the thirteen sacred weapons of Cadaria. The wooden stocks held a pair of enchanted blades collectively known as Temperance. While anyone could have picked up the weapon and held it, only its chosen wielder could separate the staff and reveal the hidden blades. Temperance was supposed to negate the effects of any mind or body altering material when in the hands of its wielder, as well as fortifying his body against the ravages of time and injury. The wielder of Temperance found all of his emotions held in check so long as the weapon was in his hands, and no rage, sadness, or joy could cloud his mind. In the right circumstances, it was a very useful ability, however, most of the time it was absolutely useless in Jaccob's opinion. Jaccob laughed to himself. The two of them fit together perfectly, Temperance and his wielder, both useless most of the time.

Lifting his mug to take another drink, Jaccob found the mug empty, regarded it for a moment, and then pounded it against the top of the bar to get the barkeeper's attention. A room full of eyes passed across the intoxicated man, who seemed not so much different from the rest of the patrons. His clothes looked slept in, his hair was mussed, and his face showed several days' worth of a beard. Slowly the barkeeper approached his customer and put his hand over the top of Jaccob's mug.

"I think you should probably move on tonight, sir. You've had quite enough, and you're starting to disturb the other patrons."

Jaccob sneered. He knew that he looked rough, but found it hard to believe that in his own kingdom, he could not be recognized. Granted, he had only been recently appointed to the post as the Topaz Knight, but after the ceremony and all the fanfare, someone should have taken notice. Jaccob pulled the mug back away from the barkeeper's hand and then pounded it upon the bar again.

"I have money, you have ale. Fill my mug, let me pay you, and then leave me alone."

The barkeeper stood straight and frowned.

"I'm not going to tell you this again. Find somewhere else to get so drunk you can't walk. My patrons don't have to put up with slobbering drunks like you, and I don't have to serve you, no matter how much coin you have in your pocket. Besides, you probably stole it from the look of you. Now, get out of here before I call the Flying Guard."

Just then Jaccob felt a hand rest on his shoulder from behind.

"Come on," the man's rough voice said, "let me help you out of here, pal."

Jaccob quickly swatted the man's hand from his shoulder.

"Leave me alone. Go away. I'm not bothering anyone, I just want another drink."

The large rough hand returned the next moment, and Jaccob felt himself being turned around. There before him were three men, obviously from one of the regiments of the Flying Guard, or perhaps even trainees. All were considerably larger than Jaccob. Instinctively, Jaccob kicked with his foot, forcing the leader of the men back, and then reached for Temperance. As soon as his hand touched the weapon, the fog of alcohol on his mind cleared and he could see and feel everything clearly. The accosting man recovered from the kick quickly and smiled.

"Now, don't be hasty young man…we don't want to hurt you, but we will if we have to…"

* * * * * * * * * * * * *

"There is no reason to be so hasty, Jaccob," Alistair Ravenheart said relaxing back in his chair at the head of the Council of the Arcane. "To make such a decision based upon the evidence at hand is both irresponsible and rash."

Jaccob had been a student at the Academy of Arcane Arts for nearly four years, and was considered to be one of the most promising prospects in many years. However, as his studies delved into the more destructive and dangerous schools of the arcane, it seemed that his tolerance and patience suffered. When the Crawling Plague began to ravage the countryside, Jaccob took it as a personal challenge to not only find the cure, but to find the source. His mind had been made up from the time he had heard the symptoms, the only possible source was the Dark Gods of Mythryn.

"The evidence is conclusive, Master Ravenheart," Jaccob replied. "The outbreak of this plague as well all of the sightings of this Grey Man in the surrounding countryside coincides with reliable eye-witness accounts of agents of the Dark Gods being spotted in the same areas. I would agree that this evidence would be easy to discount if there had been only one sighting. But, to be honest, it seemed that nearly every account of the Grey Man has a corresponding account of an agent from Mythryn or an agent for Galateria not being far away."

Fiona Ebonsight, considered by many to be the next in line to become the Headmaster of the Academy of Arcane Arts, shook her head.

"I agree, Jaccob, that this evidence is strong, but one of the points you are missing is a true connection other than that of geography. There are many possible reasons that the agents of Mythryn were in that vicinity. Only one of those possibilities is that they were responsible or in collusion with this so-called Grey Man. Perhaps they had become alerted to the threat this plague posed and were gathering intelligence in case this Grey Man decided to loose his venom upon the Dark Continent. Given our current state of diplomatic relations with Mythryn, it is unlikely they would be willing to share their findings or their motivations."

Jaccob slammed his hands upon the table.

"Why does this council continue to defend the practices of the enemies of the empire? At this point it should be assumed that Mythryn is involved until there is evidence that they are not. This council must recommend to the Emperor that a strike is made against the Dark Continent, and at the front of that strike should be all mages from the Academy who are of adept rank or higher. With us at the vanguard, it would allow the armies of Cadaria and the Knights of the Flashing Blade to cut a swath through the forces of the Dark Continent, and minimize losses on our side. A single, brutal, swift strike is the only way to guarantee victory."

Alistair Ravenheart stood, and locked his eyes on his student.

"There is no need for us to have this argument again, Jaccob. You have already been stripped of your rank three times because of these beliefs, and if you are not careful, it will cause your expulsion from our order. The arcane abilities learned here are not to be used in any enterprise that would cause the death of another. Only in self-defense should we ever take another's life, and that is only when our own is in danger. You know these teachings, and yet your rabble-rousing and cavalier attitude toward the death of your so-called 'enemies of the empire' persists."

Jaccob left his position at the foot of the council table and moved toward the revered master of the academy.

"And just when does it become enough of a threat, Alistair? How many more have to be killed by these plagues and dark magicks from Mythryn? Does it take the whole of the dark army invading the grounds of the Academy of Arcane Arts and killing novices left and right before you will allow us to use the simplest of parlor tricks to defend ourselves? Does it take the whole-sale slaughter of thousands of innocents before we use the gifts we have been given?"

"You are out of line, Jaccob," Fiona cautioned.

"Why?" Jaccob countered. "Because I am speaking the truth? We are not clerics, we are not priests or monks, and we are not sworn to non-violence or purely peaceful pursuits. If we were, why do we all learn how to call upon the power of fire? Why do we learn to call down lightning from the sky, or project ice? Why is it that I know how to make the blood of my enemies boil, or make their heart seize in their chest, if I am not to use it in combating the enemies of my Empire?"

Alistair stood silent, horrified by the words of the man who could have become the greatest student in the history of the academy.

"The learning of those dark arts has been forbidden for centuries for just the very reason you are illustrating," Fiona Ebonsight countered. "We are not here to learn more effective ways of taking a life, and it seems that your independent studies have become a danger not only to yourself but to the academy and to the empire. It is someone reckless and depraved such as you that will turn this uneasy truce with Mythryn into a full-scale war. I move for the Council to strip all titles and privileges from Adept Jaccob Aldora, and expel him forthwith from the Academy of Arcane Arts forever."

The door slammed behind Jaccob before the vote was even concluded.

* * * * * * * * * * * * *

Jaccob did not hesitate to let the power of the arcane fill him. He could have killed these men with only a thought, but that would be no fun, and would be difficult to explain. Though, in the eyes of the law, they had assaulted a member of the Flashing Blade, which was akin to the assault on the Emperor, an offense punishable by death. Jaccob accelerated his movements with a silent spell, and then shot toward the three men, tripping them quickly and leaving them sprawled out on the tavern floor. When his charge ended at the other end of the tavern, he picked up a tankard from a nearby table and took a long drink.

"I think it is you who are being hasty my friends. And I think you have underestimated how well I can hold my liquor."

The leader of the group stood quickly and drew the short sword from the scabbard at his hip.

"I don't think you really want to do that," Jaccob said softly. "You'll only get hurt."

The answer came in a quick charge. Still feeling the energy coursing through is body, the charge looked as though it were in slow motion. Jaccob sidestepped the attack and took position behind the attacker, pushing him face first into the back wall of the tavern. The impact broke the man's nose, and left a splatter of blood on the wall. A quick swipe from Temperance knocked the man unconscious and left him sprawled across the floor. The other two stood quiet for a moment, and then exchanged a quick glance. They were about to charge together when Jaccob pointed to the floor and a small burst of power leapt from his finger and exploded between their feet. That was enough to send them scampering for the door. Shaking his head, Jaccob walked slowly back to the bar, took his seat, and looked up to the barkeeper.

"Now, my mug of ale?"

The barkeeper stayed silent and filled the mug again, setting it in front of his patron. Inwardly he hoped that the guards would arrive quickly and that there would not be too much damage done to the tavern.

* * * * * * * * * * * * *

Jaccob couldn't help thinking that the scroll that had been delivered was a mistake. The imperial page had arrived at his modest cottage just after dawn with the summons from the new Emperor of Cadaria, Kaitain Lorien. The proclamation was a simple one, Jaccob had been appointed to the position of Topaz Knight, a member of the Flashing Blade, and he was to report to the Imperial Palace in Aldere to receive the official title, station, and duties, as well as the weapon of Hedorah, Temperance. While Jaccob had been born and raised in Hedorah, too many of his years had been spent in the Academy of Arcane Arts in Jelan which fell under the offices of the Kingdom of Knowledge, Menoris, and the Tiger's Eye Knight, Xaran

Firesoul. Jaccob always found it odd that a monk and not a sorcerer had been appointed to the post of Tiger's Eye Knight, and the fact that the only sorcerer in the ranks of the Flashing Blade was Orren Eldrath, a cast-off and shunned former member of the Academy of Arcane Arts. Now, Jaccob would be ascended to the level of sorcerer and would become the second expelled member of the Academy to gain a position as a Knight of the Flashing Blade. It didn't seem that the new emperor was concerned with appearances or the opinions of the Academy of Arcane Arts.

It was many days' travel from the outskirts of Menoris back to the Imperial Palace of Aldere, and when Jaccob did arrive, he was met with the fanfare usually reserved for conquering heroes and emperors. Though the land was still being ravage by the Crawling Plague, Jaccob was treated to a feast, and a full dress ball in his honor. After which, Alistair Ravenheart, standing proud and looking very annoyed delivered the weapon Temperance, and congratulated Jaccob upon his appointment. Jaccob was sure that Alistair had nearly choked on those words. By becoming a member of the Flashing Blade, Jaccob had to be accepted as one of the most powerful sorcerers in Cadaria and at least the equal of any of the Masters in the Academy of Arcane Arts. The irony was not lost on Jaccob.

* * * * * * * * * * * * *

Several mugs of ale, and several minutes later, a small detachment of the Flying Guard entered Hawk's Head Tavern looking for the perpetrator of an assault. Still seated at the bar in his normal seat, Jaccob Aldora sat, oblivious to the new arrivals. When the captain of the detachment approached Jaccob, he stopped short and then snapped a quick salute.

"Sir Aldora," the captain said quickly, "we received a report of an assault here in the tavern. We were not made aware of your presence. Have you already attended to the situation?"

Many of the patrons seemed shocked, and the barkeeper's face went blank. Jaccob sat up straight, Temperance in hand and turned to face the captain.

"It was a minor confrontation captain, and has been dealt with. There will be no charges filed, and no need to pursue it any further. You and your men are dismissed."

The captain saluted again, turned on a heel, and led his men out of the tavern. Jaccob stood up after a moment, annoyed. That made twice during the evening that he had to stop drinking and let Temperance clear his head. What was the use of drinking if you weren't allowed to stay drunk long enough to enjoy it? Jaccob pulled a pouch from his pocket and let it hit the bar.

"This is for my drinks and whatever damage the little fight caused. Make sure to tell your patrons that you are the preferred tavern of the Topaz Knight…I'm sure it will increase your business, and the thieves will leave you alone."

Without another word Jaccob left the tavern to seek his bed. Perhaps he would take the side street down to the local brothel, or perhaps he would find his way to another tavern and try again to escape the tedium of his new life in a mug of ale. Becoming a member of the Flashing Blade did not bring the fame, power, or glory that he thought it would. He had done exactly nothing since gaining the title of Topaz Knight to advance his own cause, or the cause of the Emperor. He had not been dispatched to deal with the dragons, had not been called upon to combat the Wasting Disease, had not been sent to fight the hoards on the continent of Mythryn, had not even be consulted to assist in the relief efforts in any of the other kingdoms. His orders had been to stay and protect Hedorah, the most boring and tedious assignment possible. Once, just once, he wished that he would be given an assignment befitting his position.

Several minutes later he found himself standing before the doors of the most well-known brothel in the kingdom.

* * * * * * * * * * * * *

The sky above the battlefield was blood red, clouds of smoke blotting out the sun. The smell of death was thick in the air, and all across the ground lay the broken bodies of soldiers. Many different banners and colors littered the battlefield, all of the major kingdoms were represented with dead, and as Jaccob Aldora found himself, there was little left that he recognized. The Imperial Palace of Aldere was in ruins, a smoking crater where the throne room had once been. Behind him stood Emperor Kaitain Lorien, clutching a young girl in his arms. She struggled against his grip and screamed. Beside Jaccob, he vaguely recognized some of the members of the Flashing Blade. They were all covered in blood, the price of executing their charge as defenders of the Emperor. But when Jaccob looked around for the beasts of Mythryn, the enemy, all he found were more bodies of imperial citizens, the armies of the empire.

Approaching was Gregor Quicksilver and Hannah Ironheart. Behind them was a contingent of creatures from Mythryn and a group of the Dark Gods.

"You cannot stop me now!" Kaitain called. "I have it, it is mine! You will never prevent my ascension to god-hood! I will unseat the Creator and this world will become mine! I will save us all from the Dark Gods!"

A maniacal laugh tore from the throat of Emperor Kaitain as the reality around them began to become distorted. Fire emerged from thin air, and breathable air became poison. The next moment the world would turn mad, ripped upside down and inside out by the desires of the man who called himself Emperor of Cadaria.

* * * * * * * * * * * * *

Jaccob awoke with a start. The nightmares were getting worse. As he began to untangle himself from the three naked female bodies that shared his bed, the headache began to fill his head again. Ever since Temperance had been laid into his hands, the nightmares had come. Each night they were different, but they all showed new and different horrible ways that the planet would die. Sometimes it was the Emperor, sometimes it was himself, other times it was the Dark Gods. The only common thread was the level of death and destruction, and the presence of a nameless faceless girl in the middle of it all. Jaccob had begun to believe that they were glimpses into possible futures, and in all of these nights, he had never seen one that ended well. A great deal of death was on its way to Cadaria, and there did not seem to be any way to prevent it.

CHAPTER 47

Quietly Jaccob dressed and then left the brothel. He was sure that he was late for some appointment or another at the capitol, not that it mattered. As he entered the grounds, the sentries on guard snapped to attention, and a middle-aged man carrying a lute approached. Jaccob scanned his memory for the man's name and finally found it. He was the Imperial Poet, Geoffry Aramour.

"Sir Aldora, it is agreeable to see you again," Geoffry said pleasantly.

Jaccob nodded and began to walk past. However, Geoffry took a step to the right, back in Jaccob's path.

"What can I do for you?" Jaccob asked shortly, the headache still pounding his brain.

"The Emperor has sent me on a matter of some urgency. I have an assignment for you from the Emperor himself."

Jaccob paused for a moment.

"And why would the Emperor send you to deliver his message?"

Geoffry frowned.

"I do not believe that is any of your concern. The Emperor commands and you obey."

The tone in Geoffry's voice bespoke power and a not-so-lightly veiled threat. There was certainly more to this man Geoffry Aramour, a dangerous something.

"Very well, poet. What is this assignment?"

Geoffry pulled Jaccob out of earshot of the guards and recovered a scroll from his pouch and opened it.

"You are to travel to the port city of Escan in the Kingdom of Water Thorigald to meet an emissary from the Dark Continent of Mythryn. Her name is Tess Annis, and she is to be conducted with all haste to the Imperial Palace of Aldere to meet with the Emperor on a matter of great urgency. This mission is to remain secret. You may request any aid from another member of the Flashing Blade, but they are under no circumstances to know the details of your mission, or the identity of the woman you are escorting. If any harm befalls this woman, or your mission is discovered, the punishment will be severe. Do you understand this mission?"

Jaccob was puzzled. Why would he be conducting a representative from Mythryn to Aldere while they were in the middle of a war? It made no sense.

"I understand," Jaccob said, taking the scroll from Geoffry.

His puzzlement deepened as he made his way from Hedorah to Thorigald. Nothing seemed to make sense any more, and perhaps he had made the wrong choice after all to become a member of the Flashing Blade, as if it were ever really a choice.

CHAPTER 47

Chapter XLVIII

Truth, Lies, and Legacy

Year Two of the Just Emperor Kaitain "Dragonsbane" Lorien, Creator's Calendar Year 1869

The Academy of Arcane Arts in Jelan stood at the foot of the highest mountain range in the Kingdom of Menoris, on the opposite side of the mountain chain from the capitol city of Menoris itself. As the twin suns began to peek over the snow-capped peaks of the mountain range to the east, a flurry of activity had already begun in and around the many buildings that comprised the academy proper. Novices and Apprentices alike made their way to classes and conducted their research under the watchful gaze of Teachers and Acolytes. There was always something going on at the academy, and this day was no different. However, away from the bustle and din of the academy grounds, in the highest tower of the academy, the Masters' Council met to discuss the recent events in the Empire.

The Council historically was made up of five masters, one for each of the prime elements of the Arcane: Stone, Energy, Fire, Water, and Wind. However, since the death of Alistair Ravenheart, the council was incomplete. It would take some time to find a new Master of Water, time the council did not have considering the circumstances and the current position of disfavor the Emperor held the academy in. So, on this day, the fifth seat remained empty as the four remaining masters filed into the room. This council had turned out to be different than many others of the past. It seemed that the more inclined and powerful students enrolling in the academy were women, and there were much fewer male students than in previous generations. An alarmingly fewer number. To this end, as the four masters sat to begin their discussion, it was no surprise that all of the remaining masters were women.

"I call this meeting of the Masters' Council to order," Fiona Ebonsight said quickly and then reached for the logbook that held the minutes of previous meetings. The logbook kept itself through the use of simple spells, and was always perfectly accurate to the second and to the word.

Fiona had been fostered to the Academy of Arcane Arts on her fifth birthday, much as her brothers and sisters had been before her. It was a family tradition in the Ebonsight family. For a time, Fiona struggled to adjust to the rigors of the life of a Novice, but in time she adapted and became a promising student on the verge of breaking out of the pack and becoming truly exceptional. However, Fiona in her second year as an Apprentice became romantically involved with an Acolyte who had been directing some of her independent studies. Within a matter of months, Fiona was pregnant, and had to withdraw from the Academy. She would prove her strength, determination, and dedication several years later when she returned to the Academy with her five year old daughter in tow, and petitioned for re-admittance to the academy. Both Fiona and her daughter Aris were admitted to the academy, and together would become two of the most formidable students the academy had ever seen. In a matter of successive years, Fiona, and then Aris would gain the title of youngest woman to ever attain the rank of Sorceress, and then the youngest to attain the rank of Master. It also marked the first time in the history of the council that family members sat on the Masters' Council at the same time. Fiona, as the oldest member of the Masters' Council took over control of the Academy after Alistair Ravenheart's death, and as the Master of Fire, was perhaps the most dangerous and respected member of the Masters' Council.

Aris Ebonsight while her mother's daughter in many ways, was also the complete opposite of her mother in many ways. While Fiona's abilities centered around the carefully restrained destructive natures of the Arcane, Aris's centered more around the healing aspects of the Wind element. Aris was also far more skilled at the subtle arts of diplomacy and courtliness, while Fiona valued brevity and directness. Aris often thought that her mother could have used more subtly and tact in some matters, especially when dealing with the Imperial City of Aldere, but all in all, Aris knew that her mother was a more than capable leader.

The third member of the Masters' Council was the only appointment from the Imperial City of Aldere, however, she did not owe her appointment to the current emperor, but to the Just Emperor Ender Lorien. As a favorite niece of the Just Emperor, Ashinica Maupin was admitted to the Academy of Arcane Arts as a favor to the Emperor, however her advancement was upon her own merits. A member of the royal family of Lordhill, the richest producer of all types of metals in the empire, Ashinica had received as many advantages as were possible in her life, most of which had been earned in one fashion or another, whether she had to or not. She knew that her family's appointment to the stewardship of Lordhill could be revoked at any time by the Emperor, and so she was always careful to do as she was asked, even if it became uncomfortable for her. Much to Ashinica's disgust, it seemed that Kaitain Lorien had no qualms about using her family's position as blackmail. However, now that Ashinica had been elevated to the position of Master of Stone, there was little that even the pig emperor Kaitain could do to touch her.

Beautiful and stoic, Jastra Mythryn, the Master of Energy sat quietly, waiting for the meeting to progress past the reading of the previous meeting's minutes. The only member of the council not of noble birth, Jastra had to work five times harder than anyone else to achieve the rank of Sorceress. The middle child of farmer parents, with three boys both younger and older than herself, Jastra had to equate herself by learning to defend against the jibes and prodding of her brothers. Never a lady and never proper, Jastra fit in more as "one of the boys" instead of playing with the other girls in the village. When her talents began to blossom, Alistair Ravenheart fostered her admission to the Academy of Arcane Arts, and became like a foster-father to Jastra until she became acclimated to her new life. Once that had been accomplished, Jastra roomed with Fiona Ebonsight, and the two became fast friends. While many apprentices and novices in the Academy had talent with fire, a very few had the touch to deal with the raw energy of the universe. Many who tried failed with disastrous results. Most of the deaths in the Academy of Arcane Arts came from experimentation with the realm of energy and its every changing properties. But what was dangerous and fearsome for most was child's play for Jastra. The building blocks of the universe, the stuff of stars and suns were molded in her hands like simple clay. Before long, Jastra and Fiona's friendship became a friendly rivalry that continued as each attained new ranks. Fiona would have the last laugh though, being promoted to Master three weeks before Jastra.

"As many of you have already heard by now," Fiona said after the reading of the minutes concluded, "the war with the dragons goes poorly for the Empire. Losses are numbered in the tens of thousands, with the loss of crops and property a nearly incalculable amount. Soon, the request will come from the Imperial Palace in Aldere for the Academy to lend its support to the Imperial Legions. I expect that the Moonstone Knight himself will be dispatched to bring the order and to form companies."

"This cannot be allowed to occur," Ashinica said slowly and deliberately. "For as long as the Academy of Arcane Arts has stood here in Jelan, the first rule of any who study here is to never use what we are taught for destructive purposes, except when our lives are in danger. While I agree this threat of the dragons is a dire one, it is one of our own making. The Emperor began this war, and now that he is losing, he is going to do everything in his power to make sure we have no choice but to assist in his foolishness. Perhaps we should bar the gates to the Academy and defend ourselves against everyone, including the Emperor and his Knights of the Flashing Blade."

Jastra frowned.

"You come dangerously close to treason, child of the Empire."

Ashinica bristled at the label. Though she was noble born, the fact that it was well known her appointment came from the Emperor was never far from the thoughts or the lips of her rivals. Ashinica and Jastra had never seen eye to eye on anything, and while Ashinica was more traditional in her beliefs, Jastra was more progressive, feeling that the nature of the universe was that of growth through conflict.

"We are free to speak our minds here, Jastra," Aris countered. "There is no treason and no fear of repercussions from our words. Only through the free exchange of ideas can we be sure that the Masters' Council is taking the correct action in all things. Sometimes those thoughts are unpopular, and even distasteful. But as you say, only through conflict can we grow."

Jastra felt her cheeks flush. Aris was an adept diplomat and usually played peace-maker in the council sessions. Her memory was nearly flawless, and she could recite back everything she had ever read or heard with few if any mistakes. She also had the gift to perfectly mimic any sound she had ever heard, including voices. While she never had an aptitude for music in her life, if she were to hear someone sing, she could reproduce their performance perfectly with only a moment to prepare. Had Aris had a more devious mind, she could put her talents to a more clandestine use.

"There is wisdom in barring ourselves away from the rest of the Empire," Fiona said after a moment. "But there are complications. We could not deny entry to anyone who was a member of the Academy, and we could not deny any member the ability to leave. Additionally, we would need a more militant force to protect us from the eventual response from Aldere. As there is no diplomatic solution to this issue, because of the Just Emperor's decree, I will have to support the initiative to bar the gates of the Academy."

The three women turned their heads to look at Jastra who still seemed to be mulling over the options. While Jastra had never had any love in her heart for the Empire itself or for the nobles who ran it, her concerns harkened back to her roots and others like her who were just coming into the knowledge of their abilities.

"And what is to stop the Emperor from taking those who are less than novice level from the villages and towns of the Empire and thrusting them into battle expecting them to help turn the tide against the dragons. We could be responsible for assisting him in murdering the future of this Academy and of the Empire. An alternative would be to take a few of the Sorcerer and Adept level students and lend them to detachments of the Imperial Legions. They would be able to defend themselves and the units they are with, and have a much better chance of returning alive. That way we would not have to sacrifice our future to save our present."

Ashinica shook her head.

"The Emperor has already begun to form an arcane training program of his own. That much cannot be disputed. That is why there are so many fewer male students with any talent. Only the weakest make it to us, with few exceptions. There is only one place they could be, and that is under the watchful gaze of the Emperor."

"Alistair would never have let that happen," Fiona countered.

"Alistair would not have known about it if it was being done by Kaitain and his allies. Now that he is the Emperor, and he has the talents of Orren Eldrath and Jaccob Aldora at his disposal, the destructive capabilities of those under his command increase tenfold. We both know the boy had designs on the throne long before his father contracted the Crawling Plague, and I am sure that he would have tried to make a grab for the throne in time without the intervention of the plague," Ashinica replied.

"We shall have to research this more fully," Aris said finally, "which strangely enough brings me to the next topic that we must discuss. Ayden."

Jastra growled.

"That boy must be expelled. He has no interest in being here at the Academy, and I can think of no reason why we should ask him to stay. His disciplinary file is larger than most spell books I have seen, and that is just the things we know about and can prove. From flooding the girl's lavatory, turning the water in the cisterns into ale, using the wind to lift the dresses of the female students that pass by, to using unseen forces to pinch girls in improper places. He is the worst kind of troublemaker, and is utterly and completely unapologetic for anything he has ever done."

Fiona stifled a small laugh.

"Ayden is a hand-full, that much is sure, but he has never done anything overtly harmful or too indecent. He seems to know just where the line is, and how much he can bend the rules. But you must admit, that his progress is nothing short of stellar, and if he were to ever really apply himself, he could rival any of us."

"Need I remind you," Ashinica replied, "of the time that he made frogs spontaneously appear in all of our drinking glasses at dinner? Or the time that he discovered that the wind could be used to unlace anything he wanted? Or when he inverted the gravity in the novice hall?"

"We all know there are special circumstances that keep Ayden here. While Alistair has taken those secrets to his grave, I believe that we owe it to Alistair to work as best we can to preserve Ayden's enrollment in the Academy," Fiona responded with a chuckle.

Despite herself, Fiona had always liked Ayden. He reminded her of her older brother once upon a time. Ayden was only seventeen years old, and going through the rebellions phase of most young men his age. However, Fiona had always felt something more from Ayden, something deeper and darker. Perhaps that is why Alistair fostered him into the Academy despite the objection of the rest of the Masters' Council. Many times Fiona had tried to get Alistair to confess the secret behind Ayden, but every attempt had been rebuffed. Ayden certainly wasn't talking.

"Then let us kill two birds with one stone," Ashinica said finally. "Let us publicly expel Ayden from the Academy, and send him off on his own. Privately we will give him instructions to attempt to find whether or not there is a secret force of adepts and sorcerers under the control of the Emperor. Given his history with the Academy, it will not be difficult to convince everyone that he earned his expulsion, and I am sure that Kaitain could not resist snapping up yet another fallen member of the Academy to do his bidding."

Fiona took a deep breath.

"So, this council had concluded the following: the gates of the Academy of Arcane Arts in Jelan will be barred to protect the sanctity of our cause, and that a defense force will be founded to ensure the protection of the students, faculty, and grounds. Additionally, we will dispatch Ayden on a mission to infiltrate the Imperial Legions to learn if there is a covert training school for those with arcane ability under the offices of the Emperor. If these conclusions are agreed upon, signify to the affirmative."

"The Master of Wind agrees," Aris answered.

"The Master of Stone agrees," Ashinica followed.

There was a long pause while Jastra stood with her eyes closed. She seemed to be battling within herself as to whether or not they were taking the right action. Finally, her eyes opened, and she nodded.

"The Master of Energy agrees," Jastra said finally.

"The Master of Fire agrees," Fiona concluded, "and so it shall be done."

Aris stood and began to retrieve the minutes scrolls from the table.

"I will inform Ayden as to his mission," Aris said after a moment. "I think he will take it better coming from me."

Jastra shook her head.

"I don't think that is a good idea, Aris. It's been obvious for some time that Ayden has a bit of a fancy for you, and there is no telling what he will do if you are that close to him for that amount of time. He and I may not have the best of relationship, but I can handle Ayden for the few minutes that will be required."

Jastra and Aris left the room a few moments later, followed quickly by Ashinica; still mumbling about Ayden's many offenses. Fiona sat back at the table again, chuckling to herself about Ayden and her daughter. They would probably make a good couple if times were different. Ayden just wild enough to keep Aris on her toes, while Aris might be able to introduce some temperance into Ayden's life. Fiona was about to get up and leave the room when the door to the Masters' chamber suddenly closed.

"You should really be more careful about who you let in here Fiona," a female voice said from the direction of the window. "You would think that four talented women such as yourselves would not be so careless."

Suddenly the room went dark and was filled with a cold mist. Fiona steeled herself and channeled a small amount of fire into her body, bringing her body temperature back up to normal despite the near freezing temperature in the room. When light returned, Fiona was not alone in the room, and standing across the table from her was a lovely young woman with dark hair and crystal blue eyes with a yellow border that shone cold and nearly lifeless. Power radiated from the woman in a way that Fiona had never felt before, and a shiver ran through Fiona as she prepared herself for combat.

"There is no need to fear from me, Fiona Ebonsight," the woman said after a moment, "I am not here to quarrel with you or your academy. I am here simply to deliver a message."

Fiona swallowed hard. The fear and uneasiness had not left her yet.

"A message from whom?"

"From the Council of Darkness, the ruling body of the Continent of Mythryn."

Fiona felt as though she had been struck. An agent of the Dark Gods stood not far from her, and Fiona felt overwhelmed. With a thought, Fiona reached for the power of Fire in her mind and channeled a blast that would have melted the strongest shield of any warrior. The woman simply raised her hand and the fire struck her flesh and then simply dissipated. Once the flames were gone, there was not even a scratch left on the woman's pale skin.

"That was foolish," the woman said coldly, "if I had wanted to, I could have crushed your entire council with a thought. You do not face some petty sorceress, or even the child of a Dark God, you face a member of the Council of Darkness, one of the true rulers of Espre, you face Serrina Mistic, the Voice of Darkness. And I am surprised, Master of Fire, that you would so quickly break your Academy's own rules and lash out. I see that the influence of Kaitain Lorien has already been felt out here. Humans, your principles become so malleable so quickly."

Fiona fell back into her chair, conceding defeat, but the real cause of her weakness was her own shame. She stood no chance of defeating one of the Dark Gods on her own, and it had been folly to even try. There was little she could do but sit and listen.

"I have no choice but to listen then," Fiona said disheartened.

"You had no choice to begin with, and if it weren't for your petty attempts to harm me, we could have had a civil conversation. Now we will simply have to stop being cordial and come right to the point. The Council of Darkness extends amnesty to the Academy of Arcane Arts in Jelan. Provided that your students show a better adherence to your rules than their Masters and take no role in any military action against the Continent of Mythryn, the Council of Darkness will view the Academy and its members as non-combatants and avoid any confrontation with you. Additionally, we will offer protection and sanctuary to any member of the Academy that requests it. However, should you or any member of the Academy take up arms against the Dark Gods or their forces without provocation, we will crush this place and all within it into dust."

Fiona was dumbfounded. Before she could respond, the door to the chamber burst open, and in the doorway stood a formidable woman, dressed in a flowing white dress, and holding a short staff with a long curved blade at the end. The naginata known as Wisdom was an inelegant weapon, but when in the hands of the Jade Knight Leonora Wastri, it was a fearsome instrument.

"I see that I was dispatched with good reason," Leonora said coldly looking at the dark woman standing before her. "I had received warning of a dark sorceress who had been attempting to infiltrate the Academy of Arcane Arts, and now I see that those reports were not in error. Identify yourself woman, before you are brought to justice."

Serrina laughed.

"So, this is one of the vaunted members of the Knights of the Flashing Blade. I am not impressed. So tell me, lowborn, what did you do to gain your position of honor? Did you also sleep with the Emperor as your Court Sorceress did to gain favor, or did he not find you attractive enough to bed?"

Leonora's face remained calm and serene in the face of the insults.

"Your jibes will have no effect on me witch. It is clear to me that you are evil, and it is clear to me that the only recourse I have is to destroy you. Let us not let petty insults stand between us any longer."

"I like a confident opponent, Leonora Wastri of the Kingdom of Oradrim. It is all the more tragic when you discover that you have no chance against me."

Serrina stood, her arms outstretched to either side, and her head tilted back.

"Strike me down, if you can."

Without hesitation, Leonora shot forward, Wisdom's blade streaking toward the exposed throat of the invader. Mere inches from its target, Serrina's hand swooped in and took hold of the blade, stopping it as the point barely scraped her throat. With a single push, Leonora was sent sprawling across the room, and Wisdom landed beside her. However, without any time to recover, Leonora was back to her feet, charging again, this time sidestepping the attempt to parry, and landing a clear blow to the side of the dark woman. However, instead of the plume of blood that both Leonora and Fiona had expected, the blade was stopped by the woman's garments, and Serrina laughed. The taunting smiled disappeared, and Serrina's eyes glowed red for a moment before an unseen force slammed against Leonora's cheek. Fiona could hear the breaking of bones and watched as a stream of blood flew from Leonora's open mouth, accompanied by several teeth. Another unseen blow struck the Jade Knight in the side and sent her sprawling to the ground again, gasping for breath.

"I just broke your jaw, eye socket, and five of your ribs," Serrina said coldly. "I'm quite sure you have a punctured lung and quite a bit of internal bleeding. A lesser woman would be dead by now, but it seems that you are tougher than most."

Leonora forced herself to her feet and took up Wisdom. Expelling the pain from her body, Leonora drew strength from Wisdom and from her many years of training and reached deep into her reserves of powers gifted to her by her position. With a thought, her body became insubstantial, a faint silhouette of her shape still holding Wisdom firm. The next strikes would find their target, but as before, causing no obvious damage to her opponent. However, the inevitable counter attack would send Leonora sprawling to the ground again, this time her leg broken in three places.

"A nice parlor trick," Serrina scoffed. "This battle is over Leonora. I could take your life if I wanted, but that is not our way. I will spare you, and let you live with the shame of your defeat. Know that the Dark Gods of Mythryn are not to be trifled with, and if your Emperor continues his provocative actions against us, we will be forced to retaliate and level his precious Empire. We only wanted peace, and now he brings us war. Very well, if that is what he wants, that is what he gets. Take this message back to your Emperor. If one more attack is leveled against Mythryn or any of its people by any military asset controlled by Emperor Kaitain Lorien, the Dark Gods will personally return to Cadaria, and this time, there will be no truce, and it will end with the Dark Gods assuming the throne."

With those last words, Serrina faded from the room, and the temperature returned to normal. Fiona was at Leonora's side the next moment, trying her best to tend to the woman's many wounds.

"I'm afraid the wounds are severe Lady Wastri," Fiona said after a moment.

"The wounds are of no consequence," Leonora said finally. "Heal me as best you can, for I must make the journey back to Aldere as soon as possible to return these tidings. I must also face my fate for failing the Emperor."

"We can send a messenger to relay the message while you heal. You will not be fit to travel for some time."

"I will leave in the morning," Leonora responded. "Whether I can ride, or must be pulled along in a litter, it must be so."

Fiona knew at that moment she was not going to be able to talk Leonora out of her decided-upon course of action. Part of Fiona knew what would come next. Leonora would be disgraced and exiled from the Empire, forced to live out her days with the memories of her failure. Or, the unthinkable could happen, Kaitain could order her execution, and for the first time since its inception, the Flashing Blade would have to put one of their own to death. Fiona did not know which thoughts were worse, the fact that Kaitain was slowing destroying the fabric of the Empire, or the fact that the Dark Gods could snuff out their existence as quickly as snuffing out a candle.

Audience

Year Two of the Just Emperor Kaitain "Dragonsbane" Lorien, Creator's Calendar Year 1869

Travel from any of the great kingdoms to the Imperial Provinces of Aldere was difficult, and travel papers had to be signed not only by a local magistrate of the Great Kingdom, but also by a magistrate of Aldere. Therefore, only those people who had power and influence could come and go as the pleased. The Knights of the Flashing Blade had standing right to do as they pleased and were never questioned. Sometimes though, when new members were introduced into the ranks of the Flashing Blade, there were miscommunications. As Tolon Morr stood on the side of the road being questioned by a group of Aldere Magistrates, he thought to himself that lines of communication would need to be improved.

"Just one more moment, Sir Tolon, we just need to get confirmation of your status as the Amethyst Knight," the magistrate said smiling.

Tolon tried to suppress a growl.

"This would have been much easier if you had the seal of your position."

After a moment, Tolon balled his fist and resisted the urge to draw Strength from his belt. Every moment he was delayed, the longer the

Emperor would have to wait for the message from the Triplets. Granted the Emperor would not be thrilled by the less than genial response from the three women, but being made to wait for bad news would reflect poorly on the messenger.

"Carrying the seal of my position on a covert mission for the Emperor of Cadaria could have serious consequences. Though I doubt someone of your limited intelligence and experience could make that determination without having it written down and signed by a superior," Tolon muttered.

"What was that Sir Tolon?"

Tolon laughed.

"Simply complimenting the fine work of the Aldere Magistrates."

The magistrate smiled and then went back to his conversation. It was quite a few minutes later that the situation was finally resolved, and Tolon was back on his way toward the Imperial Palace of Aldere. Things had gotten bad all around Cadaria since the open war was declared with the dragons and the rumors of conflict with Mythryn was brewing again. Tolon was sure that the Emperor was under an immense amount of stress, and with these new demands from the Maldovrin Triplets, it was about to get considerably worse. Upon entering the grounds of the palace at Aldere, Tolon remembered fondly the first time he had been to Aldere.

Tolon had not been born in to the best circumstances, and the life of a commoner actually looked like royalty to him. Tolon's mother had been sold into slavery when she was old enough, and started as a simple servant girl to one of the royal houses in the Kingdom of Steel, Celidar. In time, one of the young masters of the house would take a liking to the girl and would take her as his own. Her station never changed, and she became his personal pleasure slave and companion. Before long, she was with child. Because it was a shame on the family to have a child with a bound servant, Tolon's heritage was hidden and eventually expunged from any records, and Tolon was raised in the palace of Celidar as a slave. When he was old enough, his father sold Tolon to the brutal gladiatorial games to train. Tolon was sure that his father had simply been trying to finally dispose of his illegitimate son. However, unlike most of the cattle that were sold to the gladiatorial arena, Tolon did not wilt under the pressure and threat of death. In fact, Tolon thrived in the environment. The persistent and pervasive threat of death around every corner, the constant fight for the basic right to exist, it seemed to invigorate Tolon and drive him to become more than his station demanded.

As the months passed into years, Tolon became a feared force in the gladiatorial games, racking up win after win, and kill upon kill. In time, Tolon became one of the best known and most beloved gladiators in the Empire, always good for a show, and never too quick to kill his opponent. It seemed that he had a gift to toy with his opponents and skirt the very edge of death and still retain the victory. The first time Tolon was in Aldere was for the gladiatorial games on the anniversary of the rule of Emperor Ender Lorien. That day he killed seven opponents and escaped with only a scratch. Two years later, Tolon had won his one hundredth match, and from the Lord of Celidar had received the greatest gift a slave could ever be given, his freedom.

However, for Tolon, the years of blood and death in the role of a gladiator could not simply be washed away with a few words from a faceless lord. Tolon could never become a farmer or a simple commoner. His very being thirsted for death, he needed to feel the cold steel of a weapon in his hands, and he needed to be in the thick of battle where his life was on the line every moment. There was no life unless that life was at risk every moment. And so, Tolon traded the garb of a gladiator for that of a soldier and joined the Steel Legion of Celidar. As a soldier, Tolon was a monster. He volunteered for every dangerous mission, every treacherous post, and was the first to step on the battlefield for any confrontation. On the battlefield, he was a terror, dispatching opponents by the dozens and striking fear into the hearts of all who saw him fight. He had an affinity for blood, either his own or that of others, and he would wear it with pride. He was a terrifying sight, bounding across a battlefield, his armor stained with the blood of enemies, screaming a savage war cry, looking for his next opponent. Eventually he was given command of an elite unit of warriors, the Red Steel Brigade. Their specialty was ending confrontations quickly before they could escalate to full-scale warfare. They were very good at what they did, and it kept Tolon where he wanted to be, right in the thick of conflict. Finally, when the position of Amethyst Knight of the Flashing

Blade opened, Tolon was the only one considered, and he took his place of honor as one of the most revered warriors in all of Cadaria, and it seemed that he joined at just the right time, when the empire was becoming embroiled in the midst of two bloody wars. Hopefully, his days as messenger were over, and he would be sent to the front to make the enemies of the empire pay.

Tolon entered the receiving chamber outside the throne room of the Imperial Palace and waited. The Emperor was hearing petitions for aid from most of the Great Kingdoms of the Empire, and with their forces scattered all over Cadaria, it was difficult to give aid to any but the most needy of groups. Even then, there was only so much aid that could be offered. As Tolon looked around the room, his eyes found a beautiful woman wearing a bright blue gown. However, while the gown was quite in fashion for the imperial palace, the apparent light chain mail bodice underneath her dress was not. Along with the slightly oversized sword on her hip and the telltale look of a warrior in her eyes, Tolon felt this new arrival could be an interesting distraction for him as he waited for an audience with his master. Tolon walked over to the woman, only to be greeted with a defiant stare.

"What is it you want?"

The greeting was definitively not one of a lady of the court, it was much too direct and forceful. Tolon liked it.

"You are quite an interesting sight for these halls of power. You dress like a lady and a warrior at the same time. Reminds me a lot of Hannah Ironheart, though the sword is all wrong. Perhaps closer to Chelsea Zarova. Allow me to introduce myself, I am…."

"Tolon Morr, Amethyst Knight of the Flashing Blade. I saw you fight in the gladiatorial ring some time ago. You were quite impressive then. I am sorry to say that much of your luster has worn off in the years since. Do you not know that you are supposed to bathe after you travel if you are going to meet someone of importance such as the Emperor?"

Tolon smiled.

"I'm sure I have a few minutes before my audience, if you want to bathe me."

The woman smiled and laughed, then struck Tolon firmly on the cheek. The strike hurt, and hurt far more than he thought it would. Then he noticed the faint glitter of metal at the edges of the woman's gloves. They had obviously been lined with something, probably chain mail. Tolon was about to respond to the assault when the doors to the throne room opened, and the page called out over the din of the crowd.

"Emperor Kaitain Lorien will now hear from the Amethyst Knight of the Kingdom of Steel, Celidar, Sir Tolon Morr."

Tolon glared at the woman for a moment, and then smiled a wide smile.

"Maybe we can have that bath afterwards."

Tolon laughed to himself and then walked up the long flight of stairs that led to the Imperial Throne Room. Though the day had been busy, aside from the imperial guards that were always stationed in the palace, the throne room seemed empty and cold. Most of the tapestries that had hung in the throne room during the rule of Ender Lorien had been removed, and all of the other decorations other than the seal of Cadaria that hung behind the throne had been removed. It was said that Kaitain Lorien had received threats against his life, and that he had all of the tapestries and drapes removed to keep assassins from using them as cover. However, it had also been said in many circles that many of these precautions were nothing more than rampant paranoid brought on by the war with the dragons and the coming war with Mythryn. Tolon strode down the center of the room as he had been instructed long ago, approached to within ten feet of the throne, and then dropped to one knee with his head bowed.

"Rise and report, Sir Tolon Morr."

The voice had not been that of the Emperor. When Tolon rose, he saw that the Emperor sat looking through a series of scrolls, and that it had been the Ethereal Sorceress, Irene Drage who had addressed him. Irene was strikingly beautiful, and wore thin, almost transparent dresses that would have caused a scandal. However, Emperor Lorien would not allow any such slander to be spoken of Irene.

"As ordered, I made my way to the lair of the Maldovrin Triplets and delivered the request of the Emperor. I was received warmly, and the Triplets did entertain the request."

At those words, Kaitain sat up and fixed his eyes on Tolon. There was something different about the man since the last time that Tolon had seen him. His hair was slightly unkempt, and his eyes were bloodshot. It looked as though Kaitain had not slept in many nights, and the fatigue was beginning to weigh on him. At first, Tolon thought it was only the stress of the situation, but as Tolon felt the Emperor's gaze wash over him, and his stare locked upon the younger man's eyes, a shudder washed through Tolon, like something, inhuman, was staring back at him.

"So, Sir Tolon Morr, you have the location of the Dragon's Tear?"

Tolon swallowed hard, and then shook his head.

"After delivering the request to the Maldovrin Triplets, as well as the proposed payment for the information, they responded with a demand of their own for the information."

Kaitain was visibly annoyed by the development.

"They have the audacity to make a demand of the Emperor of Cadaria? Very well, what is this demand?"

"In order to impress upon the Emperor of Cadaria the gravity of the request made, the Maldovrin Triplets request that the Ethereal Sorceress, Irene Drage be put to death by the hand of the Emperor himself, and that her head be delivered to the Maldovrin Triplets. At that time, the information will be delivered. If this request is denied, the Maldovrin Triplets have decreed that they will hear no more requests from the Cadarian Emperor, and any who approach with such requests will be destroyed long before they reach their destination."

There was no reaction from Emperor Kaitain for a moment; he simply sat on the throne as if he did not hear what Tolon had said. For several long minutes this silence continued, the Emperor, unmoving and unblinking on the throne, staring at Tolon. Finally, Kaitain laughed, a high maniacal laughter.

"And so you executed them as ordered. I am sorry that you had to destroy them Tolon, but at least the information will fall to no other."

Tolon remained silent. Kaitain locked his eyes back upon Tolon, reading the expression of his servant.

"You did carry out your orders and execute them, didn't you?"

Finally, Tolon shook his head and fell back to one knee.

"I am sorry my Emperor. I knew the orders that I had been given, and though I tried to obey, I was unable to carry out your orders. There is no excuse to be given. I was the one who failed, and therefore I deserve whatever punishment you see fit to levy against me."

Kaitain nearly leapt from the throne, the Imperial Sword in hand. His intention was obvious, and Tolon prepared himself for the strike, but it never came. When Tolon looked up, he saw Irene whispering into the Emperor's ear, and a wide smile suddenly came to Kaitain's face.

"It occurs to me," Kaitain said moving back toward the throne, "that you did well in attempting to fulfill your orders. However, faced with three women as powerful as the Maldovrins, it seems unlikely that you would have been able to harm them. At least now I know the truth. They do know the location of the Dragon's Tear, and I cannot allow that knowledge to be possessed by anyone other than myself. Tolon?"

Tolon stood the next moment.

"Tolon, you have done well to this point, but now I must ask you to return to the valley of the Maldovrins and carry out your original orders, no matter what. The Maldovrin Triplets will surrender the information they have about the Dragon's Tear, or they will be destroyed. Kill two of them, which two, I do not care, but you must bring one of them back to be questioned. If you fail in this task Tolon, do not bother returning. Simply return your weapon to the Kingdom of Celidar and then disappear, for if I ever see your face ever again, I will make sure you suffer for your failure. Do you understand your orders?"

"Yes, my Emperor."

"That is a good soldier," Kaitain said dismissively. He then waived his hand as he turned his attention back to the scrolls that lay on the low table beside the throne. "You are dismissed."

Tolon stood fast for a moment, and then began to turn to leave.

"Was there something else, Sir Tolon?"

The Emperor's voice was thick with anger and annoyance.

"No, my Emperor."

"If you are worried about the threat of destruction by the Maldovrins," Kaitain said after a moment, "you needn't do so. Irene assures me that the powers of the Triplets does not stretch far enough to make good on any threat. And I have faith in your abilities as the Amethyst Knight. Return with one of the Triplets and you will be well rewarded. Now, go."

Tolon bowed low, and then turned to make the long walk away from the throne. He had a sickening feeling in the bit of his stomach, and he did not know how he would be able to carry out his assignment. If his weapon Strength would not allow him to act against the Maldovrins, how was he going to execute two of them and hold a third long enough to return her to the Emperor. To wield Strength was to wield no other weapon, and even the thought of holding another weapon could sever him from Strength's power forever. Tolon was in a no-win situation. As he exited the throne room, his head full of worry and doubt, Tolon barely heard the page call for the next audience.

"The Just Emperor Kaitain Lorien will now hear from Jillian Corven."

There was a small murmur through the crowd, a murmur that grew louder when there was no answer to the summons. Tolon began to look around the room as the page called again.

"The Just Emperor Kaitain Lorien will now hear from Jillian Corven."

Again there was no answer to the summons. After a moment, the page descended the steps and moved toward the lady in blue that Tolon had spoken with briefly before his audience. She looked confident, yet annoyed with the proceedings. The two exchanged some quick words, which Tolon could not hear. The page began to grow agitated, at which point Tolon moved closer.

"I cannot announce you that way, miss, it would not be proper."

The woman frowned.

"I am here because I was summoned; however, I will not be insulted this way. You will either announce me as the Lady of Cadaria, or I will not answer this summons. I will sit here all day, and make the vaunted Emperor wait. I am here by his decree, which I had no choice by to answer. Now, do your job and announce me, or explain to your Emperor why he is being kept waiting."

The page was about to launch into another tirade about protocol, when Tolon stepped between them.

"Thank goodness Sir Tolon. This common woman wants to be announced as a lady in the Imperial Palace before she will take her audience with the Emperor. He is being kept waiting now, and he will not like that one bit. But she says if she is not announced as the Lady of Cadaria, she will not answer the summons. Please talk some sense into this woman, Sir Tolon."

Tolon scratched his chin softly.

"I think you should do as she asked," Tolon said finally.

The page simply stared.

"If there are any repercussions, you can tell them that I ordered you to do it. Now, go make your announcement so that the Emperor is not kept waiting any longer."

The page bowed and returned to the top of the stairs.

"The Just Emperor Kaitain Lorien will now hear from…" the page took a deep breath and nearly choked on the next words, "…the Lady of Cadaria, Jillian Corven."

Jillian finally smiled, and began to walk toward the steps leading to the throne room. Tolon cleared his throat and then spoken.

"I think you owe me that bath," Tolon said smiling.

Jillian turned for a moment, looked over Tolon and then smiled.

"Alright."

The next thing Tolon knew, a large glob of spit hit him on the side of the face.

"Start with that, and we'll see about the rest."

Jillian turned on a heel and walked toward the steps. Tolon's blood boiled for a moment, and the on-lookers could do nothing more than gasp in shock and dismay. Finally, a smile crept onto Tolon's face and he began to laugh. He would have to find out more about this woman who called herself the Lady of Cadaria, if he survived his current mission.

* * * * * * * * * * * * *

Jillian Corven strode confidently toward the throne, no fear in her heart, and no hesitation in her steps. This meeting would be very brief, and then she could get back to what she needed to be doing, finding vengeance for herself and all who had fallen to the scourge of the dragons. When she reached the dais, Jillian stood firm and waited to be addressed. The woman in the clear gown stared at her for a moment and then smiled. Jillian ignored her and focused her eyes on the man seated on the throne. He looked like he hadn't slept in a week, and smelled as though he hadn't bathed in a month.

"You are the infamous dragon hunter, Jillian Corven? The woman who calls herself the Lady of Cadaria?" the man said coldly. "There must be some kind of mistake."

Jillian smiled.

"Very well then, if there has been a mistake I will leave. I have better things to do then stand here."

Jillian turned to leave, and two of the Imperial Guard quickly moved to impede her departure. With hands on her hips, Jillian turned back to face the Emperor, who by now was beginning to tire of the willfulness of his guest.

"No one leaves my presence without permission," Kaitain said rising from his throne, "especially not a common woman such as yourself, whether you call yourself a lady or not."

Jillian frowned and then mockingly curtsied.

"As you wish, oh great and powerful emperor."

Kaitain looked as though he had been struck, and then breathed deeply letting the anger pass through him.

"I see all of the stories I had heard about you are true. Your attitude must be what has kept you alive all this time. But no matter. I require you to assist me in my war against the dragons. You will be paid a modest fee for each of the dragons that you kill, and you will also turn over any information you have about locations of nests and any other research you have done in your time as a hunter. The fee I will pay is five-hundred per dragon."

Jillian laughed.

"Five hundred won't pay for the supplies I need, or for my crew. I get more from the local villages, and I like the company better there."

Kaitain sat on his throne and then leaned forward.

"You don't seem to understand, this is not a request. This is a decree from your Emperor. You will comply, or you will be considered of no further use to me, and I will have you put to death for the treasonous acts you have committed over the past few years. Impersonating nobility is a serious charge."

Jillian stood firm. Everything had gone as she had expected to this point.

"I will agree to help you against the dragons, Emperor Kaitain, but these are my terms. First, you will recognize my title as the Lady of Cadaria. Secondly, you will grant me sole title to the village of Seredil. Thirdly, I will be paid a fee of one thousand gold per dragon, and an additional five hundred gold for every dragon killed as a result of the information I provide."

Kaitain seemed amused with the woman. He sat back on his throne smiling.

"Very well, those seem to be fair requests."

"Also," Jillian continued, "the members of my crew will require Imperial postings. Kiara Aren had been excommunicated from the Temple of the Creator. I want her reinstated and allowed to continue her research in peace. Jacqueline Escandi is to be made a general in the Iron Legion, and Angelina Lynn Sador is to be given the title of Lady in Galateria with a modest estate."

Kaitain's smile continued.

"You are very devoted to your companions that is admirable. Now, what are you willing to do for these boons?"

Jillian stood firm, disgust and revulsion passing through her.

"I will hunt dragons for you, nothing more."

Kaitain rose, sword in hand.

"Oh, I think you will do much more than that. You will do whatever I tell you to do, whenever I tell you to do it, Lady of Cadaria. You belong to me now, and you will bow and scrape at my every whim."

Jillian took a step back and let her hand fall to the hilt of the Scaleripper.

"I bow to no man, and I serve no man's bidding. If you do not agree to my terms, we will go our separate ways."

Kaitain lifted his blade and pointed to the sword that hung on Jillian's hip.

"Are you threatening me, little girl?"

Jillian's blood boiled.

"Draw your sword, Lady of Cadaria. If you are good enough to draw my blood, I will grant all of your requests, and if I draw yours first, you will be the next trophy to find its way into my bed, and you will stay there as long as I still have use for you, and then you will be discarded like all the others."

Kaitain turned and laughed his eyes resting on Irene. She did not seem amused by his tyrannical outburst, but as he continued to laugh, Jillian drew her sword and struck. Kaitain was not caught off-guard as she had expected, and the blow was easily parried. The two crossed swords several more times, each time, Kaitain getting the upper hand. After a moment, it was obvious Kaitain was toying with the smaller woman. Jillian let Scaleripper fall to her side, and she lowered her head.

"I guess I am not as good as I thought…" she said after a moment.

Kaitain turned around and laughed hard, Jillian quickly capitalized, letting the blade of Scaleripper tear through his arm. The shock of pain was accompanied by a scream, and Jillian took several steps back laughing.

"Well, Emperor, thank you for the amusement. You're not bad for an amateur, but I would practice before you try to fight a dragon. They won't be as easy on you as I was."

As the Emperor fumed, Jillian walked toward the door to the throne room, and finally turned back before exiting.

"I will see your page about my agreement. I'll want all of it in writing. And thank you for being so generous."

Duty

Year Two of the Just Emperor Kaitain "Dragonsbane" Lorien, Creator's Calendar Year 1869

Deep in the heart of the continent of Mythryn stood the Citadel of Darkness, the capitol of the Dark Gods' domain in Espre. Very few, other than those who lived to serve the Dark Gods had survived long enough to see the tall spires that threatened to scrape the sky, and of those fewer still would survive to tell of what they had seen. Within one of the many large chambers, Gregor Quicksilver stood, an island of light amongst darkness, his faith and heart shaken by the revelations of the past. His father, and the woman that was in some ways his sister were before him, shattering the foundation of everything that had served him in the past. The two children of the Dark Gods, Darrien Annis and Alderin were passive observers to the proceedings, but their role was no less influential. Ivan had been correct, Gregor was never intended to succeed in his mission, and surely the Just Emperor Kaitain Lorien must have known the amount of power the Dark Gods possessed. This was a suicide mission, plain and simple, a way to remove Gregor from the game. Yet, even knowing the depths of the betrayal, Gregor could not abandon his duty. The Knights of the Flashing Blade were sworn to defend the Empire for all enemies, even those from within. Gregor could not say for certain if Kaitain Lorien yet fell into that category, but he certainly knew that the Dark Gods were not allies of Cadaria.

Gregor took a long deep breath and pulled his shoulders back instinctively. Pride, duty, and responsibility, all of those filled him, and yet conflicted with one another. Gregor knew what he had to do, but did not know how yet to do it. Taking one long last look around the room, Gregor locked his eyes on Sadrina Annis again and began to speak.

"Assume for a moment that I believe you, and that it is Emperor Kaitain Lorien and not the Dark Gods who have chosen to break the millennia-long truce. That does not change my mission, nor does it change my duty to the Empire. I am sworn to protect the Empire from all threats, and if the Just Emperor Kaitain Lorien has started a war with Mythryn, it is my duty to defend the Emperor and the Empire as best I can, even to my death. What you have told me changes nothing. The Dark Gods and their followers are still the enemies of the Empire, and so are my enemies."

Ivan shook his head after a moment.

"Duty is not all there is son…"

"I stopped being your son the day you joined forces with the Dark Gods."

Ivan stepped back as if struck. The anger had won out in Gregor, and it would only be a matter of time before his sword was drawn, and either Darrien or Alderin would be forced to destroy him.

"Gregor," Sadrina started, "does your duty also tell you that you must protect the Empire from itself when the need arises?"

Gregor nodded slowly.

"Then think about this. You have seen the power of the children of the Dark Gods, and I am sure you can imagine the power of the Dark Gods themselves. Emperor Kaitain Lorien must also know what he is facing. If the greatest of the members of the Flashing Blade can be defeated so easily, what do you believe will befall the rest of the Cadarian Empire if there were to ever be a full scale war with Mythryn? Cadaria would be crushed, and all of the people who continued to fight in the hopeless battle would be destroyed as well. Just think of the hundreds of thousands who would die. If a war can be prevented, is it not your duty to the Empire and not the Emperor that must win out?"

Gregor stood silent for a moment. While the argument did have merit, it was flawed. War between Cadaria and Mythryn was inevitable it seemed. The truce had been in place for nearly two millennia, and still there was tension between the two factions. There had constantly been accusations of assassins, sent by both sides. So long as both sides remained, they would be spinning ever closer toward confrontation, a confrontation so terrible that the number of dead would outpace the number of living. Gregor was sure that Sadrina was correct on one point. If the Dark Gods did become directly involved in the conflict, it would be over before it began.

"And what assurances can you give that Mythryn will not become the aggressor that we have been bred to believe they are? Can you promise me that if Cadaria ceases their assaults on Mythryn that there will be no retaliation?"

Sadrina pulled herself from her throne and strode over to Gregor. The man was a full head and shoulders taller than she, but Gregor felt as though her power and her stature dwarfed him.

"The Dark Gods do not want this fight. The Dark Gods have their own agenda that does not concern the people of Cadaria, therefore, as the queen of the Continent of Mythryn, I give you my personal assurance that the forces of Mythryn will stop this confrontation if Cadaria agrees to continue the truce. If Cadaria refuses to honor the conditions of the truce, then we will have no choice but to remove Cadaria from the face of Espre."

There was no boasting in the words of the regal woman, nor was there any fear in her eyes. It was not a threat, that much Gregor could tell. She meant what she said, and if her words were to ever to come to fruition, Cadaria would suffer.

"I shall take this offer of peace to my Emperor," Gregor said finally.

Ivan took a step forward and rested his hand on Gregor's shoulder.

"And what will you do if Kaitain refuses?"

Gregor's jaw tightened.

"I will do my duty."

Ivan patted Gregor on the shoulder and then watched as the proud man turned to leave. Sadrina wanted to say so much more to Gregor, wanted to tell him of her young daughter who sped to give this same message of peace, but she thought the better of it. Tess had her own path to walk, and in time they would all know if it was the correct one. Gregor left much more silently than he arrived, and they knew the weight on his shoulders and on his heart would be difficult to bear. Greatness sometimes is not measured by the deeds that are accomplished or the fame won, but rather by the quiet victories of the heart and spirit. These battles would determine the next course of action for Gregor Quicksilver, and could mean the difference between life and death for the whole of Cadaria.

When the doors to the receiving hall finally closed, Sadrina felt that she could breathe for the first time since she received the news that Gregor was in Mythryn. So many had died, and yet they may not have accomplished anything more than a delay of the inevitable.

"I'll need to speak with the council," Sadrina said to no one in particular. Her voice simply filled the silence in the room.

"Do you really think that is a good idea, mother?" Darrien said after a moment. "They have not been very receptive lately, and even father has begun to think that the only way that anything will be accomplished is if we wipe out Cadaria. What is the point in pursuing peace with people who want nothing more than to see us destroyed? The best course of action may simply be to wipe them out and save ourselves."

Sadrina turned and scowled at her daughter.

"Darrien, death is never the way to solve these issues. Your father knows this as well as I do. The only thing that is motivating this confrontation is fear and misunderstanding. The people of Cadaria fear us because they have been conditioned by the ruling body to see us as an ever-present threat. They are taught by their parents, their clergy, and their rulers that everything we stand for is evil and counter to that of the vaunted Cadarian Empire. The Council thought once that the creation of Galateria would help the humans to understand who and what the Dark Gods are, but it has done little to increase our reputation."

A rustle from one of the corridors caused Sadrina to turn her head.

"We were wrong," a cold voice said finally. "And it seems that ever since we fell to this world, we have been nothing but wrong."

Sadrina watched as the Dark God entered the room. He was supposedly nearly three millennia old, as were the rest of the Dark Gods. However, it was not evident in his features. He could have been the ruler of the Council, but he had never wanted the position, and was just as content remaining in the background. Part of it may have been the destruction he had seen during his life, and another part may have been the lame left arm that hung at his side.

Sadrina bowed slightly and smiled.

"I take it the Council is not meeting any more today."

The Dark God shook his head, his loose blond hair moving slightly.

"We have broken for a moment to reflect upon some recent news. Serrina has again gone too far in the execution of her duties, and we must deal with the issue. She has injured a member of the Flashing Blade very seriously, and while Gregor returns to Kaitain with our message of peace, Leonora Wastri will return with a message of war. It will of course be omitted that Serrina was provoked. A war now appears to be inevitable, and we have proven to be the enemy of our own best intentions."

Sadrina frowned. Serrina Mistic was the Voice of Darkness, the speaker for the Council, but many times she exceeded the authority of her station when dealing with others, and fancied herself far more important than she really was. She was the youngest member of the Dark Gods, a child among ancients. Unlike the other members of the Council, Serrina was born with her godly abilities, she did not attain them through ascension to the Heavens. Sadrina had always felt that had bred a dangerous feeling of entitlement. Another disadvantage was the fact that Serrina's parents were no longer members of the Council, they had left to find their own peace long ago, not long after the death of their leader over a millennia ago.

"What shall we do now, father?" Alderin said quietly.

Alderin, like Serrina was the product of two gods. His power was greater than that held by Serrina and Darrien, however he did not thirst for status or glory. Much as his father was in his previous life, Alderin was content to be the protector of those who could not protect themselves, and those important to the future of Espre. Alderin had taken the duty of guarding the life of Sadrina Annis very seriously and graciously. No one would ever harm her so long as he lived. Though, as he stood in the quiet audience chamber, he regretted not following Tess Annis on her mission to Cadaria. However, he took solace in the fact that Tess was not alone, and that her protector, Camille, would guard her well.

"We shall wait, deliberate, and argue as we always do, Alderin. Your mother and I will take some time to pool our resources and try to gain support to keep the peace for as long as possible, but I believe that the push for war will outweigh any argument that we can put forward."

Sadrina shook her head.

"So there will be war then."

The blond god shook his head, resting his lame arm on the back of Darrien's throne.

"There may be a way to prevent it still. There is one man on the face of Espre who your husband will listen to without question. The problem is, he can't help us, at least not openly. We need a way to get his attention without breaking any rules."

Sadrina was confused.

"What rules are you talking about?"

"It all goes back to the reason we were expelled from the Heavens, and why we are here on Espre. We are forbidden to discuss it openly, but in time it will have to be confronted."

Sadrina sat back on her throne after a long look at the scarred and damaged left arm of the Dark God. It was still strange to her that a wound this severe could have befallen a Dark God. She knew that it had happened before his ascension, but she would have thought that his ascension would have healed any imperfections of the body.

"So, who is this man that my husband trusts so much?"

The Dark God smiled.

"All in good time. We couldn't approach him directly anyway, he would burn whoever we sent with a thought."

The shock on Darrien's face told the story.

"He's that powerful?"

"More so than even he remembers. It's been a long time since he met anything that would have caused him to draw upon the fullness of his abilities. Even the strongest of us would have problems, but it doesn't matter, we won't be approaching him."

Sadrina sighed. Even though she was married to the head of the Council of the Dark Gods, there was still so much she did not know. There were so many secrets and so many rules.

"Then who will approach him, Aryx?"

"An old friend."

* * * * * * * * * * * * *

Jaccob Aldora sat in a dockside bar waiting. He detested waiting. For three days he had sat in the bar, waiting for a boat to arrive, a boat that ferried a messenger from the Dark Continent of Mythryn with a message of peace. For three days he had waited, and for three days he had been disappointed. The drink was not even comforting anymore, and the nightmares were getting worse. Ever since he had set foot in the sleepy little harbor town, his mind had been filled with blood and death, and it was only the power of Temperance that kept him sane with the lack of sleep.

As the barkeeper brought the next round of ale, the doors to the bar opened, and the harbormaster entered.

"Sir Jaccob?"

Jaccob at up the next moment and took hold of Temperance again. Instantly the cloud of drunkenness lifted from his mind, and whatever exhaustion had seized him was dispelled.

"Sir Jaccob, the boat you were waiting on is putting into port now."

Jaccob was off the stool in a moment, letting a small bag of coin clatter onto the bar. It was surely enough to pay for the drinks of everyone in the bar several times over, but Jaccob didn't care. He was not in need of money, and the Imperial stipend was quite generous every month. Passing the harbormaster, Jaccob pulled another bag of coins from his pocket and shoved it into the man's hand.

"Your service to the Emperor will be noted," Jaccob muttered walking past.

When Jaccob emerged from the bar, the bright sunlight shone into his eyes and temporarily blinded him. He hadn't realized the bar had been so dark, but then again maybe he had. Though Temperance could clear the haze from his mind and make him sharp again, it did not have talent enough to clear the haze from his memory. Those portions were most likely lost forever, not that Jaccob cared most nights. As promised, Jaccob could see the small vessel docking at the closest port, and in a matter of moments he watched as two woman disembarked. As Jaccob saw their faces, horror filled him.

For the next few moments, Jaccob was paralyzed. Images from his nightmares filled his head, the blood, death, horror, murder. The mad Emperor clutching the young girl to him, his own maniacal laughter as fire rained down from the skies. The world twisting itself inside out, ripping itself apart. The younger of the two women, it was her face he had been seeing for the past few months in his dream. She was the one whom all coveted, even himself. Fear and confusion clouded his mind, and no level of intervention from Temperance could change it. Just as Jaccob found his feet again, he watched as another man approached the two women. He was obviously from Galateria from the devices that he wore on his tunic, but the leathery wings that protruded from his back, and the rough, nearly leathery skin shown that he was not a mere mortal, he was one of the half-demons with blood of Mythryn flowing through his veins. Jaccob moved quickly toward the trio. Their conversation ended when Jaccob approached.

"Tess Annis?" Jaccob said calmly.

The younger woman looked toward Jaccob and smiled.

"Yes, I am Tess Annis."

Jaccob took a moment to finally drink in the features of the girl who had haunted his dreams. She was beautiful without a doubt, but it was an eerie, nearly unsettling beauty. As with most denizens of Mythryn, Tess was pale, almost white, and her body was very lithe. Her long brown hair hung loose falling to one side and resting on her right shoulder. However, it was her eyes, those golden eyes that pierced Jacob's soul. Her features were flawless and her skin looked smooth and supple. Pale rose colored lips, and high cheekbones. She easily would have fit the description of a goddess for most, and Jaccob could not have argued the point.

"I am Jaccob Aldora, the Topaz Knight of the Flying Kingdom of Hedorah. I have been sent by the Just Emperor Kaitain Lorien to commend you to the Imperial Palace of Aldere where you are expected by the Emperor himself."

The winged man made the first move, stepping between Jaccob and Tess, hand on the sword on his hip. The man was much taller than Jaccob, and looked to be much more muscular.

"Sir Jaccob, I am afraid there has been a change of plans."

"And you are?"

"Careful now Devlin…don't do anything reckless."

"I am Devlin Rannoch, the Onyx Knight of the Kingdom of Night, Galateria. My mission is to escort the princess here. Your services will no longer be needed."

Jaccob fumed. This was his chance to actually do something, and more than that he might be able to find out why this girl tormented his dreams. Why was she so important? What was it about her that everyone wanted?

"I'm afraid I cannot allow that, Sir Devlin. The Emperor was very clear in his instructions, and an Imperial Summons is not something to be taken lightly. If you wish, you can accompany us to Aldere, and I am sure the Emperor will reward you for your service."

Devlin drew his sword and took a step back.

"I'm afraid the princess is not going to Aldere, Jaccob. Now, if you don't want to get hurt, I would suggest you stand aside and let us pass. Otherwise, I will have to make sure you won't follow us."

"Now you've done it. You just drew your weapon and threatened another member of the Flashing Blade. So much for your stealthy approach to this treason you've embarked on. If you let him live, the rest of the Empire will be coming after you. You know you are going to have to kill him right?"

Devlin shook away the voice and kept his focus on Jaccob. The short-staff in his hands separated in a moment and the dual blades were revealed. It seemed that this Jaccob Aldora was full of surprises.

"So, the Onyx Knight of Galateria is a traitor to the throne. You know that is what you have become by defying me? You are defying a direct order from the Emperor, and if you do not stand aside, I will be forced to kill you."

Devlin charged the next moment. The time for talk was over. The quick hard downward slash was met by the crossed dual blades, a perfect block. Devlin continued attacking, strike after strike of his sword Discipline being met by the steel of Temperance. On one strike, Devlin overextended, and Jaccob countered, landing a solid blow to Devlin's side. Blood flowed freely from the wound, thick dark red, nearly black blood. However, Devlin did not recoil in pain at the strike, he stepped into his opponent, seizing his arm and digging razor sharp claws into Jaccob's bicep. The flesh and muscle were torn quickly, and Jaccob's right arm fell limp, one of the dual blades clattering to the ground. Pain flooded through Jaccob's body, but Temperance would not let him relent. Jaccob took a quick step back.

"Burn."

With the word of power, fire erupted from around Devlin. Thinking quickly, Devlin's wings enclosed around him, keeping the heat of the fires at bay. After a quick moment, the wings opened and then flapped hard, sending the rising flames arcing back toward their source. Jaccob stood firm, and the flames dissipated shortly before reaching their new target. Devlin regarded his opponent and then smiled.

"Nice trick."

"You'll find I'm full of surprises," Jaccob taunted.

At the next moment, the remaining blade of Temperance was wreathed in white hot flames. Devlin braced himself. The attack would come the next moment, and Devlin prepared himself to mount a defense against his opponent. It seemed that he had underestimated Jaccob Aldora.

"I hate Sorcerers. They can never just die. Bore you to death with their parlor tricks and then burn you to a crisp. Why is it always fire? Why does it always have to be fire? Hey, speaking of fire, you're half-dragon right? Aren't you supposed to breathe fire or something? Oh that's right, you didn't get the good part of the dragon did you? You just got the wings, bad skin, and bad breath. I keep forgetting."

Devlin blocked out the voice again. It was right though, some of those dragon abilities would have been very useful right about now, especially that invulnerability to fire that he had heard so much about. Jaccob charged quickly, blade poised for the kill.

"Stop."

The voice came from the robed woman beside Tess. Neither Devlin nor Jaccob had paid much attention to her, but now they were both forced to. Jaccob stopped mid-charge, and Devlin could tell from the position of his feet and his body that it was not his idea. Some unseen force had seized the Topaz Knight and rendered him immobile.

"This conflict solves nothing. Lead on Devlin Rannoch. This one, this Jaccob, will bother us no more."

The second woman pulled back the hood of her robes and looked to Devlin. There was something about her, something familiar. Deep auburn eyes, beautiful features, long brown hair pulled back into a tail. While not as striking as her companion, the robed woman was a beauty without question. Devlin looked back at the unmoving form of Jaccob Aldora.

"And what about him?"

The robed woman shook her head.

"He will not follow us, Sir Devlin, in fact, he will return to the bar and have a long drink wondering why the boat he had been waiting for didn't contain the passengers he was told it did."

Devlin smiled.

"That is amazing."

"We all have our duties, Sir Devlin," Tess answered. "You have yours, I have mine, and Camille has hers."

Devlin locked his eyes on Camille and spoke.

"And just what is your duty?"

Camille pulled the hood back over her head and started walking toward the street.

"To make sure that Tess fulfills her duty, and to make sure that no one interferes."

Devlin watched as Camille and Tess passed and made their way toward the road that would lead out of town toward Galateria.

"Did that sound like a threat to you?"

* * * * * * * * * * * * *

Jaccob Aldora stood at the edge of the dock, looking at the small boat in port, waiting for someone to disembark, but no one other than crew ever left the vessel. A matter of minutes later they had taken on new supplies and were on their way back out to sea. Perhaps the information he had been given was wrong, and perhaps there would be another vessel in a few days that would have the passenger he waited for. It just meant more waiting. He hated waiting. As he turned back to head for the bar, the strange pain filled his right arm.

Strange, Jaccob thought as he walked slowly toward the bar, *I must have slept wrong last night.*

Obsession

Year Two of the Just Emperor Kaitain "Dragonsbane" Lorien, Creator's Calendar Year 1869

The tents of the Army of Fire sat dangerously close to the border with their ancient enemy and sometime-tenuous ally Saldarine. The majority of the soldiers from the army wandered the perfectly symmetrical paths between the lines of tents, ensuring that nothing would catch them by surprise. Only weeks before the scum from Thorigald had launched a sneak attack on the capitol city of Saldarine. The unwarranted and cowardly attack had caused the death of hundreds before it was finally repulsed by the brave soldiers of the Army of Fire stationed there. The soldiers of Thorigald had been unselective in their targets, killing soldiers and commoners alike. It seemed as though their entire purpose had been to inflict as much damage as possible before retreating. Many homes, temples, and places of commerce were burned to the ground, and the standing army needed to stay behind and could not chase the retreating army. By the time a pursuit force had been formed, there was no sign of the force from Thorigald. While a hit and run attack was not in the normal pattern for Thorigald, who often preferred to attack in force and overwhelm their enemies, it seemed that the recent losses were causing them to change their tactics. Envoys were sent immediately to Thorigald demanding an explanation for the strike, but naturally the ruling council of

Thorigald denied the fact that the attack happened, calling it more Saldarine propaganda. The reply was met with the immediate mobilization of the Army of Fire under the capable command of the Garnet Knight, Chelsea Zarova of the Knights of the Flashing Blade.

In the command tent in the center of the camp formation stood the Garnet Knight. For the better part of the last two hours, she had stood in the same place, reviewing the best maps available of the area, and trying to work out a plan for the morning's battle. Fighting on the Plains of Steam was never an easy proposition, and with the amount of troops that both sides would inevitably commit to the conflict, the peril became much pronounced. Saldarine was called the Kingdom of Fire because of the amount of active volcanoes that existed both within the confines of the kingdom, but also dotted the coastline and nearby waters. Conversely, Thorigald got its title as the Kingdom of Water because of the unusual amount of rivers and lakes that dominated much of the kingdom's terrain. The several mile strip of land that separated the two kingdoms became known as the Plains of Steam. Throughout the region there were a series of geysers and geothermal vents which released the pressure from the cooling molten magma that coursed through the border between the warring kingdoms. Most days the Plain of Steam was filled with a light watery mist that was warm to the touch, while other days the mist could scald the skin. Because of the ambient heat, fighting in armor was problematic, and fatigue would set in within a matter of minutes. Holding the Plains of Steam was impossible, but to combat the enemy, the crossing would have to be made. Many attempts would be made to trap the opponent in the Plains of Steam to force them to surrender or flee, but extensive fighting always hurt both sides equally. Protracted engagements were the rule in the Plains of Steam; a series of feints, skirmishes, and voluntary retreats, tactics that accomplished nothing but frustration. However, there were more dangers in the Plains of Steam than just the weather and the enemies from the other Kingdom. One of the great dragons of Cadaria made its home in the desolation of the Plains of Steam, and at any time the great lizard calling itself Nessus the Hovering Rain could swoop down and make an impact on the conflict. And Chelsea knew well that it didn't matter whether the soldiers wore the device of Thorigald or that of Saldarine, they would be murdered by the hundreds.

On the table lay the dual weapons, the katars collectively known as Tenacity. They had served Chelsea well through many battles in the past, and far too many lives had ended at her hands. The continued conflict between Thorigald and Saldarine should have ended with her marriage to the Emerald Knight Seraph Kore, the champion from Thorigald. Their pairing had been ordained by the Just Emperor Ender Lorien, and though the two members of the Flashing Blade only knew each other in passing, it was considered a good match. It would have ended the longest feud in the Great Kingdoms, and Cadaria would finally know peace within its borders. For a time the uneasy truce held. The bickering and infighting was kept to a minimum, and there was even commerce between the two sides. Great lengths were met to secure passage through the Plains of Steam, and the Armies of Fire and Water spent most of their time guarding caravans through the treacherous passage. During the time of peace, both kingdoms flourished as never before, able to use their resources to build instead of destroy. However, everyone knew it could not last forever.

While the relationship between the kingdoms of Saldarine and Thorigald prospered for a time, the relationship between Chelsea and Seraph never did. Chelsea was a pragmatist. She saw what needed to be done and devised a way to do it. If she could benefit her kingdom and the empire through her actions, she would make sure to do her best to gain the most benefit from any action. Planning and strategy were her strong suit, and many of the most learned generals in the whole of Cadaria would seek to train under her. Seraph was her polar opposite in many ways. He was impulsive, emotional, and passionate. Rarely did Seraph consider the consequences of his actions and he let the moment rule him. On the battlefield he was an amazing and inspiring soldier, choosing to lead his troops on the field, rather than through plans and tactics. This difference in style translated to their relationship was well. They spent much more time apart than they ever did together, maintaining their separate residences in their respective kingdoms. Arguments were frequent, and the only place they seemed compatible was in the privacy of their bedrooms. There was passion to spare to be sure, but passion would not sustain their alliance, and surely would not foster good-will between two kingdoms that had hated each other for centuries.

Running her hand absently though her long blond hair again, Chelsea sighed. The idea had been a sound one, the match between Chelsea and Seraph, but it was doomed to fail from the beginning. They were as different as night and day, and the suns and the moon could never share the sky, and when they did, as on the Days of Star Fire, the results were explosive. Chelsea laughed to herself as she returned to study her maps. There was something pulling at the edges of her thought, a familiar sensation. Tenacity, even when not in her hands, would inform her when she was not alone. That next moment, the flap of the command tent opened. Chelsea's senses were alive the next moment, heightened by her connection with Tenacity. Every creak and shuffle was magnified in her ears, her nostrils filled with every scent in the room, and her eyesight sharpened to see impossible details at hundreds of yards. Her sense of touch became so heightened she could actually feel the changes in the ambient temperature and air in the room as the pressure changed on her skin. The feeling was exhilarating every time she felt it, and after a time, Chelsea had learned to control it. The man who entered the room was a simple page, but from the smell of salt on his skin and in the air, it was a page from Thorigald, not Saldarine.

"Speak," Chelsea said, her back still turned to the page.

Chelsea could hear the man tremble. From the sound of his heart and the amount of sweat rolling from his brow, he couldn't have been much more than in his late teens, rushed into service for the new war. Fear rolled off of him like a mist, and Chelsea could smell it permeate the room.

"Sir Seraph Kore, the Emerald Knight of the Flashing Blade and General of the Army of Water requests amnesty for a meeting with the Garnet Knight, the Wolf of Saldarine."

Chelsea felt the smirk tug at the corners of her mouth. The gifts given to her by Tenacity were not without notice by her opponents. Chelsea had gained a reputation on the battlefield. She was known as the Wolf of Saldarine to her enemies, a hunter who was relentless in stalking her prey. The name was useful if not inaccurate. Chelsea was quick to let the amusement pass. If Seraph wanted to talk, then perhaps they could avoid the confrontation. Perhaps no one had to die this time. There would be the typical taunts traded before any agreement was reached of course, but that was to be expected any time the married couple was together.

"Very well," Chelsea replied after a moment. "The Emerald Knight will be given safe passage into and out of the camp of the Army of Fire. I shall receive Seraph here."

The page bowed and left the next moment, no other words were required. Meetings such as this were common practice, and most often some kind of accord could be reached to prevent an escalation in hostilities. This time though, with the gravity of the attack launched by Thorigald, there was very little chance that the fight could be avoided this time. There was too much bad blood, too much pain and suffering. The people of Saldarine wanted retribution, they wanted the people of Thorigald to pay with blood. For the next several minutes, Chelsea waited, not moving from her appointed spot at the side of her planning table. The more she looked at it, the more it infuriated her. There was no way that any army could win a battle in the Plains of Steam, unless they were inhuman or dragons. Even then, the chances of victory were slim. It seemed that the perpetuation of holding actions was the only course. Finally, the flap to the tent opened again. This time, Chelsea turned to face the visitor, and could do nothing to contain the frown on her face.

Chelsea could not deny that Seraph was handsome. His dark brown hair was short and seemed to go whatever direction it willed, and his brown eyes burned with fire and passion always. The start of a beard on his face was little more than coarse stubble that coated his chin and cheeks, making him look older than his forty years should have. However, any desire that Chelsea would have had for her husband was destroyed the next moment as the scent of him filler her nostrils. She could smell the sweat from his skin, the salt...but there was another scent there, layered under the salt and sweat, under the heat. There was a faint scent of lavender, the scent of Seraph's lover. He had shared his bed with her before coming to meet with Chelsea, and her blood burned because of it.

The worst kept secret between the couple was the existence of the woman named Dominique Arais. Seraph and Dominique had been together long before Seraph and Chelsea first met. However, there was a complication in their relationship. Dominique was a common woman, and for Seraph to marry her and elevate her to the position near that of royalty was fraught with complications and peril. And so, the two kept their relationship simple. When Seraph married Chelsea, it was expected that the relationship with Dominique would end, but it never did. Chelsea had known from the first time she met the woman that the scent she had often picked up on her husband's skin had been hers. It was a slap in the face, but even more insulting was the fact that it did not seem that Seraph cared. Much like on the battlefield the Emerald Knight took what he wanted when he wanted without thought of the consequences.

"Hello, Chelsea."

Seraph's tone was light, even placid for him. The type of person that he was, courtesy was never an easy skill to master.

"Hello, husband."

Seraph felt the word pass through him like ice. He hated it when she called him that. They were married out of convenience and duty, nothing more.

"We seem to have a problem, Chelsea. Your leaders have gone off the deep-end again, and they are forcing us to fight."

Chelsea shook her head.

"I guess you should have thought of that before sending that sneak attack of yours."

Seraph walked across the floor of the tent quickly and stopped a few inches from Chelsea. The scent of him filled her again. She could smell the passion, hear the beat of his heart, it was intoxicating.

"There was no sneak attack. At least not by my order or the order of any of my generals. You and your people are just making excuses so that you can force a confrontation. It doesn't make sense that we would break the peace."

Chelsea pushed Seraph away and then pulled a parcel from her planning table and threw it at Seraph's chest.

"Open it."

With a deep frown on his face, Seraph tore the parchment from around the contents of the parcel and held in his hands finally a torn and soiled uniform of a soldier from Thorigald.

"What is this?"

Chelsea fumed.

"What do you think it is, Seraph? We took this off the body of the one soldier from your little sneak attack that we managed to kill before the rest retreated. Do you still think we're making the whole thing up, or are you just a fool?"

Seraph dropped the tunic to the ground.

"Doesn't mean anything, Chelsea. You could have gotten that tunic at any time. It could be one of mine for all I know."

Chelsea's anger burned brighter. There was no one in the world who could get to her like this, other than Seraph.

"Then I suppose we have nothing more to say to one another."

Seraph stood his ground and reached into his shirt and produced a folded piece of parchment. He tossed it onto Chelsea's planning table and then moved toward the chair at the other end of the tent.

"What's that?"

Seraph sat down and looked up at Chelsea.

"Read it."

Chelsea didn't know what she was more of, annoyed or angry. Exhaling deeply, Chelsea recovered the piece of parchment from the table and unfolded it. As she read the words, she could not help but feel the anger fill her even more.

CHAPTER 48

Seraph Kore, Emerald Knight of the Kingdom of Water, Thorigald

By decree of the Just Emperor Kaitain "Dragonsbane" Lorien, all hostilities between the forces of Thorigald and those of Saldarine are to cease immediately. As soon as this decree is received, the Emerald Knight and the Garnet Knight are to present themselves to the Just Emperor in Aldere.

Irene Drage

Imperial Sorceress

"So we just tell our armies to go home, just like that?"

Seraph frowned.

"This new Emperor wants to make an impression I guess."

Chelsea threw the parchment back at Seraph.

"Ender never would have done this. The sanctity of the kingdoms is not to be encroached upon by the Emperor except in times of war.'

Seraph waved his finger.

"Remember, we are at war, with the dragons."

Chelsea growled. At least this way, Chelsea could ask the Emperor for reparations from the sneak attack and force Thorigald to acknowledge their treachery. The Emperor would then probably order them to assist in the war with the dragons, which meant a full scale invasion of the Plains of Steam, a worse nightmare than a simple battle of vengeance.

"Well, I suppose we have a lot of work to do then. Shall we travel together?"

Seraph's expression never changed, but Chelsea knew there was something he wasn't telling her. There was something in his scent, something dark, not fear, but close. He was too calm about the situation.

“There is a problem Chelsea, and we need to solve something here, between the two of us before we meet the Emperor. We haven’t been a married couple in a long time, and you know about Dominique, I’ve never tried to hide that from you.”

Chelsea sighed.

“I would have thought less of you if you were trying, Seraph. You’ve never been good at hiding thing, especially from me. But I don’t see what that has to do with our meeting with the Emperor.”

Seraph swallowed hard.

“Dominique received a summons too.”

Chelsea’s blood ran cold. It was one thing for the Emperor to be involving himself with a conflict between the great kingdoms, but something else to be involving himself in the conflict between a married couple. This level of interference was intolerable. Chelsea had never met Dominique, but she almost felt sorry for the woman having to be summoned by the Emperor to resolve a domestic dispute.

“Seems like we do have much to discuss,” Chelsea said finally, and pulled up the other chair across from Seraph.

* * * * * * * * * * * * *

The Gray Man Pestilence stood in the middle of a field looking up at the sky. This had been where it all had started for him. Kalid had once been a peaceful little town in the middle of nowhere, unnoticed by anyone in the Empire of Cadaria. It was the perfect place to loose the Crawling Plague upon the land. It was the last place that such destruction would have been expected, and it would have struck fear into the hearts of even the most secure in the Empire. The service of Dorovar deserved no less than perfection from all of his tools, and Pestilence served his master with distinction. Pestilence felt the winds beginning to coalesce around him and before long, the Gray Man was not alone. The Serpentine Knight, Vallic Ultiv stood in the field, looking at the Gray Man, no emotion on his face.

"I have been waiting for you, Serpentine Knight of Cadaria," the Gray Man said coldly. "I came here to feel the souls of the fallen, to hear them sing. Can you hear them, Vallic? Can you hear the beautiful voices raised up in dedication? Do you hear them thanking me for being released from the dank and miserable lives they once led?"

Vallic shook his head.

"I hear nothing but your madness. The Emperor has sent me here to destroy you, Pestilence, and I intend to carry out my orders. I was surprised that you made yourself so easy to find."

The Gray Man continued looking at the sky. If the creature known as Pestilence felt anything, it did not show it by its actions or its expression.

"You found me, because I allowed you to find me, Serpentine Knight. For the moment, I have accomplished my task. Many thousands have died by my hand, and the legacy of the fear and pain caused by the Crawling Plague will persist for generations to come. My purpose is served."

The Gray Man then locked his fiery red eyes upon Vallic and smiled a wicked toothless smile.

"You may strike me down if you wish, Vallic Ultiv, and then take your triumph back to your puppet Emperor. But my death will mean nothing in the grand scheme of things, Serpentine Knight. I am but a harbinger of things to come. Even now, my beautiful sister Famine spreads her gifts upon Cadaria, filling the world with hunger and suffering once more. By curing my Plague, you have brought more suffering than you could ever imagine upon your people. I caused only fear and death, Famine will bring a suffering unlike any have seen before, and none will see again. Death is a release from the suffering she causes, and when the souls of her victims are released, they will sing loudly to the Heavens, proclaiming their freedom and their love. The bonds to this dying world broken, they will thank us with their angelic voices. Your puppet Emperor can never understand. Even if you stop Famine, the suffering will continue. The next in line will take up the banner. We are saving this land from itself, for when we are done, those who still live on the face of this world are the damned souls without redemption, and there will be no release for them for the hell that will follow. We are about the work of the true god, the force that will reshape the universe in his image and save us from the blight the Creator has place upon these worlds."

A dark maniacal laughter rolled from the Gray Man's chest.

"The dragons will suffer for their crimes against the true god. They will suffer an eternity of pain and damnation, and so too will those who are the enemies of the new order. Pray, Vallic Ultiv," Pestilence said pointing a finger at the chest of the Serpentine Knight, "pray that when the touch of Dorovar visits you, that you accept willingly and add your voice to his chorus of souls, otherwise you shall suffer with the rest of the vermin."

Pestilence collapsed the next moment, falling to the ground as if struck from the Heavens. For several long moments Vallic watched, the body of his prey unmoving. Whatever force had breathed life into the abomination had taken it away. Pestilence had been correct in his words, his purpose had apparently been served, and he was no longer needed upon Cadaria. However, the threat that Famine posed was still out there, as well as this Dorovar that Pestilence had spoken of.

"So," Vallic said walking to the east, "Famine was born when the Crawling Plague was cured. So, what new abomination will we cause by curing this Wasting Disease? I must find this Famine before she awakens the next terror. But I am afraid that I cannot proceed alone any longer."

The next moment, the field outside the once quiet town of Kalid was empty accept for the body of the Gray Man Pestilence. Moments later, a foul wind rose in the field. Lightning flashed in the sky, and the sky grew dark despite the absence of clouds. Moments later drops of blood fell from the sky, and Dorovar stretched out his power to reclaim the fallen form of his servant. Where the body fell a single spike of obsidian rose from the ground, crowned with a wreath of green fire. From everywhere in the countryside an eerie laugh could be heard.

* * * * * * * * * * * * *

The Imperial Palace of Aldere seemed colder than the last time that Chelsea stepped foot inside. The smell of death still lingered in the hallways, and no amount of scrubbing could have removed the stench. The

Crawling Plague had left a permanent scar on the heart of Cadaria, and no matter what, the wound would never be healed. Chelsea Zarova and her husband Seraph Kore walked stride for stride through the receiving hall toward the audience chamber. A step behind them walked the common woman, Dominique Arais.

As much as Chelsea hated to admit it, Dominique was a beautiful woman, and she could see why Seraph was so enamored with her. From her blond hair, to her long legs and perfect features, she was a vision of beauty. Chelsea would have problems seeing any man choose her over Dominique. The common woman was soft-spoken and humble, all due to her station in life, and it also seemed as though she genuinely loved Seraph. In a way, Chelsea was a little jealous of the woman, but could not hate her though she tried. Despite the difficulty of her situation, the young woman seemed to be taking everything in stride, and was not shaken or unnerved by the situation.

Finally, the three entered the audience chamber of the Imperial Palace of Aldere and were greeted to the sight of only the Imperial Sorceress Irene Drage waiting for them. The summons had been signed by her, but both Chelsea had expected to see the Emperor upon their arrival.

"Welcome to the Imperial Palace," Irene said gently. "The Just Emperor has been called away to deal with a matter of some urgency, but will return when the opportunity presents itself. I have been empowered to act in his stead to resolve this issue between the Kingdom of Water, Thorigald and the Kingdom of Fire, Saldarine."

Chelsea was stunned. This was unprecedented. The Court Sorcerer was an advisor only and was never given the ability to speak for the Throne in a matter that concerned one of the Great Kingdoms. By decree, the only person empowered to speak for the Emperor was a member of the Knights of the Flashing Blade in matters of law, or the Voice of the Emperor, the chosen heir. This woman spoke well above her station.

"However, before we come to that issue…Dominique Arais, step forward."

The pretty blond commoner took a deep breath and moved passed both of the members of the Flashing Blade and stood two steps from the dais. It was clear she was nervous now, and the look from Irene was one of cursory examination.

"You will follow this guard to a private antechamber until you are summoned."

Seraph's hand clenched around the hilt of his sword Patience. They were a strange paring, Seraph and Patience. The rage of emotions that constantly filled Seraph were a power that was difficult to control, but with Patience in hand, Seraph could navigate the jungle of his jumbled thoughts and hold firm to the brink of insanity. In battle, he could seize the emotion of the moment, and never felt as though a situation was out of hand. It could seem as though time slowed for him, and he could see all of the strings of time and motion, and the emotions of all the moments intersecting his. Like a spider web of thought and intention laid out before him. Seraph had tried to explain it to Chelsea once, but his gift had never been with words. The summation was always the same though. The world never felt right or in order unless Patience was at his side.

Dominique bowed to Irene, and with a quick sideways glance to Seraph, she followed the guard to the antechamber. Both Chelsea and Seraph were more confused than they had been when they received the strange summons from the Emperor, and now alone with the Imperial Sorceress, they awaited word of the fate of the dispute between their two kingdoms.

"Now," Irene said after the door to the antechamber closed, "to the matter between Thorigald and Saldarine. As there has been a state of war declared in the Empire of Cadaria, the petty disputes between the Great Kingdoms must be stopped at all costs. There cannot be a divided front in the face of the enemy. This is an Imperial Decree that has been in effect since the time of Emperor Terrik Lorien, Lorien the First. To violate that decree is to incur the wrath of the Emperor and the Imperial Legion. As the champions from the two kingdoms and as members of the Knights of the Flashing Blade, it is your duty to enforce the peace between Thorigald and Saldarine until the war with the dragons has been concluded. If you fail in this task, the Just Emperor has decreed that you will be held responsible and your positions as well as your lives will be forfeit."

Chelsea took a step back. Never before had conditions such as these been placed on a member of the Flashing Blade. Chelsea found it hard to believe that these orders had actually come from the Emperor.

"I wish to hear these words from the Emperor himself," Chelsea said stepping toward the dais.

"I speak with full authority of the Throne, Lady Zarova. Do you question the orders of the Just Emperor of Cadaria?"

Chelsea chose her next words very carefully.

"I would never question the orders of the Just Emperor, whom I will serve to my death, however what I question is why the Imperial Sorceress, who has no power to give orders to any Imperial citizen, and certainly not to a member of the Flashing Blade, is threatening the lives and stations of two of the Just Emperor's most devoted servants. It is that, Irene Drage, that I question."

Instead of reacting with anger or frustration, Irene simply smiled and folded her hands before her. The next moment, the doors to the right of the audience chamber opened and the Emperor emerged, Imperial Sword in hand. As soon as Chelsea and Seraph saw the Emperor enter the room, they both fell to one knee, and bowed their heads.

"Chelsea Zarova," the Emperor said as he sat upon the throne, "you have a very good reputation for a member of the Knights of the Flashing Blade, and you are not known for acting out of ignorance. Therefore, I will let this slight pass. From this day forward, you may inform the rest of your order that I have given the Imperial Sorceress Irene Drage comparable power to that of the Voice of the Emperor. There are only two people in the whole of the Empire that can countermand an order that she gives, and that is my daughter Marlae, the heir to the throne, and myself. Now, this issue between your kingdoms ends here, I want to hear no more of it."

"Yes, my Emperor," both Chelsea and Seraph said in unison.

"Now, go." Kaitain said rising from his throne and moving toward the antechamber. "Return to your kingdoms and take the fight to the dragons instead of each other."

As the Emperor left the room, Chelsea and Seraph were left more confused than they had been before arriving in Aldere.

* * * * * * * * * * * * *

Dominique Arais stood in the center of the antechamber feeling like a fish out of water. The trappings of the royal palace of Aldere were beyond her station, and she knew that she did not belong. When the summons to the Imperial Palace had been received, she thought it was a mistake. Only the confirmation from Seraph let her even think that it was real. Then, when the door opened to the antechamber, and the Just Emperor Kaitain Lorien entered the room, her head felt as though it were going to explode. Her body obeyed before her mind could, and she fell to her knees, her head low, and her hands before her. The Emperor required her respect, and a woman of her station in life was not blessed enough to look upon his face.

"Rise, Dominique Arais, and let me look at you."

Slowly, Dominique found her feet, her knees shaking, and her body as unsteady as a new-born deer trying to stand for the first time. She kept her eyes on the floor, not willing to look up into the face of the man who held her fate in his hands. The fact that he even knew her name made her head spin.

Kaitain was fascinated by the beauty of the woman who stood before him. She was the most beautiful woman he had ever seen. Her beauty was not accentuated by jewels or finery, no satin or silk, not pampering or perfume. It was pure beauty, untouched by any corruption of station or arrogance. As the blush filled her face and bosom, Kaitain's enthrallment deepened. Irene had been correct. She said that Kaitain needed to find something to take his mind off the pressures of the court, he needed to go on with his life and put the death of his wife and father behind him. Irene promised to find him the most beautiful woman in the whole of the Empire, one that would deserve as much attention as he saw fit to lavish upon her without demanding more than she deserved. Dominique Arais was all that, and far more. Kaitain put a finger under her chin and forced the woman to meet his gaze. Her dark eyes shown like jewels in pools of white, filled with fear and uncertainty, but a sparkle that could not be dulled by the darkest nights. The blush in her cheeks deepened.

"How is it that you are only the mistress to an adulterous Knight of the Flashing Blade?"

Dominique's breath caught in her throat. How could he know? Why did he know? She felt as if she could not breathe, she had to get away, had to escape the situation. Her body was rigid, frozen by fear and embarrassment.

"You deserve so much more than to be the pawn in a game between Seraph Kore and Chelsea Zarova. You should be here in Aldere, gracing us all with your beauty every day. This palace has been filled with so much ugliness over the past few months, with the Crawling Plague and the wars and other issues. How can the beauty and purity that is Cadaria shine through when its heart, its very center is corrupted with all that ugliness? I want you to become the light of Aldere. I want you to show the rest of Espre the beauty that we all aspire to."

Dominique's head swam more. What was he asking her to do? Was she to become the mascot of the Empire? Was she being given a title? Adopted into the Imperial Family? Her body shaking, Dominique finally found her voice.

"I serve at the leisure of the Just Emperor Kaitain Lorien. Whatever he shall ask of me, I shall endeavor to perform."

Kaitain smiled.

"Good, Dominique, very good."

****

Sitting at his desk at his estate in the capital city of Thorigald, Seraph Kore's knuckles went white as he read the imperial proclamation that had been delivered. His heart broken and tears streaming from his eyes, he threw the parchment onto the fire and took up the blade Patience that lay on the table. There was only one thing left to do.

To all Citizens of the Empire of Cadaria,

Too long has the Empire been without a complete royal family. As long as the Emperor endures, so shall the Empire, but the Emperor cannot endure without his Empress. On New Year's Day, the Just Emperor, flying in the face of the danger posed by both the dragons of Cadaria and the Dark Continent of Mythryn will wed the common woman Dominique Arais. Their pairing has been blessed by the Creator, and their marriage will begin a new era in the history of the Empire of Cadaria. All who can attend the wedding and celebration are welcome.

Irene Drage

Imperial Sorceress

CHAPTER 48

Chapter XLIX

Old Friends

Year Two of the Just Emperor Kaitain "Dragonsbane" Lorien, Creator's Calendar Year 1869

Deep in the bowels of the Citadel of the Dark Gods, yet another argument raged. A thousand years ago, the temperaments of the men and women around the Council Chambers had been more even. However, after years of bickering, the polarization had deepened. Finally, the bickering was brought to a sudden stop by the raised voice of the leader of the Council and yet another adjournment had been called. For the past few weeks, there had been only two topics of debate. The situation with the Empire of Cadaria, and the mysterious plagues that were ravaging the lands. Thus far they had only touched Cadaria, but it was only a matter of time before they visited Mythryn as well. Though few in Cadaria ever would have spoken of it, the lands of Mythryn were not populated with mindless beasts and monsters that defied description. Just as with Cadaria, there were common men and women in towns and villages trying to lead normal lives. The difference was that the Dark Gods encouraged their citizens to rule themselves as best they could. Self-determination was the gift of the Dark Gods' rule. However, there was not lawlessness or anarchy. It was a delicate balance of freedom and structure. As the Council broke, Aryx found himself wandering aimlessly through one of the many abandoned corridors of the Citadel, trying to collect his thoughts from the long day.

A hundred lifetimes ago, the situation could have been different. They could have taken Cadaria, or at least tried to be something other than the Fallen Gods from the Heavens. But Gwydeon never would have allowed it. They were not to interfere. They had to deal with their expulsion and return to where they had come from. They had to make things right. But now Gwydeon was gone, and it had been nearly two thousand years. They were weakening, and it seemed that things would never be set right. How long ago had it been that he had use of both of his arms? How long had it been since he had been riding high, fighting the good fight, and putting an end to the enslavement and destruction of the innocent? And now, he had been robbed, by the greatest thief of them all. He had been robbed of his life, his power, even his name. No longer was he the great and powerful Aryx Terian, White Lightning, Knight of the Kingdom of Marcwell, chosen protector of the world of Onea. Now, and forever more, he was Aryx Parran, a member of the Dark Gods, with a lame left arm, and seemingly no voice. The ignominy and shame of it pressed against his soul and made his head hurt.

"I know that look," a female voice called from the other end of the chamber, "you're going to do something foolish."

Aryx sighed. Most mortals could not imagine being married for twenty years. Aryx had been married to his wife Diana for two-thousand and twenty years. Their friendship had long out-paced their passion, and they had been content to let their children speak for their legacy. Between Lissa and Alderin, they knew they had done very well by their children, though Aryx's relationship with his daughter had been strained for a time. However, they had been blessed with more than enough opportunities to make up for lost time. Diana too had become disenchanted with the way the Council had been turning, and while neither of them relished the thought of fighting in yet another war, they would do their duty if it got them one step closer to reclaiming what had been taken from them.

"Just don't take my other arm, ok? I wouldn't be of much use then."

Diana laughed slightly at the very old joke. It had been a long time ago, another world, and several wars ago. Aryx had been lost, and it was only Diana who could bring him back to his senses. The cost though had been the use of Aryx's left arm, his long-time and long-feared sword arm. When he had ascended to the Heavens after the destruction of Onea, Aryx had been given the opportunity to heal the wounds that he had accumulated in life, however, he had chosen to remain as he was, the symbol of humility ever hanging by his side. Diana had always admired her husband for that.

"What are you going to do, Aryx?"

Instinctively, Aryx looked around the empty corridors around him and then walked toward his wife. There were always eyes and ears in the Dark Citadel, and Aryx could not afford to be discovered before the time was right. His actions would fly in the face of the rest of the Council, and the only chance to overt a war was to change the mind of their leader. Though the Council always acted as a whole, it was their leader who had the final say in all actions. Right now, he leaned toward an open war with Cadaria, a decision that would seriously impact both sides, but not for the same reasons. Cadaria would be decimated by the conflict, and the estimates said that only five percent of the peasants would accept the rule of the Dark Gods; the rest would have to be destroyed. It was a high price to pay. On the other hand, the Dark Gods would be consigning themselves to the fate that was handed down by the Creator. They would be damned to spend eternity on Espre, hated, resented, and without their names. They would never be able to find the redemption that they had dreamed of for so long. It was a decision that could not be made, no matter the infuriation that Emperor Lorien caused them.

"I'm going to do what I should have done a long time ago. I can't let Serrina and the others influence the Council to damn us here for eternity. I need to go see him, and I need to convince him to help us. You have to buy me some time. Delay, do something. Get Lissa to help you, I know she will."

Diana nodded.

"How long will you need?"

Aryx thought. With his powers, he could have been to his destination with a thought, but the whole Citadel would be alerted to his movements. He would have to leave by conventional means, and then make the trek by foot across Mythryn to the south. The Pritan Islands were just outside the veil to the south, and were very private and often forgotten. They were said to be uninhabited, but Aryx knew better.

"Seven days at least to get there, maybe eight. After that, I can come back using my powers, the others won't be able to find the source. Do you think you can delay them that long?"

Diana shook her head.

"Even with Lissa assisting me, it will be difficult. It will be more so once Serrina returns from her mission, after that the Council will be forced to make a decision. I am sure it will remain neutral until then. I could always sway our allies to our side if I told them what your intentions were."

"You can't do that Diana," Aryx responded strongly. "No one can know what my plans are. I shouldn't have even spoken about them generally to Sadrina and Darrien. I know they won't speak of it, but the chance was too great to take."

"Very well, Aryx. Just promise me you'll be careful. It's been a long time since you've been on an adventure, and the last time you destroyed a world, so please be careful."

Aryx smiled and then kissed is wife on the cheek. As he turned to leave, he looked back over his shoulder.

"Just for the record, it wasn't my fault the world got destroyed. I just happened to be there. Hopefully this time we'll have better luck."

As Diana watched Aryx walked through the corridor until he disappeared out of sight, a pang of regret filled her. They had all lost so much since they had started out. In the beginning their only thought was to do their duty and save the world from a great evil. Now, they were the great evil. It was strange how the fates had conspired against them after all this time.

* * * * * * * * * * * * *

The Pritan Island chain, a group of seven small islands in close proximity to one another had always been largely ignored by the populous of the world of Espre. For the citizens of the Empire of Cadaria, the fact that the islands were so close to the Dark Continent of Mythryn meant that they were most likely corrupted in some form or another. Those who lived in Mythryn rarely caught a glimpse of the islands due to the high southern mountain ranges, and the ever-present veil of the Dark Mist. However, there were those brave enough to call the southern seas their home, and the traders and pirates of those waters also gave the Pritan Islands a wide berth. Many ships had mysteriously disappeared in those waters, while still others had received damage trying to get close. On occasion a trade ship would leave Mythryn and make port at the Pritan Islands, but that was a rare occurrence.

The largest of the Pritan Islands was densely covered with trees and rocky peaks. It was said that there was a massive underwater volcano that caused the formation of the Pritan Islands, and that the majority of the island chain had simply been a part of a mountainous underwater formation that was forced to the surface. Some of the cliffs, while not as high as most of the mountain ranges of Cadaria or Mythryn, were the home of some of the rarest wildlife on Espre. The Pritan Islands had one other distinction, it was a place untouched by the dragons of Espre. Legend said they had never touched the beautiful islands, and they never would.

Near the middle of one of the smaller of the Pritan Islands was a breathtaking vista centered around a high cliff of near-crystalline stone covered with vines and flowers. Over the top of the cliff rushed a stream of water fed by a permanent geyser to the north. The waterfall emptied into a beautiful clear pool whose bottom was littered with the remnants of a coral reef that had once been on the ocean floor. Nestled into the wall of the cliff, only a few feet from the waterfall and lake stood a small cabin. The walls of the cabin were made from stone, and the roof from thatch and fronds from the nearby trees. A simple wooden door stood in a makeshift doorway. The inside of the simple cabin was as humble as its exterior. A small table sat in one corner, with a shelf slightly above it that held a set of clay plates. The only ornate portion of the cabin stood in the opposite corner, a large stained wood wardrobe with intricately carved designs on both doors. While three of the walls of the cabin were made out of stones, the fourth wall was made from the cliff-face itself. That wall of the cabin was dominated by the large wooden frame of a bed. Under the covers on the bed, two forms lay wrapped together, their bodies pressed tightly to one another.

Slowly, one of the forms began to stir. With gentle ease, the form extricated itself from the other and slowly sat up. Sitting finally, with both feet flat on the floor, the man yawned silently and then slowly stretched his neck from side to side before reaching for his pants that hung on the foot-rail of the bed. He took one long last look at his wife before putting on his pants and silently leaving the cabin. The rich morning air caught his nostrils the next moment, and all the sounds of nature assaulted his ears at once. The crash of the waterfall, the hiss of the geyser, the chirping of birds and rustling of other wildlife. The variation and complexity of some of the sounds was amazing, and blended together, they almost formed a kind of music. Taking a long deep breath, the man moved across the short distance to the waterfall. For a few long seconds he looked down into the crystal clear lake, watching the fish make their way through the coral, oblivious to their observer. When a smile finally came to the man's lips, he turned back toward the waterfall and immersed his head in the flowing water. The semi-hot water erased whatever sleep still clung to the edges of his mind, and when he pulled away from the water, a gentle steam rose around him like a mist. He had begun to take a kind of comfort and pleasure from his morning routine, though not nearly as much as bathing with his wife. They had found a small outcropping under the waterfall where they could stand together and let the warm water rush over them. He could stand there for hours with her, her warm body pressed against his.

It was a rustle of leaves and underbrush that brought him back to reality. From living for so many years on the island, every sound made by every animal that called the island home had become familiar. This new sound brought the man's guard up. When the armor clad blond-haired man emerged from the tree-line to the east, the guard was not relaxed. It had been centuries since the two men had laid eyes upon one another, and the man wondered if it shouldn't have been longer.

"Never thought I would see your ugly face again," the man said coldly. "I'm unarmed and have no interest in fighting you, Aryx."

Aryx put his hand out as a gesture to show he carried no weapons, but he smiled a knowing smile.

"You may not have an interest in fighting, Aerith, but you are far from unarmed."

Aryx continued to approach and after another moment, the two ancient men were face to face. Finally, Aerith smiled and the two men embraced. Aerith clapped Aryx on the back hard twice before pulling away.

"It's been a long time, Aryx. Too long."

"Or not long enough," Aryx replied. "I know we all agreed to leave you in peace, but I didn't have a choice this time."

"You were never one to take your promises or your duty lightly, old man, and I knew that one day if there was anything I was needed for, one of you would come knocking on my door. I'm just glad it was you."

Aryx smiled and exhaled slowly. He was glad that this had been Aerith's reaction. Perhaps the rest of the conversation would go equally well. However, it was when the woman's voice rang out behind them that Aryx's memories and concern resurfaced.

"You know, it's impossible to sleep with the two of you carrying on like that. We go to all the trouble to come out here to the middle of nowhere, and we still have people dropping by whenever they want."

The woman who stood in the doorway was breathtaking to say the least, regardless of the fact that she was nude. Her body was flawless with perfect muscle tone, and was only a compliment to her face. With high cheekbones, flashing green eyes, full pouting lips framed by flowing brown hair with gentle streaks of red, she was a vision. Aerith smiled as soon as he saw his wife, and though the woman was naked, Aryx did not avert his eyes, nor did he drink in her beauty. He kept his eyes trained on hers.

"Nice to see you to, sister."

Aryx's words broke the silence and the tension, and while Aerith laughed, the woman did not. Her pouting lips curled into a frown.

"How I could ever be related to someone as pathetic as you, Aryx, I will never know. How Diana could have lived with you for two millennia is beyond me. I would have thought she would have killed you by now."

Aryx smiled.

"That is exactly what I thought about you and Aerith, Bryn. Haven't gotten bored yet?"

Bryn put both hands on her shapely hips.

"Oh, I've been bored for centuries, but he won't let me leave."

Aerith laughed louder and put his hand on Aryx's shoulder.

"Why don't you come in old man and sit down. I'm sure you have a lot to tell us, and you've come a long way. Bryn, why don't you put some clothes on?"

Bryn flipped her hand dismissively and turned back to the cabin. As the two men approached the door to the cabin, a small black ball of fur rolled from a crevice in the cliff face and stopped just before Aryx's feet. After a moment a low purr echoed from deep within the creature and a faint whisper-thin tail darted back and forth behind it. Aryx shook his head and looked over to Aerith.

"Now, now, that is no way to treat a guest."

The little black ball of fur purred louder and then rolled back to its cave.

"He's not used to company."

Aryx laughed softly.

"I can't believe you kept him all these years."

Aerith smirked.

"I didn't. There's a whole colony of them living in the caverns behind the waterfall. They like it here, and I can't see them getting along very well anywhere else. Besides, they make good security if anyone decides to get too close to the island."

"I'm sure," Aryx responded as the two men entered the cabin.

"Oh, they love pirate meat. Not too fond of parrots though for some reason."

* * * * * * * * * * * * *

Aerith sat at the table sipping some water slowly while Bryn finished dressing. Aryx seemed to be hesitating as to relaying the purpose of his visit, and so they had sat making small talk for the better part of an hour. Bryn had already looked through two dozen dresses in the wardrobe before finally settling on a very revealing red dress that was low cut with a long slit up the right side. While it left very little to the imagination, it was definitely one of Aerith's favorites. Perhaps that is why she always found an excuse to wear it more often than not.

"So how is your son?"

Aerith frowned.

"It's been a while since we heard from him, but he's been doing well. Top of his class at the Academy. I never thought when he went off to Jelan that he would stick it out long enough to make anything of himself, he has too much of his mother in him."

Bryn scoffed.

"It's a wonder he wasn't expelled in the first week because he has so much of his father in him. Especially after you taught him all those tricks and pranks to play. And I still do not believe you tried to convince me that there was a practical application to learning how to make frogs spontaneously appear in drinking glasses."

Aryx laughed.

"There is a practical application." Aerith said calmly and genuinely. "I just can't think of it right now."

Aerith smiled fully and then turned to Aryx.

"And how are your children? Lissa, Alderin, the grandchildren?"

Aryx rubbed his left shoulder absently.

"Lissa and Alderin are well. Lissa gets to be more and more like her mother every year."

"Thank goodness," Bryn jibbed.

"But she has her hands full," Aryx continued. "Between the rigors of the council, taking care of the twins, and taking care of Wolf, it's a full time job."

Aerith cast his eyes down.

"He still hasn't recovered then?"

Aryx shook his head.

"He's been catatonic since the Fall. We've done everything we know how to do for him, but there has been no change. The Dark Seer seems to think he will come out of it in time, but I don't know whether or not I believe that. It's been so long, and I know that Lissa is hurting every day she has to take care of him."

Bryn sighed.

"I just wish you could tell us what happened. I always liked that boy, and it's a shame what happened to him. He deserves a better fate than his father and mother."

"I wish I could explain," Aryx said finally, "but it's against the rules. I almost envy the fact that the two of you never ascended, and yet somehow you still live after all this time."

Aerith leaned back in his chair.

"It's what we were owed. Even though our powers have waned over the centuries, we are still what we are. Nothing can change that, not even the destruction of our world."

The three old friends remained silent for a long time before Bryn finally spoke.

“Maybe you should tell us why you’re here, Aryx. It must be important.”

Aryx sighed.

“As much as I have missed the two of you all these years, the last thing I ever wanted to do was involve you in the politics of the Council of Dark Gods. But I have no other choice now. The new Emperor of Cadaria is hell-bent on starting a war with Mythryn, a war he can never win. He has sent a series of assassins to Mythryn in an effort to kill either one of the Dark Gods, or Queen Sadrina. Naturally all of these attempts have failed, but the Council is growing tired of the interference. I have been acting as the voice of reason and the voice of caution, but I am afraid before too much longer my voice will fall on deaf ears. There are forces within the Council that are pushing for war, to have it done with once and for all, and those forces have taken the ear of our leader.”

Aerith shook his head.

“If the Dark Gods attack Cadaria in force, there will be nothing left. The whole of Cadaria will be swept from the face of Espre, and they will have learned nothing, neither the people of Cadaria nor the Dark Gods. I know you can’t tell us what led to the Fall, but I do know that if you take the kind of action you are talking about, that it will make the situation worse.”

Aryx nodded.

“So what can we do?” Bryn asked, frustrated. “Aside from a few parlor tricks that Aerith can still perform, we have no real power. I have been severed permanently from all of the powers I had, and Aerith gave the lion’s share of his power away. We would love to help, Aryx, but we’re not exactly what we once were.”

“Perhaps not,” Aryx said nodding slowly, “but the favor I have come to ask of you would most likely not put you in any danger.”

Aerith smirked.

“Most likely? Sounds pretty damning to me. So, what is this favor?”

Aryx frowned and took a long deep breath. This gambit had a very low chance for success, and he did not like putting his old friends into danger. However, the options were becoming fewer and fewer as the days passed, and there was a good chance they could be at war by the end of the year.

"The key to the Council is our leader. If we can somehow convince him this is the wrong course of action, then we can overt a war. However, there is only one person left on Espre that he will listen to, and I can't approach him directly."

Bryn looked puzzled, but the expression on Aerith's face never changed.

"I can't do that, Aryx," Aerith said finally. "I have nothing but respect for you and for the others and what you have all done. But, I can't. Not now, not after all this time. And not after what happened to Meredith."

When she heard the name, Bryn frowned. The connection was made, and it was not a pleasant one.

"Anything else," Aerith continued, "I would gladly do. But he's not the same man I knew all those centuries ago, and I don't know what would happen if he and I were face to face again."

Aryx stood up and pulled the cloak back from his left shoulder. The long scar that ran from the middle of his bicep up to the center of his shoulder still looked as though it were fresh, and pain seemed to radiate off it in waves.

"I wear this as a reminder of all that we sacrificed to get here. We all have scars, all of the Dark Gods, and even you Aerith, and you Bryn. However, most of the scars we wear are on the inside. If I don't find a way to stop this war, all the suffering, all the loss, and all the pain we endured will be for nothing. Can you sit here and tell me that you are willing to forsake all that has passed? Are you willing to walk away from the memories and the sacrifices of those who aren't with us anymore? Cedric? Anabel?"

"Gideon…Grawn…Ellis…" Bryn said softly.

"Logan and Caris," Aerith said nodding. "Alright, Aryx. You win. I have a feeling I know where he is and how to get to him. What do I do once I've convinced him?"

Aryx frowned.

"Bring him to the Citadel of the Dark Gods, and I'll take care of the rest. Just make sure he's in a good mood, or this could get ugly."

Aerith nodded, and the next moment, Aryx had disappeared from the table. He had no doubt gone home to stall for time. Time they did not have in abundance. After a moment to reflect, Aerith got up from his chair and moved to the long trunk that sat at the foot of the bed and opened it. There before him lay his cloak, a small bag of stones and a sword. The sword had been a gift to him a long time ago from an old friend, and as he buckled the scabbard belt around his waist, it felt good to have the weight of the Dragon Sword at his hip. He turned to his beautiful wife and gave her a slow deep kiss before turning toward the door. Bryn reached up and took hold of his arm and held on for a moment before standing and taking Aerith in her arms. After another long kiss, Bryn closed her eyes, took a deep breath and then retrieved a small silver dagger from the chest and buckled it around her right thigh.

"For Ellis," she said softly.

Aerith nodded, and the two lovers walked from the cabin and closed the door behind them. After a moment the black Snag bounced from its home in the cliff and purred. It knew something was happening. After a moment it bounded across the distance and landed on Aerith's shoulder. No words were exchanged as Aerith reached into the small pouch and pulled out a red stone. Taking a deep breath, he began to pull at the edges of the stone. It took much more effort than it had in ages past, but before long a swirling portal stood before them. Moments later, only the sound of the waterfall remained in the clearing.

Fate's Touch

Year Two of the Just Emperor Kaitain "Dragonsbane" Lorien, Creator's Calendar Year 1869

The Kingdom of Ice, Rashaleb was known far and wide as the richest kingdom in the Empire of Cadaria next to the Imperial province of Aldere. While the mines of Rashaleb produced a fair amount of precious gems, they were no match for the military precision of the shipments from the gold and silver mines of Aldere. However, there was enough wealth that stayed in Rashaleb to keep a good portion of the citizens in relative comfort. The nobles of course benefited the most from the mining operation, but Orren Eldrath, the Sapphire Knight of the Flashing Blade made sure that those who risked their lives to procure the wealth also were allowed to share in its benefits. Much of Rashaleb lay in the northern reaches of Cadaria, and the extreme northern shores of the kingdom touched a massive glacier. Mining in the extreme north had always yielded the best results, and when core samples were returned from the glacier, rich diamond deposits were discovered. However, mining the glacier was very hazardous work and one wrong step could mean the death for the entire crew. Thusly, Orren as the ranking magistrate of the area decreed that any miner who spent no less than half of a year in the mines would receive a full quarter share of whatever they recovered from the mine. Also, if any miner died through any cause other than gross negligence in the mine, that miner's family would be compensated with a monthly stipend taken from the profits of all the mines in Rashaleb. These laws and the protection of the common man made Orren very popular amongst the people of Rashaleb and universally despised by the nobility. Some of the miners had profited enough in a few years to retire from the mines altogether and buy very large estates that rivaled some of those owned by the noble-born.

Orren laughed to himself at the thought of commoner and lords alike sharing a table. It was said long ago that a man's fate was locked the moment he was born. It was said that the Creator touched those who had a destiny to do great things and ignored those that did not. When Orren's abilities over the arcane first presented themselves on his fifth birthday, it seemed that the Creator's fickle finger of fate had touched Orren squarely on the forehead. Orren's parents however did not seem to be so lucky. Three months after being fostered to the Academy of Arcane Arts in Jelan, Orren's father was killed in a mine cave-in. Working conditions had been terrible, and it was only a matter of time before something tragic happened. Orren's mother, having no real trade skills was reduced to near poverty in an instant. In order to keep enough food on the table for herself and her two remaining children, his mother worked in a brothel until the day she died, barely five years later. Orren's brother and sister also died far too young. Orren's brother, who had just been born when he left to enroll in the Academy died when he was fourteen in a mine collapse, while Orren's sister, who was only one when their mother died, was yet another victim of the Crawling Plague. It seemed that while the Creator favored Orren, the rest of his family was expendable. That thought pervaded everything that Orren touched, and he felt that there must be a way to exact some revenge upon fate.

Those thoughts led to dangerous times for Orren in Jelan. He studied everything he could find about the properties of time and fate. He delved deep into prophecies and what holy scriptures he could find. He even spent a year at the Temple of the Creator in Albitonin in an effort to more fully understand the motives of the Creator. Before long, whatever healthy respect he had for the Creator had been replaced with disdain. There seemed to be no rhyme or reason as to who was touched and who was not. No pattern to follow that dictated who was important and who was not. Why he was chosen to live, and his family was slated to die. None of it made any sense, and the sheer randomness of it all infuriated Orren even farther.

Entering his favorite tavern in Rashaleb, Orren found his seat at the corner table and reflected further on his time in Jelan. He had been such a sponge, soaking up everything he could learn from anyone who would teach him, student and teacher alike. For most of his years as a Novice and Apprentice he never saw his room, and most nights he could be found in the library reading anything he could get his hands on. Most mornings he was woken by other students in time to get his breakfast. Orren remembered missing more than a few meals during his time in Jelan, and that had cost him developmentally. Orren had been a sickly child, and he grew into a weakened adult. Though his physical frame was not rugged, the power that it contained more than sustained him. Magical energy suffused his being and compensated for the lack of physical prowess. But, it was his obsession with the touch of fate that put him at odds with the Masters Council and eventually led to his expulsion. It seemed that whoever did not agree with the Masters Council found themselves out on the street. Perhaps that was Orren's payment for spurning fate. But Orren was not content with being a casualty of that which he resented. Orren's private studies continued long after his expulsion from the Academy of Arcane Arts, and it was those studies that brought him to the attention of the Just Emperor Ender Lorien.

Ender began to hear stories of a powerful sorcerer who could make the impossible happen. It had started simply, and Orren remembered it as if it had happened yesterday. He had been sitting in a tavern, not unlike the one he sat in every morning, idly flipping a coin. It took only a small exertion of his ability to manipulate probability to make the coin flip heads every time. But as he sat flipping the coin he realized that he needed to manipulate the probability less and less. He was not making the coin flip heads by controlling how it spun in the air, or turning it as it landed. It was simply though the application of his own will, and it became so. Before long the one coin became two, then three, then more. Patrons standing near him also experienced the same effect, and for a period of several hours in that tiny tavern, a coin never landed tails. Eventually Orren expanded his sphere of influence to any game of chance. Dice, coins, cards, anything that could have a seemingly random pattern revealed itself to Orren with only a thought. However, before long, Orren's abilities changed and grew darker.

Orren began to see the strings fate that connected everyone. He could see the touch of the Creator and the time each person he encountered had left. While he was powerless to see the circumstances of that person's fate, if he was close when the time was almost up, he could manipulate the situation and give the person more time. It didn't always work, but sometimes, he could cheat fate. When asked to explain it to the Emperor once, he likened it to setting the hands on a clock. Sometimes the clock will let you move the hands forward or back, and sometimes the hands will not move at all. Eventually all of the laws of fate and probability were in a state of flux around Orren. Things that should not have happened, or were the most unlikely to happen, would. Rain would pour on an utterly cloudless day. A plate would break just at the wrong time. Hinges would break on a locked door. Every time Orren progressed deeper into his studies of the fates and the Creator, more power emerged, and it took some time to learn to control those powers.

Once the extent of his abilities were known, Orren became a favorite of Ender Lorien, and would eventually become a member of the Knights of the Flashing Blade. To Orren's great surprise, his appointment to the Flashing Blade was not met with resistance from the Academy of Arcane Arts, in fact, he had been given a favorable recommendation by Alistair Ravenheart. In the years after his appointment, Orren had many opportunities to sit and speak with Alistair Ravenheart, and the two had become close friends. His passing came too soon.

Sitting at his usual table in the corner of the tavern, he idly sat flipping a coin as he often did to amuse himself. The ripples of probability could be seen in the air before him, and a subtle shift to the left or the right could change the result. Suddenly a sharp pain struck Orren between the eyes, and the coin clattered to the table. There was something wrong in the city, something terribly wrong. Fates were being cut short, lives were being snuffed out long before their appointed time. Orren took hold of long sword that hung at his hip, the sword named Courage, and sprinted toward the source of the disturbance.

* * * * * * * * * * * * *

The bright sunlight reflected off the ice formations to the north as a gentle snow began to fall over the city of Rashaleb. The streets were filled with the normal vendors and city folk, going about their daily lives totally oblivious to the danger that was approaching. At the city gates, two guards chatted idly about their wives and families when one looked up and caught the glimpse of something on the horizon. The single form emerged from the fog of distance, as the snow began to fall harder. Though the guard squinted and tried hard to make out more detail of the approaching form, he could not. Shrugging his shoulders, he returned to his conversation. In a matter of moments, the guard looked up again, horror beginning to fill him. As soon as the Wasting Disease had begun to run rampant, the descriptions of the woman calling herself Famine began to circulate. In the snow, the guard could barely make out the wispy haze that surrounded the woman, disguising the hideous features beneath. The woman looked beautiful and captivating, completely nude and inviting. But as she approached, the beauty dissolved revealing the gaunt, emaciated form beneath. With a shout, the alarms began to ring through the city, and the two guards drew their weapons and prepared to defend the city with their lives.

Famine laughed as she approached Rashaleb. The fools thought they could resist. Many had tried, all had failed.

"Surrender yourselves to the touch of Famine," she crooned as she approached. "Your souls sing and plead to be released from your shells. You will join the chorus, you will join the raised voices singing the praises of Dorovar. Do not resist. Be blessed with the freedom that His touch can provide. Shake off this old life and embrace the eternity of peace that Dorovar will bring you. Can you not feel the hunger in your souls? The hunger for a new life, the hunger for freedom? Let me release you from this ravishing hunger, let me show you the truth and the love of Dorovar."

The two guards steeled themselves against the fear that rocketed through them. When the demon approached, the first of the guards struck, thrusting his sword directly at the heart of the woman. The tip of the blade pierced her skin, and was accompanied by a hideous laughter that resounded through the city. As the guard withdrew his blade, his stomach twisted. He was so hungry. In a matter of moments, he was searching for something to eat, chipping his teeth as he attempted to bite into the steel gauntlets shielding his hands. As his companion watched in horror, the guard collapsed, the hunger enveloping him and reducing him to a shell. Famine laughed as she continued to walk slowly toward the other guard who was retreating into the city. A line of archers had formed just at the mouth of the city gates, and as the guard cleared the line of fire, a hail of arrows sped toward Famine. With a wave of her hand, the arrows were knocked from the air, and the archers all felt the touch of the Wasting Disease. Commoners in the streets scattered, screaming. Everywhere Famine looked, several people fell to the ground, screaming, crying, eating everything in sight. The carnage was incredible and the death-toll mounted as the moments passed. People cowered in their homes, praying that the hideous woman would not visit their door.

* * * * * * * * * * * * *

The physical rigors of the position of Sapphire Knight did not seem to be something that Orren could handle from his years of bookishness and poor physical health, but as he sprinted through the streets toward the source of the screaming and fear, he looked down at Courage and smiled a knowing smile. Like all the sacred weapons which had been gifts to the Knights of the Flashing Blade, Courage had special powers that seemed to know what Orren needed to be successful. Orren often laughed when he thought that Courage was fated to find its way into his hands. The power that flowed from Courage coursed through his body, hardening his muscles, supporting his lungs and heart, letting air flow freely to him regardless of the exertion. Fear never touched him, and no matter the trial, Orren knew that his body would never falter due the rigors of his duty. Clutching the hilt of Courage tighter, Orren sprinted through the streets until he saw her.

When Orren looked at any person, he could see the gentle tendrils of fate wrapping around them. Each time they made a decision, some of the tendrils were broken while still others were created, or divided by the new course. However, this woman, this Famine, was not touched by the tendrils of fate, and there was nothing but a void around her. Orren stopped in his tracks and held Courage ready to strike.

"In the name of the Just Emperor Kaitain Lorien," Orren called, his voice strong and proud, "I demand that you cease your incursion into this city and submit to the justice of the Emperor."

Famine cocked her head slightly and fixed her eyes upon Orren.

"The Sapphire Knight calls to me," Famine cooed. "You more than anyone knows the unjust touch of fate upon the souls of all men. You know the misery and horror that can be caused by fate. If you had the power, you would change all those bad fates, I have seen it in your soul."

Orren held his ground as the woman began to approach.

"I hear your soul, Orren Eldrath. I hear the cries of pain that your soul makes in the night. The loss of your family, the loss of those you wish you could save. Would you unmake fate? Would you save those who cannot be saved? You may not have the power to free them, but I do. I set their souls free for my master. Dorovar's touch is the love that the Creator's fate denies them."

She was close now, close enough to strike down. A single stroke from Courage and the horror of the Wasting Disease would be at an end.

"That's right, Orren," Famine continued to woo, "strike me with your sword. Become a hero. Give in to the fate that surrounds you. Dorovar has given me my task, and I have added thousands of voices to his choir. The Heavens will open and he will rise to face the Creator on the wings of a million souls. Send me to meet my master, and bring this chapter to a close. Bring the next of Dorovar's children to this world, and let all of Espre know the touch and freedom of Death."

Orren raised Courage and struck, but before the blade reached its target, a blast of wind caught Orren in the chest and sent him sprawling backwards. When he regained his senses, he looked up to see a robed figure standing between him and famine, a large scythe in hand. It could only have been Vallic Ultiv, Orren's longtime friend and fellow member of the Flashing Blade.

"If you wanted the kill Vallic," Orren said getting to his feet, "all you had to do was ask."

Vallic shook his head, his eyes never leaving Famine.

"You fool, she wants us to kill her. We must take her prisoner, and we can't allow her to be harmed."

Orren was back to his feet in a moment, Courage in hand. This made no sense. If they killed Famine, the Wasting Disease would be over, it would all be over. Vallic locked his eyes on Famine and scowled.

"It was something the gray man said before his death," Vallic said coldly. "He said that it was our curing of the Crawling Plague that set forth the Wasting Disease on Cadaria. If we destroy Famine, something else will come, another of Dorovar's servants, something far worse."

Orren felt his heart sink. What could be worse than the unpreventable suffering and eventual death of tens of thousands? Who or what was this Dorovar? There were only questions and no answers to be found.

"You are wise, Serpentine Knight," Famine said, laughter filling her ghostly voice, "but no matter what you do, the will of Dorovar cannot be denied. His hand will reach across the cosmos and all that he touches will know the joy of his love. But know this, you have prevented nothing. Already my touch and my gifts have killed tens of thousands, and before this Wasting Disease has run its course, a quarter of your Empire will have felt its ravishing hunger. We are culling the herd, Serpentine Knight, and only the most wicked will be left behind to suffer their fate at the hands of Dorovar. The innocents have been judge so, and will be released from their shells before they can be corrupted by your Emperor Kaitain. Let him fight his dragons, and let him taste the same miserable failures as millions of others that came before him. It is only Dorovar who can have his revenge against the dragons. Kaitain aspires to be the sun himself, and he will only find himself burned by his inadequacy."

Vallic grinded his teeth. This woman was maddening. If she was right, and that many were dead…it was impossible to fathom. Suddenly the haze of white around Famine flashed.

"Dorovar calls, and I must answer his call, and bring with me more souls for his chorus. Rashaleb has been judged pure. Except for the two of you."

The veil of haze exploded in a brilliant green fire, and a shower of white particles joined the falling snow. Vallic looked on in horror and then felt the pain racing through his mind and body. All he could do was stand there, cold and impotent as a statue as the whole city of Rashaleb died around him. Later the death toll would be in the thousands, an entire city wiped clean by the Wasting Disease, and by the touch of the woman known as Famine, and her mysterious master called Dorovar. The capitol of the Kingdom of Ice had been turned into a cold and desolate cemetery. Suddenly the ground rumbled, and then split before the two knights, a single spike of obsidian rising from the ground where Famine had stood only a few moments before. A haze of white crowned the tip of the spike, a last monument to the damage caused. After a moment, Orren took hold of Vallic's shoulder and spun him around. Orren was filled with anger and rage, but when he saw the tears streaming from Vallic's eyes, the anger fled.

"There was nothing we could have done," Vallic said finally. "If we would have struck her down, I am sure the result would have been the same. Rashaleb is no more, and for that I am sorry dear friend, but we must shift our focus now. I am sure in a very short time, Famine's threat of a new terror will come to pass."

Orren swallowed hard and nodded.

"So, what do we do?"

Vallic lowered his head and then sighed.

"The deaths of more innocents may not be preventable, my friend. But we must try our best. The true villain here is the one known as Dorovar, and we must endeavor to find out all we can about him and his agenda. The first clues have begun to fall into place, but we will need help for the rest."

Orren let Courage find its way back to its scabbard and then he looked closely at the spike of obsidian. Dorovar, Famine, Pestilence, dragons, Kaitain, all of them were connected somehow, but none of it made sense.

"We will seek out Xaran, and perhaps we will be able to learn more about this Dorovar and his history."

Orren was confused.

"How can you be sure Xaran knows anything about this Dorovar?"

Vallic smiled.

"I don't think he does, but those he is with certainly do."

****

From his position high on the glacier, Erik Relcan watched in horror as the entire city of Rashaleb was destroyed by the woman calling herself Famine, and the touch of the Wasting Disease. Two members of the Flashing Blade had been present, but they had been spared the horror that befell the innocent citizens. Erik's heart was breaking, though it seemed to no longer beat. As he looked around the frozen plain upon which he stood, he realized that he was not cold, in fact, he felt very little.

"It is a horrible thing, to see all those people dying."

Erik turned to look back at the man who had brought him back from the dead. Dimitri Sulano, the Voice of the Lost, as the man called himself, seemed to know a great deal about a great deal of subject, but did not ever seem inclined to comment further than the most basic of information. He stood unmoving, dressed in a black shirt, black vest, black overcoat, and black pants, his black hair untouched by the cold breeze. This was the man who had rescued Erik from the darkness of death, the one who had given him his new purpose.

"This is the kind of suffering that your precious Hannah will be drawn to, Erik, this kind of death and destruction."

Erik looked back at the city of the dead, imagining Hannah trying to save them all, her love and her devotion wasted on those who did not deserve it.

"The next terror will be coming soon, one much more vicious than Famine. Hannah will be duty-bound to combat the suffering head-on, but she will only prove in sacrificing herself. Is that what you want Erik?"

Erik shook his head violently. He could not give voice to the grief and sadness that filled him at the thought of Hannah dying. She could not be allowed to sacrifice herself, not for anyone, not ever.

"You must go to her now, Erik. You must save her from herself. Do not let her go to Albitonin, not under any circumstances. If you do, she will die. And if she dies, it will be your fault, because you had the opportunity to prevent it."

Erik fumed, his heart and blood were on fire. He knew what he had to do, and without thought for himself, cast himself down the face of the glacier. He had to find Hannah, he had to save her.

Dimitri watched dispassionately as Erik Relcan hurled his body down the glacier, and smiled. Xavier had done his job well, causing Erik to fall into their hands, and had certainly earned his title of Corrupter of Souls. It was then that Dimitri realized he was not alone. The next moment, a woman's soft voice broke the silence.

"Report."

Dimitri kept his eyes trained on Erik's struggling form.

"He will do as he was instructed, and will not fail us. Hannah Ironheart will be nowhere near Albitonin when the catastrophe strikes. You can inform Seraphina that everything is going to plan."

"She and her mother will be pleased," the woman replied, "pity though, I was hoping to kill Erik again."

Dimitri smiled.

"Don't worry Syren, I am sure that you will get the opportunity whether he is successful or not. I shall now move on to this Tess Annis and her bodyguard."

Syren shook her head.

"There has been a change of plans. Seraphina doesn't want the Annis girl touched. We are to bide our time and wait for the next of this Dorovar's servants."

Finally Dimitri turned around.

"Do you understand any of this?"

Syren's evil smile was answer enough.

"Seraphina's mother wants Dorovar to succeed until the Dark Gods become involved, then it will be our time. The more fractured and distracted the Cadarian Emperor and his lackeys are, the better it is for all of us."

Syren turned to leave.

"And what of you and your brood?"

Syren simply laughed.

"We have little dragon hunters to play with."

With that, Dimitri was left on the glacier, his own evil smile growing as the moments passed.

Choices

Year Two of the Just Emperor Kaitain "Dragonsbane" Lorien, Creator's Calendar Year 1869

Galateria looked far different than it had the last time that Tolon Morr made the trek through the swamps and mountains. Scars had been gouged into the walls of the mountains from assaults by the dragons in the area. The whole kingdom had been turned into a war zone, and Tolon knew that two other members of the Knights of the Flashing Blade were embroiled fighting the dragons and trying to heal the wounds in Galateria, and though Tolon wished he could help, he had to return his focus to the hopeless mission he had been dispatched upon. The last time he was faced with the Maldovrin Triplets, he was powerless to take action against them, rendered impotent by the power of his weapon Strength. He hoped for a better result this time, but did not have high hopes for any type of success.

Tolon began to believe that this time the path to the lair of the Maldovrin Triplets had been somehow easier. Perhaps it was just his familiarity with the route, but something inside of him questioned that assumption. Every step of the way was less treacherous, from the undergrowth, to the wild animals, to the tearing thorns, nothing seemed as difficult or arduous, and at times it almost seemed like the Maldovrin Triplets were parting the way for him. Perhaps they thought he returned with the head of Irene Drage, but it they were as powerful seers as they were supposed to be, that could not have been the case. They already would have known of his mission, and perhaps they were going to make an example of him to the Emperor. The broken body of a member of the Flashing Blade would make an effective point. Of course, Tolon knew that it would not be the end of the issue for Kaitain Lorien, it would only be the beginning. He would send another member of the Flashing Blade and hundreds of troops to take the women by force, and no matter their power, Tolon was sure that eventually they would fall to a prolonged assault. The Emperor had his mind set on getting the information and not letting it fall into anyone else's hands. Even if the Triplets chose to let the Emperor know about this Dragon's Tear, the end for them would be the same. It was then that everything finally fell into place for Tolon. Why hadn't he seen it before? The Emperor wanted the information about the Dragon's Tear, and if Tolon had been able to extract the information from the Maldovrin Triplets, the Emperor would have known that anyone who paid the right price would have had access to the information. That was something Kaitain never would have allowed, and so Tolon most likely would have been dispatched to remove that possibility by killing the sisters. Strength for some reason had known the true motives of the Emperor and had not allowed Tolon to strike. Just what was behind these sacred weapons, and how did they function?

His thoughts clouded, Tolon finally reached the mouth of the cavern that led to the Maldovrin Triplets. As he walked through the dank and cold mist, he waited for the dim light to appear in the distance, however, he was disappointed when it did not appear. Finally he reached the large open area, and found it nearly empty. The crafted gold lanterns and tapestries were gone, while the rug and the ornate chairs remained. It looked almost as though the Maldovrin Triplets were moving to another location, one where even the Emperor of Cadaria could not find them.

"You are most perceptive Tolon Morr," a familiar voice said from the darkness, "we are indeed on our way to more friendly territory."

The Triplets appeared the next moment, standing before their chairs as they had during his last visit. After a moment they sat. Jania, the tallest of the sisters, and apparently the one who led the group had been the one who had spoken before their appearance, Tolon was sure.

"Great Seers," Tolon said after a moment, "by now you already know why I have come."

Jordyne frowned.

"Yes, we certainly do, and this cannot end well for you by any stretch of the imagination. If you attempt to strike us down, we will have no choice but to destroy you. If you return to your Emperor in failure again, you will find your death as well. It seems as though fate has not smiled upon you Tolon Morr, and your death will come quickly as a result of this meeting."

Tolon steeled himself. There was so much riding on his next words, and if he had miscalculated the benevolence of the sisters, he would find himself very much dead as Jordyne had described.

"Great Seers, I have learned much through this endeavor, and I believe there may be another way to resolve this dispute. I know that no matter what course of action of the two I have been provided that I follow, it will end in my death, and so I must find another. To that end, it is something that you, Jania, said the last time I stood before you. You said that it is my weapon itself that prevented me from striking you. And it was you, Jordyne who said that the value of the information about the Dragon's Tear was more than any amount of land or goods could pay for. But you, Jerrica, said that the life of Irene Drage would pay for the information. All of these things are tied together, and though I do not fancy myself a very intelligent man, I think the pieces are starting to fall into place."

Jania tried to stifle a smile.

"And what is this puzzle of words and memory telling you, Sir Tolon Morr?"

"The only way I am going to escape this is to find this Dragon's Tear myself, and find more understanding about the sacred weapons of the Flashing Blade. And to do that, I have to uncover the fate of Arturious Demascious."

Silence filled the room, but Jerrica smiled. While the sisters had foreseen this moment in time, it was always interesting to watch the humans come to their conclusions. Perhaps there was hope for them yet, but for every Tolon Morr, there were hundreds of Kaitain Loriens.

"That is a very dangerous course," Jania commented.

"And perhaps a very foolish one," Jordyne cautioned.

"But still a wise one," Jerrica concluded.

Jania stood the next moment and took a step toward Tolon. Though he did not know why, fear struck his heart. While he had never seen any of the power that these three women possessed, he could perceive it, and it scared him to his core. Tolon had met Orren Eldrath once long ago, and when talking to Orren, he could feel the power rolling off the man like a mist, and Tolon had respected that power. However, there was no such palpable sensation coming from any of the sisters, and that made it all the more terrifying.

"So, Sir Tolon Morr, Amethyst Knight of the Flashing Blade, what request do you have to make of the Maldovrin Triplets to aid you on your quest for knowledge and survival?"

Tolon felt his mouth go dry. He hadn't thought it possible that he would get this far, or that the Maldovrin Triplets would even hear his request. It wasn't actually until this moment that he had even begun to conceive what he needed to make his plan come to fruition. It was a pipe dream, a fool's errand. But fate at times favored the foolish, and perhaps he was due a favor or two.

"There is little about the Dragon's Tear or the Sacred Weapons that I know and understand. I only know that the Dragon's Tear is valuable and that it is desired, and nothing more. As far as the Sacred Weapons, I know that when Strength is in my hand, I feel powerful enough to move a mountain, and that any enemy who stands before me has no chance for victory. But it is the rest of Strength's powers, the fact that it steels me against fear, allows me to feel the weakness of those around me, shows me where there are helpless innocents in need of my protection, these are the parts I do not understand. When I grew in the gladiatorial arenas, I thought of little more than destroying my opponent to defend my own life. I had strength then, strength to defend myself, and crush my enemies. But this is different. It almost feels as though Strength belongs in my hands, as though it were meant for me and no other. How could a man, almost two millennia ago, know what I would need?"

Jordyne stood and took a step forward and stood beside her sister.

"You see two paths before you, Tolon Morr, one that leads to the Dragon's Tear, and one that leads toward the Sacred Weapons. However, the Maldovrin Triplets may only grant one request, so you must choose. Which of these paths do you choose to follow? Which of these paths calls your heart?"

Tolon looked to the ground, and when he looked up, his eyes caught Jerrica's. There was sadness in her eyes, a sadness that she tried to hide. But almost as soon as Tolon caught a glimpse of it, it was gone. She had no doubt felt his thoughts and hidden her momentary weakness. They knew what he would choose before he even knew himself.

"I must find the source of these Sacred Weapons."

Jania nodded. In the back of Tolon's mind, he could hear one door slamming closed while another creaked slowly open. Perhaps he had just thrown away his career and life as the Amethyst Knight, perhaps he would become a fugitive from the justice of Emperor Kaitain Lorien, but that mattered little now. What mattered was the truth, a truth he could not find being held down by the trappings of a position he no longer felt he wanted.

Jerrica finally stood and joined her sisters.

"Your choice is made, Tolon Morr, and now you must face the consequences of your actions. Far to the north, far past the Ice Fields of Rashaleb, and deep into the reaches of the Great Glacier, there is a refuge of sorts. It is said that in his last days, after the forging of the sacred weapons, that Arturious made his way to this refuge to escape the world and the darkness that was coming. It is not known what became of him then, but perhaps there is information there that will lead you to your answers. There is a woman there, a woman who has accumulated great knowledge, and she will hold the key to your fate.

Tolon nodded.

"And how will I know this woman?"

Jania looked to Jerrica first and then back at Tolon.

"You need not know her," Jania answered. "She already knows you."

Tolon noted the information deep in his mind and did his best to suppress the discomfort that the ominous pronouncement brought to his heart. The journey that the Triplets had laid out for him would be a treacherous one, spanning the entire length of the Cadarian Empire in to the farthest northern reaches of its borders. It would be the ultimate test of his dedication to his new path, and perhaps that was the point. If he faltered during the journey, if he did not have the desire or fortitude to carve his way through the miles and hazards, then he truly did not want or deserve the information he sought. It was a quest of the highest order, the kind that children's tales used to recount. However, in the versions that were told in the gladiatorial arenas, the heroes never made it to the end of their journeys. Heroes had to die before you knew their names, and a heroic death was usually the label for meeting ones end while doing something incredibly foolish. Shaking himself away from old and pointless thoughts, Tolon bowed deeply to the three women, and turned to leave. He was suddenly struck with great concern for the three women. Tolon paused at the edge of the cavern and turned back.

"And what becomes of the Maldovrin Triplets?"

Jania smiled.

"We shall move on. There are many places on the face of Espre where we will be safe, and many allies that will shield us from those that would misuse the information that we possess. Worry not, Amethyst Knight, we shall remain as we have for all this time."

Tolon nodded and then made his way from the cavern.

* * * * * * * * * * * * *

Jordyne watched Tolon go, and turned to face her sisters.

"Do you realize what we have done?"

Jania shook her head and walked back toward her chair.

"We have done nothing that would not have occurred normally. We have not broken any rules."

"Not broken any rules?" Jordyne fumed. "You gave him the location of the refuge, you told him that a woman who knew who he was would be waiting. You practically pushed him to solve the riddle. If he learns the truth…"

"He won't," Jania replied sitting down and folding her hands in her lap.

Jordyne rounded on her sister.

"Sister, you may be the older by a few seconds, and you may have inherited the majority of the Sight, but you do not know that much more than I do about events that are in motion. How can you be so sure that he will not find the answers?"

Jania sighed.

"Jordyne, you were always too content to look at the future, and never enough at the now. There are not only the actions of Tolon Morr that you must consider; you must also look at the actions of those around him."

The look of confusion on Jordyne's face was all the answer that Jania needed, and after a moment, she pointed in the direction of their younger sister, who still intently watched the opening of the cavern, watching as the last glimpses of the young knight passed out of her sight.

Jordyne put her hands on her hips and frowned.

"You can't be serious."

Finally Jerrica turned around, totally oblivious to the conversation that had been taking place behind her. She was greeted with the frowning face of Jordyne, and the placid expression of Jania.

"Your fate is not hidden from me, sister," Jania said after a moment. "No matter how you try to hide it, it hangs upon you like a robe. We all must make choices in our lives, and now this choice is yours to make."

Jerrica looked into Jania's eyes, and at that instant her decision was made.

"I have to go with him. He will fail without me."

Jordyne's frown deepened.

"You don't know that. You know that our abilities are limited when we put ourselves into the situation. As soon as you bias your own vision by adding yourself to it, the vision becomes worthless. You could either assist him, or doom him, you have no way to be certain."

"Sister," Jania said in a soothing voice, "you cannot dictate reason in matters of the heart. Jerrica has made her choice, and she much go with our blessing. Fate has spoken, and as always we must cede to its will, even when it calls our name. Go to him Jerrica, go to him and aid him as best you can. Know that once you leave us, your abilities will be limited, and that you must still abide by the rules laid down by the first of our clan."

Jerrica smiled, tears filling her eyes, and she quickly hugged Jania. After standing, she wiped her eyes and turned toward Jordyne. Jordyne stood, frowning, and then finally spoke.

"Take care of yourself sister, but don't let him be bad to you. If he hurts you, I will know before he does it, and I will make him suffer for it."

Finally Jordyne opened her arms, and the two sisters embraced for a moment. Jerrica then pulled away and began a fast walk toward the mouth of the cave. She allowed herself one last look over her shoulder at her two sisters before passing out of sight, and into the unknown.

* * * * * * * * * * * * *

Tolon Moor stood at the edge of the cave opening, trying to quiet his racing heart. For a moment, he had felt the touch of death, and for a moment, he did not believe that he would find another path to follow. But now, his mind was clear of the turmoil and pain that had been caused by his brief service to the Emperor of Cadaria. There were more important questions to be answered.

Reaching into the bag that hung at his side, he recovered the seal of the Kingdom of Steel, Celidar. The crossed sword and axe over a tower shield, crafted from pure amethyst with steel inlay sparkled in the dim light. This was the seal that marked his position as the most powerful warrior in all of Celidar. The one who had ascended to the rank of Knight of the Flashing Blade. But that was not what Tolon was any longer. He was not a protector of the Emperor or Empire, he was not a knight. However, he was also not the slave or the gladiator that had come before. He was now on a quest, a quest that filled his heart and mind. Looking one last time at the seal in his hand, Tolon let it drop to the ground, where it slowly began to sink into the mud. Holding onto the strap of the bag at his side, Tolon took a long deep breath and then began his long walk north. It was a quiet and soothing voice that stopped him.

"Won't you be needing this?"

Tolon turned and was surprised to see Jerrica standing behind him. Before his mind could even form a question, he watched as she bent down slowly and recovered the Seal of the Amethyst Knight from the mud. She looked at it for a moment, holding it cautiously as though it would shatter in her hand, and then looked back up to Tolon.

"Some of the places that you must travel, may be difficult to explain. However, as long as you are in the Empire of Cadaria, and hold this seal, there are none that would bar your path."

Tolon smiled. She was right of course. Had he thought things through more clearly, it would have come to him too. That seal could provide him with shelter and passage anywhere in Cadaria, and as soon as Emperor Lorien learned of Tolon's betrayal, it would be the only refuge left.

"Thank you, Jerrica. The Maldovrin Triplets have been very kind to me, and I do not know how I can ever repay that kindness. When I first came here, I was ready to kill all of you, and now, I am thankful that it never came to that. For the first time, I feel as though I have a real purpose."

Tolon extended his hand and waited for Jerrica to return the seal. She hesitated for a moment, and then extended her hand. Tolon took hold of the seal, but Jerrica did not release her hold upon it.

"Perhaps there is a way you can repay us," Jerrica said looking at the seal, and not at Tolon.

"If it's in my power to do," Tolon said without hesitation, "I will gladly do it."

Finally Jerrica looked up, her eyes sparkling.

"Take me with you."

Tolon smiled, his mind never stopping to think about the ramifications of the request.

"Gladly."

Jerrica smiled, a joy that she had never known filling her. She released the hold on the seal, and stood silent, her hands folded in front of her. Tolon put the seal away and then turned back toward the path. After a second he looked back over his shoulder at Jerrica.

"Ready to go?"

Jerrica nodded wordlessly, the smile still on her face. Tolon smiled himself and then began walking. Jerrica quickly followed, keeping about two steps behind Tolon. Tolon could feel her behind him, her perfect gown untouched by the nature around them, and her footfalls nearly silent on the mud. He slowed his gait and felt her getting closer. Finally she walked beside him. As they walked together through the destruction of Galateria, keeping their course northward, Jerrica would eventually find herself walking arm in arm with the man once known as the Amethyst Knight.

* * * * * * * * * * * * *

Jania sat alone in the darkened cavern, contemplating the changes to the future that Jerrica's decision had brought. Where so much seemed to be rigid, there was now fluidity. By taking this action, Jerrica may have unbalanced all of fate, but Jania could not find it within her to condemn the actions of her sister. Every person, even the great Seers had the right to follow their heart, wherever it led them. After a few minutes of quiet contemplation, Jania began to realize that she was not alone. Jordyne had gone to make final preparations for their move, and the power accompanying this new presence was not that of her sister.

"So, she made her choice."

The voice was familiar.

"She has, cousin. We did not expect you for some time yet. Have the ripples from Jerrica's defection reached you already?"

The Dark Seer Jehna Feris pulled the hood of her cloak back and walked slowly across the dark cavern. Though she was old by the standards of normal humans, her body and face still retained all of the beauty of youth. However, it was on the inside that she felt the age pulling upon her. Her legs did not move as freely as they did once upon a time, and so the long walking stick that always accompanied her became less for decoration and more for function.

"Though Jerrica's decision does complicate matters, it is not the reason for my visit. My time grows shorter and shorter sister, and it will only be a matter of time before the three of you are the last of our clan. With Jerrica off with Tolon Morr, she will not be able to hear my words, or be given the secrets left to us by the founder of our clan. You and Jordyne must come with me now. The legacy of our clan must be protected, and the two of you are the only ones I can trust."

Jania looked to Jehna, curiosity filling her. Those of the Clan Forer were always gifted with the Sight, but it touched them all in different ways. What was always consistent though was the fact that no other member of Clan Forer could use the Sight on any other member of the Clan. However, it had become obvious on many occasions that Jehna could. This made her both intriguing and dangerous.

"The legacy of our clan?"

Jehna's eyes went cold.

"Something that must be protected at all costs if any of us are to survive the storm that is coming."

Hold the Line

Year Two of the Just Emperor Kaitain "Dragonsbane" Lorien, Creator's Calendar Year 1869

The voice of the Moonstone Knight rose over the din of metal against scale and the roar of dragons. Covered in blood and gore from head to toe, Bernhardt Yeoman stood tall on the fallen body of a black-scaled dragon and surveyed the situation on the battlefield. Most of his army lay slaughtered, and those veteran soldiers that still stood were trying desperately to hold the line against and advancing horde of hatchlings and one very upset mother dragon. The nest they had discovered was far more populated than anyone expected, filled with four different families of dragons and guarded by five males. The first assault had been the best of the day. Catapults and well placed bolts from crossbows had felled one of the massive beasts in a surprise barrage. When Bernhardt ordered the charge, the bloodshed started in earnest. Hundreds of his troops were engulfed in the blazing fires the massive creatures belched forth, and the dragons rained death upon them with vigor and vengeance. The Legion of Iron was well trained and they did their job to the best of their ability, taking on the massive creatures when they finally were forced to the ground by a continuous volley of archer and catapult fire.

However, even as the battle seemed to be drawing even, Bernhardt could not help but feel like a colony of ants attacking an anteater. The sides were hopelessly unmatched, and though they tried their best, the Legion of Iron was suffering far too many loses. Faced up against the larger of the guardian dragons, Bernhardt set his feet and swung his heavy war hammer Gravity with all his might. Though light to the touch, the head of Gravity could be any weight the wielder chose on contact and could defy the very forces of nature where necessary and anchor itself in mid-air. When the head of Gravity struck the flank of the massive beast, the dragon howled in pain and scales shattered, pieces flying in all directions. With the soft skin below revealed, some of the other soldiers pressed in, drawing the dragon's blood and sending it roaring to the ground. Though laying on its side, it was still dangerous as it clawed and thrashed, crushing some of the more rash soldiers with its tail. A single blow from Gravity to the side of the dragon's skull would end its onslaught and Bernhardt set his sights on his next prey.

More and more of the guardian dragons fell, but not before most of the archers and all of the catapults and ballistae had been destroyed. By the time the female dragons and hatchlings began to pour from the entrance of the nest, a quarter of the Legion of Iron had fallen and all but one of the guardian dragons had met its end. That was as even as the sides would be for the rest of the battle. While most time was spent dispatching the mother dragons, the hatchlings ripped apart soldiers by the dozens, tearing through armor and weapons like wet paper. Thousands were dead now, reduced to quivering piles of broken flesh and blood-soaked earth. Bernhardt waded into the hatchlings, swinging his war hammer wildly in all directions, collecting hatchlings at the end of the hammerhead and sending them flying into others of their kind, or crashing to the ground in a heap. On the battlefield, with Gravity in his hand, Bernhardt was nearly unstoppable. Or at least he thought he was until the large claw from the remaining mother pierced his defenses and ripped through his left leg.

The wound was deep, almost deep enough to be fatal. If it wasn't treated in a few minutes, Bernhardt knew he would bleed to death. However, the mother dragon was too certain of her kill and stuck her head in just far enough that Bernhardt could bring Gravity to bear, and a single strike to the side of the creature's head sent it tumbling to the ground like a felled tree. Lightheaded from the loss of blood, Bernhardt too fell to the ground, the bodies of his men and fallen hatchlings littering the ground around him, blood oozing into all the cracks in the ground. The darkness began to creep in at the edges of his vision as the seconds passed. Sounds of death and dying began to fade from his ears, until Bernhardt Yeoman saw and heard nothing any longer.

* * * * * * * * * * * * *

Year Sixty-Four of the Just Emperor Ender "JustHand" Lorien XI, Creator's Calendar Year 1846

"I've been what?"

Bernhardt Yeoman stood at his forge working on repairing the damage to his sword after the latest round of training with the new recruits. Some of them had potential, but not many of them would end up in the service of the Kingdom of Iron, Pellatori. It was a great honor to train with the general of the army, but few of the men seemed to take full advantage of the honor or of the opportunity to impress. Too many of them felt that they would earn a position simply because of their status in the kingdom. Family name got them everything, and what they couldn't get with their name they got with a healthy dose of coin. It turned Bernhardt's stomach to think that duty could be bought with gold, or that honor could be found with jewels. He had earned his position the old fashioned way. Bernhardt was the son of a blacksmith, raised in virtual poverty in one of the richest regions of Cadaria. However, hard work and perseverance had gained him a spot in the Army of Pellatori, and eventually an appointment to the Legion of Iron, the most prestigious detachment in the kingdom. Working his way through the ranks had been hard and had brought many scars and broken bones, but eventually, Bernhardt was elevated to the position of General of the Legion of Iron.

"You've been summoned to the Imperial Court of Aldere, General," the lieutenant said proudly. "Rumor has it that you will be promoted to the position of Moonstone Knight."

Bernhardt turned back to his forge and finished his repairs and then let the hammer rest on the edge of the anvil for a moment before sitting on the small wooden stool and taking in the words of his subordinate. There had to be some kind of a mistake. Bernhardt was a competent soldier and a better than average tactician, and though he had been the youngest ever to be named as the General of the Legion of Iron he did not feel qualified enough to be on the same level as the other members of the Knights of the Flashing Blade. In time, perhaps, and with more experience he would be ready for such an honor, but that time was not today.

"Prepare my horse. I will leave as soon as preparations are made. The rest of the command structure will remain as it is for now, until my return."

The lieutenant snapped a quick salute and then left to carry out his orders. It was going to be a long day, and there would be much to do. Bernhardt made his preparations and after a quick meal left for the Imperial City of Aldere and his chance meeting with a new fate.

****

The sounds of dying and pain suddenly filled Bernhardt's ears again. Blinking his eyes rapidly, he was able to force away some of the blood and dirt with tears, but even as his eyes opened, his eyesight was blurred. Try as he might to focus, all he could see was a great light blur surrounded by a wide blue blur. His mouth dry, and filled with the taste of death, Bernhardt tried to force his way to a sitting position. Pain racked his body, and as he repositioned his left leg, a long sharp pain greeted his attempts. It was then that he remembered where he was. He was on the battlefield. Dead men were all around him, men that he had served with for many years before that fateful day all those years ago. The day he first met Ender Lorien, the day he became the Moonstone Knight. Why had his thoughts been drawn to that moment in time? There had been so many important days that had led up to that one. His days at the training grounds where he earned his stripes. His day of ascension to the Legion of Steel. His recognition as General. Had becoming a member of the Flashing Blade dulled the importance of all those other acts?

Pain began to overtake Bernhardt again, though he began to hear stirring around him. Groping out through the mud and bodies, Bernhardt found the handle of his war hammer again. It felt good to have Gravity clutched back in his hands again. The muscles in his left leg contracted hard, a response to the loss of blood, and caused more pain. Bernhardt could feel his hold on consciousness beginning to slip. It would only be a matter of moments before the veil of darkness would descend on his vision again. Blood must have still been flowing freely from the wound in his leg. How many more minutes did he have left before there would be no chance of saving the leg? How many more after that before there would be no chance of saving his life? The great Moonstone Knight thought he heard voices approaching as he fell into unconsciousness again.

* * * * * * * * * * * * *

Year Sixty-Four of the Just Emperor Ender "JustHand" Lorien XI, Creator's Calendar Year 1846

The Imperial Palace at Aldere was one of the most impressive structures that Bernhardt had ever seen. Though it had taken some time for his travel papers to be validated by the local magistrates, the momentary aggravation had given Bernhardt time to reflect on the beauty of the high towers and palisades of the palace. It was a truly impressive structure designed to resist any type of attack, whether it be from the air or the ground, and armed guards and archers constantly patrolled the grounds both within and without the walls, their duty to be ever vigilant and to identify any possible threat to the Emperor or the Imperial family.

Upon entering the Imperial Palace, Bernhardt was led to a receiving hall full of courtiers and others who were waiting to be called into the presence of the Emperor to put forward a petition or some other form of request. Bernhardt began to feel uncomfortable in the sea of people, and he most certainly felt out of place. Even when he was back in the comforts of his home kingdom, Bernhardt had never been at ease in the arena of the court. On the battlefield, the rules were simple. The person who charged at you was your enemy. However, there was no such cut and dry rule in the Imperial Court or in any courtly setting for that matter. Every courtier had their own agenda and could be either friend or foe in the same breath. This was not a place for a warrior to be, it was a place for flatters and those who plotted in darkness.

Several of the courtiers spoke to Bernhardt and while Bernhardt tried his best to make polite conversation, he did not feel like he was in the same world as they were. His mind was not filled with the news of the different kingdoms, and he rarely had anything interesting to add to the conversation. While he could have spoken of tactics and the art of war for hours on end, he did not have a gift for small talk. Finally, a friendly face came to save him from his misery.

Gregor Quicksilver was well respected by every military man in each of the thirteen kingdoms of Cadaria. He had led several successful campaigns against bandits and creatures from the Dark Continent of Mythryn. Never had an army that Gregor led been defeated, nor had they ever suffered a significant number of casualties. The man was possessed on the battlefield. It was as though the Creator touched the man with the divine strength and determination to defeat his enemies, while the Great Dark One possessed him with the ruthlessness and singleness of purpose to crush them into the ground without pity or remorse. It was a dangerous combination; one that teetered on the brink of a type of enlightened madness. At the same time, Gregor when not embroiled in battle was one of the most generous and caring men on the face of Espre. Taking Bernhardt by the arm, Gregor led him toward a smaller group standing at the far side of the receiving chamber.

"You looked a bit out of place, my friend," Gregor said after a moment, "perhaps you would like to meet those that you will be serving with in the near future."

Bernhardt's head spun.

"So, it is true, I am to be elevated."

Gregor smiled.

"Yes, my friend. Your experience and mastery over military tactics will be a welcome addition to the Knights of the Flashing Blade. Besides, it has been a long time since we had a pure military man in the group. Perhaps you can help the rest of us brush up on our skill, though I hope they are never needed."

Bernhardt smiled, and for the first time since he had arrived in Aldere, he felt as though he was where he was supposed to be. There was still discomfort, but there was a gradual acceptance of the situation.

The group that Bernhardt was being led to was made up of five other members of the Flashing Blade. Three of them Bernhardt knew on sight, their fame had reached even the most remote sections of Cadaria. Hannah Ironheart needed no introduction to any person who worshiped the Creator. Her love and zeal in the service of the Creator was legendary, and it was said that she gave all of herself to heal and comfort those who could not fend for themselves. She was a tireless protector of the innocent and disadvantaged. As Bernhardt regarded the woman for a moment, it was hard not to find her attractive, and yet her pious nature made it difficult to think of her as anything more than a chaste and pure woman. To even try to envision this woman indulging in the pleasure of the flesh was impossible, and though she was beautiful to be sure, it was more the beauty seen by a son looking at his mother.

The woman who stood beside Hannah also had a type of ethereal beauty, but hers was more intimidating than it was chaste. Leonora Wastri, the Warrior of the Soul, and Jade Knight of the Flashing Blade had earned her fame through her legendary studies and furthering of wisdom and enlightenment. While she did not look much like a monk with her long flowing hair and delicate features, her eyes told a different story altogether. There was an age in her eyes that belied her youthful appearance. The eyes were those of a woman who had seen much in life, and eyes that saw more than just the outward trappings of life. Leonora looked as though she could see the world within, the one that created the shadows of reality that the rest of the human race took as substantial.

Like Leonora, Xaran Firesoul had a wisdom about him, but as Bernhardt looked at the blind man, it was hard for him to imagine anyone mistaking the Tiger's Eye Knight for a cripple. He stood proudly, his shoulders pulled back as he took in all of the sounds around him. Bernhardt watched the way the man moved for a few quick seconds, and had he not known the man was blind, he never would have believed it. Xaran moved as though he was sighted, deftly and gracefully, never searching for a footfall, and always looking directly at the person speaking to him.

Gregor was greeted with smiles by the five as he approached, but when Bernhardt got closer, one of the members of the Knights of the Flashing

Blade brought Bernhardt's defenses up quickly. For as long as Bernhardt could remember, he did not like the idea of magic. The very thought of the arcane forces of nature being bent to anyone's will brought a sick feeling to Bernhardt's stomach. In fact, as he grew older, every time he had been exposed to magic or had been close to one who wielded arcane power, the sick turn in his stomach returned. It was as though he could feel the subtle flows of the arcane all around him, and when they were collected in any amount over that found in nature, Bernhardt had an adverse reaction. As he approached the group, and got closer to the blond man in the white cloak, the sickened feeling returned.

"Friends," Gregor said after a moment, "let me introduce you to the General of the Legion of Iron, and soon to be the newest Moonstone Knight of the Flashing Blade, Bernhardt Yeoman."

There was a polite applause from the group, and Gregor quickly made the introductions.

"Bernhardt, you most likely already know Lady Hannah Ironheart, the Celestine Knight. Beside her, the Jade Knight, Leonora Wastri and the Tiger's Eye Knight, Xaran Firesoul. The two others here, you may not know, as they are more reclusive than the rest of us."

"For good reason at times," the man in the brown cloak said slowly, "some of us do not desire the glory that the rest of you seem to require in vast amounts."

Leonora laughed, a sound that could have been the laughter of angels.

"Pay no attention to Vallic, Bernhardt. He is just upset that Ender pulled him away from his frolicking in the woods to attend your ascension ceremony."

"I do not frolic," Vallic replied frowning. "And don't you know that it is impolite to refer to the Just Emperor by his first name in mixed company?"

The man in the white cloak smiled.

"Ladies, Gentlemen, it is rude to have such a conversation in front of our new friend. Pleasure to meet you, Bernhardt, I am Orren Eldrath, the Sapphire Knight of Rashaleb."

Orren extended his hand as a token of friendship, but Bernhardt did not. Sensing the tension, Bernhardt coughed and smiled.

"I'm sorry, Sir Orren, but my hands are oily and dirty from the ride in, I'm afraid there was not time to properly clean up."

Orren smiled and nodded.

"Well, you should get used to being in a hurry like that my friend; there will be little chance for finery and ceremony for you after today."

Bernhardt returned the smile in kind, the sickened feeling in his stomach never relenting. There was something about this Orren Eldrath that Bernhardt did not trust, and it was more than his obvious mastery over the arcane forces.

"The grumpy member of our little troop is Vallic Ultiv, the Serpentine Knight," Xaran said after the awkward silence.

Vallic smiled.

"I neither frolic, nor am I grumpy."

There was a bit of a laugh among the group, but it was quickly silenced as was the rest of the receiving hall by the voice of the page rising above the din.

"The Emperor will now receive Bernhardt Yeoman of the Kingdom of Iron, Pellatori, and the next Moonstone Knight of the Knights of the Flashing Blade."

There was applause through the receiving hall, and the sickened feeling in the pit of Bernhardt's stomach intensified.

* * * * * * * * * * * * *

CHAPTER 49

Pain racked Bernhardt Yeoman's body again, this time because a set of hands were manipulating his badly injured leg. When his eyes opened, he saw the face of one of his soldiers looking down at him. The haze in his mind would not allow him to recall the soldier's name.

"Just try to relax sir," the soldier said, his voice sounding so far away. "The healers are on the way, and they will do what they can for your leg."

Bernhardt's mouth felt as though it had been full of sand, and even as he croaked out a question, his own voice sounded alien to him.

"Report."

"We've held the line as you ordered, sir," the soldier replied proudly. "The nest has been cleared, and all of the dragons and hatchlings have been accounted for. But there was a heavy cost. Eighty percent of our standing forces have been destroyed, all or our catapults and ballistae are out of commission or worse, and all of the reserves have been exhausted and routed. There are only about five to six hundred troops that are battle ready, the rest are either wounded or dead."

Five or six hundred. The number did not set well in Bernhardt's mind. He had thirty-five thousand troops when he had marched from Pellatori to the north. The first nest had been cleansed with only ten percent casualties, but now, the army that had been under his command was no more. They had succeeded in their mission, but the cost had been too high to be believed. Even in success, they had failed miserably. Bernhardt kept chewing on the numbers in his mind as the healers arrived. The horrified look on the older man's face was the only prognosis that Bernhardt needed.

"We must move him," the healer said finally.

Bernhardt steeled himself for the pain that would rocket through his body. Even as he felt himself being lifted by the strong hands of his soldiers, the pain robbed him of consciousness again.

* * * * * * * * * * * * *

Year Sixty-Four of the Just Emperor Ender "JustHand" Lorien XI, Creator's Calendar Year 1846

Bernhardt knelt at the foot of the Just Emperor Ender Lorien and felt humbled. Never before had he felt so in the shadow of another man in his life, and looking up at the great and powerful Emperor of Cadaria made Bernhardt feel like a boy looking up at his father in awe. Even as the massive war hammer known as Gravity was placed in his hands and the title of Moonstone Knight pronounced to the assemblage, disbelief filled Bernhardt's mind. When finally he stood and looked into the eyes of the Emperor for the first time in his life, Bernhardt felt as though he was truly where he was meant to be.

"I give you now the most important order I shall ever give you," Ender said with a regal and powerful voice. "You are to be the general of all armies that serve under the banner of Cadaria, and all troops of all kingdoms are yours to command. Just as Gregor Quicksilver is my Fortitude, Hannah Ironheart is my Faith, Leonora Wastri is my Wisdom, Xaran Firesoul is my Vision, Vallic Ultiv is my Objectivity, and Orren Eldrath is my Discretion, so shall you be my Strength. From this day forward you shall be my sword arm against all enemies both within and without my realm. Never shall an enemy subvert or impede my will so long as you are in my service. As I am the light of the Cadarian Empire, henceforth and forevermore you Bernhardt Yeoman will hold the line against the darkness. You shall hold the line with every breath in your body and until death comes to claim you. Even then you shall take up arms against death itself and hold until all of my enemies have been returned to the fires of hell from whence they came. Do you understand and accept this charge, Bernhardt Yeoman of Pellatori?"

Bernhardt swallowed hard and took a deep breath, his heart swelling with pride.

"I shall hold the line, my Emperor. No matter the cost."

Dark Secrets

Year Two of the Just Emperor Kaitain "Dragonsbane" Lorien,
Creator's Calendar Year 1869

Rain began to fall harder on the plains outside the Kingdom of Thorigald. Heavy rains were a common occurrence in the plains of the Kingdom of Water, and caused the banks of the rivers to swell to nearly twice there size during the hurricane seasons when the moon passed the closest to Espre. A small detachment of soldiers made their way through the rice fields and bamboo forests looking for the bandit who had been responsible for a series of deaths in some of the small villages near the borders of Saldarine. It was surmised that this bandit was truly an agent from the Kingdom of Fire sent to increase tensions along the border and to cause riots. While this kind of dirty-fighting and destabilization were not normal tactics for the Kingdom of Fire, the recent Imperial Mandate that put an end to open warfare encouraged new types of combat. Carefully trudging through the mud and water, the soldiers tried hard to get a glimpse of the bandit's trail, but it was all but hopeless at this point.

Cold, nearly dead eyes watched the soldiers from a distance, hidden in the shadows deeper in the forest. His sharp eyesight analyzed each of the soldiers in turn, making note of each of the weak points in their armor and where their defenses would be most vulnerable to attack. Because of the rain and mud their reaction time would be slowed, and it would be possible to kill all six of them before he would even be spotted. This would be a glorious kill to be certain. Reaching into the pouch that hung at his side, the man withdrew three small darts that dripped a slimy green liquid from the tip. The poison on the dart would make quick work of three of the soldiers and would cause enough of distraction for the others to be made easy prey of. Three quick and deft motions delivered the darts to their targets, the soft exposed necks of three of the soldiers causing them to fall into the water and mud. The distraction would be an effective one to say the least, the sound of them splashing in the water masked the assassin's approach. Barely another sound was heard as the sword leapt free from its scabbard, and with three quick precise strikes, the remaining soldiers fell. Death was quick and painless.

After a moment to ensure that all of the soldiers had met their deaths, the assassin returned to the tree line and retrieved two other bodies. Though they were heavy to carry, the wet conditions made it easy to drag them from the tree line to the area where the Thorigald soldiers lay. The two additional bodies, clad in the garb of soldiers from Saldarine would spark yet another incident and stoke the fires of war between the two old enemies. Careful to cover not only the drag marks but also his own footprints, the assassin staged the scene, recovering his own darts and making the proper cuts on the fallen bodies to make it look as though a fight had occurred. It was a masterful stroke. Within a few moments Saldarine had been successfully framed, and the assassin would escape without being spotted. His employer would be most pleased.

* * * * * * * * * * * * *

Midnight in the Kingdom of Blood, Zevarit was normally as safe as any other time in the city, however things had changed since the disappearance of the Ruby Knight, Gregor Quicksilver. The local militia had many issues on their hands dealing with beggars and thieves, not to mention the more powerful criminal element that had decided that it was more than a perfect time to move in on the city. As long as the famous knight was missing, lawlessness could flourish for a time. With all the petty criminals roaming the streets, few took notice of the woman who carefully made her way through the streets and alleyways. Her muscular form encased in tight blood red leather and her auburn hair pulled back tight against her head, she could move swiftly and silently. Only a few of the passersby even looked in her direction, and by the time they realized something was there, she was gone. It took only a few minutes to travel by alley and rooftop through the city to the area where most of the royal households were. Though this area of the city was far nicer and well-guarded, it was still little effort for the woman to maneuver her way to the area where her target slept. Slipping behind the house and into the shadows, she recovered a simple set of lock picks from her belt and deftly opened the lock that held shut the doors that led to the cellar. After allowing her eyes to adjust to the low light in the cellar, she quickly found the location of the four barrels of wine that sat in the far corner.

There was to be a great feast the next afternoon to recognize the ascension of the next lord of Zevarit. This wine that had sat in this cellar for over fifty year was supposed to be a gift to the new lord, and with certainty would be drank with great pleasure at the banquet. Without a word, the woman retrieved a long metal needle from her belt and carefully pierced the seal at the top of one of the barrels. The long slow process would ensure that the damage to the seal would not be detected and a small bit of sealant added after withdrawing the needle would ensure that there would be no leakage. Once the needle had been inserted, the woman retrieved a small vial from her belt, a vial that contained the sap from an exotic flower. This sap, a very potent poison would mix with the wine perfectly, adding no flavor, but killing anyone who imbibed of the wine within three hours. The deaths would be quite painful, and would mimic that of the Wasting Disease close enough, as the victim would feel hungry and thirsty no matter what they ate or drank for the last few moments of their life. It would be a fair enough cover to the mass assassination. It took only a few moments to empty the contents of the vial into the barrel, and only a few minutes more to repeat the procedure with the other three barrels. Deftly the woman left the cellar and relocked the doors behind her. The exit from the royal quarter was as simple as the entrance, and as she quickly made her way out of town she knew that she had certainly earned her wage for this mission.

* * * * * * * * * * * * *

The capital city of the Kingdom of Steel, Celidar had long been thought of as impregnable. Where most castles and towers were made of brick, stone, and wood, the one in Celidar was made of pure steel. However, the rest of the village that had cropped up around Celidar was made of thatch and wood, much like the villages in the rest of the world. This was the vulnerability that the red-haired woman was ready to exploit. Normally her abilities were used for simple assassinations that would make it look like an accident, usually fires. That had been her ability since she had been a little girl. Fire was her friend, her plaything, and as her body matured, her control over fire enhanced. Instead of simply being able to control fire where it already existed, she gained the ability to spark a fire anywhere that it could be sustained. Out of nothingness, fire would appear and burn so long as it had fuel.

Walking through the village in the middle of the night, she began to allow the powers of fire to course through her veins, she could feel the heat beneath her skin, and suddenly the two houses on either side of her began to burn. One by one, each of the houses on the block began to burn. The fire was spreading out of control, and the screams of pain and terror soon began to rise from the burning houses. It took only a few seconds before the streets were filled with the terror-stricken residents, and the assassin easily blended in with the mob, where she escaped the scrutiny of the Army of Steel.

* * * * * * * * * * * * *

Geoffry Aramour walked through the streets of the Port City of Escan in the Kingdom of Water, Thorigald taking in all the local sites. It had been a long time since he had been given the liberty to go where he wished since entering the service of Emperor Kaitain Lorien, but that was not a bad thing by any stretch of the imagination. Geoffry was the type of man that liked to stay busy, and as soon as there was no challenge or nothing to do, boredom set in quickly. Geoffry often feared that his skills would diminish if he sat idle for any period of time, so in the times of peace were there was little work to be done in his field, Geoffry found himself inventing accidents for local commoners. Of course it did not have the same challenge as assignments for the Emperor, but there was a type of beauty in concocting the perfect murder. Then of course, planning was not enough, as a plan that is not put into action was worthless. Geoffry had been careful not to cause the unexplained deaths of too many peasants, but there were times when a few had to be sacrificed for the sake of his art.

The bar near the docks had been the planned meeting place for Geoffry and his new flock of assassins. The Emperor Kaitain had been clear about the mandate for the creation of this new force of assassins. They could not be members of the Shadow Guild, nor could they be on anyone's recruiting list. They had to be unknowns, stable enough to not be a threat, but eccentric enough that no one from the Shadow Guild would ever think of using them. Behind the bar was a suitable meeting area, and as expected, the three people stood waiting for Geoffry to arrive.

The youngest of the women sat on a wooden beam by the ocean, her feet bare dangling into the waters below. Wordlessly she drew little circles in the water with her toe as she flipped through the pages of a book. Her dress was common, but even through the clothing of a peasant, her muscular frame could be seen. She had kept herself in superb physical condition, and could likely best some of the elite male warriors in most of the kingdoms of Cadaria. Her auburn hair hung tied back tight and braided. While she would not be considered beautiful or pretty by most, she had an exotic look about her that some might find attractive. Geoffry had found her in small farming community in Menoris, where she happily stayed out of everyone's way tending to her many gardens. She was quite well known in the area as a bit of an herbalist, and if she was so inclined, and well paid, she could create an antidote to nearly any poison, or cure nearly any sickness. However, what most of the villagers didn't know was that her true calling was the creation of exotic organic poisons, those derived from the roots and petals of rare flowers which she cultivated like her own children. It took only the promise of the resources of the Imperial Gardens to convince Liandra Nightshade to leave her meager village and join the new group of Imperial Assassins, and it was easy to see how she earned her nickname of Death Blossom.

The other woman of the group had been discovered purely by accident in the Kingdom of Hedorah. Her fire red hair had caught Geoffry's attention, and the attention of many others at the brothel at the edge of the capital city, where she had been sold into service. She stood not far from

Liandra, her back to a tree, looking out onto the water. As Geoffry had come to learn about the woman in white, she had been born as the daughter of a whore and an unlucky soldier from Bellnoc. When she was old enough, she was cast out of the orphanage that had raised her, and it was only a matter of time before she found herself selling her body on the streets to survive. As she aged, her talents began to emerge over the powers of fire, and that is what brought her to the attention of a somewhat moronic young mage who thought that he could trade lessons in the arcane for the use of the young woman's body. She was more than willing to tolerate him long enough to find out what she needed before he was found in the gutter one morning, burned to a crisp. From there, Rhain Feirbran lived two lives. Most of the time, Rhain was a feared assassin and mercenary for hire, however when business was slow, she still supported herself through her old habits in a brothel. However, over the years she had begun to detest the touch of men. For that reason, she restricted her client base to women who wanted to torture and then kill the men in her life. She had become an angel of vengeance for wronged women, and more than lived up to the name Firebrand.

Cole Breon, the man called the Living Shadow, stood with the hood of his cloak pulled up over his head, looking down at the ground. Anyone who passed by would think that he was sleeping, but they would most certainly be mistaken. Cole had one of the most developed senses of hearing that Geoffry had ever come across, and with his eyes closed, he could perceive everything that occurred around him almost as clearly as one could with their eyes opened. Nothing escaped his notice, and along with his perfect memory, there was no detail that he could not see, hear, or remember. The most uncanny ability in his repertoire was the ability to mimic any sound that he had ever heard with perfect accuracy. When dealing with Cole, one often wondered if they were hearing his voice, or one of the hundreds that he had perfected over the years of his life. It was this uncertainty and mystery that made Cole all wrong for the Shadow Guild. He could not be reliably controlled, and his memory could be a threat to those within the organization. More than all of that, Cole loved his work. Moreover, Cole loved to kill. It didn't matter if there was a reason or not, he loved to feel the blade of his sword pass through the flesh of his prey. Cole cared not for payment or even for the comforts that Geoffry had offered him in the Imperial Court. All he wanted was to kill, a weapon to be used at leisure. Well, there was one concession. Geoffry would have to attend to that in time.

When the three saw Geoffry approach, they stayed as they were. Assassins meeting in the open was uncommon, but not unheard of. In fact, hiding in plain sight often proved to be the most prudent and effective course of action.

"Report."

Rhain smiled.

"There was some interesting news out of Celidar this morning. It seems that there was a fire that raged out of control in the merchant's quarter. It killed dozens of people and left most of the market district in ruins. It's going to be some time before they are going to be able to replace all of the supplies that were destroyed. And with the rations being cut so short because of the prolonged war with the dragons, it could be a very harsh winter. But I guess the Imperial Stores are going to supplement them through the coldest months."

Liandra laughed.

"Well, isn't that too bad? Kinda makes you wonder what happened to cause the fire. But then again, most people are talking about the outbreak of the Wasting Disease that happened in Zevarit. Though it was not as impressive as Rashaleb being leveled, it did leave a large percentage of the royal families dead. And with the Ruby Knight missing there is going to be great turmoil in Zevarit for a long time to come. It was a good thing that the Emperor installed that regional governor and took full control over the kingdom himself, otherwise, who knows what could happen."

Geoffry smiled. The new agenda of the Emperor was brilliant in its simplicity. In order to reduce the bureaucracy that had pervaded the kingdoms for centuries, and to reduce the reliance on the members of the Knights of the Flashing Blade, Kaitain had launched a series of surgical strikes that would cause all of the kingdoms to look to Aldere for leadership and support. The outbreak of the Wasting Disease that had leveled Rashaleb had given Kaitain the idea, and Geoffry's new assassins seemed to be the logical people to carry out the new plans. It served as a good test of their mettle, while at the same time furthering the overall agenda. Rashaleb's whole royal family had been wiped out along with their capital, and so Kaitain had been forced to take direct control over the kingdom. Now the same course of action could be taken in Zevarit, especially without Gregor Quicksilver to interfere. Celidar had been embroiled in the fight with the dragons, and with Tolon Morr the new Amethyst Knight on a mission for the Throne before he had been able to truly entrench himself in the minds of the commoners, they would turn to Aldere for support. Now that most of their food stores had been destroyed, the peasants would see Kaitain as a savior and would begin to love him more for his mercy and benevolence. Galateria was already fully dependent upon Imperial troops to protect them from attacks from the local dragons, and it was only a matter of time before more of the kingdoms had no choice but to see Kaitain as a savior as well as their Emperor. He would be universally loved, and then he could make a move to eliminate the Flashing Blade once and for all. The plans were already in motion to dispose of Gregor, Hannah, and Seraph. Soon the rest of them would fall by the wayside as well.

After a moment Geoffry looked over at Cole. The man's cold features never changed, and never seemed to show any type of emotion.

"And what have you heard from Thorigald?"

Cole looked up for a moment, met Geoffry's eyes, and then looked back down to the ground.

"It seems there have been quite a few ambushes along the border with Saldarine. A great many soldiers from both sides have been found dead, and there is quite a bit of finger pointing. War seems inevitable now."

Geoffry smiled. This was the master stroke. Kaitain had forbidden the two great kingdoms from making war on one another, but with Cole's master manipulations it wouldn't be long before there would be nothing that could stop the two bitter enemies from being at each other's throats. Once open war broke out, Kaitain could mobilize the Imperial Legions to restore the peace, execute the royals from both kingdoms and then rid himself of the married members of the Flashing Blade. Finally the two old enemies would know peace, and Kaitain would be the cause. They were brilliant tactics to say the least. Of course, Geoffry knew that these plans did not come from Kaitain himself. He was too infatuated with this new woman that he planned to marry, the woman that would become the new empress, Dominique Arais. Rumors persisted that she was already with child, and it would only be a matter of time before there was a new heir to the throne. Irene Drage practically ran the Empire now, and was accepted as the Voice of the Emperor without question. Geoffry wondered how the Imperial Princess Marlae Lorien would react to this when she returned to Aldere. If it became too much of a concern, Geoffry was sure that his talents would be called upon to remove one of the thorns from the Emperor's side, and which one did not concern him in the least.

"It seems there is quite a lot happening in the Empire these days," Geoffry said finally. "Perhaps we should see if there is more unrest that should be reported to the Emperor."

Geoffry pulled three scrolls from the inside of his long coat and looked them over for a moment before handing one to each of the gathered assassins.

"Inside you will find your…"

Cole raised his hand to silence Geoffry. He had heard an echo from the other side of the wall.

"Someone comes."

Geoffry turned and walked toward the side of the tavern to investigate, and was met with an interesting sight. The Topaz Knight Jaccob Aldora stumbled out of the tavern, obviously drunk, and ran headlong into Geoffry.

"Excuse me…terribly sorry."

Jaccob's speech was horribly slurred, and he looked and smelled as if he had not bathed or changed clothes in several days, perhaps several weeks.

"Sir Jaccob, what are you still doing here?"

Jaccob took a step back and looked over the man he had bumped into. There was something familiar about the voice. Inwardly cursing, Jaccob took hold of the hilt of Temperance and felt his head began to clear. His vision sharpened and the cloud over his mind lifted, and he was face to face with Geoffry Aramour.

"Ah, Geoffry," Jaccob said after a moment, patting the other man on the shoulder. "It seems your information was wrong. The boat that you mentioned was here, but the person I was supposed to meet was not on it. No one seems to know anything about it, so I've been waiting here to see if they were on another ship."

Geoffry frowned.

"You should have reported back to the Emperor when they didn't arrive, Sir Aldora. Didn't you think that would have been the proper course of action?"

Jaccob smiled brightly and laughed.

"That wasn't part of my orders, you know that, Geoffry. Besides, who are you to tell me what I should and should not be doing? I am a member of the Knights of the Flashing Blade, and you are just the Imperial Poet. Now, either sing me a song, or leave me in peace. I have to go check the docks yet again."

Jaccob pushed past Geoffry, as the older man felt his blood begin to boil. Never had he been insulted that way by anyone. Jaccob walked to the back of the tavern where the three assassins had been. Geoffry followed quickly, ready to dismiss his charges, but was surprised when he saw only one of them still there. Cole and Liandra had already disappeared, obviously gone to follow their assignments. Rhain remained, still leaning against the tree, looking beautiful and distracted by the sea, like a woman looking for her long lost love to return. Jaccob fixed his eyes on her immediately, and smiled.

"I've seen you before, haven't I?" Jaccob said walking up to her quickly. "Yes, I never forget a face. You work in Hedorah in the trade quarter. I've seen you, but always seem to miss you and get occupied with one of your co-workers."

Rhain let the practice blush color her cheeks, and where her voice had been strong moments before, Geoffry was shocked to hear the pensive and fluttery voice of a common woman.

"I'm so flattered you remember me, Sir Jaccob." Rhain looked down to the ground as her blush deepened. "I never thought you even looked in my direction. You always seemed to be more interested in the other girls."

Jaccob smiled wider.

"Perhaps we should make up for lost time then…"

Jaccob leaned in and began to kiss Rhain's neck passionately. Though she moaned and giggled at his advances, her eyes were cold and her face a mask of hatred and disgust. She locked eyes with Geoffry the next moment, and with a nod, the plan was hatched. Jaccob Aldora would not survive the night. Rhain giggled again, and the warm embarrassed face of a peasant girl returned and she pulled away from the knight.

"Sir Jaccob! Perhaps we should go to your room?"

Jaccob laughed and shook his head.

"You can't tell me that you are shy. I've seen you do far more in the common room of a brothel."

Rhain smiled a wicked smile.

"Yes, Sir Jaccob, but what I want to do to you is best kept in private."

Taking the woman by the arm, Jaccob pulled her up the street toward the inn where he was staying. Geoffry watched all of this with a detached awe. Another member of the Knights of the Flashing Blade was about to be removed from the game, while this one was unexpected, he was sure that the Emperor would be pleased all the same.

****

Jaccob's head hurt. All he remembered was drinking all that wine and ale, and laying down in bed with that beautiful woman, and then everything went black. Still lying in bed naked he groped around for Temperance, but he could not find it.

It's so hot in here…Maybe I shouldn't have had all of that to drink…is that smoke?

It was then that his mind began to comprehend what was happening. There was indeed smoke filling the room, and the walls were on fire. The pounding in his head continued as he tried to pull himself out of the small bed. The attempt to stand failed, and Jaccob tumbled to the floor, his legs weak, and his sense of balance destroyed by the drink. Naked and covered in sweat, Jaccob crawled across the impossibly hot floor trying desperately to find the sacred weapon that would clear his head and allow him to escape yet another embarrassing and treacherous situation. The next moment, the door burst open. Jaccob looked up, but all he could see was fire and smoke billowing into the room. Then a figure emerged from the flames, leaping into the room. In a single deft motion, the young man ripped the blanket from the bed, wrapped Jaccob in it and began to lead him toward the window. Jaccob looked up and finally saw the glint of steel out of the corner of his eye. He tried to form the words, but the cough from the smoke would not allow him to speak. All he could do was grunt and point in the direction where Temperance lay. The young man whirled away into the smoke, retrieved the weapon and took Jaccob under his arm again. The glass of the window had already begun to melt from the heat and the fire in the room. Not hesitating a moment, the young man extended a hand and the whole wall exploded outward in a flash. Reflexively, Jaccob covered his face, and then felt the exhilaration of dropping out of the third story window and plummeting toward the ground. However the impact was as soft as a feather falling to earth, and when the watering of his eyes finally cleared, Jaccob looked up at the young face of his savior.

"Here you go, Sir Jaccob," the young man said handing over Temperance.

Jaccob took hold of the weapon, and all ill effects were erased from his mind. The blurry contours of the young man's features were suddenly sharpened, and Jaccob noticed that though the young man had just come from the heart of the inferno, not a single hair on his head was singed, and not a single bead of sweat rolled from his face. There was something special about this young blue-eyed man, and Jaccob resolved to find out exactly what it was.

"Do I get the pleasure of my savior's name?" Jaccob asked standing straight and wrapping the blanket firmly around himself.

The young man smiled.

"My name's Ayden, Ayden Seth. Pleasure to meet you."

Chapter L

Storms on the Wind

Year Two of the Just Emperor Kaitain "Dragonsbane" Lorien, Creator's Calendar Year 1869

Xaran Firesoul could feel the power around him as he followed the lead of his friend Khalas into the domain of the dragons of Cadaria. Their travels through the air had been long, and finally they came to an end near the southernmost tip of Cadaria, an island long referred to as the Island of the Lost. It had been the domain of one of the greatest of the dragons of Cadaria, a creature known only as Skyfire, but it had been slain centuries ago. Since then, the spawn of Skyfire and other dragons had kept this place sacred, shielded from the dominion of man. Xaran felt nature all around him, full of life and full of question. It was as though the creatures around him questioned the incursion of the hated human upon their land. He could feel their agitation growing with every step. After a few moments of walking, Xaran heard the wings of his large friend fold back against his body.

"Do not worry, my friend," Khalas said in a low voice, "the creatures of these woods will not act against you so long as you are with me."

"Comforting, my friend," Xaran responded in an equally low voice.

The undergrowth in the area was thick, but walking behind Khalas allowed Xaran to find the path through the most difficult areas. Though unable to see his surroundings, Xaran knew they were breathtaking. All of the smells and sounds filled him with a picture of such life and motion. Holding Faith tightly, Xaran followed Khalas though the last bits of the forest until they emerged into a clearing.

"Take my sight if you wish, my friend," Khalas said after a moment of silence. "You may not be able to see something so beautiful ever again."

Faith had given Xaran many abilities, and much clarity in the time since he became the Tiger's Eye Knight. One of the most useful had been the ability to see through the eyes of others. While Xaran could use this ability at will, his teachings would not allow him to invade another without permission. On many occasions, Khalas had allowed Xaran to look through his eyes, to see the vastness of Cadaria from above, to feel the exhilaration of flying. When Xaran opened his mind and reached out to the vision of his large companion, he was not prepared for what he saw. All around were large trees, the forest ending in a massive clearing. The grass changed from a thick green underbrush to a gentle silver moss that covered the ground of the entire clearing. In the center of the clearing was a massive white structure in the shape of a tree, but it appeared to be made of a stone that Xaran had never seen before. A comforting glow emanated from the structure. While all his life, Xaran had been able to perceive and commune with the spirits of long-dead ancestors, he was struck by the spirits that circled the great tree. They were the spirits of the long dead dragons that had once dwelled the world and they served as guardians for the sacred grounds.

"This is the Great Tree, my friend," Khalas said after a moment of reflection. "It has been here since the birth of this world, and stood before even the dragons came to Espre. It is holy ground of the highest order, the touch of the Creator himself upon Espre. Here we meet and put aside all that separates us. Here there can be no war, and no conflict. Blood can never touch this hallowed place, it can never be allowed to be corrupted."

From a clearing to the east of the great tree emerged a woman. However, she was like no woman that Xaran had ever seen or ever known before in his life. Practically naked with the exception of a simple leather loin-cloth, the woman walked proudly across the silver moss, the orange and brown stripes that ran across her entire body evident. Her bright reddish-orange hair hung like a mane around her head and shoulders, falling down across her breasts. A stark white patch extended from her throat down the center of her chest and across her stomach, with thin stripes flanking it on either side. She looked like a tiger, a tiger that walked on two legs with the beautiful face of a woman. Her tail swung behind her with the rhythm of her steps.

"Lord Khalas," the woman said in a rough, growl-laden voice, "the Council awaits your return."

Khalas nodded its large head.

"Sir Xaran Firesoul, let me present to you the last of the Tigrelle, Tera Dawnrunner. She is known throughout this region of our domain as Wild Grace, and is the Guardian of the East. She is one of four guardians appointed to ensure that this holy ground remains pure."

The woman nodded slightly in Xaran's direction, her yellow cat's eyes gleaming in the calm light of the Great Tree. Quickly, Xaran released his hold on the sight of his friend and allowed himself to recover his bearings in blindness. In a moment they would begin walking toward the Great Tree again, only to be met by another voice, a large voice, one larger than Khalas.

"You have been gone too long, Khalas," the voice said coldly. "Much has happened and we must speak of it. I must say that you have picked an interesting time to bring with you a human. Perhaps it is advantageous, and perhaps it is also ill-advised. Shadowweaver will certainly not be pleased."

"Shadowweaver is never pleased, my lord Tarot. Lord Tarot, this is my friend that I have spoken of on many occasions. This is Xaran Firesoul."

There was a sound of scales moving through fine hair. Xaran had heard it many times when Khalas would run its clawed hands through its beard. He could feel the dragon looking down at him, taking in all of his features as he thought.

"Ah yes, the blind Knight of the Flashing Blade. Perhaps he will add some interesting perspective to the proceedings. Come Khalas, we have already begun. Leave your friend here, and Tera can attend to him until he is called to give his testimony to the council. Stay with Tera, human, or you may not like what awaits you in these chambers. The spirits of our dead can have strange effects on those not chosen to walk these hallowed grounds."

Xaran heard the two massive creatures walk off together toward the center of the Great Tree. Tera then took Xaran by the arm and led him closer to the tree.

"Can you function going up stairs, human?"

Xaran smiled.

"Perhaps not as gracefully as you, but I can manage."

There was a low grown from the woman.

"We shall see."

As the two began to ascend a rather small and rather steep set of stairs, Xaran began to question his confidence. The stairs seemed to twist and turn at odd angles and seemingly without rhyme or reason. It was almost as if the stairs formed organically with the contours of the Great Tree, an afterthought for those who could not simply fly. Eventually, the two reached a terrace of sorts, and Xaran could feel the altitude. He had spent many days sitting on the tops of the Peaks of Patience, and while not nearly as high as that, it was an impressive distance that the two had traveled in a relatively short time.

"We are at the edge of the chamber used by the Council of the Winds. From here you will be able to hear all of the deliberations. You may speak if you wish, simply keep your voice low as to not interrupt those speaking below. Your voice will not carry here if you do not project."

Xaran nodded silently, and let his ears fill with the sounds below. Though he could not see them, the scents and sounds were unmistakable. There were dragons below him, dozens of them, in a massive room. Some were seated, as Xaran could hear the sound of scales moving slowly across what must have been stone, while other stood. There was much discussion in languages that Xaran could not understand. They must have been speaking in some draconic dialect. Finally a voice raised over the din, and the whole chamber came to a quick silence.

"As the last of us has returned to the Council, we may now continue our deliberations."

That had been the voice of the one that Khalas called Lord Tarot. From the tone of his voice and the way in which he spoke, he must have been the leader of this Council of Winds. Xaran's suspicions were confirmed the next moment.

"That is Lord Tarot," Tera said quietly. "He is the oldest of the dragons still living, timeless by human standards. He leads this council."

"My fellow dragons of Espre, for two millennia we have called this ball of rock home, watching the sub-species and humans grow, watching them stumble through their lives, and fall in their ignorance. They have begun, as we all expected them to, to make war upon us. It is in small measure for now, but it will begin to grow as time goes on. To that end, we have received an envoy from the Creator, and have been given a mandate."

Xaran felt his heart jump. Belief in the Creator was mostly an abstract construct for most of the human race, but the dragons spoke of the Creator as a person they had seen, touched, been in the presence of. It was an awe-inspiring thought.

"If I may, Lord Tarot?" another voice rang out.

"The Council recognizes Krangoth Granitewill."

"It has been a long time since we have received an envoy from the Creator with any tidings that were not poor for the race of dragons. The fact that this envoy comes now, with all that has occurred in Cadaria and elsewhere, perhaps we should give the words of this envoy more weight than we have in the past."

There was a lot of talking among the dragons in the council, lots of rustling and obviously angry voices. Though the words were not apparent, the meaning was clear.

"The Council recognizes Shadowweaver."

The name brought silence to the gathering. It was the kind of silence born from great respect or great fear, Xaran could not tell which.

"With all due respect to my friend Krangoth, he needs to pull his head out of the ground a little more often. You aren't the one being attacked by these pathetic humans. They are no threat. They argue and bicker, fight amongst themselves. Chasing after these little plagues and diseases of theirs. Chasing after ghosts. We can hold them at bay long enough that they will distract themselves with something else before too long. Besides, if this whelp emperor of theirs continues on his course of action there will be nothing left of this Cadarian Empire to worry us."

The argument began again, dozens of voices clashing in both common language and in the draconic dialects. The argument raged for several moments seeming to build hotter and hotter.

"Is this common?" Xaran asked quietly.

"No," Tera commented, "it's usually much worse."

Finally Tarot's voice rose above the din again.

"The Council recognized Serentis."

Silence entered the Council chambers again. This time however, Xaran knew the source of the silence. There was a great power that emanated from the next speaker, the kind of power that Xaran had felt from people like Orren and Vallic, but to a much greater extent. This dragon had command over the very primal powers of nature as well as the arcane forces that held them together.

"Shadowweaver speak truth…Cadaria…Kaitain…watches...Dark Gods come…destroy…inevitable…Greater threat comes….Old threat…ancient enemy… ripples in the arcane…great death coming…death with old name…"

The voice of Serentis was equal parts hissing and language. The broken fragmented words and thoughts came in one long stream, and perhaps lost much in the translation from the draconic dialect. However, the purpose and the meaning were quite clear.

"Which leads us back to the original purpose of this Council," Tarot interjected. "The emissary from the Creator has informed me of a threat unlike we have ever seen before. An ancient enemy of the dragons, one that holds the very secrets of the Creator in his hands is bent on the destruction of the entire race. He will not be content with just killing one of us, or a dozen, or a hundred. His goal is nothing less than the extermination of the entire species. According to this envoy, he has the power at his disposal."

"So, let us just kill him," a voice rang out above the rest.

"Guarded….hidden…waiting…." Serentis answered. "Tools do his work….waits for freedom…prison….waits…patient….eternal…Cadaria will suffer…Cadaria bleeds…"

"So what, may I ask, does the Creator's envoy suggest we do?" Shadowweaver asked, his voice dripping with venom. "We are tied to this forsaken rock with no way off thanks to our agreement. An agreement, I don't need to remind you was forced on us by the Creator and by the actions of these infernal humans. I for one would be all in favor of abandoning this place for another, if it were possible."

The shouting came again, this time much louder, and much more violent. It persisted for some time until it finally subsided when a much softer, feminine voice rose above the din.

"We have been given a way, we have been given a path."

"That is Mariti Brightblade," Tera said in the silence. "She is the betrothed of Tarot and next in line to rule this Council."

"The Creator has allowed us to attempt to take an action that would grant us permission to leave this world. However, to do this we must take action that many here will find abhorrent. It is an action that very well may cause a war that will follow us from this world to whatever other we may choose to inhabit, and could become a portent of our destruction. The

Creator will release us from our tie to this world if we destroy the leader of the Dark Gods."

A wave of shock and horror passed though the Council. The Creator had given permission for the dragons to murder the leader of the Dark Gods, the once chosen and favored of the Creator's. Those fallen warriors who had been sent to Espre in disgrace.

"You know what this means," another dragon called out, "it will mean a war between the dragons and the Dark Gods. They will not simply allow us to destroy their leader and not retaliate."

"Brux is right," Krangoth called out the next moment. "The humans may not be a threat to us now, but the Dark Gods could kill us by the hundreds even in their weakened condition."

"So, we will not do it," Shadowweaver said finally. "At least, we will not allow the Dark Gods to know that we were behind the action. Let the humans tend to it. This Kaitain is bent on destroying the Dark Gods and fighting anyone that he perceives as a threat to him. Give him the means to defeat the most powerful of his enemies as his ancestor did, and he will jump at the chance. This whelp is a fool, and fools can be used for our purposes. We have proven that many times over."

Xaran's heart ran cold. Shadowweaver's assessment of the new Emperor may have been correct. Kaitain's hatred for the Dark Gods knew little bounds, and he still blamed the Dark Gods for the Wasting Disease and the Crawling Plague. If he suddenly came in possession of a means to destroy even one member of the Dark Gods, he would surely use it, and use it with great vigor. It could tip the balance of the war and give Kaitain more power than he could imagine.

"Are there any who object to this course of action?"

Xaran could feel a set of eyes peering at him from below.

"We have a human with us from the Empire of Cadaria," Khalas said after a moment. "He is my guest, and he should be allowed to speak."

There was a great grumbling in the chamber until the voice of Lord Tarot rang out again.

"The Council of Winds recognizes the Tiger's Eye Knight, Xaran Firesoul."

The one set of eyes became a hundred, all peering through Xaran. After a moment, Xaran cleared his throat and began to speak.

"While I do not pretend to know the politics of the Council of the Winds, nor the information that has been provided to you by this envoy of the Creator, I cannot help but fear any course of action that would give Kaitain Lorien control of the type of power that you propose. Had it been his father, Ender, I would not have hesitated, but the ravages of these plagues and diseases, as well as unforeseen turmoil and strife had made this Kaitain a broken man, a man on the edge of madness with such power under his disposal that he is a danger to anything that he does not control. A power that would find its way into his hands would surely be used for the purpose that you devise, but it would eventually be perverted and used against first the dragons, and then the rest of Kaitain's enemies. I understand that you are all trapped here against your will with danger looming closer. But I must ask you, please, the danger that you would create may be the greatest faced by any of us."

"So what do you purpose, human?" Shadowweaver countered. Xaran could feel the beast's hot breath on him, as it had turned to face Xaran's position. "While I care not for the fate of humans, if you are right about the instability of your Emperor, I would not want to see any of my brothers or sisters harmed by the actions of this council. So, we will give you the means, Xaran Firesoul. You will become our assassin, and you will create our opportunity to leave Espre."

Xaran's blood ran cold. His good intentions may have doomed him.

"What shall it be, Xaran Firesoul?" Tarot seconded after a moment. "Shall you carry death to the leader of the Dark Gods, or will you allow that knowledge to fall to your Emperor? Choose now."

Xaran hung his head, there was no choice.

"I shall do as you have asked."

Tarot lifted his great arms.

"Are there any objections in the Council to this course of action?"

The floor was silent.

"The Council has spoken."

****

Xaran sat on a stump outside the hallowed area of the Great Tree, a dagger sitting in his hands that was wreathed in a smoky haze. The dagger, once plunged into the heart of the leader of the Dark Gods, would consign his soul to the depths of hell for eternity and would allow the dragons to escape the face of Espre before the great threat could claim them. Inwardly, Xaran tried to rationalize his next course of action. One life taken could save the lives of thousands. Still, Xaran felt cold. There had to be another way, though it was not quick in presenting itself.

"You were cheated in there," Khalas said finally.

Xaran looked in the direction of his friend, and tried his best to smile.

"What happened was meant to happen my friend, and no matter the discomfort this act will bring me personally, it does not compare with the damage that would have been caused by Emperor Lorien if he would have inherited this power."

Khalas shook his head.

"I never expected it to come to that Xaran, and I am sorry that you are in the middle of our squabbles. Shadowweaver is very adept at getting his way in the Council, and had I know the conditions I was stepping into, I never would have brought you here. But as you say, fate has a strange way of rearing its head when it is least convenient. But as I mentioned to you earlier my friend, I have a gift for you."

Xaran heard a rustling from Khalas, and then after a moment, felt something being placed into his hands. After a moment of inspection, it felt like an ordinary belt, however, it seemed to be made out of a leathery substance that he could not identify. The clasp was also unique, like ivory in smoothness.

"In the beginning, the god of dragons granted each of the first ninety-nine of us, the rulers of the dragons a great treasure to guard. These treasures could be given as gifts to those who proved themselves as worthy to the cause of dragons. Because of this great burden you have chosen to bear, you have more than proven yourself worthy of this gift. The item you hold in your hands is known as Kadan. It is made from a strip of skin from the first dragon, and the clasp is made from a tooth donated from the supreme dragon. While wearing that belt my friend, you may use any ability that is granted to any dragon that walks this world, and you may also change your shape to that of any dragon. I hope my friend that is serves you well in the task you have chosen to undertake."

Xaran bowed his head.

"Thank you my friend for this thoughtful gift. I will treasure it and use it in the furtherance of my mission. Perhaps in time, I will be able to show more of your kind that there are humans that can be trusted without being used as pawns in a game."

"I hope you are right," Khalas replied. "I must return to the council, as there is more business to attend to. Two of your compatriots will be here in a moment, on a matter of some urgency it seems. Let them not approach the Great Tree, for they will not be as lucky as you were when Tera and the other Guardians see them."

* * * * * * * * * * * * *

The recess from the Council of the Winds would not be a long one, but Shadowweaver took the opportunity to meet with two of his long-time allies. Charnada Ivorytooth, the skeletal dragon was evil as the day was long, and had no love for many members of the Council of the Winds, or anyone else it would seem. Stormbane was also not trusted by many. He was known as the Traitor in most circles, and was known to never keep any commitment once he had profited from it. Shadowweaver could use them for his purposes well enough.

"Tarot is a fool. The time for us to take action is now," Charnada said softly.

"I agree that this course of action is foolish," Stormbane replied. "But the Council has ruled, and there is little we can do about it now."

Shadowweaver smiled.

"Not true, my impetuous friend."

After a moment, Shadowweaver raised one of his massive hands and opened it to reveal a silver dagger whose blade was wreathed with a smoky haze.

"It seems the envoy of the Creator gave the Council two of these daggers, just in case something went wrong. They will not miss this one for some time, as it was easy enough to create a facsimile. I will ensure through one of my agents that this makes its way to the Imperial Court of Aldere and into the waiting hands of Emperor Kaitain Lorien. It should be easy enough with the right manipulations. The chaos he will cause will be enough cover for us to take action."

"What about Tarot?" Stormbane worried.

Charnada stuck Stormbane hard.

"Coward. If you do not have the stomach for this, then go back to the Council with your tail between your legs. You always were a weakling."

"Enough." Shadowweaver interjected. "But you are right Charnada, it is our time. Begin to mobilize our allies. When the time is right, it will be time to unseat Tarot and his bride, as well as their simpleton supporters. Whether we leave this rock or not, the next council will be mine to control.

* * * * * * * * * * * * *

Xaran could feel the flows of power around him began to distort and then suddenly his two allies, Orren Eldrath and Vallic Ultiv stood before him. It was always easy to tell the two men by the amount of power that exuded from them, though Vallic tried his best to hold back his level of ability.

"Good to see you my friends," Xaran said smiling.

"The practiced jest of a blind man," Orren replied. "But I am afraid I have no time to spar with you today my friend. Something terrible has happened, something that I cannot even put into words now."

Xaran stood.

"What has happened?"

Vallic was the one to answer.

"The creature calling itself Famine came to Rashaleb, and though she fell by her own hand, the whole of Rashaleb has been laid to waste. The capital city is now a tomb. Tens of thousands are dead."

The wave of horror passed through Xaran.

"But that is the end of the Wasting Disease, is it not," Xaran asked. "Now that Famine has fallen, there will be no more outbreaks."

"That may be true, Xaran," Vallic replied, "but I am afraid, that we are not out of danger. We have begun to put many of the pieces together. These creatures, this Pestilence and Famine were tools put forth by a greater evil that calls itself Dorovar. Both Pestilence and Famine alluded to something else, another servant of Dorovar that would be born from the death of Famine. I am afraid it is only a matter of time before another kingdom knows the touch of Dorovar."

"Bellnoc was hit hardest by the Crawling Plague, Rashaleb lost tens of thousands to the Wasting Disease, and Galateria has been gutted by the attacks of the dragons. It seems as though these forces are conspiring to eliminate Cadaria piece by piece," Orren said finally. "We hoped you would be able to help us to learn more about this Dorovar, and maybe to prevent the next disaster that is going to happen."

"I am sure your new friends have more information than we do," Vallic said knowingly.

Xaran shook his head.

"I am sure you are right," Xaran replied finally. "But as of now, their concerns are elsewhere. There is a threat to the dragons, one that I do not hesitate in saying is this same Dorovar of which you speak. They will not hear us now, as their concern is their own preservation. Dorovar is in some type of prison, a prison that he cannot or will not escape until the path for him has been cleared. His tools are doing the work for him, but I do not think that he would dispose of his tools so easily. If this new tool has not emerged yet, perhaps one of the others will return to bring it into the fray. I would continue to track Pestilence and Famine though they seem to be gone. Perhaps they will lead you to this new threat, and you will be able to stop it before it causes more damage."

"Will you not come with us then?" Orren asked.

Xaran shook his head again, and instinctively looked down at the new dagger at his hip.

"I am afraid we all have our path that we must follow."

"Each to his fate then," Orren said putting his hand on his friend's shoulder.

"Each to his fate," Xaran answered.

Xaran stood in the silence of the forest as his two friends and companions disappeared in to the ether. As he silently ran his hand over the hilt of the dagger, we wondered if fate would ever reunite the old friends again.

Burden of Position

Year Two of the Just Emperor Kaitain "Dragonsbane" Lorien, Creator's Calendar Year 1869

Three weeks….three weeks on the road from Menoris to Aldere, and Gabriel Shadowfall began to wonder if he would survive the rest of the way. The normal time to travel between Menoris and Aldere was a week by horseback, a week and a half at the most, and that was only when inclement weather was involved. Then as Gabriel began to think about it, a hurricane was involved in their slowness…Hurricane Marlae. For the past three weeks, the Celestial Princess's mood worsened by the day. Due to her position, she refused to ride on either a horse or in a common carriage, and so her royal litter had been prepared. Before they had even been able to leave Menoris, the cushions in the litter had to be changed three times, and after that the curtains and drapes were changed twice before they finally were to the young woman's liking. After that, there had been stops because the wind was rocking the litter too hard. If Marlae had gotten tired, they had to stop while she slept because the movement on the road could wake her. If a road was too bumpy, they had to find an alternate route. Every time she was hungry, the caravan stopped, and her personal chefs prepared a meal for her. Most of the time the food was not fit to eat in the Celestial Princess's opinion, and so the caravan made a stop at the nearest village or town in order for better food to be procured. Then of course the Princess would want to sleep in the village in a proper bed, which at times also proved to be difficult in finding the right pillows, sheets, bedding, mattress, and everything else under the suns. Naturally also the Princess would need to bathe at every opportunity as she could not stand the smell of the road on her clothes or her skin, which precipitated more stops along the way. The maddening slowness of their voyage had started to grate on Gabriel's nerves, but when the wandering herald met them two weeks into their journey, Marlae became even more unbearable.

The news of her father's impending marriage hit Marlae hard, and her anger could be plainly seen by all, and she made no attempt to hide it. It had been a week since she had seen the notice provided by the herald, and even as Gabriel stood guard, facing the door as her two female servants bathed her in the inn at the outer edge of Aldere, she fumed and fussed. The two ladies in waiting knew enough never to repeat anything they heard, and Gabriel's practiced adherence to his duties had earned him enough of the trust of the Celestial Princess that she often spoke freely around him as though he were not even there.

"I cannot believe the nerve of that whore," Marlae said out loud to no one in particular. "She is nothing more than a common tramp trying to intrude on the fortune of the Lorien family. First she seduces a member of the Knights of the Flashing Blade, a married man no less, and then when she grows tired of him, she sets her sights on the Emperor. And where were his advisors and protectors when he was being drawn to her bed? They were usurping his power at every turn. That harlot Irene and the other charlatans at court... All they want is to control the Empire while my idiot father is bedding that sow. Well, once I get there, all of that will be put to an end I can assure you. If not for all of these moronic delays I could have been there to prevent this, but no, we have to stop at every single town to spread the good name of the Emperor to these filthy beggars. What a waste of my time. When we get to the palace I should have the caravan master executed for his incompetence."

There was a loud splash and the sound of something hitting the floor.

"Gabriel!"

Gabriel spun around, and the Celestial Princess looked at him impatiently. She looked in his eyes and then down at the floor where the bar of soap lay. Without a word Gabriel dutifully retrieved the soap from the floor and extended it back to the Princess. Frowning, the young woman slapped the back of his hand and sent the bar falling back to the ground.

"That one is dirty, Gabriel. Are you truly that incompetent? Fetch me a new one right this second or I am afraid I shall never be clean."

"As you command, Princess."

Gabriel choked down his pride as he left the small room. The room had brought no end of protestations from the Princess, regardless of how many times the innkeeper had told her that all of the rooms in the inn were the same size. This was not one of the richer cities on the edge of Aldere, in fact it was by far the smallest. Most of the people who stopped here could not afford much more, or this was the only place they could find in the middle of a late night. This small inn catered to anyone who could pay, without question, and so often it housed some less than reputable clientele, most of which had been scared off by the sudden appearance of the royal caravan.

Within a few moments, Gabriel had procured another bar of soap and made his way back to the Princess's room. However at the top of the stairs, he heard the raised voice of the Princess screaming at her ladies-in-waiting.

"You stupid hag, be careful. You pulled my hair!"

Gabriel stopped at the door for a moment, closed his eyes and then took a deep breath before pulling the door open and returning to the room. Keeping his eyes to the ground, he approached the side of the tub and extended the bar of soap to the Princess.

"I swear, Gabriel," Marlae said snatching the bar from his hand, "if you were any slower one would mistake you for a doddering old man."

"My apologies, Princess," Gabriel said calmly, repeating a phrase he spoke quite often, "I shall endeavor to do better next time."

Marlae looked at Gabriel for a moment before sliding back under the water.

“See that you do. Otherwise you will be scrubbing my chamber pots for the best years of your life.”

Gabriel bowed slightly and then returned to his position by the door. Though he tried his best to not allow the taunts and abuse to affect him, since the news of her father’s impending wedding, Marlae had been more vicious than usual. Her attacks were personal to be sure, not the normal taunts and jibes, and her patience for the mundane failings of her servants was non-existent. A perfect example of that was about to happen.

One of the ladies-in-waiting was simply washing the Princess’s hair, but when the Princess turned her head unexpectedly, a tangle of hair caught the young woman’s fingers. The Princess yelped in pain.

“I told you, you worthless cur to be careful. You nearly pull the hair right out of my head. Get out of here, both of you, you are worthless!”

The two women, the younger one trying to hide the tears that streamed down her face fled the room as though they had been whipped. Gabriel simply stood to the side and let them pass. They were not the first, and certainly would not be the last to suffer the wrath of the Princess, but they would be back at her side in a matter of minutes helping her dress as soon as she found something else to be angry about. Behind him, Gabriel heard the sound of some splashing water and then a scream. When he turned, Marlae lay on the floor, one foot cocked against the edge of the bath. She had apparently tried to get out and slipped. Gabriel rushed to her side and took hold of her, helping her quickly to her feet.

“Are you hurt, Princess?”

The concern for the young woman was genuine. Though the Princess could be annoying and wicked to any who served her, Gabriel took his duty to the young woman very seriously. He knew that if anything were ever to happen to the Princess, he would be to blame, and that the stain upon his honor would never be cleansed, no matter what he did.

The Princess winced and held her elbow that would obviously show a bruise within a few hours, and a pair of tears rushed down her cheek. When she looked up at Gabriel, for a moment, the cold and uncaring look was replaced by a vulnerability that Gabriel had never before seen. The hard façade had been pulled away to reveal the softness of the girl beneath. Gabriel held the Princess close for a moment, protecting her from the invisible threat. She was naked against him, vulnerable and real. Gabriel had seen the Princess nude on many occasions, one of her more common teases, but this was different. There was no motive and no malice in her nudity, it was pure and disarming. He could feel the softness of her skin beneath his hands, the faint floral smell from the bath oils flowing from her skin.

Remembering himself, Gabriel allowed the distance befitting their difference in position to return. As if suddenly remembering where she was, and who she was, the vulnerability in her eyes disappeared, and the prim and proper Princess of the Cadarian Empire returned. Marlae pulled away and put her hands on her hips, staring directly into Gabriel's eyes.

"How dare you touch me in such a manner. I should have you hung for that."

Gabriel allowed his glance to fall down to the floor, calming his nerves for the onslaught that was about to be loosed on him. However, the torrent of insults and jibes never came.

"Bring me my towel, Gabriel," she said after a moment. "It's cold in here."

Gabriel nodded his head.

"As you wish, Princess."

Taking a step past her; Gabriel took hold of the soft cloth towel and handed it to the young woman. Without a word, she wrapped it around her lithe body and then stood silent for a moment before sighing deeply.

"Leave me, Gabriel. Have the caravan prepared. I want to be in my own bed tonight."

Gabriel bowed low.

"As you wish, Princess."

As Gabriel made his way to the door, Marlae spoke again.

"And send those worthless cows back in here, I don't intend to ride naked in my litter all the way back to Aldere, no matter how much you would enjoy it."

* * * * * * * * * * * * *

The royal palace of Aldere bustled with activity. Ever since the announcement of the impending wedding, people from all around the Empire had put their lives on hold to make the journey to Aldere. The finest bakers, tailors, chefs, and other workmen from all fields had been hired to make this wedding the grandest event in the history of Cadaria, and at the center of it all, was the soon-to-be Empress, Dominique Arais. Her days had become more and more full since her arrival in the court of Aldere, and since the announcement, she had begun to take on more and more of the responsibilities that would soon fall to her as the Empress.

Dominique found her day starting before dawn, and her four ladies-in-waiting roused her from her slumber in her spacious satin covered bed, in which she often slept alone after her short torrid scenes of passion with her soon-to-be husband, and whisked her off to the massive bathing chamber. For a common woman who was used to bathing in a river or a stream, the scented candles and oils in the bathing chamber took some getting used to. Adding to that the fact that she could have fit her little house into the bath made it even harder to come to grips with. Floating nude in the luxurious warm water was one of the most pleasurable experiences of her life, and when her servants began to rinse her with the finest soaps and perfumes, she began to feel as though the entire world was meant for her and her alone. The humility of her station was never lost however, but enjoying such pampering was the one indulgence she allowed her soul.

After the bath, the servants dried her quickly and led her to her chambers where she would be dressed and her hair would be done. For most of her life, Dominique worried and cared little for her long blond hair. Since she spent most of the time in the fields with her brothers and with the animals of the field, it was not unusual for her hair to be filled with mud, sweat, and sometimes blood. Because she was the only girl born to her parents, her five brothers often found it amusing to abuse their sister. Dominique, while not muscular or masculine by any stretch of the imagination had found ways to defend herself against her brothers, and often had the upper hand on them, relying on her smarts instead of brawn. Those days were long gone, as the ladies in waiting took great pains in making sure her hair was just so, just as the Emperor liked, and that her makeup was applied with equal precision. For the woman who would be given the title of Empress and the Beauty of Aldere, there could be nothing out of place. With her hair, makeup, and clothing perfect, her education on the rules and customs of the court could commence.

Over breakfast, which rarely consisted of more than mixed fruit and bread to conserve her figure, Dominique received instruction from tutors in language and etiquette. For a common farm girl to be elevated to the status of royalty was not unheard of, but it did require much in the way of remedial learning of those things the rest of the royal court would take for granted. Everything from how to sit, when to sit, how to cross and uncross her legs, when to speak, and how to speak were discussed. With great care she was re-taught everything from how to walk to how to eat in a ladylike fashion. After breakfast were riding lessons. Before coming to Aldere, Dominique's only exposure to horses had been the ones that pulled the wagon to market after harvest. Riding one had always been outside her comfort, but now it was expected of her status. Learning was difficult and had resulted in more than one tumble. These falls were invariably met with gasps of horror from those in attendance. Everything Dominique did was closely scrutinized, and every difficulty was quickly noted by those who firmly believed that she did not belong there.

However, after the lessons and the tortures of her new station, there was an island of calm in the hurricane of insanity. Her lunches with the young woman who would become her daughter upon her marriage, Quyhn Ravenheart, were a blessing. Quyhn, though raised in the finery of court, had not allowed the opulence to touch her sense of simplicity. Together the two women could speak openly and honestly about the matters of the day, or issues that Dominique was having difficulty with. Quyhn was often able to provide Dominique with tricks to get past some of the difficulty. Quyhn was only about four years younger than Dominique, and the woman who would soon be Empress found it almost impossible to look at the younger woman as a daughter. They were becoming more like sisters with every passing day. Sometimes Quyhn would even join Dominique for her lessons in an attempt to add some sanity and perspective to the proceedings. However, such things could only be tolerated in the morning sessions. The afternoons were always more difficult, and those were the times that Dominique dreaded the most.

As Empress, Dominique would be expected to mediate some disputes and hear petitions that did not require the full attention of the Emperor. Learning how to handle these situations was at the heart of Dominique's new position, and while she did not mind the added responsibility, the instructor in these matters bothered her very much. Irene Drage could have been a wonderful woman had she truly wanted to be. However, while it seemed that everyone else in the royal court, including the Emperor, was enamored with her, Dominique saw her for what she was, a manipulative charlatan. Dominique had never met a person with more faces in all her life. The whispers around the court said that she had gotten her position as the Imperial Sorceress by having a sexual affair with the Emperor. Dominique believed every word of those rumors, and after seeing the way Irene always seemed to get what she wanted, she was sure that it wasn't just her limited physical charms that bewitched the Emperor. Whatever arcane power was at her disposal kept the Emperor wrapped around Irene's little finger, a situation that Dominique fully intended to put an end to. While inwardly Dominique had no true reason to detest Irene as fully as she did, the hatred burned within her nonetheless. For hours the two women sat together, talking of matters of the court, with Irene putting on her best fake smile while Dominique smiled back, the sick feeling in the pit of her stomach growing stronger as the day passed into night.

Most nights, after the lessons with Irene, Dominique would have a quiet dinner. Sometimes Quyhn would join her, and still other times Kaitain would grace her table. Other times however, she would be required to attend a state dinner of some kind, usually welcoming a person of great importance who had come to Aldere for the wedding. Within the next week, the Celestial Princess, Kaitain's daughter was expected to return to Aldere. This was a meeting that Dominique was not looking forward to in the least. Besides the fact that Marlae had a reputation of being a bit difficult, Dominique felt for the young woman's position. She had lost her mother, and now a woman that she had never met was going to try to fill that position. It had to be hard for Marlae, and Dominique did not want to make an enemy of her.

After an often too-light dinner, Dominique would read the accounts of the court matters of the day before retiring to her bed for the evening. Sometimes Kaitain would come to her in the middle of the night, but more often than not, he slept in his own room at the other end of the palace. Most said that he was up working until the late hours of the evening, but Dominique knew better. Irene still had her hooks deep into Kaitain, and there were nights when he would come to her, and she could still smell the stench of the repulsive woman all over his skin. She did her best to tolerate those moments of lovemaking, though it often felt like she was in the room watching them. Dominique was always relieved when Kaitain left her, and she could fall into an often-troubled sleep. Her thoughts in these private moments often went to Seraph. Her love for him had never diminished one iota, and often she wondered how he had reacted to the news of her upcoming marriage. Some nights she dreamed that he would come to rescue her from her position, with other nights it would turn to a nightmare where Kaitain would have him put to death. Both trapped and blessed by her position, Dominique cried herself to sleep many night, dreading the dawn of the next morning.

* * * * * * * * * * * * *

Irene Drage sat in her chair looking out over the moonlit waters that surrounded the Imperial Palace of Aldere. Things were going exactly as she planned. The kingdoms of Cadaria were falling into place, seeing Kaitain as the next great savior of the Empire, and the importance of the Knights of the Flashing Blade was being reduced more every day. Kaitain was distracted by Dominique Arais, and the new Empress would find herself embroiled in a bitter battle with Marlae Lorien soon enough. Irene was free to act with near impunity. Her revelry was interrupted by a quiet knock at the door.

"Enter."

The door opened slowly to reveal a man dressed from head to toe in dark crimson robes. His face was partially covered in mask, cold eyes glaring out at the Ethereal Sorceress. Irene stood and smiled. She had met with this agent on many occasions. Though she did not know who Torda Safrick called master or what agenda he truly followed, he had provided very accurate information in the past. Torda had been the source of the information about the relationship between Sadrina Annis and Hannah Ironheart, as well as the source behind the information that led to the discovery of Dominique Arais. Irene had heard Torda called the Master of Secrets in some circles, and Irene had been in no position as of yet to dispute the title.

"Torda, so nice to see you. What do you have for me?"

Without a word, the masked man reached into his robes and produced two scrolls. The second scroll was attached to a small package. He placed them on the desk and then closed the door as he left the room. A knowing smirk appeared on Irene's face. In the nearly two years that Irene had been dealing with Torda Safrick, she had never heard the man speak a single word. Perhaps that was his power. He who did not speak could never have his own secrets revealed. Smiling at the thought, Irene retrieved the two scrolls. She opened the first as there came another knock at her door. She knew that knock, it could be none other than the Emperor.

"Please enter, my Emperor."

The door opened quietly, and Kaitain Lorien entered the opulent dwelling of the Imperial Sorceress. He had gone to some expense to make sure that Irene had all the luxury that she could ever want. Without a word, Kaitain made his way to Irene's bed, and lay down, his shirt quickly discarded.

"Not sharing a bed with your Empress this evening, my Emperor?"

There was no need to ask the question, Irene already knew the answer. For months, Irene had kept Kaitain satisfied in her bed, and the spells spoken in his ear in the middle of the night kept him coming back as long as she wanted him to. She still had use of him if her plans were going to succeed, and it would only be a matter of time before she would no longer require him in her bed. By that point, Dominique could have him if she still wanted him.

"What news, Irene?" Kaitain said, ignoring her question.

Irene finished reading the first scroll.

"It seems that your brother Feyd and his daughter Felicia will be arriving just in time for the wedding."

Kaitain groaned. Feyd Lorien was Kaitain's annoying younger brother. Though the two were only born seven minutes apart, Kaitain was the older of the two, and therefore was the heir to the Throne of Cadaria. Feyd would soon be forgotten in the cogs of the Imperial machine, set to be the envoy of the Throne to the province of Lordhill. He could cause no problems there. However, because Feyd's daughter Felicia was born some months before Kaitain's wife finally became pregnant there was some concern in Kaitain's mind for a while whether or not Feyd would make an attempt to seize power from his older brother. However, Feyd proved to not be devious or opportunistic enough to take advantage of the situation, a mistake that he would suffer for in obscurity for the remainder of his days. Felicia and Marlae were polar opposites, much as Feyd and Kaitain were. Where Marlae was prim and proper, loving subtle manipulations and the battles of court, Felicia, still recognized as a Princess of Cadaria, loved physical confrontations and the lure of the sword. She was known throughout Cadaria as the Warrior Princess. Marlae bristled at even being mentioned in the same sentence with her cousin.

"I suppose I will at least get some amusement from Marlae and Felicia sparring for a while. What else?"

Irene opened the second scroll and nearly choked. What she was seeing before her could not be true. It was impossible. Impatiently, Irene tore at the wrapping of the package and revealed a small dagger whose blade was wreathed in a smoky haze. Kaitain sat up as soon as he saw the blade and looked at Irene quizzically.

"What is that Irene?"

Irene smiled a wicked smile and took hold of the dagger. As she curled her slender fingers around its perfectly smooth hit, she could feel the power coursing through the blade.

"This, my Emperor, is the tool to kill a god..."

Growing Darkness

Year Two of the Just Emperor Kaitain "Dragonsbane" Lorien, Creator's Calendar Year 1869

The Kingdom of Gold, Bellnoc was aptly named, as that it housed some of the richest gold mines in the whole of the Empire of Cadaria, with the exception of the mines of Lordhill which lay in the Imperial province of Aldere. The riches of the kingdom brought it a great deal of attention from all sorts throughout the Cadarian Empire; merchants, thieves, mercenaries, pirates, and an assortment of other characters. However, while most of these men and women had only profit on their minds, others had more nefarious schemes.

Since her birth, Natalia Pressen had been destined for great things. Her father was a fairly important member of the court of Bellnoc and had been the ambassador to the Imperial Court of Aldere for many years. Natalia's mother kept the tradition of her family by being a member of the mysterious Shadow Guild, the Empire's foremost assassins. When Natalia was old enough, her mother retired from the Guild and fostered her daughter in her stead. This had become a common practice in the Guild for as long as it had existed. Eventually, Natalia's skills advanced to the point where she would be named a master in the ranks of the Shadow Guild, and along with her recognition outside the Shadow Guild as a skilled trade negotiator, Natalia became an easy choice for the position of

Sunstone Knight of the Flashing Blade. Though none but the Emperor knew of her position in the Shadow Guild, her exploits and successes outside the Guild were enough to warrant her ascension on their own.

As Natalia hung by her heels from a beam of wood extending from the back edge of the roof of an inn, her mind went back to many of her days in training where her master would have her hang like this for hours on end. She would stay there as long as possible until the blood rushed to her head and the blackness of unconsciousness tugged at the corners of her eyes, demanding them to close. More than once in her training she had given in to the light-headed sensations and fallen to the ground unconscious, but in time she learned to compensate through slight movements of her neck and back. Now though, she worried little. She could stay perfectly still for days if necessary and never lose consciousness. That was but one of the gifts granted to her by the rapier that hung at her side, the Sacred Weapon known as Perseverance. As long as Perseverance was by her side, there was no physical trial that Natalia could not endure. She could run at full speed all day and night, and never feel the touch of fatigue or pain through her muscles. She could hold her breath for nearly infinite stretches of time, and her hands never cramped while holding firm to the side of a mountain face by just her fingertips. In her line of work as a master of the Shadow Guild, these added abilities became extremely useful. While her prey would eventually tire, she never would relent.

Steadying her mind, Natalia closed her eyes and whispered a nearly silent incantation. When she opened her eyes again, the world around her seemed insubstantial with the exception of the faint outlines of bodies of men and creatures that radiated heat. Taking a silent count of the number of people in the small building below her, Natalia closed her eyes again and released the spell. Much to the chagrin of the Academy of Arcane Arts in Jelan, the Shadow Guild had created their own type of arcane power, and taught it to every one of the their members, each of which would have been considered adept by the Academy. However, unlike the banal spells taught by the Academy, the Shadow Guild found more direct uses for arcane ability. Picking locks, seeing body heat, and even a few offensive surprises were the purview of all members of the Shadow Guild. However, the masters were given access to the more advanced abilities that would make men choke as air was wrenched from their lungs, blood stopped flowing from their heart, or they found their memories ripped from their mind. All were useful in eliminating their targets or ensuring that their deeds were never seen by the public at large.

This occasion, Natalia knew that she would need all of the powers at her possession in order to carry out her mission. Her target turned out to be a man by the name of Karak Gill. Karak had been a smuggler and mercenary most of his life, sometimes employed by both Mythryn and Cadaria to either ensure the delivery of goods, or to ensure that goods never reached their destination. In the wars between the kingdoms of Cadaria, Karak amassed a small fortune harassing the supply lines of both sides and then selling the items he stole to the highest bidder. While this type of profiteering was frowned upon, it was not an offense that would draw the ire of the Emperor. The source of the contract on this occasion turned out to be something much more heinous. Karak had turned his attention from simply raiding supplies to becoming a cog in the wheel of an assassination plot against the Emperor himself. The plot had been discovered when another member of the Shadow Guild carried out the assassination of a bandit leader in the south of Aldere. There were many correspondence from Karak found in the bandit's effects, and it was only a matter of time before the termination order found its way into Natalia's hands. The orders were simple, to eliminate Karak and all of his associates, as well as to determine the extent of the plot against the Emperor. This was her first assignment for the new Emperor Kaitain Lorien, but with the rumors on the wind, she was sure it would not be her last. The new Emperor seemed to have a way of collecting enemies, and it would mean a busy few years for the Shadow Guild.

Taking a deep breath, Natalia whispered another incantation, and her body disappeared from view. Her feet released the beam the next moment, and she fell slowly from her high perch to the ground where she landed without a sound. Stepping normally, her footfalls obscured by her spell, Natalia moved toward the small building and crouched just outside the closed door, and waited. It would be only a matter of time before the guard opened the door to check the perimeter as he did every hour. Natalia had taken great pains in tracking Karak and his group, and then spent many days watching their operations. They had not been easy to track at the beginning, and Natalia had spent nearly six weeks aboard a freighter before one of Karak's known associates led her to a meeting site where she found another of Karak's associates. This broken trail had been followed for another few weeks until finally she identified Karak. While she had wanted to make a move on him then, the opportunity never presented itself, and she had to follow him to this small base of operations in her home city of Bellnoc. Perhaps this would be the best place to strike and more incriminating evidence on his co-conspirators could be uncovered.

After several minutes, the door finally opened and the guard stepped out to check the perimeter. Timing her movements, Natalia sprinted toward the door as soon as the guard emerged, and just as the door began to close behind him, Natalia leapt and tumbled through the closing door before landing on her feet in the well-guarded room beyond the door. Three low tables were set up in the room around the walls, laden with weapons and armor, as well as some items that Natalia could not identify. They seemed to be arcane supplies of some type or another, wands and staffs, but there were other items probably necessary for dark rituals. Natalia made a mental note to have some of the items shipped to the Academy of Arcane Arts in Jelan for study, while others would go to the Shadow Guild for possible use in later missions, if they could be saved without endangering the mission. At the very least they could be hidden away or destroyed so that they could never be used in another plot against the Emperor. Three men stood in this room, heavily armed and armored. Once she struck, Natalia knew that her cloak of invisibility would be broken, so she closed her eyes slowly and whispered another incantation.

Within a matter of moments one of the guards sat down on the edge of one of the low tables, his eyes drooping. One of the other men yawned slightly before he slumped slowly to the floor fast asleep. The third man however showed no sign of tiring and went to check on his fellow guards. With one quick deft motion, Natalia bounded the distance between the door and the third guard and upon drawing Perseverance let its razor sharp tip pierce his heart and lung from behind while her free hand covered his mouth to stifle the attempt to cry out. Though she was now visible to the world around her, she had yet to be discovered. Silently moving across the room, she quickly broke the necks of the other two guards and returned to the shadows by the door to await the fourth guard. He would be returning any moment and she would have to act quickly to ensure that she would remain undiscovered. Knowing the limitations of her craft, it would be another hour before she would be able to recreate her invisibility shroud, so Natalia quickly calculated the best course of action to her as she crouched by the door.

Because the door opened inward, Natalia knew she had an extra few seconds before the other three guards would be discovered. After a few moments of silence, the door cracked open, and Natalia quickly spoke another incantation, and the world around her slowed. While still retaining her normal speed, she waited and watched as the door opened inch by inch. Finally when the fourth guard came into view, Natalia lurched forward, taking the guard by total surprise, snapping his neck and pulling him into the room before letting time return to its normal speed. After closing the door to the building, Natalia smiled to herself at her handiwork and silently made her way down the nearby corridor to the deeper portion of the building.

Four guards had been eliminated, and five remained not including Karak. Skulking slowly down the corridor, keeping to the shadows, she watched as a form moved in the distance. Whispering another incantation, the shadows in the hall seemed to wrap themselves around Natalia as the lantern from the approaching guard tried to banish the darkness. He only moved about half-way down the corridor before turning back. This was Natalia's chance. She whispered another incantation robbing all sound from the room. Then, putting her speed and mastery of acrobatics to use, Natalia sprinted down the corridor, leapt into the air, her back nearly scraping the ceiling. As she flew through the air over the unwitting guard, she took hold of his head and wrenched it unnaturally, ending his life with a sickening snap. The guard fell quickly, and Natalia flipped around kicking her feet forward. The guard fell, but the lantern landed on Natalia's outstretched legs instead of shattering on the floor. A smirk graced her face as she blew out the lantern and set it gently by the guard's body. Five guards down, and only four to go.

The next portion of the assault would prove to be the greatest challenge. The last four guards held the room before Karak's office, and would most likely be the most elite of them all. Additionally the room would be quite well lit, and keeping her assault a secret from Karak would be most difficult.

However, she did have a plan. Taking the lantern from the ground, Natalia walked to the door to the next section of the building and gently opened the lantern and began to pour the oil along the floor. It took only a few seconds to spread the oil in a fitting amount. Pulling her waterskin from her belt, she added a small amount of water to the wood ensuring a slow and smoky burn. Then, after whispering another incantation that enhanced her hearing, Natalia ignited the oil with her flint and tinder, and then waited for the smoke to begin to rise. As the smoke gathered, Natalia whispered a spell, increasing the production of smoke tenfold. Already on the other side of the door she could hear the voices of the guards as they talked about the smoke. Smoke had begun to fill the room and their voices began to raise as the shouts of fire increased. Natalia crouched, ready to strike, and when the door opened she did not hesitate. Smoke had already filled the room, and in a matter of heartbeats, Natalia launched into the room, slicing the throat of the first guard as he stood shocked by the door. Their vision impaired by the rolling black cloud of smoke, the other three guards could do nothing by cough and choke as Natalia used her enhanced hearing to track them down and end their lives. Just as she had finished dispatching the fourth guard, the door to Karak's office sprang open as he came to investigate. Natalia leapt for him, her shoulder striking him in the gut and forcing him back into the room. A single kick from her foot closed the door, and Perseverance found its way to Karak's throat as Natalia hovered over him.

"What is this?"

Karak's voice was filled with a mixture of fear and anger. He had no doubt been utterly surprised by the woman's assault, and as he looked up into her cold blue eyes, her dirty blond hair hanging down into her face, there was no doubt in his mind that she could end his life at any moment.

"Karak Gill, your termination has been ordered, and I am here to carry it out."

The blood drained from Karak's face.

"Termination?"

Natalia's expression remained fixed, her eyes locked on her target.

"You are charged with conspiring to assassinate the Emperor. If you cooperate now and name your co-conspirators, mercy may be shown and you may spend the rest of your life in the Imperial Dungeons at Aldere. Otherwise, your life ends here and now."

A knowing smile came to Karak's lips, and Natalia found herself surprised at the man's reaction. Usually there was begging and bribe attempts, and often there were quite a few tears. A smile was last thing that Natalia ever expected.

"Oh that…Go ahead and kill me then. You'll never get me to talk."

Natalia smiled.

"I don't need you to talk to take what you know. But just know that the last moments of your life will be filled with such pain that death will be a blessing when it is over."

Karak's features hardened and then he spit into Natalia's face.

"For you and your Emperor."

Natalia buried the tip of Perseverance into Karak's throat and waited. It would take but a moment to finish the job and end his life, but quickly Natalia closed her eyes, and put her free hand on the top of Karak's head and concentrated. The technique of Thought Stealing was perfected by the Shadow Guild, but it was unpleasant for both the assassin and the victim. As each person's mind worked and organized information slightly different, it was difficult to find a single thought or stream of thoughts in a short amount of time. To that end, the Shadow Guild created a way of taking all of the memories from the target for a temporary amount of time. The maximum amount of time that a member of the Shadow Guild could hold onto these stolen thought varied depending upon the person and the amount of information stolen from the victim, but the longest known duration was three days. If the transfer didn't fail outright, the thoughts received were jumbled at best, and took quite some time to sort out. Far too often the thoughts were lost just as they were starting to find some organization. However, Natalia hoped that between her experience and the assistance of Perseverance, she would be able to find the information that she needed before it was too late.

Holding tight to Karak's head, Natalia began to feel the burning sensation through her hand and arm that told her the information was beginning to be drawn from him. Finally, Natalia heard the blood-curdling scream wrenched from Karak's chest as the pain began. The procedure was truly horrible for the victim, a pain that defied description other than feeling like dying over and over again as each second passed. The transfer took only a few moments, but for Karak, Natalia was sure it felt like hours of intense pain. Finally, when she was sure it was done, Karak's throat was slit, and Natalia stood alone in the small building, her mind awash with alien thoughts, confusion filling her. The disorientation was extreme, but even as her thoughts swam, she quickly returned to the corridor taking with her three more lanterns. She broke one against the wall, adding a massive amount of fuel to the small fire, causing it to lick the walls. The other two lanterns were broken farther down the corridor, ensuring that the blaze would spread quickly. As she stood in the far room of the building near the exit, Natalia looked down the corridor and spoke one more incantation and watched as the blaze rose higher and burned hotter. In a matter of seconds it would rage out of control and engulf the whole building. Smiling to herself, Natalia opened the door quickly and raced into the streets before leaping into the shadows of the inn once more. After she was sure that no one had witnessed her escape, Natalia pulled the hood of her cloak over her head and began her trek back to Aldere to report her findings. She hoped by the time that she returned to the court of the Emperor that she would have the answers that he would want to hear.

* * * * * * * * * * * * *

Kaitain Lorien sat at his desk in his private study, the enchanted dagger sitting before him untouched. The possibilities boggled the mind. With the tool that lay before him, he could strike down any of the Dark Gods, but the mission was clear. It was the leader of the Dark God that would have to be robbed of his life by the blessed weapon, a message sent to the rest of the Dark Gods that the Cadarian Empire would not tremble at the machinations of the Dark Continent of Mythryn any longer. The Cadarian Empire would stand for eternity, and if that meant that the blood of all of the Dark Gods would be spilt, then so be it. Irene had cautioned that using the weapon offensively could ruin the element of surprise, and it should be used as a defensive measure when the Dark Gods and their armies chose to strike. However, Kaitain rejected that on principle. Kaitain refused to be caught, huddled in his palace while the armies of Mythryn descended on Cadaria like a plague. No, he would strike at the heart of the Dark Gods before they could move against him, and he would end the war before it ever started.

As Kaitain smiled to himself, there was a knock at the door of his study. It was a late hour for anyone to be paying him a visit, and so Kaitain quickly covered the dagger and took hold of the Imperial Sword.

"Enter."

The door opened to reveal the exotic features of the Sunstone Knight, Natalia Pressen. Kaitain relaxed little upon seeing the woman's face, but smiled. Natalia took a step into the room, closed the door behind her, and then fell to one knee, her head bowed.

"Lady Natalia Pressen, Sunstone Knight of the Kingdom of Bellnoc reporting, my Emperor. I bring news of a matter of some urgency regarding a plot against your life."

Kaitain frowned. These assassination plots seemed to grow in number by the day, no matter how magnanimous and cautious he had been in his actions. The commoners seemed to love him on the surface, but there were elements everywhere that resented his wars against the dragons and Mythryn that caused so much death. No matter how good they may have been for the long term health of the Empire, some could not see past the moment. However, if they thought that his death and replacement would end the wars, they were sorely mistaken. All around Espre, forces were conspiring to destroy the great and shining empire that was Cadaria, and Kaitain was fighting tooth and nail to keep all of it intact for the people. They would have to be made to understand that.

"Rise, and report, Lady Natalia."

Natalia stood and bowed again before speaking.

"The Shadow Guild discovered the threads of a plot whose logical conclusion would be your death, my Emperor, and so I was assigned to track down one of the supposed architects of the conspiracy, terminate him, and extract whatever information I could about the plot. As per my orders, I tracked the criminal Karak to his lair and upon infiltrating eliminated all of his guards, and then extracted the information from Karak before ending his life. The hideout was burned to the ground, destroying all of the items they had gathered in furtherance of this plot."

Kaitain smiled. Though Natalia may not have been the favored assassin of Kaitain, her abilities could not be denied. Perhaps it would be advantageous to keep her around a little longer.

"And what did you discover, Lady Natalia?"

Natalia's features remain cold and unreadable.

"It is clear from what I extracted from Karak's mind that he was but a minor player in the overall scheme. This conspiracy stretches through a great many smaller hands before reaching their architects. At this point I know that Karak was involved in procuring certain arcane items that would then be sent via a courier to Saldarine where they would be received by another agent and then forwarded to another destination. Each member in the chain only knew two to three other people in the web so to protect the whole organization from discovery. I did however uncover what I believe to be the name of the organization as well as the name of the person who recruited Karak. The name of the organization is the Hand of Chaos, and the recruiter used the name Xavier Cormea."

Kaitain pondered for a moment. If this conspiracy was as vast as Natalia suggested, the attempt could come at any point in time and without any kind of warning. The whole of the resources of the Shadow Guild would have to be mobilized in order to combat this threat. To make it public with orders to the military would bring to much attention and would weaken the position of the Throne. Also it could cause more people to flock to the banner of this Hand of Chaos.

"Send dispatches to your agents, Natalia. This Hand of Chaos represents and clear threat to the Emperor and to the Empire of Cadaria. Tracking down the members of this conspiracy and terminating them is now the primary focus for all of the Shadow Guild and the mission will not end until every last one of these traitors is hunted down and destroyed."

Natalia bowed.

"By your word, my Emperor."

Natalia stayed bowed for a moment before lifting her head again and locking her eyes on the Emperor. There was an uneasy silence before Natalia spoke again.

"With your permission, my Emperor, I will track this Xavier Cormea and uncover his role in this Hand of Chaos."

Kaitain thought for a moment and then caught the covered form of the dagger in the corner of his eye. Natalia was a very skilled and very impressive assassin. Perhaps she would be able to succeed where so many others had failed.

"No, Lady Pressen, I have another task for you…"

* * * * * * * * * * * * *

Xavier Cormea sat a tavern in the city of Bellnoc gently sipping from the tankard of ale he held. The reports of the death of the mercenary Karak brought a smile to Xavier's face as he read the small scroll of news that had been circulating for several days. No doubt the news of Karak's involvement in a plot to assassinate the Emperor had reached Aldere. All was going according to plan. Looking out the window, Xavier saw the raven perched on the tavern's sign, and knew that his contact had arrived. Standing slowly and running his fingers though his stark white hair, Xavier dropped several gold pieces on the table before walking slowly out of the tavern.

"You're late," a voice said from the darkness of the shadows to Xavier's left.

"You have a gift for overstatement and the dramatic my friend. I trust you have heard of our successes here?"

Dimitri Sulano emerged from the shadows and watched as the raven lifted from its perch and returned to its familiar place on Dimitri's shoulder.

"I did. And are you sure all of the proper information found its way back to Kaitain?"

Xavier smiled.

"Have you ever known me to fail?"

Dimitri shook his head. Xavier was as arrogant as the day was long, but he always got results.

"And the second phase of the plan?"

"It is in place, and will be put into action as soon as Korin arrives. It should prove a fair enough distraction before the Emperor's wedding. Between searching for me, dealing with these phantom issues in Thorigald, Saldarine, Galateria, and now Bellnoc as well as protecting Aldere for the wedding, our target should be quite undefended."

Dimitri smiled.

"Good. Torda delivered his package, and so that should rob another few resources from the Emperor and should give us just the opening we needed. I will be sure to give your good wishes to Seraphina."

Xavier did his best to suppress a shiver.

"Any word on the next gift from our friend Dorovar."

Dimitri turned away.

"Only that very soon, Albitonin will suffer as never before."

To Save the Soul

Year Two of the Just Emperor Kaitain "Dragonsbane" Lorien, Creator's Calendar Year 1869

Gregor Quicksilver had given himself ample time to clear his head and focus on the ramifications of his next actions. Not so long ago he had wandered the countryside, fighting the enemies of the Emperor, now though his journey through the kingdoms of the Empire had a much different motivation. It had been nearly three months since his return to the mainland from Mythryn, and nothing he had heard since his return quelled the darkness that filled his heart or the sick feeling that rumbled in the pit of his stomach. Emperor Kaitain Lorien was taking great strides to ingratiate himself to the people of Cadaria, but there were disturbing undertones in each of the orders given. Most of the imperial proclamations were not even signed by the Emperor himself, but were issued by the Imperial Sorceress, a woman who had begun calling herself the Ethereal Sorceress Irene Drage. Perhaps the Emperor was simply too busy with preparations for his wedding that would be taking place at the end of the month, or perhaps the festivals for the upcoming New Year's celebration demanded too much of his attention. However, the implication was clear, the Emperor was less interested in the disposition of the Empire than he was about his personal life. Perhaps this Dominique Arais, this common woman that he planned to marry would be a calming influence on Kaitain, but Gregor began to see her as nothing more than another distraction placed in his path by the supposedly loyal Irene Drage. The woman was quickly consolidating her power, and whether it was by design or not, the real ruler of Cadaria was emerging, and it was not the rightful member of the Lorien line.

More disturbing to Gregor was the news and rumors about the members of the Flashing Blade and the horrors loosed by both the Gray Man Pestilence and the woman called Famine. Rashaleb was in ruins, reduced to a series of regional governors reporting directly to Aldere, and the Sapphire Knight, Orren Eldrath was nowhere to be found. Some said that he disappeared after the destruction of Rashaleb with Vallic Ultiv while still others said that Orren had died of the Wasting Disease like the rest of Rashaleb, and that the Throne was simply covering it up so that the rest of the citizens of the Kingdom of Ice did not lose faith. Either way, Aldere was going to great lengths to turn Orren into a symbol in order to keep the rest of the governors in line. Word from Albitonin was not much better. The Temple of the Creator seemed to be in disarray. Hannah was long overdue from her mission in Galateria, and there had been no word from her since the latest round of attacks. The only news from Galateria had been that she, while wounded, had insisted on leading a charge into the phalanx of dragons that attacked and was not seen after. Her body was not recovered after the battle was over, and most rumors said that she was dead. Gregor could not believe that Hannah would be that reckless. There were more disappearances reported as well. Xaran Firesoul, Tolon Morr, Seraph Kore, and Devlin Rannoch were all missing, and while most assumed that they were on secret missions for the Throne, Gregor had his doubts.

Xaran was not the kind of resource that would be dispatched on a secret mission, he was too valuable in the open as a symbol of solidarity and accomplishment. Ender always understood that having the blind man visible to all of Cadaria was a greater tool than any of the other assets that the monk brought to the table. When the citizens of Cadaria saw Xaran Firesoul, they did not see a monk, or a member of the Flashing Blade, they saw a common blind man that had risen above his dedicated station in life and it inspired them to do better, and to be the best that they could be in all things. He was a lightning rod that captured the hearts and imaginations of the Empire, and that was a greater weapon against rebellion than any amount of gold or favor. Perhaps Kaitain was not as wise as his father, or perhaps Xaran was embroiled in something that prevented him from serving his standard position as mascot for the Empire. Gregor had no doubt that if Xaran was missing, Vallic would not be far away. The two men shared a strange bond. Often they would sit at the summit of the Peaks of Patience for days at a time, never exchanging words, but still having whole conversations. When they returned they often said that they had been contemplating the nature of the universe or some other such nonsense. They were a secretive pair to be sure, but none of the other members of the Flashing Blade were as trustworthy, save Hannah.

Gregor did not know enough about the new members of the Flashing Blade Tolon Morr and Devlin Rannoch to know if they were on extended missions for the Throne or not. When Gregor had left Cadaria, he knew that Tolon had been dispatched on a secret mission, but he had heard rumors upon his return that Tolon had been spotted in Aldere as well as in Galateria. Some said that he was in the company of a woman, while others said that he was traveling alone. Devlin Rannoch on the other hand had been having nothing short of miraculous success against the dragons in Galateria. However, upon his disappearance, it seemed that the battle against the oversized lizards had gone from bad to worse. The whole kingdom of Galateria had been gutted from one end to the other, and the death tolls were said to be in the tens of thousands. Only in the most remote pockets of Galateria, where the denizens were mostly creatures from the Dark Continent of Mythryn did the battle still go well. It seemed that the monsters of Mythryn were able to hold their own in battle with the dragons, and perhaps the remoteness of their location gave them advantages as well. Gregor shuddered at the thought that perhaps an alliance with Mythryn would serve more than averting a war that would be the end of Cadaria, but also would bring a force to bear that would be enough to combat the mass of dragons.

It was the disappearance of the Emerald Knight Seraph Kore that concerned Gregor the most. While Gregor did not know Seraph as well as he knew Seraph's wife Chelsea, Gregor did know that Seraph was a hothead and often acted rashly. Gregor was perhaps one of the handful of people in the Empire that knew of Seraph's affair with Dominique Arais, the soon-to-be Empress, and while the relationship had always been a sticking point between the married couple, they had always found a way to co-exist. Now though, with Dominique set to wed, Gregor was certain that Seraph had let his emotions get the better of him, and perhaps his disappearance was the first step on a road to an action that he could not possibly take. Seraph was an accomplished warrior to be sure, and tenacity was one of his main assets. Few knew that he was once an acolyte in the Temple of the Creator before he became a soldier in Thorigald, and in that time he developed abilities that made him both a suitable healer, but also a quite capable warrior. He was trained by one of the best warriors of the temple to bring his abilities to bear against the undead, the greatest enemy of the Temple. After years in the service of the Temple, Seraph returned to Thorigald to become the General of the Army of Water, and eventually a Knight of the Flashing Blade. However, while everyone thought of Seraph as a master swordsman because of his skill with the sword Patience, Seraph's greatest gift was with a bow in hand. It was said that he could make impossible shots with regular consistency, and that he could kill a man from a thousand yards in high wind with a single arrow. If he had set his mind on assassinating the Emperor, Seraph had all the skills at his disposal.

Finally, Gregor's travels brought him back to Aldere. Upon his return, Gregor was immediately conducted to the Great Receiving Hall of the Imperial Palace of Aldere. Gregor sat alone of the far side of the room, the hood of his cloak pulled over his head lost deep in thought over the many pieces of information he had received during his travels. There were patterns developing, alarming patterns. Just as Gregor was beginning to tune out the world around him and become lost in the introspection of his own thoughts, the doors to the Great Receiving Hall burst open. There was a great commotion from outside the palace, and Gregor looked up to see a sight that chilled him to the bone.

Leonora Wastri had always been a friend to both Hannah and Gregor, though Hannah had known her longer. Leonora had been one of the few people who were allowed to attend Gregor and Hannah's wedding, and she was one of the few that Gregor counted as an ally in even the worst of times. Never in all the years that the two had known one another had Gregor seen Leonora as anything other than a calm and rational agent of the Empire whose only goal was the steadfast advancement of the

Emperor's agenda, and the defense of her kingdom. However, the woman that entered the Great Receiving Hall was neither calm nor capable. Leonora walked slowly, leaning on her sacred weapon Wisdom for balance. Her left leg looked to be intact, but from the way it dragged behind the woman with every step, Gregor could tell that it was lame. Cuts and bruises covered her face and arms, but there was still a quiet determination in her eyes. A page rushed to her, but Leonora's clear voice rang out before the page could speak.

"I must speak with the Emperor, now."

The page stopped dead in his tracks and nearly ran up the long flight of stairs to the Audience Chamber and then disappeared behind the imposingly tall wooden double doors. Gregor took the next moment to approach his old friend, and when Leonora saw him, she exhaled slowly and smiled, though pain still tugged at her features.

"Gregor," she said slowly, "at least I know I have one friend in Aldere."

Gregor looked over Leonora once more. Her body had been contorted due to pain for a long period of time, and with but a glance, his powers allowed him to see the amount of damage. He could heal her of course, but it would take quite some time.

"What happened, Leonora?"

Leonora looked down to the ground and shook her head.

"I am afraid that we are all doomed, Gregor. The Dark Gods of Mythryn have their sights set on our destruction and even we, the Flashing Blade are powerless to stop them."

Gregor shook his head. However, this was no place for a disagreement, nor was it a place for Gregor to share what he knew.

"Shall I take your pain?"

Leonora looked up and into Gregor's eyes. Long had she relied on her own inner strength, and even though the powers of Wisdom allowed her to escape even the most basic needs of a mortal such as the need to eat, sleep, or breathe, it did not insulate her from pain or injury. After a moment, Leonora nodded slowly. Gregor closed his eyes and pulled upon his own powers as well as those granted to him by Valor. While healing his own wounds took no effort, channeling that ability to heal the wounds of others had never been easy. Hannah had tried to teach him to focus his ability to become a more effective healer, but it seemed that her gifts in that area were always more pronounced. Taking a moment to focus, Gregor's hard strong hands began to glow with a yellow aura, before he placed them without a word on Leonora's shoulder. Unlike the healers at the Temple of the Creator, Gregor could not simply take pain away. It was not that easy. Gregor did not have the power to heal the wounds of others, and that was something he could never make Hannah understand. Gregor could only heal his own wounds, but in order to help others, Gregor had to transfer the pain from the victim to himself. In his mind, Gregor could see the many pains throughout the body of the Jade Knight, and he slowly began to pull the pain from her body into his. After a low, deep breath, the stinging pain in his side would begin, and though he tried his best to suppress the pain, it would not relent, and his face contorted. The wince on his face went without notice to anyone in the room. By the time the page returned from the Audience Chamber, Gregor had finished his ministrations and though pain racked his body, he tried his best to retain his calm and placid façade.

"The Emperor will now hear from the Jade Knight of the Flashing Blade, Leonora Wastri of the Kingdom of Soul, Oradrim."

Together Leonora and Gregor ascended the long flight of stairs to the Audience Chamber, an uneasiness filling both of them. With the news that both Leonora and Gregor possessed about the machinations of the Dark Gods, the Emperor would most likely be enraged all the more, and Gregor could not see the conversation ending with anything less than a declaration of war against the Dark Continent of Mythryn. However, there was something darker in Leonora's eyes. There was a doubt that Gregor had never seen before, one that bespoke death on a grand scale. That look scared Gregor more than anything he had ever seen in his life.

When Gregor entered the Imperial Audience Chamber with Leonora by his side, he was shocked at the starkness of the room. All of the massive tapestries that had once covered the walls had been replaced by the mounted heads of dragons that had been felled in the defense of Cadaria. Each had a small placard beneath them that noted the name of the person responsible for the death of the creature, the creature's name, where it was killed, and when. Most did not have names, but some of the larger heads did. As Gregor took a sideways glance, he saw that most of them bore the name Jillian Corven, Lady of Cadaria. A good number of the others had the name Devlin Rannoch or Bernhardt Yeoman. These trophies made it appear that the war against the dragons was going well, but Gregor knew better. The war was a disaster, as one-sided as it could have possibly been. Kaitain was deluding himself if he thought these trophies meant otherwise.

The dais that stretched before the two members of the Flashing Blade had changed a bit since their last audience. Now two thrones stood on the dais, the Emperor's obviously larger than the one made for the Empress-to-be. On a lower level of the dais, a smaller still throne sat, reserved for the Celestial Princess. Each member of the royal family were seated as the two knights approached. Marlae looked bored, a book in hand. Her personal guard stood behind her, his eyes constantly scanning the room, a tray in his hands holding both food and drink for the Princess. Dominique Arais looked extremely out of place, and Kaitain Lorien looked more like an impetuous boy than an Emperor, foregoing the royal robes of his position and wearing only a loose fitting shirt and riding pants and boots. Beside the throne stood the Imperial Sorceress Irene Drage, looking every bit her position.

The two knights approached the dais slowly and bowed low.

"Gregor Quicksilver and Leonora Wastri, two of the finest members of the Knights of the Flashing Blade," the Emperor said slowly. "I trust by your presence here you have reports on the missions I sent you upon."

Leonora rose and took a step forward.

"My Emperor," she said proudly, "I have returned from the Academy of Arcane Arts in Jelan, and I bring with me chilling news."

Kaitain waved his hand dismissively.

"In due time, Jade Knight," he said, his eyes locked on Gregor, "I want to hear about Gregor Quicksilver's journey to the Dark Continent of Mythryn."

Many of the guards in the room were obviously taken aback by the news of Gregor's trip to Mythryn. There were not many who had ever returned from that place alive. Marlae too seemed to be intrigued by the news, enough to hand her book over her shoulder to her guard.

"My Emperor," Gregor said bowing again, "as you ordered, I made my way to the Dark Continent of Mythryn and engaged many of the troops there. Many hundreds found their deaths at my hands, and I was taken to the Citadel of Darkness where I met with the Queen of Mythryn, Sadrina Annis and her daughter Darrien. I know that my mission was to find and defeat a member of the Dark Gods, however, after my confrontation with Darrien Annis, a half-goddess herself, I think that perhaps I would not have returned if I had attempted to carry out my orders."

Kaitain's cheeks filled with crimson. Anger was beginning to rise within the man.

"Explain," Irene Drage said after a moment.

"Even after dispatching hundreds of the dark guard, my confrontation with Darrien Annis could not have been more one-sided. She easily disarmed me, and could have destroyed me with a thought. The power at her disposal was amazing, and she was the child of a Dark God and a mortal. Even at my best, with surprise as my ally, it is doubtful that I would have been able to succeed in defeating her, let alone a Dark God. However, I believe that my meeting with Sadrina Annis could have been fruit enough from my journey."

Kaitain was furious, but choked back enough of his anger.

"I will listen to this a little longer, Gregor," he said coldly.

"The Dark Gods of Mythryn and their servants do not desire war, and deny any involvement with the Crawling Plague or the Wasting Disease. You know me, my Emperor, and I do not believe there is any duplicity within them. I truly believe that they wish to be left in peace."

Leonora took that moment to speak up.

"I agree with Gregor, my Emperor. On your orders I traveled to the Academy of Arcane Arts in Jelan in an attempt to uncover whether or not there was a plot by a dark sorcerer or sorceress to assassinate the Emperor. What I found there was a member of the Dark Gods, a woman named Serrina Mistic. She had come to deliver a message, a message largely of peace. However, there was a warning. She said that if another incursion was made upon Mythryn by any force of Cadaria, the Dark Gods would have no choice but to level Cadaria. I tried my best to defeat this woman, but much as Gregor described, my abilities were no match for hers. I was but a child that she chose to toy with for a while. My injuries are proof alone of my complete and utter defeat."

It was then that the restraint in Kaitain snapped. He sprung from his throne and pulled the Imperial Sword from the low table and moved down the dais quickly. His aim was clear and he intended to strike at Leonora.

"Are you telling me that you were defeated by a member of the Dark Gods in the Academy of Arcane Arts in Jelan? That she was there upon your arrival, and perhaps she had corrupted the whole of the Academy."

Leonora bowed her head.

"I do not know of her level of involvement with the Academy, my Emperor, but from my dealings with the Master's Council in the few hours after my confrontation with the Dark God, my impression is that there was no corruption. The Dark God was there to declare amnesty to the Academy in order to prevent them from becoming involved in a conflict with Mythryn."

Kaitain smiled.

"They are afraid of the Academy."

Kaitain turned back to Irene.

"They are afraid of what the Academy could do to them, Irene. Ha ha ha...... Perhaps it is time to mobilize our troops and the members of the

Academy into an all-out strike against Mythryn. We could level them in a single blow…"

Gregor was shocked.

"My Emperor," Leonora said quickly, "even if there is concern about the amount of power possessed by the Academy, I doubt seriously that they pose a threat to the Dark Gods. If one of their youngest and weakest members could have killed me with a thought, and one of their children could have destroyed Gregor, the strongest of our order, what hope do the children of the Academy have?"

Kaitain rounded on Leonora.

"How dare you! Just because your failure has stained your honor does not mean that you can impugn the rest of the Imperial Legions with your traitorous speech."

"I did not…" Leonora started.

"Silence!"

The room fell silent at Kaitain's words, and he stood before Leonora, his sword in hand and his eyes filled with fury. Gregor could feel the restraint in the man close to snapping.

"Leonora Wastri, your failure and shame are more than enough for me to strip you of your position as a member of the Knights of the Flashing Blade, but the words that you have spoken here today do more than that. You are a traitor to the Throne, and your failure to protect the Throne and the Emperor from all threats, and your inability to find the level of corruption in the Academy of Arcane Arts of Jelan shows a dereliction of duty and lack of respect for the Emperor. This slight will not go unpunished, Leonora Wastri. I hereby strip you of all title and claim to the position of Jade Knight of the Flashing Blade, and I will execute you here and now for your crimes."

Kaitain held his sword high, and for a moment Gregor was about to pull Valor from its sheath. He was not sure what he would do, but he could not let this happen. However, it was the soft voice of Dominique Arais, and not Valor that stayed Kaitain's hand.

"Husband, a word if I may?"

Dominique's voice was a calming wind that passed through the whole room. It was as though all of the nerves and rages were silenced when she spoke, and Kaitain took a deep breath and turned back to the beautiful young woman for a moment.

"What does the Empress-to-be request?"

Dominique smoothed her dress as she stood and took two steps down the dais toward Kaitain, her eyes never leaving Leonora.

"While I agree that Leonora has failed in her task and that she should be made to suffer for her crimes, perhaps now is not the time to end her life. Let there be a public proclamation of her failures and let her punishment be viewed on the night before our wedding. It will signal to the people of Cadaria that no such failure will be tolerated and that the Cadarian Empire will prevail over all enemies. If you were to kill her now, all the people would hear is that she was defeated by a member of the Dark Gods, and you killed her for it. It would strike more fear and breed more doubt. If you wait, and control the facts that are released, you could win more support and have thousands more ready to take the fight to Mythryn."

Gregor tried hard to suppress a reaction to the words. Dominique had deftly tamed the beast inside of Kaitain without seeming weak at the same time. Though she was a common woman, Gregor could see that she was going to be a force to reckon with in the Imperial Court. Perhaps she would be powerful enough to combat the growing influence of the Ethereal Sorceress. As Gregor looked over to Irene, he thought he saw a look of annoyance for a moment, but if faded quickly.

After a moment, Kaitain smiled.

"My wife, you are as wise as you are beautiful. We will indeed make an example of this miserable failure."

CHAPTER 50

Kaitain returned to Leonora, and uncaringly pulled Wisdom from her clutches.

"Leonora Wastri, you will be confined to the Imperial Dungeons until the evening before the Imperial Wedding three weeks from this date. That night you will be executed as a traitor to the Throne, and you will confess your sins to the public so they know the full and complete failure that you have become. Upon your death I shall elevate another to the position of Jade Knight, and that person will lead the members of the Academy of Arcane Arts in the war against Mythryn."

Kaitain turned as two guards took hold of Leonora's arms and began to lead her toward the dungeons. Gregor and Leonora locked eyes for a moment before she disappeared from view. Gregor could not let this stand.

"My Emperor," Irene said after a moment. "Should not Gregor Quicksilver meet the same fate as Leonora Wastri for his failure?"

Gregor felt the rage begin to rise inside him. The woman obviously saw him as a threat and was going to use this as an opening to exploit the Emperor's anger. Kaitain turned and looked at Gregor for a moment before smiling.

"No, Irene," he said finally. "Gregor has brought me a great deal of information about the Citadel of Darkness and how to attack it successfully. Gregor, you will have to redeem yourself in my eyes or you will share the same fate as your former cohort. You will detail for me everything you saw in your journey to Mythryn, and you will create for me a plan of attack. If we fail in our goal, the failure will be on your head, and that head will be the price for failure. And just to ensure your head is clear, you will spend the next few weeks in the dungeons….to prevent you from being distracted."

Gregor tried not to scowl, but as he was being led toward the dungeons, he was sure he failed.

* * * * * * * * * * * * * *

Marlae Lorien walked toward her chambers, fuming. Never had she seen her father more completely manipulated in all her life. First it had been Irene, now this new bitch Dominique was planting her own flag. Before long she wouldn't have any influence over her father. That was unacceptable. Walking slowly down the corridor, Marlae caught sight of a woman out of the corner of her eye. She was pretty, for a commoner, her fire red hair dancing in the torchlight. Marlae had seen her many times before, always in the company of Geoffry Aramour. That meant she was an assassin. Perhaps there was another way to create influence and control.

"Gabriel?"

Gabriel Shadowfall moved closer to the Celestial Princess.

"Yes, Princess?"

Marlae pointed in the direction where the woman had been.

"Find me that red-haired woman, and bring her to me."

****

Kaitain sat in his private chambers in the middle of the night. As usual he couldn't sleep. The dark nightmares continued to plague his mind, and the voices were beginning to get worse. But it mattered little. His course was clear and the spells and potions that Irene had given him were doing their job. He could continue indefinitely if necessary. On his cluttered desk were writings, some from his own hand, and some from the hand of the madman Arturious Demascious. All of the writings had the same subject though, the legend of the Dragon's Tear. Kaitain had done nothing but research about it since he had learned of its existence. A knock at the door broke his concentration.

"Enter."

Kaitain knew the scent of Irene Drage before she fully entered the room. Her beauty and her scent were intoxicating, and though his mind was cluttered, being near her always seemed to bring clarity.

"How fares my Emperor this evening?"

Kaitain ignored the question.

"Send orders to Bernhardt Yeoman. He is to break off his engagement with the dragons and lead a force to Jelan. I will have the cooperation of the Academy of Arcane Arts even if I must secure it by force."

Irene bowed and then moved toward the small bed in the corner. Kaitain looked over to Irene and frowned.

"Now, Irene."

Irene smiled and sat on the edge of the bed.

"Perhaps my Emperor could use a bit of a distraction for his mind so that he can sleep?"

Kaitain stood and flung some papers that he was reading onto the table. He walked to the door of his chambers and opened it slightly.

"Carry out my instructions, Irene. I will find all the distraction I need in the bed of my Empress this evening."

Irene smiled and gently left the room. However, the rage and confusion that built inside her with every step could never be fully measured.

Chapter LI

Time Heals All

Year Two of the Just Emperor Kaitain "Dragonsbane" Lorien, Creator's Calendar Year 1869

The battle was going poorly to say the least. All around Evan people were dying, and dying by the dozens. For months the agents of the Creator had been on the trail of the creature that had been destroying whole worlds and leaving a trail of bodies in its wake. The death tally was in the millions and the amount of damage caused boggled the imagination. So much death, and regardless of what the agents of the Creator tried, it seemed that none of it could be prevented. For a time it seemed that the trail had gone cold, but in the unrelenting darkness a clue had been found, a clue that led them closer to their goal. At last they had found it, floating among the stars between worlds. They thought they had taken the beast by surprise, but they had been wrong. Dead wrong. The first three envoys of the Creator had been snuffed out before they could get close. The life had been sucked from them, their bodies left to float in the void of space for eternity. It had taken only a wave of a hand and the flash of eyes, and three agents of the Creator were gone. That kind of power should not have been possible. There should have been nothing that could have stood up to the combined might of the task force that had been dispatched. But even with the superior numbers, the battle looked to be doomed to failure. When more agents arrived, they tried to take the creature by force, but they too failed. The life had been crushed out of them by the madman's already bloody hands. Evan and his wife Meredith held back the next group of envoys, waiting for the opportunity to strike.

"You have to flank him, Evan," Meredith called over the cackling laughter of the madman. "I'll take my group in while you circle around him. We take him from both sides and he can't get us all."

The plan sounded good at the time. Meredith and her group rushed in while Evan and his group came at the creature from a rear angle. Evan tried his best to retain his focus as the screams of pain and torment rose around him. The smell of death filled his nostrils even in the vacuum of space. Finally Evan got close enough to take hold of the madman. With two other envoys holding his arms, the murderous rampage was finally at an end. His power had been robbed through the use of a tool provided by the Creator. He would be led away to his prison where he would spend the rest of eternity to toil in his madness. When Evan turned to look for Meredith, he saw her body floating in the void, a gaping wound in her chest. The madman had struck her down.

"Dorovar….what have you done?"

****

Evan Sinn woke with a start. He had been sleeping, and as usual the nightmares had crept into his mind. They had been the same for millennia, constantly relived the death of his wife, and each time, his heart was left raw and burning. There was no peace or healing awaiting with time or with sleep, only pain, and only heartbreak. Suddenly Evan felt a pull in the corner of his mind, a pull that could only mean the approach of someone with power. He could feel the portal forming in the back of his mind, and in a matter of seconds he turned as it winked into existence. However, he was not prepared for the two people that emerged.

For a moment Evan felt as though he had woken from one dream into another. Long ago he had been a simple man who desired nothing more than to serve his lord and do his work. It was good work for a time, but like so many things in life, it became corrupted by lies and half-truths. It was then that he was granted another chance, a chance to make things right. A legendary warrior had passed his mantle to Evan, and through the adoption of those powers, Evan found his way to the service of the Creator. And now, the man who had started the whole cycle, Aerith Seth and his wife Bryn stood before Evan. But so much had changed since those times. So many worlds had fallen, so many lives destroyed.

"If I'm dreaming, I don't think I want to wake up from this one for a while," Evan said finally.

Aerith smiled and approached his old friend and the two men embraced for a quick moment before Aerith pulled back with his hands on Evan's shoulders. Bryn remained a respectful distance from the two men, hands on her hips and a blank expression on her face.

"It's not a dream my friend, I assure you. Bryn and I thought a great deal before we came to see you. I knew it wouldn't be easy for either of us."

The warm smile on Evan's face suddenly faded, and the cold eyes returned. It was as though Evan became a different person in that moment.

"You shouldn't involve yourself in matters that no longer concern you, Aerith. You could find yourself in a very unfortunate position."

Aerith frowned.

"Doesn't concern us," Bryn piped up approaching the two men. "There is nothing that affects this world that doesn't concern us. We live here too, remember?"

Evan turned and scowled at Bryn.

"The two of you are still alive by the grace of the Creator, and though your usefulness and worth were well proven on Onea during those times and during that war, it has been a long time since those enemies were put to their graves. We did what we could to combat that threat, and we were there when it all ended. Though we couldn't save our world, we saved what pieces we could."

"And you did a fine job of it, Evan," Aerith said stepping toward his old friend, "but that was then, and this is now. I'm here to talk about now, not relive the old days."

Evan turned his back to Aerith.

"You have no standing to talk to me," Evan said coldly.

Bryn felt her blood boil. If she still retained her powers, she would have lashed out at Evan. Even in her days as a member of the phasia she would not have had enough power to strike him down, but never would she allow herself to be talked down to. The insult was almost too much for her to bear. Looking at her feet, she found a small stone. With a single deft motion, she picked it up from the ground and flung it at the back of Evan's head. Inches from him, the stone exploded, the dust from the rock filling the space between Evan and Aerith for a moment. Evan shook his head slowly and then began to walk away.

"Take her home, Aerith, before she starts to make me mad."

Aerith turned to look at Bryn for a moment and then turned back to Evan. This was not the man that he had known all those years ago. The cold and bitter anger had slipped into his heart, and whatever was left of the kind man was long since dead.

"What happened to you, Evan?"

The question was as simple and as complex as any question could be. So many years had passed, and Evan had seen so much death. Seeing that much death in a lifetime eventually puts a stain on the soul, one that can never be cleansed.

"Meredith is gone, Aerith. Now all I have is my work. And it seems that the longer I serve the Creator, the more death I see. All I am trying to do now is prevent death where I can."

Bryn stepped up again, gently resting her hand on Aerith's shoulder.

"That's why we are here, Evan. We want to help prevent deaths on this world. I know that we aren't what we once were, and we don't have the powers that once made us both feared and respected, but we do have our minds and our memories, and we know what it takes to win these wars. You are doing what you must, we understand that, but perhaps we can help you in ways you have not considered."

Evan took a deep breath and finally turned to face his old friends.

"I'm listening."

Aerith took a deep breath.

"The Dark Gods, our old friends, are leaning toward an invasion of the Cadarian Empire. You know what will happen if they follow this course of action. The whole of Cadaria will be wiped out."

Evan nodded slowly.

"It was only a matter of time before this occurred, and there is no course of action that will prevent it. The Council of the Dark Gods will not listen to anyone."

Aerith shook his head.

"That's why we're here. Aryx came to us and asked for our help. Their leader will listen to reason, but only from the one person that he still trusts. We came to convince you to talk to him. Tell him what is going on and hold him from this course of action a little longer."

Evan sighed. There was so much going on, and so much that Aerith and Bryn didn't know…couldn't know.

"I'm afraid that is impossible, my friends. There are plans in motion that prevent me from involving myself in the politics of the Dark Gods. They were cast from the Heavens by the Creator, and I am still an agent of the Creator. Besides, there are other plans in motion that may solve the problem for us."

There was a cold shiver that ran through Aerith.

"What are you talking about?"

Evan's cold and heartless voice rang out.

"This world is going to be ripped apart, and the Creator wants to save those that he can, and so I was sent to give the dragons of Espre the ability to leave this world before the threat claimed them. But, in order to conclude the agreement that binds them here, they must murder the leader of the Dark Gods. I have given them the power to do so."

Aerith couldn't believe his ears.

"He's your friend, Evan. How could you do that?"

Evan turned again. This conversation was at an end.

"I am doing my duty to the Creator."

Evan heard the sound of steel being drawn. Closing his eyes, Evan chuckled to himself until he began to feel a familiar twinge of power coming from behind him. It was an old power, close to that of the Creator, but impure. When he spun around, Evan saw Aerith clutching the Dragon Sword tightly in his hands, his body in a classic dueling position, and Aerith looked ready for a fight.

"It's been a long time since this sword was drawn in anger, Evan, and I don't do it lightly. Several great men wielded this sword before it found its way to me, and I owe it to their memory, to their legacy, to not let you continue on this course you have taken. I will not let a good man die just because the Creator wants to save a few overgrown lizards."

Evan frowned and let the pure golden sword, a gift from Aerith all those years ago, appear in his hand.

"You don't understand, Aerith. I don't have a choice. Dorovar is about to be freed from his prison, and I have to be here to stop him. I still owe him for Meredith. I am going to follow my orders, free the dragons, and then wait for Dorovar to emerge. Then I will settle my score, no matter the cost."

"Are you even listening to yourself," Bryn shouted. "Meredith is dead, and that was a horrible tragedy, but are you really talking about trading the lives of everyone on this world, including your friends for a chance at revenge."

Evan's scowl deepened. A moment later, a bolt of energy emerged from Evan's eyes and sped toward Bryn. Taking a quick step to his left, Aerith intercepted the bolt with the blade of the Dragon Sword. For a moment Aerith could feel the sting of the energy in his palms, but after a few seconds the energy dissipated.

"Go home," Evan said coldly. "Don't make me kill you."

Much to Evan's surprise, Aerith smiled. It was more of a smirk than a smile, but its presence on Aerith's face unnerved Evan.

"Been dead once already," Aerith said rounding on his opponent, "wasn't very impressed with it, so I don't think I'm up for an encore."

The two men circled for a long few moments, their eyes never leaving one another. Suddenly Evan struck, the pure golden sword slashing downward in a hard attack. Aerith to his credit brought his sword up to block, and was sent sprawling to the ground. The force of Evan's strike was unbelievable.

"You can't beat me, Aerith," Evan said finally. "You gave away all your powers, and I have added the powers of an envoy of the Creator. I could snuff the life out of you without so much as a thought, but in deference to our friendship, I have humored you thus far. But, I do not suffer fools lightly. Keep up this charade of a fight, Aerith, and I will have no choice but to destroy you."

Aerith picked himself up of the ground and lightly dusted the soil from his pants.

"You know, I pride myself on my appearance, and you have gone and ruined another good pair of pants. I'll have you know, living on that island, there are very few chances to replenish my wardrobe."

Evan tried to suppress a growl. He knew Aerith's tactics, almost better than Aerith knew himself.

"I know all your tricks old man, you taught me yourself. Now take Bryn and go. Never let me see you again, or you may not live to regret it."

Aerith cocked his head and stuck the tip of the Dragon Sword into the ground. The smile grew quickly on his face.

"So, you think I taught you all of my tricks huh? How about this one?"

* * * * * * * * * * * * *

Deep in the Citadel of the Dark Gods in a guarded room, lay the sleeping form of a Dark God. Unlike the rest of the Dark Gods, this one had been affected by the fall in a way that no one could explain. He lay slumbering, unresponsive to the world around him, lost in an oblivion that seemed to have no cause and no resolution. Every day, he was tended to constantly by his wife and children. As the Council had broken for the day, Lissa sat beside the bed of her husband and gently stroked his hair as she ran small chips of ice across his lips. This was his only form of nourishment, with the exception of clear broth on rare occasions. Still his condition plagued her, and tears began to well in her eyes as she looked down at him. For two millennia she had been without him, without his touch, without his kind heart.

"How are you holding up?"

Lissa looked up at the sound of her father's voice. Aryx had been gone for some time to enlist the help of some old friends in an effort to avert a war, and his absence had not gone without notice. The whole of the Council was in an uproar, and the recess had been called to let some of the anger and frustration abate before the vote that would determine the next course of action was taken.

"It's hard, father," Lissa said finally. "I just wish we could do something more than just be here."

Aryx nodded and looked around the sparse chamber.

"Where are the girls?"

Lissa sighed and then smiled.

"They are out in the garden tending to the flowers. They try to keep a bright bouquet beside their father's bed at all times. They are so sweet, they think it makes him feel better."

Aryx nodded.

"And I'm sure it does. Is there anything I can do?"

Lissa shook her head.

"Unless you can make Wolf wake up, I'm not sure there is anything that anyone can do right now."

Off in the distance there was an explosion. Lightning seemed to fill the sky and it fury course through the clouds and even the protective haze that covered Mythryn. As Lissa and Aryx moved to the window to try to figure out what was going on, the sleeping form lay unobserved; his hand beginning to move slightly.

* * * * * * * * * * * * *

Evan stood watching as the Dragon Sword began to glow slightly. With his enhanced vision, Evan could see his mentor Aerith channeling all the power that remained in his body into the blade of the sword.

"What are you doing, Aerith? You can't possibly believe that you have enough power left to do any sort of damage to me. Compared to what I can draw upon that little trickle you have there is like comparing a candle to the sun."

Aerith continued to smile though the signs of the physical exertion were beginning to show on his face.

"You never did pay attention, did you, Evan? See you have to learn from everywhere you can, and this is a little trick I picked up from a former wielder of this sword. You might remember him. Of course, in his last few days he went by a different name. He called himself Lord Phoenix for a while."

A sudden knowing look flashed across Evan's face, and he tried to strike out at Aerith, but it was too late. There was a flash from the Dragon Sword and the two men were engulfed in the flash. Evan stood transfixed, the golden sword slipping from his hand. Lightning flashed all around, and the ground below their feet began to rumble.

"What I have given," Aerith said over the din, "I now take back."

Pain racked both Aerith and Evan's body the next moment as the light that engulfed them turned to a light shade of red. Aerith's mind was on fire and he felt as though his body was going to explode. Only holding onto the hilt of the Dragon Sword kept him from losing consciousness. Familiar sensations began to flood his body as lightning, ice, fire, and smoke enveloped both of the men. Out of the corner of his eye, Aerith could see Bryn inching closer to the field. They had discussed this eventuality long ago, and now it seemed to have come to pass. They both knew the risk, they both knew that it could mean their death, but after Meredith's death, every contingency had to be explored. Bryn leapt into the field as it began to change color from red to green, and every cell of their bodies began to be modified by the power infusing them. The transition felt like death, and the whole world shook at the effort. As the colors changed again from green to blue, the burning sensations began to cool and the mind-shattering pain began to ebb. Aerith began to feel again the power that shook the heavens in his youth, he felt the power that had been his birthright begin to return. As the lightning and fire began to creep across his skin, Aerith felt the blissful pain return, intense and jarring, but at the same time familiar and soothing. His heart beat fast in his chest, so hard that it threatened to burst out of his ribcage. At times it felt like he had to drag the breaths in and out of his lungs, but as the pain finally came to an end, Aerith's smile returned. He was whole again.

Bryn too began to feel different. The long cold coals of power within her were stoked again, and as she stood beside Aerith, she snapped her fingers and watched the spark of fire appear. She was whole again, the thread of power that had been blessed to her as a member of the phasia had been reignited, and she was the Mistress of Fire once more, the Lady Fox. Evan slumped to the ground and breathed hard. He felt as though he had been turned inside out, and his mind and insides were on fire and freezing all at the same time. His thoughts raced as he tried to make sense of what had just happened. He had been violated in the most primal of ways, tricked by his former friend.

"What have you done?"

Aerith moved to Evan's side and reclaimed the sword that had been a gift to him. Justice had returned to its owner, and it felt good to have the smooth hilt back in his hand.

"You left me no choice, Evan," Aerith said finally, a new power filling his voice. "I had to take back the powers that I gave you once upon a time, and I had no choice but to take up the position as *Chosen One* once more. There are no prophecies to bind me, and no bloodlines to satisfy in some grand scheme. You forgot the lessons that I taught you all those years ago, Evan. There are no absolutes. Though Dorovar may be evil and you may think you represent good, as soon as you descend into the depths of vengeance you have become that which you fight against. You must exist in the gray Evan, you must be the champion of balance. By choosing to serve the interests of the Creator and sentence your friends and your kind to the kind of death you have, you left me no choice."

Aerith and Bryn turned to leave, but both felt an incredible power explode into existence behind them. When Aerith turned, he saw Evan begin to levitate into the air, his body on fire with a white flame that licked every feature. This was the pure unadulterated power of the Creator, and Evan's anger had ignited it. Within a matter of seconds, a perfect blade of crystal appeared in Evan's hand, and as his feet found the ground once more, Evan locked his gaze on Aerith. All of the vestiges of the man were gone. Where once human eyes had looked upon the world, Evan's eyes had been replaced with white fire. Evan had become a tool of the Creator, his envoy and his Voice. No longer human, and no longer in control of his actions.

"Aerith Seth," the powerful and tortured voice spoke, "you have committed an unthinkable sin against the chosen vessel of the Creator's Might. For that you must pay the ultimate price in this life and all others. Your end shall be here, and shall be at my hands."

Aerith tightened the grip on both his blades and took a half step toward the vessel of the divine.

"I've killed gods before. Don't think you'll be much different."

Aerith felt Bryn side up beside him, silver dagger in hand.

"This isn't your fight, Bryn," Aerith said after a moment. "If we both fall here, there will be nothing that will stop the Creator's agenda for the Dark Gods. You have to get to Pike and warn him about the assassination attempt. Go. I'll hold here as long as I can."

Bryn wanted to protest, but she knew her husband was right. He had given up so much to give them a chance for success, more than he ever let on. Readopting his powers would have a price, one that could be far more terrible than anything they could ever imagine. With a thought the swirling blue portal appeared and Bryn stepped through, a long last look at her husband and the man she loved without question. Though her heart no longer beat, she still felt the love there, and it seemed to rage all the stronger.

With Bryn safely out of the battlefield, Aerith felt his smile grow at the corners of his mouth. It had been a long time since he had been in the middle of a good fight, and this had the possibility of being the fight of his life. Easing back into a defensive stance, Aerith let the golden blade of Justice sit poised over his head, ready to strike while the blade of the Dragon Sword lay in wait beside him, prepared to parry any strike that came his way. The Voice of the Creator took one long step forward, the bright crystalline blade sheathed in white hot power and ready for the kill. There was no subtly in its movements. It was a tool, a tool that would destroy all who dared to stand in the way of the Creator. The Voice pointed the tip of the crystalline blade at Aerith's heart and spoke in an eerie almost mechanical voice.

"Submit," the Voice said, "and you shall not suffer."

Aerith smiled.

"Let's have some fun."

Extended Family

Year Two of the Just Emperor Kaitain "Dragonsbane" Lorien, Creator's Calendar Year 1869

Preparations for the royal wedding were in full swing, and only two days remained until the blessed event. There had been a great deal of commotion after the imprisoning of two of the members of the Knights of the Flashing Blade, and a great deal of petitioners begging for clemency for Leonora Wastri. However, all of these pleas fell on deaf ears, and the Emperor had no intention of allowing the treasonous acts of one of his subordinates to go unpunished. The execution would continue as planned, and Kaitain did not feel anything other than elation that his plan was proceeding so smoothly. As he sat in his private audience chamber, Kaitain lightly read over a series of dispatches from Geoffry detailing the successes that his new charges had created. Kaitain was more than pleased with the abilities of his new assassins, and it would only be a matter of time before they would be utilized for more important endeavors than sewing unrest in the kingdoms. They would help him consolidate control over the Empire piece by piece. The unilateral destruction of the regional governments would follow in the coming years, and within five years' time, the whole of Cadaria would be in Kaitain's grasp, utterly at his mercy. The thoughts brought a smile to his face, but a knock at the door broke him from his reverie.

A page entered the room sheepishly and waited with his head bowed to be acknowledged by the Emperor.

"What is it?"

Kaitain's tone was dismissive and filled with a bit of frustration and annoyance at being interrupted from his pleasurable thoughts. However, that aggravation would deepen with the page's next words.

"My Emperor, Lord Feyd and Princess Felicia wish the honor of an audience with the Just Emperor of Cadaria. Does my Emperor wish to allow such an audience?"

Kaitain wordlessly scratched his chin, a frown beginning to tug at the corners of his mouth. He detested his meddlesome younger brother and had it not been for the open invitation to the wedding, Kaitain would have preferred if he never set eyes on Feyd again. It was only seven minutes, seven impossibly short minutes that had put Kaitain on the throne over his younger brother. Of course, Feyd would never let any of his ambition show, but he never had to. Kaitain knew full well that if anything were to ever happen to Marlae, it would be Feyd who would stand next in line to ascend to the throne, and the girl Felicia would follow in his footsteps.

"Very well," Kaitain said with a sigh.

The page disappeared the next moment, and Kaitain waited in silence for his brother to appear. Each second that passed was an agony, and unconsciously Kaitain shifted in his seat. Several moments later, three people entered the private audience chamber.

Kaitain's eyes first fell to the smiling countenance of his younger brother. For twins, Kaitain and Feyd could not have been less alike. Kaitain's hair was dark brown almost black like his father's while Feyd's was lighter, almost auburn like their mother. Kaitain's eyes and features were cold and hard, while Feyd retained an almost boyish glow. Unless a person knew what to look for, they never would have guessed that the two men were brothers. As they grew together, the two were never close. Kaitain preferred the company of the soldiers and the people of the court, while Feyd always seemed to find distraction in art and poetry like their mother. What sickened Kaitain the most was the fact that Feyd could have been so much more if he would have applied himself. He showed such a great aptitude for the blade and could have been the general of the Imperial Legion, but he was content with being a bureaucrat and ambassador to the province of Lordhill. Granted it was a lucrative and visible position in the Imperial Court, but it was nothing compared to what Kaitain could have offered had Feyd decided to be more like his more powerful brother.

Felicia Lorien on the other hand was more the daughter that Kaitain always wanted. Marlae was cruel and manipulative which were important traits for one that would eventually become the Empress of Cadaria, however Felicia was more direct and forceful. She was not one that would ever use the manipulations of the court to prove her point, she respected force and understood its applications. Against the advice of her father, Felicia had accepted a post with the Imperial Legions as a magistrate of Aldere. She spent most of every year traveling the countryside of Aldere adjudicating disputes and meting out the Emperor's law. From all indications she was quite adept at her duty, and before too long could ascend to a much higher station. It would only take a word from Kaitain for it to happen much quicker, and perhaps he would, for no other reason than to annoy her over-protective father. Like her father, Felicia had auburn hair and bright eyes, and was the spitting image of her mother, a woman of great beauty that had died during childbirth. Felicia's mother had been Feyd's childhood sweetheart, a girl that in all respects Kaitain should have had. The thought of it still turned in the pit of Kaitain's stomach, the old grudge coming back to the surface.

Standing two steps behind Felicia was her appointed personal bodyguard, a man by the name of Galen White. Galen was an accomplished soldier in the Imperial Legion and had been handpicked for the detachment that would be responsible for the protection of the Imperial Family. While Feyd had always bristled at the thought of constant protection and scrutiny, he demanded it for his daughter. Perhaps it was this close proximity to warriors that had caused Felicia's choice of vocation, no one would ever be truly sure, but as was his station, Galen ensured that no one would ever harm the Princess.

"It's good to see you, brother," Feyd said, purposefully ignoring Kaitain's title in an effort to aggravate him, "and congratulations on your engagement and forthcoming wedding."

Kaitain forced a smile.

"Thank you for coming, Feyd, I wasn't sure you were going to be able to make it with the recent threats of violence against Lordhill."

Feyd's smile widened.

"Not to worry, brother, Connor and I have everything under control. There will be no interruption in the shipments, and no loss of time in the war effort. We can't have the Imperial Legions running out of arms and armor, can we?"

His nerves beginning to grate, Kaitain tried hard to suppress a frown. Feyd certainly had the fangs bared this day. It was no secret that production from Lordhill was vital to the war against the dragons and the upcoming war with Mythryn. If production stopped or slowed, it could mean utter defeat. Feyd held production in the palm of his hand by Imperial Decree, a decree set down by their father, a decree that Kaitain could not rescind. Felicia, sensing the tension in the room, bowed slightly and smiled.

"You look well, my Emperor, and I am sure that with a beautiful woman like Dominique at your side, your just rule will continue for a long time to come."

Unlike her father, Felicia knew her place. Her position as a magistrate demanded that she use the Emperor's title at all times when addressing him, even though as a member of the royal family she was entitled to call him by name. Kaitain smiled despite himself and rose from his chair.

"Have you met Dominique yet, Felicia?"

Feyd interjected.

"We were hoping to pay our respects, but it seems that the Empress-to-be will be unavailable until the banquet tomorrow night. It seems that the

Imperial Seamstress has been having some issues with her wedding gown and the Ethereal Sorceress wants to make sure everything is perfect for your wedding."

Kaitain's teeth ground together unconsciously. Irene had been taking a heavy hand in all the preparations for the wedding, and for the most part, Kaitain was glad of it. He had little care for the finery and ceremony of an Imperial Wedding and wanted it to simply be done with. However, as Irene had said on several occasions, this was an opportunity for Kaitain to show his softer side to the people and allow them to love him for the man and not simply the position. This appearance could be invaluable in the days to come, especially as Kaitain started to consolidate his power.

"Well, I am sure that we can arrange a few minutes for you to pay your respects. In the mean time I am sure that you will want to receive your briefing on the war efforts so that you know where to send the resources in the next few shipments."

Feyd laughed.

"That is the brother I know and love. Always duty before all else. Even when it is supposed to be the happiest day of his life, the Just Emperor must deal with traitors before pledging his life to his new wife. One day you must find time for yourself brother."

Kaitain frowned, he could not suppress it this time.

"When the Empire of Cadaria stands alone and no enemy threatens its borders, then and only then shall I have time for anything other than my duty."

Silence filled the small audience chamber and the two brothers stared at one another for a long moment. It was Felicia again that brought civility back to the situation.

"With your leave, my Emperor, we shall leave you to your preparations. I would like to pay my respects to my cousin Marlae and meet my new cousin Quyhn."

The civility ended the next moment when her father spoke.

"Yes, it was a very kind thing you did, adopting Quyhn like that, brother. And what a shame it was that her father passed in such an ugly manner. I'm thankful that there was someone here who seemed to have her best interests at heart."

There was venom in Feyd's voice and to Kaitain the implication was clear. Feyd obviously suspected that the death of Alistair Ravenheart was not an accident as advertised, and that it had been Kaitain who had a hand in his demise. For a moment Kaitain remembered that the man who stood before him was not just a simple courtier in his service. Feyd was a very intelligent man, and because the two grew up together and were twins, they thought a lot alike. It was always Feyd who saw through Kaitain's plots and schemes when they were children, and if anyone would be able to foil his plans now, it would be Feyd. Perhaps an accident would have to befall his brother on his way back to Lordhill. One of Geoffry's new assassins would be perfect for the assignment. Despite himself, Kaitain smiled. Yes, this would work out perfectly. With his brother out of the way, the proclamation would be null and void, and Kaitain would be able to exercise complete and direct control over the production of Lordhill. It was too perfect an opportunity to let slip past.

"Feyd," Kaitain said finally, "sometimes you are presented with opportunities that your heart and soul will not let you ignore. It is just as mother taught us all those years ago. Our paths are so full of obstacles and ambiguous choices. When one presents itself that is so clear and so right, you must simply thank the Creator for the gift and not be afraid to act."

Feyd nodded slowly and then bowed to his brother.

"By your word, my Emperor. May we be allowed to take our leave?"

"By all means…"

The three bowed again to the Emperor and were shown quickly from the audience chamber by the page that stood near the door. Once the three had left, the page returned.

"Is there anything else that you require, my Emperor?"

Kaitain returned to his chair and after a few moments of contemplation, turned to face the page and smiled.

"Yes, there is. Find Geoffry Aramour and have him brought here. I have a special song I want performed."

* * * * * * * * * * * * *

Marlae Lorien lay in her bed comfortably, the satin sheets and comforter feeling good against her naked skin. Though her skin was still covered with sweat, she felt wonderful. Quietly, she stretched her arms, letting her back arch off the soft mattress, her toes curling reflexively. Beside her the form stirred, and as Marlae looked over, she reached out and smoothed the mass of red hair back from the pretty woman's face. Rhain Feirbran had been a more than pleasant surprise, and whatever she lacked in social graces she more than made up for in other skills. There came a knock at the door and still half-asleep Marlae answered.

"Enter…"

The door opened and a young man entered, and from the look of him, he was one of the new servants hired for the wedding preparations. He gasped as soon as he entered the room, though he tried his best to hide his shock. Marlae half-sat in the bed, her naked bosom exposed, and the obvious form of the nude woman lying in bed beside her. A look of annoyance sprang to Marlae's face.

"What do you want?"

The young man stammered for a moment.

"Princess, the Emperor sent word that your presence is requested in the Imperial Dining room for a lunch in honor of the Lord Feyd Lorien and the Princess Felicia Lorien."

Marlae felt the rage grow inside her. She hated that woman, hated her more completely than anything she had ever felt in all of her life. That next moment, her voice broke the stillness in the room.

"Gabriel!"

No more than five seconds later, Gabriel Shadowfall rushed into the room, his hand on his sword and ready to combat anything that threatened the Princess. As he was conditioned to do, he ignored the presence of the woman in the Princess' bed, especially since over the past few days it had become a more common occurrence.

"Don't these people know any better? How many times have I made it clear that no one, and I mean no one is to talk about that bitch in my presence with any kind of title?"

Gabriel, despite himself smiled and looked at Marlae.

"To which 'bitch' do you refer, Princess?"

There was no comedy intended in his comment, but despite that, Rhain laughed as she sat slowly and slipped out of bed. Color immediately leapt to the young man's face, and Gabriel did his best to keep his eyes trained on those of the Princess. As Rhain approached Gabriel, Marlae spoke.

"Little man, you may go. Tell my father I shall be there in due time."

The young man bowed quickly and retreated from the room, his mind spinning. The door shut quickly behind the young man, and Rhain found her way over to Gabriel and stood as close as she could, pressing up against him and looking up into his eyes.

"I still think he is very handsome, Princess, perhaps tonight he can join us in bed. I'm sure he knows quite well how to use more than just his sword."

Marlae laughed.

"Gabriel has his uses, but I am afraid that in the bedroom of a Princess and her consort, he would be lost. Gabriel is a man of duty and not of pleasure. Isn't that right, Gabriel?"

Gabriel felt himself swallow hard as he felt the red-haired woman's hand travel down his side and across his thigh.

"Oh, I'm sure we could find good enough use for him. Besides, duty takes all forms, doesn't it?"

Closing his eyes for a moment to steady himself, Gabriel let the wave of emotion and physical sensation pass through him.

"Enough, Rhain. Even Gabriel has limits as to how much teasing he can take in one sitting. And I must admit you are quite an accomplished tease."

When Gabriel opened his eyes again, he saw the pouting expression on the naked woman's face as she turned away and moved back toward the bed.

"Ensure that our young friend doesn't say too much about what he saw here after he relays my message to the Emperor."

A different smile came to the face of the female assassin. She quickly recovered her clothes from the floor and slipped the white garment over her head before leaning in to engage in a deep and passionate kiss with the Princess. Wordlessly, Rhain moved passed Gabriel and out the door, running her hand over his stomach as she passed. With the door closed again, Marlae rose from the bed and moved toward her wardrobe, beginning to look for something to wear.

"My dear cousin the so-called Princess Felicia is here."

Marlae shuddered at the title.

"I will not tolerate anyone using that word in front of me, Gabriel. I am the only one in this entire empire that deserves the title of Princess. So, I want you to make sure that from this day forward whenever I am announced anywhere, I am to be announced as the Celestial Princess. Do you understand?"

Gabriel nodded.

"I understand completely, Princess."

Marlae turned, and caught Gabriel's eyes passing over her naked body. She could not deny that they had shared somewhat of an intimate moment while on the road back to Aldere, but Gabriel was a servant, not an equal. She would never allow herself to debase herself by having a relationship with someone like Gabriel. Rhain was different, she was a tool, a means to an end, and a plaything, nothing more. There could have been something deeper between Marlae and Gabriel, if only he wasn't so beneath her.

"Make it known now, Gabriel, and on your way out, send in those worthless cows. I have need for my bath."

Gabriel bowed again.

"As you wish, Princess."

* * * * * * * * * * * * *

Dominique Arais stood as still and as silent as she could, trying not to breathe, not that she could if she wanted to. The seamstress told her it would be a simple process and the fitting would only take a few minutes, but as she looked in the full length mirror and felt the pressure increase through her body, she wondered if she would live long enough to get married. Two women pulled at the laces of the corset, pulling it tighter and tighter around her, and just when it seemed like it was about to burst under the strain, it was held and tied. Gasping for breath, Dominique looked in the mirror, feeling half of herself. Granted the slimmer waist was flattering to her hips and her bosom, but having an hourglass figure did not mean that she had to actually look like an hourglass. With another cough, Dominique finally was allowed to move, and to her great surprise, she was able to move with little effort.

"Does that feel as uncomfortable as it looks?"

Quyhn Ravenheart sat in the near corner of the room, watching the whole process with an amused look on her face.

"Don't laugh," Dominique managed to choke out. "You're next."

The two women finally shared a laugh and when the knock came at the door, Dominique reached for the robe that hung from the side of the mirror and wrapped it around her before finally answering.

"Come in, please."

Quickly the door opened to reveal the smiling face of Chelsea Zarova. Everyone stood at the appearance of the Garnet Knight, and none were more surprised than Dominique at the woman's appearance. These two should have been enemies, however since the announcement of the wedding, Chelsea had been nothing less than a supportive friend through Dominique's many hours of need. Dominique met Chelsea in the center of the room and the two embraced for a moment.

"It's so good to see you, Chelsea. I hoped you would be able to break away from the matters in Saldarine for the wedding."

Chelsea frowned.

"There was little choice Dominique, all of the members of the Flashing Blade with few exceptions were recalled. We have to report before New Year's or we will be considered traitors to the Throne."

Dominique could not believe the words that came from Chelsea's mouth. There was so much happening in the Imperial Palace, so much that she did not know, but she resolved at that moment to make sure that nothing else escaped her notice ever again, no matter what it took. There was an unspoken question that lingered between the two women, a point of contention and pain that would never quite go away. Before Dominique could give voice to the question, Chelsea shook her head.

"There has been no word from Seraph. He just simply disappeared. I only hope that he hasn't done something rash."

Dominique sighed. Chelsea's concerns were well-founded. Seraph was a very emotional person, driven by the passions of the moment. She was sure that as soon as he got word of the impending wedding that he would make some kind of move against Kaitain. Perhaps he was biding his time, or perhaps he just needed some space to let the raw emotions cool. That moment the seamstress interjected between the two women.

"Empress, you must be ready to attend the lunch in honor of your visiting guests. They must all wait upon you, my Empress, and it is never good manners to keep guests of such stature waiting. After all, they will soon be your family."

Dominique sighed, and turned toward the open wardrobe. Hanging against the far right wall of the wardrobe was a dress that she had been eyeing for the past few hours of torture. It was wicked, decadent and completely unbefitting her station. It would be perfect. Without a word she took hold of the dress and was met with a shocked gasp from the seamstress.

"The Empress can't seriously be considering wearing that?"

Dominique smiled and held the dress up to her chest. It was dark maroon in color with darker streaks of black mixed into random patterns. It hung low at the chest and was cut high at the hip and would accentuate Dominique's long flawless legs and ample bosom. Chelsea and Quyhn both nodded their approval.

"That will look stunning on you," Chelsea said after a moment. It was amazing. This woman who Chelsea had hated so vehemently was growing to be one of her closest friends.

Dominique turned to Quyhn.

"What do you think daughter?"

Quyhn laughed at the shared joke.

"I think Marlae will hate it."

Dominique smiled.

"Perfect."

Democracy of Anarchy

Year Two of the Just Emperor Kaitain "Dragonsbane" Lorien, Creator's Calendar Year 1869

Hannah Ironheart sat in the small farmhouse at the edge of the Kingdom of Night, Galateria and waited. It had been some time since she had received the information from Devlin about the delays in their travels due to the increased security patrols. Ever since the arrest of both Leonora and Gregor, the Imperial Legions had been ordered to find the remaining members of the Knights of the Flashing Blade and have then brought to Aldere. It was a show of force by the Emperor that would require the remaining members of the group to either show their support for the Throne or be burned as traitors with Leonora. It was only a matter of time before the treachery of Devlin and Hannah was discovered, and they would have to make sure that Tess was safe long before that happened. According to Devlin's letter, as soon as the new orders for the Imperial Legion went out, Devlin used his contacts in Galateria to begin to spread the news of Hannah's death in a dragon raid. The cover would last for a little while, but would not hold up to scrutiny. Eventually Kaitain would send someone to look for Spirit, and when the great mace was not found, he would begin to question the validity of Hannah's death.

The days had passed quickly, and New Year's Day was just around the corner and in Aldere, it would mark a double celebration. It would be a new year under the rule of the Just Emperor Kaitain Lorien, and it would also mark the day of his wedding to the common woman Dominique Arais. However, the terrible truth was the day before the wedding, Hannah's friend and ally for many years would meet her death at the hands of the tyrannical ruler. Something turned in the pit of Hannah's stomach. There was no way that the rumors could be true. Leonora would never commit treason against the Throne, no matter the stakes. It was simply not within her character to do so. There had to be more to it, and Hannah doubted very highly that it was none other than the Ethereal Sorceress who was behind the charges against Leonora. That woman obviously had designs on the Throne and would do anything in her power to keep the rest of the Flashing Blade in line.

Finally, there came a light knock on the door, followed by two harder ones. That had been the prearranged signal, and Hannah moved quickly to unbar the door and allow passage to the three people who quickly entered. Devlin Rannoch looked a little worse for wear, but the two women who followed seemed unaffected by the length of their travel. Immediately the smaller of the two women moved quickly across the room and threw her arms around Hannah.

"Aunt Hannah!"

For the first time since her trek to Galateria, Hannah felt a smile come to her face. As the young woman pulled back and Hannah finally got a look at her, Hannah could see a lot of her mother in the young woman Tess Annis. However, the eyes of the young woman gave Hannah pause. They sparked like warm amber in the morning sunlight, bright gold and both imposing and soft at the same time. They were no doubt the eyes of her father, the one that ruled the Dark Gods.

"Tess," Hannah said softly, her hands resting on the young woman's shoulders. "It is so good to see you finally. You look so much like your mother did once upon a time. It is hard to believe you are her daughter."

Tess smiled and turned back to Devlin. She moved quickly to the larger man and gave him a long hug. Devlin looked shocked at the emotional reaction, and Hannah was sure that because of the man's physical appearance, there had not been much physical emotion shown to him in his lifetime.

"Thank you Sir Devlin for bringing me to my aunt," Tess said after a moment. "If not for you, I am afraid we would have fallen into the hands of the agents of the Emperor. Though I am here to sue for peace between our two empires, I do not believe that my words would have ever been heard if I was not brought to Aldere by the great Hannah Ironheart."

Devlin smiled despite himself, and he felt his heart begin to beat faster.

"It was my pleasure."

Keep your mind on business. She does have clothes on your know.

Tess laughed slightly, and then spoke in a voice low enough that only Devlin could hear.

"That isn't funny, Sir Devlin."

For a moment, Devlin just looked down at the smaller woman, and after a moment she winked at him. Had she heard the voice? How was that possible? It was Hannah's voice that finally snapped Devlin out of his confusion.

"How was the journey?"

Devlin let his cloak drop to the ground finally, followed by the belt that held the scabbard and Discipline. He let his wings stretch for a moment before sitting on the low bench at the far end of the room.

"Terrible. The Imperial Legion is everywhere, rounding up any of us that can be found. Orders went out to all members of the Flashing Blade rescinding their assignments and ordering them to appear at the Imperial Court before New Year's. I've done my best to make sure that the news of your death is confirmed as much as possible, but before long, I will have to follow orders, or our little rebellion may be over before it begins."

Hannah sat and shook her head.

"Kaitain will never believe my death to be genuine without Spirit."

Hannah unconsciously ran her fingers over the head of the mace and looked at it silently. Since she had ascended to the rank of the Celestine Knight, Spirit had never been far from her grasp, even in times of peace. It was a symbol of her station and strengthened her connection to the Creator's Love.

"I guess I have no choice but to take it with me," Devlin said finally.

Hannah shook her head.

"No matter the trial, I cannot let Spirit leave my hands."

Tess smiled.

"Camille can fix that, can't you Camille?"

For the first time, Hannah let her eyes find the form of the silent robed woman in the corner of the room. Hannah had dismissed her when the three travelers had appeared, seeing her as only the assigned guard for Tess, however, with Tess's words, Hannah began to see that this Camille would be more than just a simple guardian. At Tess's acknowledgement, the woman named Camille pulled back the hood of her cloak to reveal her striking features and long brown hair. Her eyes flashed for a moment, and then on the floor at Hannah's feet appeared a perfect replica of Spirit.

"That is quite impressive," Devlin said after a moment, "but I doubt it will hold up to the scrutiny that it will no doubt be subject to by the Imperial Sorceress and the rest of the Imperial Court."

Tess smiled.

"I think you are underestimating Camille's abilities. Remember, she is a daughter of two Dark Gods; so her powers are not comparable to the parlor tricks of the Imperial Sorceress or her lackeys. Go ahead, Aunt Hannah, pick it up and see what you think."

Hannah raised an eyebrow slightly and then let Spirit slide from her grasp to the floor before picking up the facsimile. As soon as she felt the weapon's weight in her hand, the familiar rush of power filled her body. It was as if she held the real Spirit in her hands. The fact that this woman had just cloned one of the Sacred Weapons in a matter of moments was nothing short of miraculous.

"Unbelievable."

That was the only word that Hannah could manage. By his own admission, it had taken Arturious Demascious the culmination of a lifetime of work to create the thirteen Sacred Weapons, and though many had tried since his disappearance to duplicate the work, none had succeeded. If this woman, from across the room, could duplicate a master's work in a matter of seconds, what else was she capable of? Hannah's mind spun as she began to think of the possibilities that must have been open to the other children of the Dark Gods. And if their children were this powerful, what did it mean for the Dark Gods themselves? Perhaps the arrogance of the Cadarian Empire had clouded their minds as to the true nature of the Dark Gods. A cold shiver ran down Hannah's spine as she thought about the possibilities.

That was truly impressive, don't you think? I would much rather have this Camille as an ally rather than an enemy. I'm sure after seeing what she did to that Aldora chap at the docks; she could have burned him to a cinder with a thought.

Tess looked at Devlin again and smiled.

"Camille is a formidable woman. Her mother and father taught her quite well to be more than capable in all forms of combat and magic. However, her mother's love affair with the bow seems to have rubbed off the most on my good friend here. Of course, she doesn't need to carry one as her mother did, because with the powers at her disposal, she can just create one out of thin air."

Devlin shook his head. Now he was certain, this woman....no...girl...could hear the voice. He didn't have time to deal with that now. He knew he would have to leave now if he was going to make it back to Aldere in time to avoid being charged as a traitor.

"Well, Hannah? Does it pass the test?"

Hannah shook herself from her disbelief and silently nodded.

"Good," Devlin said finally, "then I should be off. Since I'm the newest member of the Flashing Blade, I'm sure there would not be any protestations if I were to end up hanging right beside Leonora."

Devlin claimed the replica Spirit from Hannah and then began to move toward the door.

"Devlin," Hannah said after a moment.

Devlin turned and smiled.

"Don't worry, Hannah. I'll find a way to get them out."

Hannah felt herself sigh, and then finally found the smile again. With a nod to the three women, Devlin pulled his cloak back over his wings and set out toward Aldere. By Hannah's calculations he would get there by evening the next day, just a few hours before the scheduled termination of Leonora. Hannah silently prayed that the young half-man would not run into too many delays.

For a long time, there was silence in the little farm house, the three women regarding each other. Finally, it was the young Tess who broke the silence.

"I like him, he's nice."

Hannah could not help but chuckle a little at the young woman's words. She couldn't have been more than seventeen, and though she had been forced to accept many drastic circumstances in her life, she still seemed to retain the innocence of youth. There was energy within her that Hannah could feel from several feet away. It was as if the joy of life radiated from the young woman and she lived on the pure enjoyment of the moment. Camille on the other hand did not seem to be affected by this haze of emotion, and stood silent, her eyes constantly searching the room. Hannah was sure that even without her abilities the child of the Dark Gods would have been a formidable warrior simply by her nature.

"He certainly is unique," Hannah conceded. "So, my dear niece, perhaps you will tell me what is so important that your mother would send you all this way to attempt to broker a peace that seems to be doomed before it can begin."

Tess, for the first time since entering the farmhouse, stopped smiling. At that moment, Hannah could finally see the weight of her mission and her position began to show. For a girl of that young age to be burdened with that level or responsibility was beyond Hannah's comprehension. Hannah could not even imagine herself being able to handle the strain when she was seventeen.

"There is much happening that you are not aware of yet, Aunt Hannah, and there is much of it that I am not allowed to discuss for various reasons, but I will try my best to make sense of the madness that seems to be consuming both Cadaria and Mythryn."

At that moment, Hannah could feel a change in her niece. It was as though at that moment she became much older and much wiser. Even her features took on a much more aged look. The change disturbed Hannah deep in her soul, almost as though she could see the darkness of her half-god side beginning to emerge. The part of her that was tied to the love of the Creator screamed out. Though this young woman shared the same blood as the devout Hannah Ironheart, she also shared the blood of an abomination that Hannah was dedicated to destroying. The inner turmoil began to become a full scale was of responsibility and love, and it threatened to spin out of control at any moment.

"As you know, after the first Emperor of Cadaria, the one you call Godslayer defeated the leader of the Dark Gods in single combat, the great truce was created which eventually resulted in the creation of the Kingdom of Night, Galateria. However, what you most likely do not know is that the Emperor Terrik Lorien did not defeat the Dark God at all."

Hannah nodded. Over the years, and then again more recently after the information about Leonora's and Devlin's interactions with the Dark Gods, Hannah began to question the validity of the story of the great and powerful Terrik "Godslayer" Lorien defeating the greatest of the Dark Gods in single combat. It was obvious there was more to the story, and perhaps now Hannah would begin to solve one of the mysteries that had plagued the empire for generations.

"When the Dark Gods were cast done," Camille suddenly piped up, "my father was the first to take up the banner as leader. All he wanted was to ensure that his allies and his children would be able to exist in peace while they coped with their expulsion from the Heavens. My father and mother fought hard to create an island of sanity in a world that had suddenly gone mad. Cadaria had been thrown into absolute chaos because of the emergence of the Dark Gods, and they naturally brought war to Mythryn. Cadarian history teaches that it was the servants of the Dark Gods who brought about the War of Darkness, however the memories of those who were there, those who lived through the awful dark days tell a much different story."

Hannah simply blinked at the words of the dark goddess. If her father had been the god that Terrik Lorien slew to end the War of Darkness, which meant that this woman who looked no more than twenty years of age was almost two-thousand years old. Hannah's head swam. All of this information was too much for even the great Celestine Knight to take in. Unconsciously, Hannah reached for Spirit, hoping the serenity of the connection to the Creator would clear her mind and bring peace to her thoughts. However, instead of the peace and clarity that she hoped for, the screams for the destruction of the two women that stood before her filled her mind. There was a great red rage that threatened to seize her, an absolute need to cleanse the abominations from her sight. With a clatter, Spirit fell to the floor, the rage beginning to dissipate.

Tess looked at her aunt and frowned. She knew this situation would be hard on the woman that she called aunt. For such a devout follower of the laws of the Creator to be suddenly faced with two children of the Dark Gods, the enemies of all that she stood for must have been overwhelming. Once the fact that one of them was her own flesh and blood was factored in, it must have been nearly impossible to bear. After a moment, Hannah took a long deep breath.

"You'll have to excuse me. The Creator frowns on one of his servants conversing with the children of the Fallen. However, I cannot refuse a request from my sister, or from my niece. I shall atone later if that is possible, but for now the truth is more important than even the fate of my soul."

Tess nodded.

"As Camille said, it took some time for Gwydeon to unite the Dark Gods under his banner, and for a long time there was infighting and uncertainty. Eventually the disorientation from their new condition lifted and the Dark Gods were able to form the cohesive Council that has ruled them since. However, the death of Gwydeon was almost enough to bring destruction upon the unity that he had tried so hard to build."

Hannah shook her head.

"So this Gwydeon sacrificed himself so that there could be peace between Cadaria and Mythryn. He must have been a truly powerful leader. I'm sure his loss was tragic for the rest of the Dark Gods."

"My father was a skilled leader," Camille said finally, "and while Tess' father was able to fill the void of leadership left when my father was killed, there were some portions of my father's role that could never be filled, and Gwydeon's death diminished the Dark Gods far more than anyone could have ever known."

Hannah frowned. It was obvious from the look on her face that she did not understand. Tess turned to look at Camille and it seemed as though a silent conversation took place for a few seconds between the two women. Finally Camille nodded and Tess began to speak again.

"There are rules, Aunt Hannah. Rules that prevent the Dark Gods from speaking openly to anyone but each other about the circumstances that led to their expulsion from the Heavens. Not even the children of the Dark Gods know the whole story, with the possible exception of Serrina. The only reason she is privy to the information is because she is sitting on the Council in her parents' stead. She is the only child of the Dark Gods ever allowed to join the Council. But, while I cannot share information with you that tells you the cause of the Fall; what I can tell you is that Gwydeon was not like the rest of the Dark Gods, he was special."

Hannah nodded.

"What do you mean 'special'?"

Camille was the one who spoke next.

"My father was once a man, flesh and blood like you, but unlike the rest of the Dark Gods, his service to the Creator did not begin with his ascension to a position in the Heavens. First, my father was touched by the Creator's power and he became an agent of the Creator, known throughout the cosmos as the Brother of Angels. It was only after years of service to the Creator in that capacity that my father allowed himself to ascend and join my mother in the Heavens. When my father returned to the Heavens, I was born, one of the few children of the Dark Gods to be divine beings. But like my father, I was touched by the Creator, a final reminder of what would be lost through their expulsion from the Heavens."

Camille then slowly unbuttoned the top button of her cloak and let it slide from her shoulders. There was a harness around her chest that she gently unclasped, and Hannah watched in shock and awe as a pair of angelic white wings extended from behind the woman. Though they were a bit cramped in the smallness of the farmhouse, their majesty and beauty were not lost. Hannah could not believe her eyes. The mark of the Creator was firmly upon this child of the Dark Gods, a child born before the Day the Heavens Fell. From where Hannah sat, she could feel the divine energy radiating from the wings, and it felt as though she was being bathed in the light of the Creator. After a moment, Camille folded the wings back, but did not restrict them with the harness again.

"That is…amazing," Hannah stammered.

"So you see, Aunt Hannah, there was much more to this man Gwydeon that Terrik Lorien killed. With his death, my father did his best to hold the fragile alliance together, but as the years have passed the resentment of the mortals and their damned position have begun to grate on some of the members of the Council. As you said, war between the Dark Gods and Cadaria may be a foregone conclusion, but such an event will surely damn both the peoples of Cadaria and the Dark Gods of Mythryn."

"This war cannot be allowed to take place," Camille said finally. "And we cannot rest until measures are taken to prevent it from occurring."

There was silence before Camille finally spoke again.

"No matter the cost."

The implication was clear. Though Hannah did not understand the threat that a war between Cadaria and Mythryn posed to the Dark Gods considering their power, it was clear from the reactions of both Tess and Camille that there was a threat. Tess had been sent to Cadaria to stop a war, and Hannah was sure that no amount of talking would accomplish that goal. The only way to avert a war would be to stop Kaitain Lorien from continuing his plans. That might very well require Kaitain Lorien and his pet the Ethereal Sorceress Irene Drage to meet an untimely end.

"There is obviously more to this story," Hannah said finally, "most of which I will probably never know. For now though, perhaps we should rest and wait for a report from Devlin on the happenings from the wedding. If he is successful in rescuing both Gregor and Leonora, then we will have more assistance in whatever course of action we choose to take next. If not, we will have to find allies elsewhere."

Tess smiled.

"I understand, Aunt Hannah. And you're right, I am pretty tired. It was a long trip."

The darkness and age on Tess's features had disappeared. The girlish tone in her voice had returned. After another hug for her aunt, Tess retired to the bedroom in the back of the farmhouse with Camille close behind. Though the child of the Dark Gods obviously had strange and miraculous abilities, and though Hannah knew she was supposed to hate the woman named Camille, she could not help but be relieved that Camille had been sent to protect Tess in the days to come.

****

The night passed slowly for Hannah Ironheart. It wasn't much past midnight, and she had not slept a moment. The words of her niece turned in her mind, and the impending death of her friend at the hands of the man that she supposedly served weighed heavily on Hannah's heart. The covers a mess, Hannah finally sat up and walked out the front door of the little farmhouse. Perhaps a walk in the night air would clear some of the confusion from her mind.

A clear full moon shown over the battle-scared lands of Galateria and Hannah stood in a dew-covered field looking out into the night. So many had already died in the war with the dragons, and a hundred times more would die if Kaitain continued on his destructive path. A war with the Dark Gods of Mythryn would destroy Cadaria, and if Tess and Camille were right, it would likely bring an end to Mythryn as well. Perhaps this world had been doomed from the beginning. Perhaps it was simply the Creator's Will.

"Hannah?"

The eerie voice floated through the night on the wind. Hannah looked around quickly trying to find the source of the voice, and then suddenly found a ghostly form emerging from the late evening mist. As it approached, it gained more solid qualities, and as the man's face came into view, horror filled Hannah's heart.

Erik Relcan's face was stark white; his once blue eyes had faded to a light gray that swam in a pool of milky white. His brown hair had faded to an ash gray, and the smell of the grave and death circled him like a haze. Hannah knew that she was not looking at a flesh and blood living man, she was looking at a shade, an undead shadow of the man she had once called a friend. Without a thought, Hannah brought Sprit to bear, ready to defend herself against this unholy affront to the Creator's Laws.

"You don't need that Hannah," Erik said sweetly. "I love you; I'm here to rescue you."

Hannah stood firm.

"Be gone foul demon, or I shall take what remains of your soul and consign it to the fiery depths below for the rest of eternity."

Erik hesitated for a moment and then advanced.

"Hannah, my love," his sweet and wanting voice continued, "I saved your life back in Galateria, and now I have come to save you again. You are walking into danger my love, and I cannot allow that to happen. We are destined to be together. My love brought me to you and took the stroke of the blade that was meant for you, and now my love for you has brought me back from the grave in order to save you again. The path you are on is too dangerous and you must be saved from yourself."

Hannah stood firm, ready to strike.

"I don't understand."

Erik continued to advance, his hands held out in a gesture of peace.

"Those people who claimed to love and serve you in Albitonin, they don't deserve your love, and neither do these demons and horrific abominations in Galateria. You cannot sacrifice all that is good in you to save them. It is too dangerous here for you now, and you cannot go back to Albitonin. I have to make sure you are safe. Come with me Hannah, and I will make sure nothing can ever harm you. Let me love you. Let me take the pain away and show you love forever."

Erik was only a few steps away now, but suddenly a bright white light pierced through the darkness. The light enveloped Erik and Hannah watched in horror as the once human face of the man changed to the decaying visage of a corpse. Steam began to rise from Erik's skin as the light seared his undead flesh. Screaming in pain and horror Erik fled, disappearing into the shadows of the night. Hannah turned finally to see the source of the light was Camille and her bright extended wings. Hannah still found it strange and disconcerting that the divine light of the Creator could be found in the body of a child of the Dark Gods. As soon as she was sure that Erik was gone, Camille put her cloak back on and turned back to the farmhouse. Hannah pursued the woman, forcefully turning her around.

"What was that?"

Camille's features remained calm and serene.

"A Shadow. The spirit of one who cannot let go of the things it desired in life. It is a common servant of those who practice the dark arts. It was sent to you to prevent you from a course of action. It was a puppet, nothing more."

Hannah stood silent, still looking in the eyes of the Dark Goddess. Erik had mentioned Albitonin and how they did not deserve her love and a great danger that was coming. He said it many times. Something was going to happen in Albitonin and it was going to happen soon. It was then that Hannah felt a pain in her chest, the pain that she knew well. Spirit allowed Hannah to feel the rising pulse of the followers of the Creator, and their combined faith gave her strength. Now, all Hannah could feel was death, a great loss.

"How quickly can you get me to Albitonin?"

Camille blinked once, and then sighed.

"I shall rouse Tess, and we will all go. You'll be there before daybreak."

As Hannah watched Camille return to the farmhouse, Hannah prayed that daybreak would be soon enough to prevent the horror that was coming.

Blood from a Stone

Year Two of the Just Emperor Kaitain "Dragonsbane" Lorien, Creator's Calendar Year 1869

Deep in the bowels of the Temple of the Creator in the capital of the Kingdom of Stone, Albitonin, the guardian of the ancient tombs of the ancestors walked slowly through the catacombs and crypts, admiring the finely crafted artwork on both the walls and the sarcophagi themselves. It had been three years since young acolyte Ardis Franel had been appointed to the position of guardian, and it had been the happiest three years of his life. It was a great honor to be chosen to keep the remains of the great forebears from harm. The remains in the tombs were priceless, including the remains of each of the fallen Emperors of Cadaria and their families.

As was customary, Ardis made his rounds through each of the twisting and turning passageways of the catacombs, touching each of the sarcophagi and tombs as he passed, silently speaking the names of the person buried there to himself. He knew the names of every person buried in the great crypt by heart, and he took great pride in learning all the facts that he could about each of the people there in order to more fully appreciate the grandness of his position. These great men and women would lay in the tomb for as long as it stood, and he was the keeper of everything that remained of them, in this life and the next. He dedicated himself to becoming a living memorial. The keeper of the dead, the guardian of things lost.

When his rounds were at an end, Ardis gave way to the guardian who watched the tombs at night, and he returned to the great chapel where he was cleansed in the Pools of Loss. It was thought by those that ruled the Temple of the Creator that prolonged exposure to the remains of so many who were touched by the Creator allowed a residue to build upon the soul. This residue could allow the guardian, even one who was pure of heart and spirit, to fall to corruption. Mortals were not meant to feel the touch of the divine in such a way. And so, as Ardis bathed in the chillingly cold waters, he reflected and prayed to the Creator to remove the trespasses from his soul and to allow him to continue his service in silence.

* * * * * * * * * * * * *

Year Seventy-Three of the Just Emperor Ender "JustHand" Lorien XI, Creator's Calendar Year 1867

The unthinkable had occurred. The Crawling Plague had already claimed so many great people in the Kingdom of Cadaria, and because of the corruption of their bodies, they could not be entombed within the hallowed catacombs of the Temple of the Creator. Many nights Ardis found himself weeping the fate of those who could not find peace with those of like stature. However, when the Emperor, the great and powerful Just Emperor Ender Lorien fell at the hands of the Crawling Plague and the mysterious Gray Man that called itself Pestilence, Ardis was nearly inconsolable. This would mark the first time in the history of the Temple of the Creator that the chosen vessel of the Creator's holy power, the great Emperor Lorien could not find his eternal rest with his ancestors. It was wrong on every level, and in Ardis' mind it consigned the spirit of the Just Emperor to wander the lands of Espre for eternity without rest.

Though he tried to reason with his superiors in the Temple of the Creator, his pleas fell on deaf ears. There would be no exception to the decree, not even for the remains of the Emperor. Though a special dispensation could have been granted, the rigidity of the hierarchy of the Temple frustrated all of Ardis' attempts. Ender Lorien and all of his good works from his lifetime would be lost forever. His stories would never be told, and the power that he once ruled with would never find its way back to the love of the Creator. The situation was untenable, and totally unacceptable. At that moment, Ardis resolved to do what he reasoned had to be done. Ender Lorien must find his way to the catacombs with the rest of the Imperial family, and Ardis would simply not take no for an answer.

He stole away in the middle of the night, after the cleansing ritual and after he was sure he would not be discovered. The proposition had sounded like such a simple one when it entered his head, but with the increased security due to the death of the Emperor and the outbreaks of the Crawling Plague seemingly everywhere in Cadaria, it made it very difficult to sneak away from one of the most heavily guarded fortifications in the Empire. However, few knew the grounds of the Temple of the Creator better than Ardis, and he took his time in securing his escape without notice. The note left in his room would explain his absence, the sickness of an imaginary relative. It would buy him some time and with his spotless reputation it would be accepted without question.

It took only a few days of hard travel to reach the mass grave on the outskirts of Lordhill. Lordhill for centuries had been the richest mining area in all of Cadaria, and one of the exhausted mines seemed a suitable place for the remains of those who had been touched by the horror of the Crawling Plague. Due to the stench and corruption there was no one guarding the mine, as there were few brave or foolish enough to attempt to rob the graves of those lost in this manner. The chance of falling to the Crawling Plague was too great, and no one would risk such damnation. Ardis however, firm in his faith and service to the Creator, simply tied a scarf around his mouth and nose to block the stench and descended deep into the abandoned mine, his higher purpose filling his mind.

No matter what he had prepared himself for mentally, it could not ready him for the horrific sight that awaited him deep in the mine. Bodies were stacked like cord wood, whole lives discarded like a crumpled piece of paper. The coldness of it all brought a tear to Ardis' eye, and he could sense the restless spirits clinging to their disrespected remains. The loathing and anger over their fate was palpable, and Ardis choked on the combination of rage and foul stench. After several hours, in a small antechamber, Ardis discovered the remains of the Emperor, and the shock of his discovery shook his soul. Where all who shared his line had been given a proper burial in an ornately crafted sarcophagus, buried with honor and great ceremony in the catacombs of the Temple of the Creator, this great man, Emperor Ender Lorien lay face up in tattered clothing on a table that must have once been used for the miners to eat their meals. The ignominy and disrespect of it was intolerable. Brushing tears from his eyes, Ardis retrieved the corpse of the fallen Emperor, and after a brief prayer for forgiveness, Ardis placed the body in a long black silk bag, one used often to carry the corpse of the fallen from their deathbed to their final resting place, and made his way slowly out of the mine. This Emperor's legacy could not find its end in this way. It could not end, forgotten and lost in a mine that would eventually be buried and cast to time. Ardis would ensure that Ender Lorien would find a fitting rest.

* * * * * * * * * * * * *

"He must be expelled!"

The shouts and clamoring in the Heart of Stone were nearly deafening. Ardis stood, his clothes covered in soot and mud, his hands bound in front of him. Tears filled his eyes as he listened to the angry voices around him. Ardis' plan had been so simple and it had only been the chance encounter with a guard taking a walk in the wrong place at the wrong time that had led to his discovery. Had Ardis returned to the catacombs a few minutes earlier or later, there would have been no problem, and Emperor Ender Lorien's remains would have been tucked away safely into a proper place of honor with his ancestors. As Ardis stood, his eyes moving across the faces in the room. The faces of men and women that he knew well had judgment and hatred in their eyes. Their horror was evident. These were people he had been raised with, had served the will of the Creator with, and people that he counted as friends for all of his life. He thought that they would understand his quest, understand the purity of his actions, but regardless of his words, there was nothing but scorn that awaited him. Ardis let his eyes travel to the pulpit where the High Priestess Hannah Ironheart stood. It was she who would pass final judgment upon Ardis for his actions. Finally, Hannah raised her hand and silence returned to the sacred Heart of Stone.

"Ardis Franel, you have committed a grave sin and treason against the laws of Cadaria and the laws of the Creator. The decree to isolate the bodies of those who fell from the Crawling Plague was in the best interest of the Empire and if your intention was to honor the memory of the fallen Emperor Ender Lorien, then you first should have honored his decree. Your treason against the Throne will go unreported, that is the forgiveness that is extended to you for your lifetime of service. However, the sin of pride you have committed cannot be so easily commuted. All I have heard here since your discovery is that you must be expelled and excommunicated. To this I have no alternative. From this day forth, Ardis Franel, the Temple of the Creator will never acknowledge you and your soul may find no solace in our teachings. For the rest of your life, you must seek your redemption elsewhere, and you must find your own way back to the Creator's Love."

Ardis felt the tears roll down his cheeks as he was led out of the Heart of Stone and then out of Albitonin. The home and family he had known all of his life had been stripped from him for one action. It was an action that was called a crime, a mistake of pride and arrogance. However, no matter the evidence he was shown he would never see his actions as anything other than the will of the Creator.

* * * * * * * * * * * * *

Year Two of the Just Emperor Kaitain "Dragonsbane" Lorien, Creator's Calendar Year 1869

Ardis Franel stood at the top of a high hill, looking down at the sprawling city of Albitonin. Most of the city would be fast asleep, with the exception of a few priests in the Temple of the Creator. Lights still abounded in the Heart of Stone; the prayers for the lost of the war with the dragons would go on throughout the night as they did every night since the war began. Prayers were all that the priests of Albitonin could ever offer. Even though Ardis had been cut off from the faith and love that he had felt all of his life, he still spent all the hours that he could praying for his salvation, the salvation of those who died, and the salvation of those who had expelled him from all he ever knew and loved. But still, even after all the pain and torment his expulsion caused, he prayed to the Creator. However, for some reason he no longer felt the love of the Creator as he once did. He no longer felt that close intimate connection that he felt when he knelt in Heart of Stone. Those days were gone forever, and now Ardis would have to find comfort in those few good works he could still perform.

Turning away from the cityscape that stretch below him, Ardis took a long deep breath and let his eyes fall down to the path before him. Emptiness threatened to consume his soul. Then suddenly Ardis felt as though her were no longer alone. It was like a set of eyes was peering through him, through his soul. It was then that the green light appeared out of thin air and seemed to come from everywhere all at once.

"He cannot hear you."

The voice came from the forest, from the grass, in the very wind itself. It was a voice that seared Ardis' soul and made his skin tingle with a cold fury. Ardis spun to look behind him for the source of the voice and there on the very edge of the hilltop stood a man, his gray skin immediately sparked recognition. This had been the creature that caused the Crawling Plague, the one that had robbed so many of their lives, had robbed so many children of their fathers and mothers, and had robbed the Empire of its great father. In his own way, Ardis too had been robbed by the Crawling Plague. Anger filled Ardis that next moment, a rage that he had never felt before, and he began to understand the loss and despair. Everything he had ever known had been taken from him, and it had all be because of the Gray Man. This Pestilence had his back turned, looking over the great city of Albitonin. It would only take a hard shove and the creature would be sent plummeting to the ground below. But Ardis hesitated.

"No matter how much you pray, he cannot hear you."

Finally the Gray Man turned to face Ardis, and horror began to fill the young man. The creature's visage was terrible to say the least, and though Ardis tried to take a step back in revulsion, his body would not cooperate. He was frozen, rooted to the spot like a great tree.

"All you have ever been taught," Pestilence said slowly, "all you have ever known has been a lie. A great lie perpetrated by the followers of the Creator for a thousand lifetimes. Every world under the control of the Creator is filled with these lies, and in the end the result is always the same. Humans are nothing more than a plaything, a minor blot on the face of worlds that existed long before their infestation, and will remain long after their extinction. The Creator does not care about you, does not care about your prayers and your pleas, and does not value your souls. He had his own agenda and has his favorite creatures, and man is not counted among them."

Ardis shook his head, tears welling in his eyes.

"Believe what you will, but what I speak is the most profound truth your ears shall ever hear. The Creator does not love you. Even now the Creator is taking steps to save his chosen children, the dragons, from the destruction that will soon befall this Espre. The dragons that kill your kind by the thousands have been placed above all others and will be allowed to fly away from this world, as they have a dozen others, leaving nothing but death and ruination in their wake. The teachings of the Creator are a great lie. There is no Heaven waiting for the souls of those who fall in the service of the Creator. The Other Side is a prison of damnation and suffering. You have all been deceived and betrayed by the one who is supposed to love you no matter your failings."

Tears streamed down Ardis' cheeks, and though he did not want to believe the blasphemy spoken by the Gray Man, he could not help but feel the words stirring in his heart and his soul. The words could not be true, and yet at the same time they had to be.

"But there is one, like you, that does love you. He who would be the true god. He who waits to be ascended to his proper place in the Heavens. He loves you more completely than you could ever know. Unlike the Creator and his lies, Dorovar values the souls of all men, wicked and holy alike. Their voices fuel his chorus and will sing him to the Heavens. You should have heard the thousands of voices crying out in joy when the Crawling Plague released them from this lie perpetrated by the Creator and his agents. Even your Emperor Ender Lorien's voice spoke of the rapture and freedom of his release. It was my touch, the gift given to me by the great god Dorovar that allowed me to free them from their pain, just as Dorovar released me from my pain. Famine's touch added more voices to the chorus, but there is still so much work to be done."

Pestilence's stare bore into the heart and soul of the young man, his heart beating fast and hard. The Gray Man's voice resounded in Ardis' soul, suffusing him, holding him, and the love that he once felt while sitting in the Heart of Stone returned. He felt Dorovar's Love, and it was beyond anything he had ever felt in his life.

"Dorovar wants to give you a great gift. You will help to save the innocents from the fate that is coming. So much pain awaits those who are so corrupted by the trappings of this lie of a life the Creator cursed them with. You must release them from their bonds, Ardis. You must allow them to travel to the light of Dorovar's Love, and add their voices to the growing chorus. You shall become the third of Dorovar's chosen. You shall become Death."

The green light that had filled the small clearing suddenly condensed into a haze around Ardis, and he could feel the touch of Dorovar on his skin. Warmth filled his body, a warmth and safety he had never known any day of his life. The tears streaming from his eyes were no longer tears of sadness, rather they were the result of the fullness of emotion and joy that filled his soul and had no outlet other than to stream from his eyes. Outside his closed eyes, changes began to come over the man who was once known by the name of Ardis Franel. The tattered and soiled clothes began to glow, their fabric slowly being altered by the powers of Dorovar. The vibrant skin below became malleable and then merged with the clothing, turning darker as the moments passed. Finally the thickening armored skin settled on a color of black deeper and darker than the darkest night. It was a black that drew in all light and color around it and bespoke dread to all who laid eyes upon it. The armor continued to thicken and grow around the creature that used to be a man, until the full suit of armored skin looked like a perverted version of that worn by the holy knights of the Temple of the Creator. The only pieces of skin left exposed by the armor, his hands, nose, mouth and chin were powder white and radiated a fierce aura of cold…the cold of the grave. The man once called Ardis no longer existed, and as he fell to his knees before the Gray Man, the creature knew that he was no longer a man at all; he was now the third chosen of Dorovar. He was now Death.

A new voice spoke the next moment, a voice Death instantly knew as the voice of his master, the one who had saved his soul from a lifetime of fruitless toil and torment serving a false god.

"My child, you will take my touch to those who are deluded by the lies of the Creator, and you shall free them from their bondage. The kingdom below you has been led astray, and now you must make them see the light. The voices of their souls that once wasted their praise on the Creator shall now join my chorus and raise me to the Heavens where I shall make the Creator and his chosen suffer for the ignominy they have reduced our race to. There is no longer a need to hide behind plagues and diseases my child. Your touch and the force of your stare shall free all from their eternal chains, and finally the word of Dorovar shall be spoken openly on the lips of those wise enough to embrace my teachings."

Death smiled and moved to where Pestilence stood. Albitonin stretched below him and would soon know the touch of the true god. Dorovar had come to the Kingdom of Stone, and before mid-day, there would be none left but the echoes of rejoicing spirits.

* * * * * * * * * * * * *

Even as Hannah, Tess, and Camille emerged through the portal at the edge of the capital of Albitonin, Hannah could feel the suffering and death all around her. In the streets lay the bodies of the fallen, the life stolen from them, and the looks of horror still painted on their faces from the last moments of life. Hannah could feel the heart seize in her chest, fear and pain overtaking her. It was then that she caught a glimpse of the figure in black moving toward a huddled mass of women and children. They were pleading with him to stop, and as he approached, Hannah could hear their souls crying out in pain. With a touch they were gone, all color fading from their faces. Without a thought, Hannah pulled the mace Spirit and was about to charge the figure, but it was the trembling hand of her niece that held her back.

"No Aunt Hannah, you can't stop him. We have to run before he sees us."

Hannah pulled her arm away. She could not abandon her post, she could not abandon her kingdom without a fight. This was her duty, a duty that she was given by the Emperor of Cadaria, and more importantly by the Creator.

"Camille, get her out of here and go back to the farmhouse. Wait for Devlin to return and continue with the plan. There is too much riding on Tess to stop now."

Camille looked at Tess and then back at Hannah.

"Tess is right, Hannah," she said softly. "This creature is the chosen of Dorovar, and he cannot be stopped by you, no matter what you try. You will only be throwing your life away if you attempt to combat it. We must focus on what we can do, not what we cannot."

Hannah was torn. She could not simply turn away and let her home be destroyed. She could not leave all of these innocents to die needlessly. Perhaps there was another way. Perhaps there was something that could be done. Wordlessly Hannah turned to Camille and locked her eyes on those of the young woman. No words were needed, Camille knew exactly what Hannah wanted.

"You can stop him," Hannah said finally. "You can put an end to all of this suffering and save my city."

Camille shook her head.

"At best I could delay him. Yes, your Albitonin would be saved, but how many other cities will suffer because of what I do here? What good can come out of revealing myself for the sake of a few thousand who could be dead tomorrow?"

Hannah frowned.

"We must save all we can. You came here to avert a war…"

Camille shook her head.

"I am here to protect Tess. I will follow my orders and protect my charge no matter the cost."

Tess looked between the two fierce women. Finally she put her hand on Camille's shoulder. The look in Camille's eyes changed that next moment, and Hannah could see the love in the older woman's eyes. It was a love that was more than that just that of a caretaker and her charge. No words were needed, and none were exchanged. Finally, Camille stepped away and let the cloak and harness fall to the ground. With her wings extended, Hannah watched in awe as the fierce woman gracefully soared through the streets of the city toward the tower of the Heart of Stone. She landed at the very top and let her voice catch the wind, echoing through every street and alley.

"Hear me Servant of Dorovar! No longer shall you bring death and suffering to this city, no longer shall your fear reign supreme. Albitonin is under my protection from this moment forward, and you are no longer welcome here."

Camille's wings glowed and a faint white light began to cloak the city. However, a bubble of blackness remained visible, and it floated up until it was at eye level with Camille, and the two powerful beings stood eye to eye.

"The Dark Gods have no providence here," Death said slowly and calmly. "No matter your interference, you will not prevent me from freeing these poor souls from where they languish under the thumb of the Creator. You and your kind understand the oppression of the Creator and so you should be assisting me not prohibiting me from my task."

Camille's eyes flashed with white hot light.

"Even if it costs me my life, you shall not take these souls."

At that next moment, white light exploded throughout the city. Camille's form could be clearly seen rising above the highest point of the Heart of Stone, like a star in the morning sky. She could be seen for miles, radiant and glowing like an angel from the Heavens. Hannah could hear the scream of pain coming from the dark creature, the light pulsing and battling against the sphere of darkness. No matter the strength the creature called Death had at its disposal, the shield of darkness could not hold out against the power of the Creator, and after several moments it had been completely enveloped by the radiance spewing forth from Camille's brilliant wings. Never in her life had Hannah felt closer to the Creator than when bathed in that white light, and when the light finally receded, Hannah looked on in astonishment as the bodies of the fallen who had been touched by the servant of Dorovar began to stir. Camille had done more than prevent further loss, she had reversed death itself. However, as Hannah looked up to find Camille, she suddenly knew why the powerful woman had hesitated. There would be a price for her actions, and as Hannah and Tess watched in horrified silence, the limp form of the angelic woman tumbled slowly to the ground, feathers scattering in all directions. The only sound Hannah heard as she watched the Dark Goddess fall was that of Tess sobbing.

CHAPTER 51

Epilogue

New Year's Eve

Year Two of the Just Emperor Kaitain "Dragonsbane" Lorien, Creator's Calendar Year 1869

Another year was about to come to an end, the last few hours of the second year under the rule of the Just Emperor Kaitain Lorien. However, the turmoil and pain that had faced the new Emperor were unrivaled in the history of Cadaria. While the great feast took place upstairs in the Imperial Dining Hall, down below in the dungeons, Leonora Wastri sat in silent meditation, contemplating the fate that would meet her as the bells in the giant clock tower that sat atop the Temple of the Creator in Aldere chimed out the start of the New Year. At that moment, the final seconds of the Creator's year eighteen-hundred and sixty-nine, Leonora would have her head separated from her body with her own weapon. It was poetic justice that Kaitain had wanted, and he was sure to receive it. Thousands would be gathered in the grand courtyard, and Kaitain would have the example that he wanted of his utter and complete control of Cadaria. Not even the members of the Knights of the Flashing Blade were immune to the punishment of the Throne. No one stood in the way of the Just Emperor Kaitain. Not the dragons of Cadaria, not the Dark Gods of Mythryn, and certainly not the Knights of the Flashing Blade.

Though Leonora toiled in silence, Gregor Quicksilver one cell over, did not. For the last few days he had done nothing but pace back and forth across the floor of his cell, and Leonora was sure that before long there would be a groove worn into the floor. However, once Devlin Rannoch had returned to the Imperial Palace of Aldere carrying the sacred weapon Spirit, Gregor had become enraged. In a single motion he had ripped the door of the cell off its hinges and killed two guards. The loss of his wife had driven him mad. It took half a dozen members of the Imperial Guard and a reinforced steel door to contain Gregor's anger, and as the time inched by in the still night, Gregor could be heard again, pacing. Leonora felt for her compatriot. He had been away, away on a mission that had no purpose, and he would never again see his wife. Whether there was love between the two or not was immaterial. The loss was still profound.

A sound echoed from the top of the stairs, and the door to the dungeons opened. Leonora steeled herself. The time had come at last to meet her fate at the hands of the Emperor. Standing slowly, Leonora stood tall and proud, waiting for the contingent of guards that would escort her to the place where she would meet her end. However, when the lone form crept slowly and silently down the stairs, Leonora felt a smile creep to her face. Devlin Rannoch was proving to be full of surprises.

Holding a key ring in his hand, Devlin moved to first to the door of Leonora's cell and quickly opened it before moving to Gregor's cell and releasing the lock there. Before Leonora knew what was happening, Gregor burst from the cell and seized the winged knight by his throat and slammed him against the bars of the cells across the hall. Rage filled his eyes, and the scent of blood was in his nostrils.

"I know you were the one who did it, I know you were the one who killed Hannah. Tell me I'm wrong you worthless half-breed. Tell me the Emperor didn't order you to kill my wife."

Leonora stood fast, knowing better than to come between Gregor and his pray.

"We don't have time for this Gregor. Devlin will be judged if he had anything to do with Hannah's death. Now we must concentrate on escaping from Aldere if we are ever going to be able to have an impact upon this Empire ever again. Killing him will accomplish nothing."

Devlin tried to speak, but the crushing force against his windpipe would not allow enough air to pass to form any words. Gregor sneered and squeezed harder.

"Remember this feeling well, demon. One day, a day not too far from now, you shall find my hands wrapped around your throat once more, and I will make sure that the last thing you ever see are my eyes."

Gregor pulled Devlin away from the bars and then flung him down the hall where he slid and finally clattered to a stop against the far wall. Gregor picked up the key ring and turned to Leonora. Finally able to catch his breath, Devlin forced his way to his feet, pain wracking his body and spoke.

"I appreciate the threat, Gregor. But Hannah's alive."

Gregor and Leonora both turned to face the Onyx Knight. While Gregor's face held a look of shock and disbelief, Leonora's lips twisted into a knowing grin. It all seemed so clear. Hannah somehow had seen the darkness growing in the Imperial Court of Aldere and had enlisted Devlin's help in a scheme that would lead to the liberation of both Gregor and Leonora. It was an ambitious and bold plan.

"She's waiting for us in Galateria. Now, if I can get the two of you out of here without getting the three of us killed it will be miracle enough."

Gregor frowned.

"Our weapons?"

Devlin shook his head.

"No chance of getting those now. Leonora's weapon is on display in the courtyard waiting to be used in her execution. Yours has been locked away in the Emperor's personal study. I think he is intending on keeping it as a trophy until he finds your replacement, if he ever does."

Leonora's puzzled look asked a silent question.

No time, guards will be coming.

Devlin shook his head.

"We need to go now, there will be time enough for explanation after we're safe."

Gregor and Leonora both nodded and the three soon to be former members of the Knights of the Flashing Blade slowly ascended the stairs out of the dungeon, desperately hoping that they would escape with their lives to live to fight the growing evil that sat on the Throne of Cadaria.

* * * * * * * * * * * * *

Aerith Seth stood looking at the embodiment of the Creator's power that hovered before him and tightened his grip on both the Dragon Sword and Justice. While Aerith was still somewhat disoriented from the recovery of his powers, enough of it still was fresh in his mind that combat would be easy. The crystalline blade of the man who Aerith had once called friend flashed for a second before the floating form charged. The long hard downward slash was fast enough that it was only out of reflex that Aerith brought both his blades together to block the assault. More and more strikes rained down on Aerith and with the speed at which they came, the man once called the *Chosen One* could do little more than block and dodge. Finally, it was a hard slash that sent Aerith sprawling to the ground. The Voice hung in the air, looking down with brilliant glowing white eyes at the mortal as he pulled himself from the ground and stood. However, much to the Voice's surprise, a smile crept to the man's face.

"Is that all you've got? I was expecting something…I don't know…divine."

"You will suffer," the metallic voice said the next moment.

"Only if you intend to sing with that voice," Aerith taunted before charging in.

Letting his powers fill his body, Aerith propelled himself at great speed, surging past the defenses of the Voice and landing a clean blow with Justice on the right arm of the hovering creature. The strike severed the limb from the creature's body, and when Aerith turned, he saw the Voice still hovering in mid-air, its arm laying impotent on the ground beneath its feet. When the Voice turned, there was no expression at all. No pain etched on its face, no look of concern. Light flared from the stub of an arm the next moment, and the limb reconstituted itself, formed from the pure divine power of the Creator.

"You are only delaying the inevitable, Aerith Seth. You cannot harm me, and you cannot prevent what will occur on this world. All you do now is increase the suffering that awaits you on the Other Side. Submit now and the Creator may show you mercy for the years of service you have put forth on other worlds."

Aerith dropped Justice and pointed at the Voice.

"You get this through your thick skull. I never worked for the Creator, I never did anything other than what I had to do. I didn't want these powers. I didn't want to be a pawn in some game between the light and the darkness. But I will tell you one thing, I sure as hell won't allow what I gave to a friend a long time ago be used to destroy the very thing that I fought for. So, unless you intend on boring me to death with another long diatribe, shall we continue?"

Aerith's answer came in the form of another charge from the floating Voice. Expecting the assault, Aerith sidestepped and reached out with his powers and found what he had been looking for. It was something that Bryn had said before her departure. There in his mind, in those split seconds, he found it. There, like a tiny ember in the farthest darkness, Aerith could see the dancing green flame. Surrendering himself to it, the Blaze flashed through his body and in that next second an aura of green flame flashed around the Dragon Sword as it once had generations ago. A single strike would end the battle, as the Dragon Sword found its target, piercing the still heart of the Voice. Finally a cry was wrenched from the body of his former friend, and Aerith knew that all that was left of Evan Sinn had finally been completely destroyed. Evan's lifeless body fell to the ground, the white light banished from his form.

Aerith knelt at the sided of his fallen ally, all of the memories from their time together flooding his mind. It was such a tragedy, the loss of such a great ally and friend. Now, with the growing storm that was coming, the forces that would rally to protect humanity had perhaps lost their greatest asset.

"I'm sorry old friend, you left me no choice."

A portal opened the next moment, and Aerith was gone. He knew where he had to go next, and there was no doubt that more agents of the Creator would be waiting for him, trying to stop him from his next actions.

* * * * * * * * * * * * *

Throughout the day, rumors abounded through the streets of Albitonin. There were very few real facts about what had happened, and most were calling it a miracle, a gift from the Creator that was given to His most loyal parishioners. However as Hannah knelt in the Heart of Stone before the body of Camille Renar, the child of two of the Dark Gods, she could not help but weep. After another silent prayer, Hannah looked over her shoulder at her niece Tess Annis. Tess had been nearly inconsolable after the death of her long-time protector, but finally the tears had ceased. Now, Tess's face was an emotionless mask, her body and soul filled with pain and loss. Hannah stood from her place before the body of the Dark Goddess and strode down the aisle of the Heart of Stone and stopped for a moment, and rested her hand reassuringly on the shoulder of her niece. Tess's cold eyes looked up at Hannah for a moment before returning to where her long-time friend's body lay. Hannah could not imagine what the young woman was feeling or the sense of loss that must have filled her heart. But there would be time enough to deal with that later. The suns were beginning to set on the last day of the year, and many things were about to change throughout Cadaria. Hannah knew that the changes had to begin somewhere, so in her mind there was no better place for them to begin than Albitonin.

Hannah left the Heart of Stone and was met with the clamor of voices from clergy and parishioners alike. Quickly, Hannah ascended the steps of the dais and let her voice ring out above the din.

"All of you who know me know that I am not capable of lying to you. My faith and my belief in the utter power of the Creator will not ever allow me to lead you astray. And so it is with a heavy heart and a confused mind that I stand before you today. By now, whether you were touched by the hand of the creature that called itself Death, or you were there to witness the divine light that rained down from the Heart of Stone, you know that something miraculous happened here in the streets of Albitonin in the early hours of the morning. However, many of you do not know the truth of this, and so I will share all that I know.

"Some time ago, I was dispatched to the Kingdom of Night, Galateria to help those who had suffered so much at the hands of the dragons of the area. It was only through luck and the grace of the Creator that I escaped an attempt on my life, an attempt I am sad to say was perpetrated by the man who currently sits on the Throne of Cadaria, the Just Emperor Kaitain Lorien."

Confusion and discord circulated through the crowd with many shouts of traitor and murderer scattered about. Raising her hands, Hannah quickly recaptured the attention of the crowd and continued to speak.

"The Emperor may have been right and may have been wrong to order my death, but that is not what I am here to tell you. You see, the miracle that took place today was not accomplished by any great deed of my own hands. It was not accomplished by a member of the faithful of the Creator's flock. That divine light, that holy light that we all know as the Creator's touch was brought about by the woman whose body lay in the Heart of Stone behind me."

"I saw her," a woman cried out from the crowd. "She was an angel, a gift from the Creator."

"No," Hannah said finally, her voice cutting through the emotions of the crowd like a knife. "She was no angel. The woman who gave her life to save us all and to keep death's touch away was none other than a Dark Goddess from Mythryn."

The crowd exploded in a wave of emotion and disbelief. There would be riots in the streets as many tried to come to terms with the lies that had been fed to them for generations. For the next few hours the faithful from the Temple of the Creator would fend off those who wanted to see the body of the angel in the Heart of Stone while others called for the death of the Emperor. With her words, Hannah Ironheart had ignited a fire that could rip the Empire of Cadaria a sunder.

* * * * * * * * * * * * *

"I want them found!" Emperor Kaitain screamed as he pounded his fist at the banquet table. "Mobilize the guard. Seal the borders."

By now, word of the escape of Leonora Wastri and Gregor Quicksilver from the Imperial Dungeons had begun to circulate throughout the palace. Kaitain stormed from the table nearly immediately, barking orders in all directions. Most of the other courtiers and guests took their leave shortly after, but Marlae Lorien kept her seat, watching the chaos unfold around her. This had been an unexpected turn of events that could very well be the opportunity she had been waiting on.

After an appropriate amount of time, Marlae rose quietly from the table, dabbed the corners of her mouth with a napkin and strode regally and gracefully out of the dining hall, seemingly oblivious to the chaos that had been sparked around her. Gabriel Shadowfall was there to be certain, close enough to keep any threat from her, and in the days to come, Marlae was sure that Gabriel would have to use his abilities to their fullest to keep all threats from her person. Half-way to her chambers, Marlae was joined by Rhain, and the two women walked slowly speaking in hushed tones.

"According to sources in the palace, it was Devlin Rannoch who assisted Leonora and Gregor in their escape," Rhain said softly.

Marlae smiled.

"So, Hannah Ironheart still lives."

Rhain's face showed puzzlement.

"Devlin Rannoch is not smart enough to plan and carry this out himself. He is a stupid half-breed. No, it would have taken strategy that his mind could never comprehend. It must be Hannah. Excellent."

Marlae stayed silent for several moments before turning to fully face Rhain.

"I think the time is almost upon us my dear. With the Knights of the Flashing Blade divided, my father's enemies will take this opportunity to try to strike at him. In the meantime, we must strike at the one person who is the greatest threat to my Empire. We must ensure that Irene Drage is dead long before the blade finds my father's back. And you, my beautiful Firebrand, you are the one who is going to secure my Empire for me."

Rhain smiled and the two women walked quickly back to Marlae's quarters to plot the new course of the Cadarian Empire.

* * * * * * * * * * * * *

Deep in the Heart of Stone, Tess Annis sat looking at the fallen form of her friend, the woman that she loved as a sister, perhaps even more than she loved her own sister. They had been together as long as Tess remembered, and though Camille was so much older than Tess, they bonded as though they were the same age. Tess never felt safer than when she was with Camille. Tears began to stream down the young woman's face, and pain filled her. Never before had she felt pain like this. Never before had she felt the loss coursing through her heart, constricting her veins and causing the breath to catch in her throat. Openly sobbing Tess walked up the dais and stood looking down at the face of her friend.

It's so unfair. You shouldn't have sacrificed yourself to save these people. I never should have made you do it. You knew that you would die, didn't you? You knew that what I was asking you to do was impossible, and yet you did it anyway? Why? Why are these people so important? Why is the fate of Cadaria so important to the future of the Dark Gods? Why did you have to leave me Camille? Why?

All strength in Tess's body gave out and she slumped onto the cold form of the angelic Dark Goddess. Tears streamed from her face, and her body convulsed with pain and sorrow. Below the pain, something stirred. It was a feeling that had never been there before. It was a red searing pain, it tugged at her senses, inflamed them, held her and as the seconds passed erased the sorrow. Rage had taken hold.

There is no justice. These people who hated them, hated the Dark Gods, hated Mythryn, they would continue to profit from the death of those who only wanted an end to the war. And yet, they would continue to push for more death. Why should they be saved? Why should they bother to be allowed to live?

Cold filled the Heart of Stone. Her eyes closed, Tess could not see the haze of breath escaping her lips or hear the sound of holy water freezing in their vessels. The Heart of Stone began to feel like a tomb, but Tess's hot rage kept her from noticing the cold. Her mind was on fire, and as she finally opened her eyes, a golden glow filled the room. A long-dormant power had awakened inside of her. There was only one thought that filled her mind.

Come back to me.

The golden glow flashed in the room, and Tess collapsed onto the ground, her breathing labored and shallow. A second later another gasp filled the Heart of the Stone, and the winged woman slowly began to move.

* * * * * * * * * * * * *

Deep in the Citadel of Darkness, Pike stood looking out a low window, staring at the haze of darkness that clouded the sky over Mythryn. He took a deep breath and thought to himself. How many centuries had he stood in this same place, looking out at the same view, thinking the same thoughts? As he did on many days, he stood alone, an island unto himself, locked in the private thoughts of both his position on Espre, but also on the position that he lost in the Heavens. He heard the door open behind him, but did not turn in response. The news brought to him no doubt was the same that he felt several hours ago. There had been many changes in the Citadel over the last few days. Aryx's mysterious disappearance, Wolf's reawakening after thousands of years in slumber, Serrina's return and the fervor of war that swept through the Council like a plague. It was all beginning to grate on his nerves.

"Husband?"

Sadrina had been a good match for Pike and the two had been happy for many years. His family was the one bright spot in the new life he had been forced to make for himself on Espre. But now, it could all come to an end. The balance had been tipped again, this time perhaps it had finally tipped in the favor of the Dark Gods.

"Serrina has become quite adept at rabble-rousing, Sadrina, and if it weren't for the changes in the tides, I might have been convinced. But there is more going on than anyone knows, even the other members of the Council. Only Aryx perhaps has an inkling of what is happening, only because it was his rash actions that set it all in motion. But even he could not see the way the fates have conspired to aid us."

Sadrina's features remained placid. She had learned that marriage to one of the Dark Gods meant a life filled with mystery and unanswered questions. This day would be no different. Finally Pike turned to face his wife and smiled.

"We're finally going home."

Sadrina's face finally showed the shock and puzzlement that filled her soul.

"Isn't that right, Bryn?"

Confusion filled Sadrina even more as the woman in the red dress emerged from the shadows in the far corner of the room. The wicked smile on her lips comforted and terrified Sadrina all at the same time.

* * * * * * * * * * * * *

Evan Sinn's body lay quiet in the open plains, a light breeze stirring his clothing slightly. No creatures dared to approach the fallen form of the envoy of the Creator. However, the sound of footfalls could be heard approaching. A hawk sat down on the branch of a nearby tree and watched the form approaching. Golden hair sparkled in the sunlight, and as the form knelt by the fallen envoy, a woman's voice broke the silence.

"It's time to go home, Evan. You've been gone too long."

Appendicies

Dramatis Personae

The Imperial Court

Terrik Lorien
Emperor Lorien I

Liette Lorien
Wife of Terrik Lorien
Empress of Cadaria
Seer

Kaldawyn Lorien
Emperor Lorien X
Father of Ender Lorien

Ender Lorien
Emperor Lorien XI
Father of Feyd and Kaitain Lorien

Kaitain Lorien
Crown Prince of Cadaria
Father of Marlae Lorien
Twin Brother of Feyd Lorien

Marlae Lorien
Crown Princess of Cadaria
Daughter of Kaitain Lorien

Feyd Lorien
Prince of Cadaria
Brother of Kaitain Lorien
Overseer of Lordhill Province
Father of Felicia Lorien

Felicia Lorien
Princess of Cadaria
Daughter of Feyd Lorien

Galen White
Member of the Imperial Guard
Personal Guard of Felicia Lorien

Gabriel Shadowfall
Member of the Imperial Guard
Personal Guard of Marlae Lorien

Geoffry Aramour
Imperial Historian and Bard
Master of the Shadow Guild

<u>*The Knights of the Flashing Blade*</u>

Bernhardt Yeoman
The Moonstone Knight
Kingdom of Iron, Pellatori
Wielder of the Hammer Gravity

Chelsea Zarova
The Garnet Knight
Kingdom of Fire, Saldarine
"The Wolf of Saldarine"
Wife of Seraph Kore
Wielder of the Katars Tenacity

Devlin Rannoch
The Onyx Knight
Kingdom of Night, Galateria
Half-Dragon
Wielder of the Kopesh Discipline

Gregor Quicksilver
The Ruby Knight
Kingdom of Blood, Zevarit
Husband of Hannah Ironheart
Paladin of the Church of the Creator
Son of Ivan Quicksilver
Wielder of the Greatsword Valor

Hannah Ironheart
The Celestine Knight
Kingdom of Stone, Albitonin
High Priestess of the Church of the Creator
Wife of Gregor Quicksilver
Wielder of the Mace Spirit

Jaccob Aldora
The Topaz Knight
The Flying Kingdom, Hedorah
Former Member of the Academy of Arcane Arts
Wielder of the Double Sword Temperance

Leonora Wastri
The Jade Knight
Kingdom of Soul, Oradrim
Wielder of the Naginata Wisdom

Natalia Pressen
The Sunstone Knight
Kingdom of Gold, Bellnoc
Master of the Shadow Guild
Wielder of the Rapier Perseverance

Orren Eldrath
The Sapphire Knight
Kingdom of Ice, Rashaleb
Former Member of the Academy of Arcane Arts
Wielder of the Long Sword Courage

Seraph Kore
The Emerald Knight
Kingdom of Water, Thorigald
Husband of Chelsea Zarova
Wielder of Twin Sword Patience

Tolon Morr
The Amethyst Knight
Kingdom of Steel, Celidar
Former Gladiator
Wielder of Battle Axe Strength

Vallic Ultiv
The Serpentine Knight
Kingdom of Steam, Iltorp
Wielder of Scythe Harmony

Xaran Firesoul
The Tiger's Eye Knight
Kingdom of Knowledge, Menoris
Blind Since Birth
Wielder of Staff Faith

Ivan Quicksilver
Former Ruby Knight
Father of Gregor Quicksilver

Tutio Illik
Former Onyx Knight

The Academy of Arcane Arts

Alistair Ravenheart
Grandmaster of the Academy of Arcane Arts
Master of Water
Imperial Sorcerer
Husband of Estelle Ravenheart
Father of Quyhn Ravenheart

Estelle Ravenheart
Sorceress
Wife of Alistair Ravenheart
Mother of Quyhn Ravenheart

Quyhn Ravenheart
Sorceress
Daughter of Alistair and Estelle Ravenheart

Fiona Ebonsight
Master of Fire
Mother of Aris Ebonsight

Aris Ebonsight
Master of Air
Daughter of Fiona Ebonsight

Jastra Mythryn
Master of Energy

Ashinica Maupin
Master of Stone
Member of the Imperial Family

Irene Drage
Sorceress
Protégé of Alistair Ravenheart

<u>*The Dragon Hunters*</u>

Jillian Corven
Self-Titled Lady of Cadaria
Wielder of Scaleripper
Leader of the Dragon Hunters

Kiara Aren
Dragon Hunter
Former Priestess of the Creator

Angelina Lynn Sydor
Dragon Hunter

Jacqueline Escandi
Dragon Hunter
Former Member of the Iron Legion

<u>*The Hand of Chaos*</u>

Dimitri Sulano
The Voice of the Lost

Syren Belloch
The Priestess of Blood

Torda Safrick
The Master of Secrets

Xavier Cormea
The Corruptor of Souls

<u>*The Chorus*</u>

Dorovar
The Destroyer of Worlds

Pestilence
The Grey Man
Carrier of the Crawling Plague

Famine
Formerly Isabel Relin
Carrier of the Wasting Disease

Death
Formerly Ardis Franel
The Collector of Souls

The Court of the Dark Gods

Sadrina Annis
Queen of Mythryn
Mother of Darrien and Tess Annis

Darrien Annis
Half-Dark Goddess
Daughter of Sadrina Annis

Tess Annis
Half-Dark Goddess
Daughter of Sadrina Annis

Alderin Parran
Dark God
Protector of Darrien Annis

Camille Renar
Dark Goddess
Protector of Tess Annis

Serrina Mistic
Dark Goddess
Voice of the Dark Council

The Seers

Jehna Feris
The Dark Seer

Jania Maldovrin
Oldest of the Maldovrin Triplets

Jerrica Maldovrin
Youngest of the Maldovrin Triplets

Jordyne Maldovrin
Middle of the Maldovrin Triplets

Other Cast

Cole Breon
Freelance Assassin
The Living Shadow

Dominique Arais
Commoner
Mistress of Seraph Kore

Liandra Nightshade
Freelance Assassin
Death Blossom

Rhain Feirbran
Freelance Assassin
Firebrand